D0824003

SUSPENDED RAPTURE

"Tell me you still want me, Linette."

Hunter's lips brushed against Linette's. She made a little noise, a whimper born of passion and despair. "Hunter, no, please."

"Tell me how you think of this when his hands are on you," Hunter whispered. He kissed her, his lips melting into hers, rocking seductively until her lips parted for him. Linette could not move, could hardly breathe; yet she wrapped her arms around his neck, clinging as if she might slide from his grasp. His breath was hot against her cheek, his skin searing hers wherever they touched. Years of yearning rose up in her, and she kissed him back fervently. She felt suddenly, wildly alive, every nerve in her body tingling, a myriad of emotions exploding within her.

Also by Candace Camp

Published by HarperPaperbacks

Harper
Monogram

Flame Lily

 CANDACE CAMP

HarperPaperbacks
A Division of HarperCollinsPublishers

This is a work of fiction. The characters, incidents, and dialogues are products of the author's imagination and are not to be construed as real. Any resemblance to actual events or persons, living or dead, is entirely coincidental.

HarperPaperbacks   *A Division of* HarperCollins*Publishers*
10 East 53rd Street, New York, N.Y. 10022

Copyright © 1994 by Candace Camp
All rights reserved. No part of this book may be used or reproduced in any manner whatsoever without written permission of the publisher, except in the case of brief quotations embodied in critical articles and reviews. For information address HarperCollins*Publishers,*
10 East 53rd Street, New York, N.Y. 10022.

Cover illustrations by Roger Kastel

First printing: June 1994

Printed in the United States of America

HarperPaperbacks, HarperMonogram, and colophon are trademarks of HarperCollins*Publishers*

❖ 10 9 8 7 6 5 4 3 2 1

Flame Lily

1

The waiting seemed endless.

Hunter sat motionless on the bench in the hall, legs stretched out in front of him and crossed at the ankles. He had been contemplating the tips of his boots for the past several minutes, and his hard face looked calm, even indifferent. It was a look he had perfected over the years, one that had come in particularly handy in the Yankee prison, when you didn't want anyone, least of all a guard, knowing how you felt. In time it had become almost natural. And Hunter had found that life was easier lived that way, with no one knowing the path to his feelings.

But, whatever his face might express, the waiting was wearing on him. It wasn't even his wife, his child, yet Hunter found it hard to sit still, to wait in uncertainty. It was harder still with Gideon sitting right there, tied up in knots.

Hunter glanced across the hall at his older brother. Gideon sat on one of the lower steps of the staircase, feet planted on the floor and elbows propped on his upraised knees. His chin rested on his hands, and he stared, eyebrows knit in a frown, at some point on the floor. His blond hair stood up in little tufts, pushed awry by his anxious, clenching fingers, in a way that would have been comical if the situation had been different. His face was pale beneath its tan. He was a big man, taller even than Hunter, and with the thick chest and arms of a man who had spent his life in hard physical labor. But all his strength was of no help in this situation, and his frustration was stamped on his features.

"Why is it taking so long?" Gideon growled, pushing up off the stairs and beginning to pace the hallway.

Hunter shrugged and moved his feet out of the way. He could imagine how Gideon felt. If things had worked out the way he had once thought, it could have been Hunter himself in this situation. Linette up in that bedroom, bearing his child.

The thought sent a shiver through Hunter. He preferred not to think about it, and then he, too, jumped to his feet, shoving his hands into his pockets. "I don't know. Maggie or Ma'll come tell us if something happens."

"But why haven't we heard anything?"

Hunter shrugged again. He was frankly glad that they hadn't heard anything for a while. The few moans and cries they had heard were enough to make his skin crawl and they made Gideon turn pale, his eyes stark with fear.

"How long has it been?" Gideon went on.

Hunter peered into the parlor, where an oil lamp burned dimly on the mantel. "Eleven o'clock. Not so long."

It was five o'clock when Gideon had ridden into Hunter's yard to tell them that Tess had gone into labor. Gideon had returned to his own farm with Jo, their mother, while Hunter had ridden into town for the doctor. The doctor was married to Maggie, the only Tyrrell daughter, and Maggie had, of course, insisted on coming with him to help Tess. Hunter had gone along, too, thinking that Gideon might need masculine company during the period of waiting.

He had been right. Jo, of course, had banished Gideon from the birthing room as soon as Tess let out a moan of pain between clenched teeth and Gideon turned pale. "Go on, now," she had said, shooing him out of the room the way she did the chickens in the yard. "There's no place for a man here, except Reid when he comes. Besides, you take up too much space."

Gideon had left promptly, well aware of his mother's opinion of the complete uselessness, even hindrance, of fathers at a birth. Frankly, he had confided to Hunter later, he was just as relieved to go. Gideon had seen the worst of war, but nothing there had torn him up the way it did to see his delicate Tess in pain. It made it even worse knowing that there was nothing he could do to help her.

Now, when Hunter told Gideon the time, he sounded amazed. "Is that all? I thought it must be the middle of the night at least."

"Just seems longer when you're waiting." Hunter walked to the front door and looked out the upper panes into the still, dark night. He thought again of Linette. He remembered how he had dreamed of how it would be when they were married, of the children they would have, the life they would build together.

He turned away with a muffled curse. Why did he have to think of her now? It didn't happen much anymore. He had gotten over her and her treachery. At least the last few lonely years in Texas had driven her image out of his mind, so that he no longer dreamed about her at night or thought about her during the day. He no longer imagined her scent or the soft drift of her hair across his cheek, as he had when he had lain in that prison and only the thought of Linette waiting for him at home had kept him going. He no longer tasted her kiss or felt the velvety touch of her skin until he thought it would drive him mad with longing, as he had in those first awful days after he returned to Pine Creek and found that she had married another man in his absence. There was no longer a gaping hole in his life that only Linette's presence could fill.

But somehow being here with his brother awaiting the birth of Gideon's child was stirring up old emotions, old thoughts that should have been dead years ago. Linette was married to another man; she would never be his. Hell, Hunter knew that he wouldn't even want her if he could have her. She had proven herself to be a heartless bitch, marrying another man the moment she thought Hunter was dead. She had never loved him, that was obvious, and Hunter knew that he was better off without her. It was only the circumstances, he reminded himself, that had made him think of those old times, those old dreams. The last thing he wanted now was Linette Conway or any child by her.

A thin wail pierced the air upstairs. Hunter froze in his tracks, then turned and looked across the room at his brother. Gideon, too, stood motionless, his eyes full of a crazy mixture of hope, excitement, and fear.

"Was that—" Gideon's voice came out a croak, and he cleared his throat and started again. "Do you think—"

But he was interrupted by his sister's voice. "Gideon!"

Maggie appeared at the top of the stairs. Her face was flushed and beaming, her thick red-brown hair escaping from its careful moorings and curling around her face.

"It's a boy!" she cried. "Gideon! You have a son."

Gideon looked so stunned for an instant that one might almost have supposed that he hadn't been expecting some sort of announcement like that. He turned white, then color flooded back into his face. He let out a whoop, grabbed Hunter in a bone-crushing hug, and took the stairs two at a time to hug Maggie, too.

"You're the best sister in the world, Mags!"

Maggie chuckled, giving Gideon's cheek a loving pat. "For what, you goose? *I* didn't do anything."

"For telling me. I've been going out of my head the last few hours. Can I see her now?"

"Of course. She's expecting you."

Gideon rushed past her and down the hall to their bedroom. He walked through the door and straight to the bed where Tess lay, hardly even seeing Reid washing up at the basin by the window or his mother bundling up the bloodied cloths.

"Tess!"

It made Gideon's heart contract with pain to see her lying there, so frail and small in the great bed, almost as white as the sheets around her. She was looking down at the swaddled bundle in her arms, and at his voice, she looked up and smiled, and the joyous smile put Gideon's world back in order.

"Tess, are you all right?"

"I'm fine." Her voice was weak but full of happy wonder. "Come look, Gideon! Our baby."

For the first time he really looked at what she held and saw that it was a baby wrapped up in a white cloth. It was red and scrawny and almost bald, the tiny face screwed up. It was ugly, Gideon thought, stunned, and yet, somehow, curiously, wondrously beautiful, as well.

"Yes." His heart swelled with emotion and he stood awkwardly, gazing down at mother and child with a foolish grin. Tess reached up and took his hand, and he squeezed it hard, tears coming into his eyes. "Oh, Tess, I love you."

Maggie ran down the stairs lightly, chuckling. Hunter grinned back at her, full of an inordinate pride of family that was common with the birth of a niece or nephew.

"Isn't it wonderful?" Maggie cried, jumping down the last two steps and throwing herself into Hunter's arms, just as if she were a girl again instead of a twice-married matron of thirty-one years.

Hunter caught her easily and whirled her around before he set her down. He and Maggie had always been the closest of the Tyrrell children. Gideon and Shelby, several years older than they, had tended to stick together, excluding the younger set, or to lord it over them. So Maggie and Hunter, only a year apart, had been almost constant playmates when they were young, and even after they had grown into adolescence, there was still a close bond between them. Though the war had taken Hunter away and afterwards he had gone off to Texas, the bond between them had remained.

A year ago, after four years of roaming, Hunter had finally come home. He had done so because Maggie had needed him. Her husband, Will, had died. In some ways it had been a blessing. Will had been wounded in the head during the recent war between the North and South, and he had had the mind of a child ever since; he had been a burden to Maggie. Still, it had left her and her son, Ty, without even the nominal protection of a man about the place. More than that, Maggie had been sad and lonely, burdened with a guilt that she had been able to reveal to no one except Hunter.

"How are the children?" Maggie asked now, looking past Hunter toward the parlor.

Hunter shrugged shamefacedly. "I don't know. Tell you the truth, I'd forgotten about them. They haven't been making any noise lately, so I guess they must have dozed off.

"If that isn't just like a man," Maggie said, shaking her head but grinning in a way that took the sting from her words. Her gray eyes, very like their brother Gideon's in color, danced with amusement. Maggie was a striking woman, tall and statuesque, not classically lovely, but, with her broad, sensual mouth, dark slashing eyebrows, and expressive gray eyes, she was arresting, especially when, as now, humor touched her face.

She cast Hunter a teasing glance and walked around him into the parlor. She found her son Ty stretched facedown on the braided rug before the fireplace, head pillowed on his hands. He was thirteen years old now and seemingly all legs and arms, his former loose-limbed grace blurred by the gawkiness of adolescence.

Next to him, on the sofa, lay Tess's daughter, Ginny, curled up, clutching an old rag doll tightly to her chest. Asleep, she was a pale, delicate beauty like her mother, but when she was awake that image was quickly dispelled. Then it was easy to see that the mischievous blue eyes were like her father's, not Tess's, as was the heart-breaking grin she could turn on one. Ten years old, she was a perpetual bundle of energy, the sort of child who was always into something, and it was easy to see that in personality she took after Shelby, too.

Her father, Shelby, was the second-oldest child of

the Tyrrell family, a handsome, devil-may-care boy who could never pass up the possibility of a good time or an adventure. He had been the golden child of their family, the most handsome and charming man in all of Pine Creek and its environs, and it had seemed only fitting that he should marry Tess Caldwell, the beautiful daughter of the richest man in the county.

But that had been before the war struck. Shelby, of course, had enlisted immediately, unlike the more staid Gideon, who had waited a few months. He and Hunter had gone off merrily to fight, as if on some grand adventure. Ginny had been born four months after he left. Shelby had died after years of fighting, not long before the end of the war. And Tess, whose father lost his fortunes in the war, had been left to carry on, raising her daughter and taking care of her mother, barely managing to scrape by. Tess's strength and resiliency had surprised everyone. She had tackled the unfamiliar work without complaint, laughing at her mistakes and forging ahead. Over the years of hardship she had grown closer and closer to Shelby's family. She formed a fast friendship with Maggie, who before the war had shrugged Tess off as a frivolous, useless beauty. After Gideon returned from the war, he had helped Tess out, repairing things around her house or plowing a vegetable garden for her.

Gideon, as the oldest brother and head of the family since their father's death, had assumed responsibility for his younger siblings, and it was a duty he took seriously—which tended to irritate independent-minded Hunter and Maggie. To begin with, it had been this sense of duty that led him to help Tess in every way he could. But as the years passed, he had also fallen in love with Tess. He had tried to hide it because he was afraid that he could never win Tess's love. Everyone knew that she had been deeply in love with Shelby, and Gideon was certain that there was no way a staid, serious man like himself could hope to compete with the memory of Shelby's quicksilver charm. He felt guilty loving his brother's widow, wanting her when Shelby was lying cold in the ground.

But then Tess had almost lost her home to Benton Conway, and in the fight to save it, the two of them had been drawn more closely together, and she had discovered that she could love again. They had gotten married a year ago, and Tess had moved out to the farm with her daughter, Ginny, whom Gideon loved almost as much as he loved Tess.

Ginny loved living on the farm, where there was always something on which to expend her limitless supply of energy. She had been bored living in town with her constrictingly proper Grandmother Caldwell. She was normally a fearless child, but tonight, hearing her mother cry out in pain, she had been troubled and scared, and Maggie had sent her downstairs to play with Ty instead of going to bed only two doors down from where Tess was giving birth. Ginny had obeyed, putting on a determinedly courageous face, but she had taken with her an ancient rag doll, one she hadn't played with in years.

As if she felt her aunt's gaze on her, Ginny woke up and looked at Maggie. "Mommy?" she inquired groggily, starting to sit up.

"She's fine," Maggie assured her, putting a hand on her brow soothingly. "It's all over now. You have a little baby brother, and your mama's doing just fine. So you go on back to sleep."

"Really?" Ginny's nose wrinkled up in disgust. "A boy?"

Maggie chuckled. "I'm afraid so. But don't worry, you'll enjoy playing with the baby, all the same."

Ginny didn't look entirely convinced, but she was too sleepy to argue. She yawned and laid her head back down on the embroidered sofa pillow, closing her eyes and almost instantly going back to sleep.

Maggie turned back toward Hunter, lounging in the doorway, watching her, and smiled. She walked back to him, and he grinned, murmuring, "Boys, I take it, are not much appreciated?"

"Not at this age." Maggie sighed, stretching wearily. "Why don't we go outside to talk? That way we won't wake the children."

"Sure," Hunter agreed, opening the front door for her. "Though with all they've been sleeping through, I think it would take a cannon to wake them up."

Maggie sat down on a slatted wooden chair on the front porch, and Hunter perched on the wide railing that ran around the porch, his legs stretched out in front of him, crossed at the ankles. Ever since he returned from Texas, he never seemed quite comfortable among furniture.

It was early March and the night was cool, but the

slight chill in the air felt good to Maggie after the long hours in Tess's room. She let out a sigh and lifted the tendrils of her hair that had come loose, so that the air caressed her hot neck.

"How's Tess?" Hunter asked.

"Fine. Reid said it wasn't a hard birth."

Maggie scrunched up her nose and added irrepressibly, "'Course, a lot he knows about it—he may be a doctor, but he's still a man."

Hunter grinned. "And we men, of course, are lamentably ignorant."

"Oh, not ignorant, exactly. Reid's delivered several babies. But there are simply some things that no man will ever really understand." She smiled a little to herself, and a dreamy, almost secretive, expression came into her eyes. She looked for a moment very different and far away.

Hunter gave her a penetrating glance. "Maggie? What is it?"

Her smile broadened, and her eyes twinkled at him. "You know, it's hard to keep a secret from you."

"I know you too well. Something's going on."

"All right then. I guess it's only right that you should be the first to know . . . after Reid, that is. We're expecting."

His eyebrows shot up. "A baby? Are you serious? You and Reid?"

"Yes. Are you happy for us?"

"Of course I am. How can you ask?" He pulled her out of her seat and hugged her. He was happy for her, but the truth was that it made him feel a little strange, too, just as it had years ago when she had had Ty.

Maggie was his little sister and always would be that in his heart, no matter how old they were. "Boy, we're going to be running wild with children. First Gideon and Tess, and now you and Reid."

Maggie smiled up into his face. "And you, too, I hope, someday."

His face closed, and he stepped back, releasing her. "Don't count on that, Mags. It'll never happen."

A line creased his sister's brow. "Don't say never, Hunter. You don't know what might happen."

"I know what isn't likely to," he retorted.

"You can't let Linette ruin your whole life," Maggie told him softly.

Hunter turned cold eyes on her. "Linette has nothing to do with this."

"Oh, yes. She has everything to do with it." Maggie paused, looking at her brother, then drew a breath. "Sometimes I hate her for what she did to you."

Hunter wanted to deny it, to pretend that Linette had not left him unable to love again, but the words stuck in his throat. They were lies, and they both knew it. Whatever capacity Hunter had had to love, it was gone now; he was certain of that. His heart had been like a lump of rock in his chest for years now.

"I don't want to talk about her," Hunter said gruffly, turning away.

Maggie watched him with pain in her eyes. "All right."

The front door opened, and Reid Prescott stepped out onto the porch. Maggie smiled, reaching her hand up to him. Reid was a handsome man, with even features and a full, sensual mouth, now somewhat drawn with tiredness. His hair was brown and his eyes an odd blending of green and brown. It was easy to see from the gentle way he smiled down at his wife that he was head-over-heels in love with her. He sat down beside her, bringing her hand up to his mouth and kissing it before releasing it.

"I suppose Maggie's told you the news," he said to Hunter, and Hunter nodded. "I guess that makes us both uncles. Odd, for a while there, I had no family at all, and now I'm blessed with nieces and nephews and cousins all over the place."

"With some of the Tyrrells," Hunter commented dryly, "I'm not sure that *blessed* is exactly the right word."

"Hunter! How can you say such a thing?" Their mother appeared in the open doorway in time to hear her son's words, and she scowled fiercely at him. "The Tyrrells are the best family in the county."

"I know, I know, Ma." Hunter raised his hands in mock surrender. "Don't eat me alive."

"Well, you should be ashamed of yourself, saying a thing like that."

Jo Tyrrell joined them on the porch, and Reid jumped up to give her his seat, taking a perch on the railing himself. Hunter leaned back against a column supporting the porch, surveying his mother somewhat sardonically. Jo, though not born a Tyrrell, was a staunch defender of the name, and she had never hesitated to light into any one of her children for bringing any sort of disgrace to the name. She was equally determined to defend all her chicks, children and grandchildren alike, and her protective wings had also been spread to cover anyone her children had married.

In looks, she was an older image of Maggie, with the same vibrantly curling hair, in her case graying and more firmly twisted into a knot at the nape of her neck, and the same strong features. She had worked hard all her life, and her figure had thickened through the years with childbearing, but she was still an attractive woman, her face softened with the light of humor and love.

"Sorry, Ma."

Jo nodded, accepting his apology, then smiled. "Isn't this wonderful?" she asked, taking her daughter's hand. "The birth of a baby is the most beautiful thing."

"It's always a miracle," Reid agreed, "no matter how many times you witness it."

"That's right." Jo nodded. "And to think that I have another grandchild! It will be so wonderful to have a baby to hold again." She glanced meaningfully at Maggie. "And, God willing, I hope to have many more of them before my life's over. It's like a whole new start for this family, coming back from all that pain and loss of the war."

"We'll never have Shelby back," Hunter said tersely. A shadow touched his mother's eyes, and Hunter cursed himself for having spoken without thinking.

"No," Jo agreed. She smiled sadly. "Shelby's gone forever. But I have you and Gideon and Maggie. And now my children are picking up their lives again, starting new families. There's hope, don't you see?"

She looked up at Hunter, and he knew that she meant there was hope even for him. It hurt her, he knew, as it hurt Maggie, to see him unmarried. So he smiled at her, not wanting to cause her more pain. But he knew, as surely as he knew the sun would rise in the morning, that though Gideon and Tess and Maggie had found new loves, he would not. Hunter Tyrrell was through with love.

2

Linette Conway murmured something to her stepdaughter as they spread the cloth over Rosemary's desk, and both the women smiled. They made an interesting contrast as they worked, setting out the bowls and plates of food from the basket Linette had brought from home. Linette, the older of the two, was a woman of vivid beauty, with lush dark auburn hair, large, bright blue eyes, and a well modeled face and form. Though of recent years her beauty had lost much of its vivacity, subsiding since her marriage to Benton Conway into a kind of bloodless perfection, she was still the most beautiful woman in Pine Creek—indeed there were those who said they'd never seen a loveliness to equal hers in the whole state of Arkansas.

Rosemary, on the other hand, had never been called a beauty. She was not unattractive; there were even times, such as now when she was smiling, that she had a sort of quiet prettiness. But Rosemary was the kind of woman whom one never *noticed.* She was a perpetual wallflower, quick to recede into the background, seemingly eager to go unnoticed. She was small, even delicate. Her hair was an unremarkable brown, and she wore it skinned back into a tight knot. Her eyes were her best feature, large and warm and brown, surrounded by thick, straight lashes, but they were rarely noticed because of the spectacles she wore perched on her nose. She generally wore the dullest and plainest of dresses, no matter how many times Linette had urged her to have a dress made up of some material that enhanced the tones of her skin or brought out the color of her eyes. Rosemary obediently listened to her stepmother and even admired the dresses when they were finished, but somehow those dresses always found their way to the back of Rosemary's wardrobe and it was her plain grays and tans or washed-out pastels that she wore.

It had taken Linette some time to realize why her efforts were so quietly ignored. But gradually it had been borne in on her that whenever Rosemary wore one of the more attractive dresses, her father invariably made one of his cutting remarks to Rosemary, and after that the dress was put away. It made Linette fume, but there was no way that anyone, Linette included, could get Benton to do or say anything except exactly what he pleased—and no matter how much she cajoled and pleaded with Rosemary, Linette could not convince her that the pale gold satin evening gown turned her skin a warm, becoming golden and did not make her look as if she were trying to make a spectacle of herself.

Linette was pleased and a little surprised to see that today Rosemary had decided to wear a day dress that Linette had persuaded her to purchase last summer, a dark wine red silk that brought a becoming color to Rosemary's cheeks. However, Linette was careful not mention the dress; that was the surest way to get Rosemary not to wear it again. Rosemary's primary ambition in life seemed to be never to call any attention to herself at all. So Linette simply laid out the lunch she had brought and talked of other things.

"Isn't this fun?" Rosemary commented, her eyes sparkling behind her spectacles. "It's so sweet of you to bring me something to eat."

When her father first married Linette, Rosemary had been leery of the other woman, intimidated by her beauty and suspicious of someone who would marry a wealthy, older man like Benton Conway when she had until only recently been engaged to Hunter Tyrrell. Rosemary still didn't know what had prompted Linette to do such a thing. In fact, the more she had come to know Linette, the less it seemed like something she would do. But Rosemary had soon determined that her stepmother was a kind and generous woman, not the self-absorbed beauty Rosemary had feared she would be. Over the years Rosemary and Linette had become fast friends, and it warmed Rosemary's heart to see Linette smile and talk in this easy manner. When Linette had first come to live in their house, it had seemed as if she would never smile.

"When Benton rode off to Sharps this morning, I thought today would be a perfect time to visit you at the library," Linette was explaining her unexpected visit to Rosemary. "Then I thought, why not just bring you your meal, as well?"

"Did Papa go to visit Mr. Jones?" Rosemary asked in a colorless voice.

"I believe so." Linette cast a concerned look at Rosemary, whose gaze was fixed stonily on the utensils in her hand. "He said he would dine there before he went to see Colonel Thompson."

"I—I wish Papa wouldn't associate with Mr. Jones, and all those other Yankees. It makes me feel like a traitor."

"I know. Me, too."

Linette did her best not to think about her husband's political affiliations. Benton Conway was what Southerners called a scalawag, a fellow Southerner who had dealt with the enemy after the war, with the Union army and the carpetbaggers that followed them to make a profit off the fallen Confederacy. Benton had not gone to fight in the war, but Linette had not realized until after the war that he had no side except what would benefit him the most. It had been six years since the war ended, and the South was still struggling to survive its financial and sometimes physical destruction. Many lived hand-to-mouth, getting by on what they could raise in their gardens. Some, like Tess, had lost their land or their businesses completely. Others had found that they had nothing left to come home to. But Benton Conway and others like him had made a fortune.

Linette despised Benton for what he had done, and so did the rest of the townspeople. Because Linette was Benton's wife, they lumped her in the same category. Linette knew what the people of Pine Creek said about her, that she loved only money and it was for that she had married Benton. They said she was a perfect mate for him, as greedy and cold as he. She no longer had friends in this town, except for Rosemary, who was as tied to Benton as she was. Linette also knew that if it hadn't been for Rosemary and the fact that Rosemary's mother's family was an old, respected one in Pine Creek, both Linette and Benton would have been thoroughly ostracized by everyone in town—everyone except the northern interlopers, that is.

However, Linette realized that there was no way out. She was Benton's wife, and it had been part of their bargain that she would play the role of his wife in all visible ways: she would hostess his parties, go where he went, associate with those whom he chose. She would be the ornament on his arm, the perfect wife of a successful man. Linette was one who lived up to her side of a bargain. So, little as she liked the carpetbaggers and others, she was perforce tied to them. She accompanied him to the parties and smiled brittly and talked with the Yankee officers' wives. And she had grown adept at removing herself mentally from her surroundings, of sitting and listening, smiling, like a mannequin, while her mind roamed somewhere outside.

"I don't know what Papa sees in Mr. Jones," Rosemary went on, her brow knitting. "I wish he wouldn't encourage his suit."

For some reason, Farquhar Jones had taken a liking to Rosemary and had been pursuing her in his oily way for the past few months. He was a man of very large girth and quite bald on top of his head. He was vain about his lack of hair and tried to compensate for it by sweeping what little was left from one side of his head to the other across the long bald strip. He kept the long strands of hair thoroughly saturated with macassar oil to make them stay in this unnatural position, but even so, sometimes they would separate and flop comically into his eyes. He grew wide, long sideburns and a drooping mustache, as well. He would have been a thoroughly laughable figure had his false air of joviality and conviviality not covered a heart as hard and cold as stone.

Linette could have told Rosemary exactly what Benton saw in the man—an opportunity to make money—but she refrained from speaking bluntly about Benton in front of his daughter. Rosemary still retained some illusions about her father, and Linette hated to spoil them.

"I—I imagine he wants to see you protected and taken care of," Linette equivocated. "Mr. Jones could do that; he's very wealthy."

"But I don't want to marry him!" Rosemary gave an expressive shudder as she set out the last dish and put the basket aside. "Papa thinks money can cure anything; I think it was because he was poor as a child. But he's wrong. And I could not stand to live with Farquhar Jones the rest of my life, no matter how much money he has."

"Then you must tell your father that. Surely he wouldn't force you to marry the man if he knew how much you disliked him."

Rosemary looked uncertain. "No. I suppose not."

"Come," Linette said brightly, "let's not talk any more about Mr. Farquhar Jones. It's enough to spoil my appetite."

Rosemary smiled. "You're right. And this meal is much too nice to ruin."

Rosemary sat down behind the desk while Linette pulled up a chair on the other side, and they began to eat.

They chatted lightly as they ate, giggling like schoolgirls over the ridiculous concoction of swooping feathers that Mrs. O'Brien had worn at the ball Lilibet Thompson had given last week and speculating with interest on whether the new minister's wife would win the struggle between her and Tess's aunt Charlotte.

Suddenly, there was the sound of a cleared throat at the open doorway. Rosemary jumped, startled, and raised her head. Color flooded prettily into her cheeks, and a bright smile lit her face. Looking at her, Linette's eyes widened, and she swung around with interest to see whose presence had caused such a change in her stepdaughter's appearance.

It was Seth Manning, the new schoolteacher. He was a slight, sandy-haired young man with a pleasant, though serious, face. He carried a stack of books in one arm; the other sleeve of his jacket hung empty, turned up and pinned to itself. He had lost an arm during the war.

"Hello, Miss Conway." He smiled at Rosemary, then turned, somewhat reluctantly, Linette thought, to nod at Linette. "Ma'am."

"Oh, I'm sorry. I don't think you two have met. Linette, this is Mr. Manning, the schoolteacher. Mr. Manning, this is my stepmother, Mrs. Conway."

"How do you do, ma'am?"

Linette smiled and nodded at him. "Yes, I recognize you; you've been pointed out to me, though we've never met. You're quite a famous personage in our town, you know. Pine Creek was without a teacher for several years."

Manning had arrived in Pine Creek only a few months ago, brought by Reid Prescott, the town's doctor, who had known him during the war. The townspeople were able to pay only a modest salary, but they supplemented it by often bringing him food or firewood, and the Ladies Guild had helped by giving him the small rent house on the back of the library property to live in.

"Yes, I know. Everyone has been most kind and generous to me." Manning's eyes turned back to Rosemary. "I brought those books that I told you about."

So Rosemary had expected the teacher's visit, Linette thought, intrigued. That certainly explained why she had chosen to wear the attractive dark red dress today.

"Oh, thank you. Just set them down here on the desk." Rosemary hastened to make room for them, and Linette moved out of the way, busily trying to think up an excuse to leave the couple alone. It might not be proper, but the last thing Rosemary needed was chaperonage. She was so shy, and the more people there were, the shyer she grew.

To her relief, Linette heard the front door open. "Oh, someone's come. Don't worry, Rosemary, I'll take care of them." Linette blithely ignored the fact that she hadn't the first idea how to help anyone with any aspect of the library, and she sincerely hoped that Rosemary would ignore that fact, too. "You stay here and help Mr. Manning with those books. Perhaps he might stay and have a bite to eat, too. I brought more than enough."

Linette bestowed a smile on the two of them and hurried out of the room before Rosemary decided to be responsible and take care of the new visitor herself. She turned toward the front door, walking forward with a smile on her face, but she stopped abruptly when she saw who it was.

Maggie Tyrrell! No, Prescott now.

Linette hesitated. She knew how Maggie felt about her, how all the Tyrrells felt. She had to admit that they had good reason. What she had done had hurt Hunter bitterly, and none of them knew why she had married Benton so hastily. But realizing that didn't make it any easier to face any of them. Usually both she and the Tyrrells made certain that they didn't meet.

"Maggie . . . I mean, Mrs. Prescott."

"Mrs. Conway." Maggie's voice was cool. She looked as uncertain as Linette felt.

Linette walked over to her, saying in a low voice. "Did you want a book? I'm afraid I'm not much help, but—"

"Actually, I came to talk to Rosemary. Is she here?"

Linette cast a glance back toward the office door, biting her lip. "She's rather busy right now."

"I see." Maggie stiffened, and Linette suspected that she thought Linette was simply being rude.

"I'm sorry. Why don't you come sit down here in one of the rooms until Rosemary's done? I'm sure she'll want to see you."

Linette gestured toward the front room and walked into it, so that Maggie more or less had to follow. There were a couple of chairs at a table in the center of the room, and Linette sat down at one of them.

Maggie followed her example, and for a long moment they simply sat looking at one another. Finally Maggie said, "I came to tell Rosemary that Tess had her baby yesterday."

"Did she?" A strange mixture of pain and joy flooded Linette's chest. Her arms felt suddenly empty and aching. "What—what was it?"

"A boy. They're naming him William." Maggie's eyes were suddenly bright with unshed tears.

"After your husband? How nice of them."

Maggie nodded. "Yes, I—was very pleased when they told me. Gideon and Will were best of friends growing up."

Linette smiled, but her chest ached. She thought of a baby boy, all soft and dimpled, head covered by a fine fuzz of blond hair. "I'm so happy for them."

Maggie studied her. "Yes, I think you are." She sounded puzzled.

Linette smiled a little bitterly. "I'm not entirely heartless, you know, whatever you may think. Tess was once my best friend."

"I know. I—well, I've wanted to tell you several times, and I never have. I guess I haven't had the courage. But we all were very grateful to you for helping Tess save her house last year."

Tess, whose once-wealthy family lost its fortunes during the war, had been unable to pay the taxes on her huge house and nearly lost it. Finally, Linette had given her the idea of donating her house to the Ladies Guild to be used as the town's new library, retaining the right for her and her mother and daughter to live there the remainder of their lives.

"I'm afraid I didn't do that much," Linette demurred, squirming a little in her seat. Even though her scheme had enabled Tess to at least continue to live with her family on the second floor of her home, it had still been a very difficult thing for Tess to give up the home she had been raised in, and Linette felt guilty about it.

After all, it had been Linette's own husband who had persuaded his Reconstructionist friends to raise the taxes on Tess's house. Benton had wanted the Caldwell place for himself because it was the best house in the county. Benton always wanted to possess the best and the most beautiful. That was, after all, the same reason why he married Linette.

"Besides, anything I was able to do wasn't enough to—to make up for it."

Maggie nodded, too straightforward a person to pretend that she didn't know what Linette meant. "Still," she said, "it wasn't something you had to do."

"Yes," Linette said slowly, "you see, it was."

"Well, I know that it meant a great deal to Tess, and to the rest of us, too. And we are grateful for what you did."

"Thank you." Linette looked down at her hands in her lap. She could think of nothing to say. She wanted to ask after Hunter, but she didn't dare. Maggie's attempt at friendliness would immediately disappear.

Maggie stood up. She looked as uncomfortable as Linette felt. "I really should be going."

"I'll run get Rosemary," Linette offered. "She had a visitor, but I'm sure she'd want to hear your news."

"No, that's all right. Don't interrupt her. You can tell her about it. I simply wanted her to know; Tess is very fond of her."

Linette smiled. "It would be hard not to be."

"Of course." Maggie stood for a moment, looking at Linette, a line of puzzlement creasing her forehead. But then she straightened and smiled mechanically, as though thrusting off her thoughts. "Good-bye. I'm glad that we had a chance to talk."

Maggie walked to the front door. She hesitated, glancing back over her shoulder at Linette, then walked out, closing the door behind her. Linette remained for a moment, looking after her. Her heart felt full and sore, and emotions tumbled within her, unclear and conflicting. It warmed her that Tess had had a baby, but at the same time she could hardly bear to think of it. And Hunter, she hated to think about him, but now she could not get him out of her mind.

It was like that any time she saw Maggie. Maggie's eyes were gray, not the clear green that Hunter's were; her rich brown hair was not nearly as dark as his, which was almost black; and, of course, her features were too feminine to really look like Hunter. But there was, somehow, a resemblance to Hunter that was unmistakable. Her wide mouth was very similar to his, and sometimes a smile flashed across her face in exactly the same way that it would across Hunter's. Or a fleeting expression would touch her eyes or she would frown in a certain way, and then she reminded Linette so strongly of Hunter that Linette's breath would almost stop.

Linette went over to one of the bookcases and stood for a moment, staring blindly at the spines of the books. She chose one at random and sat down, opening it. But she could not read it. She simply sat, gazing at the page in front of her and wishing she hadn't seen Maggie Tyrrell.

As Linette had expected, Rosemary was filled with excitement and joy at the news of Tess's giving birth. She was, in fact, so pleased, that she gushed out the news to her father that night at the dinner table. Linette went still, her hand clenching her fork, and she studiously avoided looking at Benton.

Linette had long suspected that Tess's house had not been the only thing Benton wanted when he had gotten the taxes raised on the Caldwell place. She knew that he had been almost as furious when Tess married Gideon as he had been when she foiled his efforts to get the house. The fact that Tess had been Linette's best friend would have added a distinct titillation for him to bedding Tess.

"Is that right?" Benton said finally, his voice calm and cool. Linette glanced over at him. He appeared undisturbed, but there was a look in his pale, oddly colored eyes that made Linette want to shiver. She knew that Benton was not at all pleased to have his daughter tell him about Tess's happiness.

"Yes," Rosemary went on innocently, pleased to have caught her usually indifferent father's interest. "Maggie Prescott told Linette so today."

"Oh, I see." Benton turned his eyes on his wife. He was a middle-aged man with a small paunch, beginning to bald, and at first glance, he did not look either powerful or fearsome—until one looked in his eyes, and then one realized that he was not a man to cross. "So you have become friends with Maggie Tyrrell now?"

"No." Linette returned his gaze calmly. She had learned over the years that the best way to deal with Benton was not to let him intimidate her. That was Rosemary's mistake: she let her father see that he frightened her, and that only gave him more power. He enjoyed seeing one's fear. "I merely happened to be at the library when she came in to give the news to Rosemary. I think you know that the Tyrrells are not exactly friends to me."

"Yes. One might almost say that you avoided them."

Linette saw a speculative look in his eyes that troubled her. A small smile played about Benton's narrow mouth, and that bothered her even more. Benton always looked like that when he was contemplating something disagreeable.

She was sure that her suspicions were correct the next morning when Benton announced at the breakfast table that he intended to take Rosemary and Linette out for a drive.

"A drive?" Rosemary squeaked. "But I—I was planning to go to the library."

Benton turned his head to look at her. "I believe the library can get along without you for one day, don't you?"

"Yes, of course, it's just that I—" Rosemary began, then stopped as Benton raised his eyebrows at her, his gaze growing hard. "All right, Papa."

"What are we going to do?" Linette asked. "I have several tasks around the house."

"Such an admirable housewife," Benton commented sardonically. "I'm sure that your 'tasks' can wait. You have an ample number of servants to do the household chores, after all. You have to come; I planned this surprise just for you."

His words made Linette more uneasy. Benton wouldn't look so pleased and sly unless he expected his scheme to upset her in some way. For years now their relationship had settled into a quiet, unyielding warfare.

There was little she could do, however, except

mentally brace herself for whatever was about to
come. Linette and Rosemary went upstairs to put on
their hats and gloves. When they came back down,
Benton was outside, impatiently waiting for them
beside the buggy. He handed the women into the
vehicle, then climbed in himself, and they started
through the town.

Pine Creek was a small, sleepy town, the sort of
place where everyone knew everyone else. It lay west
of the Mississippi River delta and just on the edge of
the gently rolling land of central Arkansas. The
streets of the town were muddy from the frequent
spring rains, but the showers had brought out the
spring flowers and the budding green leaves of the
trees. Later, in the summer, it would be hot and
muggy, but now the temperature was pleasant, the air
stirred by a soft breeze. Before long, Linette knew,
the air would be sweet with the scent of honeysuckle
and gardenias.

The houses they passed were mostly frame, and
more than one was in need of paint, as were most of
the fences—the times were too hard to waste money
on whitewash. But with the coming of spring and
summer, colorful flowers and flowering bushes would
soften the harsh reminders of poverty, and the shadows of the trees would dapple the peeling walls.

They drove west out of town in the buggy. It was a
bright and sunny spring day, and it would have been a
pleasant drive if Linette hadn't felt so wary.

They soon reached the Whitcomb place, where
Will and Maggie used to live. After Maggie married
Dr. Prescott and moved into his house in town,

Hunter Tyrrell had taken over the place and turned it into a horse farm. Much to Linette's astonishment, Benton slowed the horses and turned into the driveway.

Linette stiffened, and in the seat behind her she heard Rosemary's quickly stifled gasp. *Benton is bringing us to see Hunter!* Linette's stomach knotted. She couldn't imagine what had possessed Benton. *What kind of a husband would bring his wife out to the house of her former fiancé?*

She turned to Benton. He was watching her, his eyes narrowed, a smile playing about his lips. Linette knew that he had done this to hurt and humiliate her. That was why he had brought Rosemary with them, too, so that there would be another witness to her reaction. Linette didn't know what he expected her to do—burst into tears or run or what—but she wasn't about to give him the satisfaction of seeing that he'd given her pain. She gave him a cool, indifferent glance and turned back to look at the house.

"Maggie's house looks well kept up," Linette said conversationally.

"Yes, indeed," Rosemary squeaked out behind her. Linette silently blessed the girl for her effort to support her.

An old farmhouse, the structure was typical of many in the area, frame and two-storied, with a porch running the length of the front and brick chimneys at either end. It had been painted white in the not-too-distant past, and the shutters were a deep forest green. There was a barn in back of the house, and as the buggy drove around the side of the house to stop in the farmyard, they saw that two large new pens had been added. Several horses milled around inside the larger pen.

Hunter Tyrrell was on the back of another horse, racing across the open strip of land between the farm and the woods. As the horse neared the trees, Hunter turned him in a wide arc, and they thundered back to the farmyard. The horse was powerful and midnight black, and Hunter rode as if one with the animal, crouched low over his neck.

Hunter saw Benton and the women sitting in the yard in a buggy, and he straightened, pulling back abruptly on the reins. The horse reared, and Hunter clung to his back, pulling him down. Hunter's muscles bunched across his back and down his arms as he fought to control the horse. There was something terribly primitive about the scene, a pitting of man against beast in a most basic way. Hunter himself looked primitive—vital, strong, and elemental. Intensely male.

The horse came back down on all fours, shaking his head in a last gesture of defiance. Hunter sat for a moment, looking at them. Then he nudged the horse with his heels, and trotted over to the buggy. Hunter was hatless, and his hair shone crow-black in the sun, thick and a little too long, damp with sweat around his face. He was dusted with a fine powder of dirt all over, but on his face sweat had washed away much of it, and his skin glistened with the moisture. He wore a shirt, but it hung open down the front, so that a wide strip of his tanned skin was visible.

Linette drew in a breath. She had almost forgotten how intensely male and powerful Hunter was. Feelings long dormant in her stirred, and she leaned forward unconsciously.

Hunter came up beside Benton, not even glancing over at Linette. He raised his straight black eyebrows at Benton in question. Linette was glad that he didn't look her way; it gave her a chance to observe him unawares. It had been so long since she had seen him. One night shortly after he had returned from Texas, he had inexplicably come by and talked with Benton, and Linette had seen him just as he was leaving. It had been nighttime, the only light coming from the flickering sconces along the hall wall, and she had not been able to see him well.

But she could remember him well from before the war. She had known his face and form as well as she had known her own, and they had been much dearer to her. She could see now how much youth and life had been drained from him—yet how handsome he remained. His face was tanned, and the years had worn grooves beside the corners of his mouth and around his eyes. His eyes were startlingly green in contrast to the tanned skin around them, with the same bright intensity they had always had. But there was a wariness and cynicism in them now that had never been there before. He looked older and harder, and there was no sign of that flashing, slightly mischievous grin that had never failed to charm any woman of whatever age.

Hunter crossed his arms and gazed levelly at Benton, waiting for him to speak.

"Good morning, Hunter. I believe you know my wife, Linette. Linette, say hello to Mr. Tyrrell."

Hunter cast her a brief glance and nodded toward her. "Mrs. Conway."

"Mr. Tyrrell." *God, he once held me against his chest, naked flesh to naked flesh, and here we are calling each other "Mr." and "Mrs."* It was absurd, but in a way that was painful rather than humorous. She wondered if Hunter still felt anything when he looked at her, if his chest tightened as hers did.

Benton looked back and forth between Hunter and his wife, as though he couldn't decide which of them was more intriguing. Hunter moved his gaze from Linette to the back seat of the buggy, and he nodded again. "Miss Conway."

"How do you do?" Rosemary replied breathlessly. Linette wondered if her manner was in response to the tension in the air or merely in response to Hunter's masculinity. He had that effect on women.

Hunter returned his gaze to Benton. "What do you want here, Conway?"

"Why, Hunter, is that any way to speak to a customer?" Benton asked in mocking amazement. "I'm afraid you'll have to learn to be more sociable if you want to make a success out of horse trading."

"You're telling me you're a customer?" Hunter's mouth curved downward in disbelief.

"Why, of course. Why else would I be here?"

"I don't know. You tell me."

"I'm here to look at your stock. I'm considering purchasing riding horses for my daughter and my wife."

Benton turned his head toward Linette, and unconsciously Hunter's gaze followed. He looked at her for the length of a heartbeat, then turned back to Conway.

"I don't sell to scalawags, Conway," he said calmly. "You're vultures. And you're wasting your time."

"My, my, you must be doing awfully well to be able to turn down business," Benton commented sarcastically.

"Least I can sleep at nights."

"Can you?" Benton smirked and reached over to lay his hand casually on Linette's thigh. "I suspect I rest easier than you."

Linette went rigid, and her face flamed. It was the height of crudeness for her husband to make such a blatant physical claim to her. He might as well have told Hunter that he owned her, body and soul. Linette felt as humiliated as if he had. Yet she could hardly protest; any attempt to deny his implication would only make matters worse.

Hunter's eyes flickered toward Benton's hand, then back to his face, and for an instant something bright and deadly sparkled in those cold green eyes. Benton had challenged Hunter, and they all knew it. A Tyrrell never backed down from a challenge, least of all Hunter.

"I guess you have a point," Hunter said, his voice as cold and sharp as a knife blade, and he swung down from his horse. "A man can't afford to turn down business, no matter what the source." He walked lithely around the buggy to Linette's side, leading his horse, and reached a hand up to help Linette down. "What sort of mount would you be interested in, ma'am?"

3

Linette didn't want to put her hand in Hunter's to step down from the buggy; she was afraid that if she felt Hunter's touch again, she would start to tremble. But she had no choice. Her only hope at retaining a shred of pride was to act as if neither Hunter nor Benton's actions embarrassed her. So she laid her hand in Hunter's. Though her glove separated their skin, she could not stop the shiver that ran through her. She only hoped that she was able to hide it.

Linette climbed down from the buggy, and Hunter released her hand, holding it not an instant longer than was necessary for politeness. His face was a blank as he walked with her toward the horse pen. Behind them Benton frowned and scrambled out of the buggy. Rosemary followed helplessly.

"Father, I don't want a horse. I don't need one," Rosemary said, hurrying to catch up to Benton.

Benton glanced at her. "Don't talk nonsense. Of course you need a horse."

"No, truly. You know I can't ride," she finished lamely as they came up beside Hunter and Linette. She cast an embarrassed look in their direction.

"Then it's time you got over your foolish fear," Benton told her decisively. He turned toward Hunter. "Rosemary, I'm afraid, is scared of horses."

Hunter slid his eyes over to Rosemary, and for the first time the faintest bit of warmth tinged his face. "Lots of folks are," he said kindly. "What you need, Miss Conway, is a good, quiet, steady horse." He climbed lithely over the fence, and taking down a hackamore from the gate post, he approached a small gray mare. Chewing stolidly, she watched him approach, only the twitch of one ear acknowledging his presence. Hunter patted her forehead, and the mare stuck her head in his chest. He chuckled and ran a hand down her mane.

"Hey, now, Prim." His voice was gentle; it made Linette's heart hurt to hear it. She knew that soft tone was something that she would never hear from him again.

Hunter slipped the hackamore over the mare's head and led her to the fence. "Here you go, Miss Conway," he told Rosemary. "This is as good and gentle a horse as you'll ever find. Here . . ." He reached out and took Rosemary's hand and guided it to the horse's nose. "Just pat her. She won't hurt you."

Jealousy twisted inside Linette as she watched Hunter with Rosemary. He was being no more than kind to her; she could hardly begrudge Rosemary his kindness. Yet it hurt her to see him touch another woman or turn his attention on her, even without any hint of sexual attraction. *How could it still hurt so after so many years?*

Linette pulled her eyes away from Hunter and Rosemary and found that Benton was watching her, his eyes narrowed, and she was aware with a sick certainty that he had seen the flash of jealousy on her face. She hated him for putting her in this situation.

Now Hunter was approaching with another horse, a palomino gelding so beautiful it took Linette's breath away. "Oh, Hunter," she breathed, momentarily forgetting herself in her appreciation of the horse. "He's lovely."

She reached out and stroked her hand up the animal's forehead. Hunter watched her, idly running the horse's mane through his gloved hand.

"I brought him with me from Texas," Hunter went on. "Rubio here is prime horseflesh, but you could handle him."

Absurdly, Linette felt herself flushing with pleasure at his compliment. It didn't mean anything, of course; he was merely speaking the truth. "I—I haven't ridden much lately. Spartan died a year ago, and before that he had gotten too old to ride."

"I'm sorry to hear that. Spartan was a good horse." He would remember Spartan, she knew; it had been the animal she always rode when they went out riding together. Or when she met him at the creek when she had told her parents she was riding or calling on a friend. For an instant, there was an aura of closeness about them, an air of intimacy bred of familiarity and a shared past.

"He looks a little spirited for a lady," Benton interjected, verbally putting himself between them.

Hunter glanced over at Benton, and his eyes held a faint amusement that stated clearly how little he thought of Benton's opinion regarding a horse. "She can ride him." He shrugged, his face bland as he went on, "Course, he's an expensive animal. Might be more than you want to spend on your wife's mount."

Benton bristled. "Price isn't a concern."

"Really? I'm glad to hear that. These days so many good folks are hard up. But, then, I guess that wouldn't apply to you, now, would it?"

Linette bit the inside of her cheek to keep from smiling. Hunter was playing with Benton. He knew that to suggest that something might cost too much would insure that Benton would have to have it. Then he followed it up with an insulting remark so subtle that it was hard to deny.

Benton looked at Hunter with narrowed eyes. Hunter gazed back blandly, as if unaware of what he'd said. "I'll take the horse," Benton said abruptly. "Both of them."

Linette looked at the palomino. It was a wonderful horse—and doubly special because it was clearly one of Hunter's favorites. For Hunter to have brought it out for her seemed almost like a gift from him. She had always loved to ride, and she thought with pleasure of being on this horse, of riding into the country, feeling the wind blowing past her. She wanted the horse so much it hurt.

"No," she said stiffly and backed up from the fence. She could not do it. Every time she saw the palomino, every time she rode it, it would remind her of Hunter. She would think about him, ache for him. Having that horse would make Hunter a real, live presence in her life, and she could not afford that. Whatever pleasure it brought her, it would bring her greater pain. She would be reminded constantly of what she did not have, what once was hers and was no longer.

"What?" Hunter glanced at her, surprised.

A smile curved Benton's mouth. "You don't want it?"

"It's a wonderful horse, but . . . but I'm afraid I'm too rusty. I might not—well, I'm not as good a rider as I once was."

Hunter gazed at her steadily, his eyes unreadable. Linette wondered if he knew why she was turning down the horse or if he thought she simply didn't want something that was precious to him. Would he think that she didn't care? That she was scorning his gift?

Linette looked at him, willing herself not to cry. It didn't really matter what she did; Hunter would think what he wanted about her. It was what he had done before. She swallowed hard and looked out across the pen. "What about that bay mare?"

"She's a good horse," Hunter responded without inflection. "No problems with her. You want to ride her?"

Linette shook her head. "I haven't a riding habit."

"Our visit was a surprise," Benton added, giving

Linette a falsely affectionate smile. He curled an arm around her shoulders and squeezed her to him for a moment. "The horse is a gift for my wife's birthday."

"That's not till July," Hunter said, surprised. Then he clenched his jaw, and a faint flush tinged his sun-darkened cheeks. He looked away. "That is, if I remember correctly."

"You do."

"I never realized you had such an excellent memory, Hunter," Benton drawled, and his eyes gleamed wickedly as he glanced back and forth from Hunter to Linette. Neither of them was looking at the other one.

"You want the bay mare?" Hunter ignored his last remark.

"For Linette? No, I think not. Give Rosemary the other mare, but I think you're right: the palomino is the mount for my . . . *adventurous* wife."

"I don't want it," Linette repeated crisply.

"Oh, yes, you do; you simply won't admit it." Benton's tone was jovial, that of a kindly uncle dealing with a recalcitrant child.

"I won't ride it." Linette's chin was thrust out mulishly, and she looked up straight into Benton's eyes. "It's no use buying it."

Benton waggled a forefinger at her. "Now, now, my dear, I know you better than that. We've been married far too long for you to pull the wool over my eyes."

"I *do not want* the horse." Linette enunciated each word clearly, glaring at Benton.

"Tie it to the back of the buggy," Benton instructed Hunter. "And give me the other one, too, the hack for Rosemary. Maybe she'll learn to conquer her terror."

"Perhaps you ought to go with the mare for Li—your wife," Hunter suggested. "Sometimes people take a powerful dislike to an animal, and then they'll never ride him."

"I'm sure I can persuade Linette to get on this horse." Benton smiled and reached out to run a caressing hand down his wife's arm.

Hunter's eyes turned as hard as marble. "Sure." He crossed his arms. "But you can't take them back today. I still need to have them shod."

Benton dismissed this inconvenience with an airy wave of the hand. "Then bring them to our house when you have them ready."

"All right." Hunter turned away.

Linette pulled her arm away from Benton and shot him a murderous glance. "What do you think you're doing?"

"Why, my dear, getting you the animal you really want."

"I meant what I said. I won't ride it."

"Then you can admire the horse from a distance, can't you?" Benton's eyes glittered palely.

Linette's fingers itched to slap the smug smile from Benton's face. Benton knew why she didn't want the horse, and that was exactly why he was determined that she should have it. He had always been jealous of Hunter, though before they were married, he had been better at hiding it from her. But his jealousy had seemed to grow by leaps and bounds since Hunter had returned to Pine Creek and set up his horse farm.

Linette had no way of fighting Benton except with

her silence and pretended indifference, which only goaded him into further remarks. The only thing that seemed to satisfy him was for Linette to break down into tears, but Linette stubbornly refused to do that. She would not let him see her cry; she would rather take the barbs.

She turned on her heel now and marched back to the buggy. Rosemary stood indecisively for a moment, then scurried after her. Benton stood watching them, his eyes narrowed.

Linette sat stiffly in the buggy until they left, doing her best not to look at her husband or Hunter while they transacted their business. She was sure that Benton took a great deal of pleasure at counting out the money to Hunter; he loved the role of a wealthy man dealing with his inferiors and to have Hunter in the part of the shopkeeper, swallowing his dislike in order to get Benton's money, would make the occasion all the sweeter. He doubtless also liked the idea of Hunter's delivering the animals to his house like a servant. There were times when Linette hated her husband, and this was one of them.

She wished she were a hundred miles from here; she wished she had never agreed to marry Benton. It would have been better, she often thought, not to have married him, no matter what the price. She could have moved away, supported herself somehow, even by scrubbing floors if she had to. Surely it would have been preferable.

But at the time, numbed with grief as she was, and naive enough to believe Benton's assurances that he would love and treasure her without demanding her love in return, it had seemed the best thing to do. The only thing.

The years had opened up her eyes, of course, but by then it was too late. She was married to Benton for life. She had made her bargain with the devil, and she had had to see it through. She took what comfort she could in the fact that, after what had happened, she wouldn't have been happy even if she hadn't married Benton. Her life had ended on that day long ago in Louisiana, and all the rest of it had just been marking time. The truth be known, Benton hadn't gotten the best bargain either, for he wound up with a wife who was nothing more than an empty shell.

At last Benton climbed into the front seat and picked up the reins. Linette didn't glance at him as he clucked to the team, and they rolled out of the farmyard. Neither did she look back in Hunter's direction. She kept her hands clasped in her lap, her eyes on the horizon, exerting all her effort on not allowing the burning teardrops to fall. She refused to let Benton see how he had hurt her. It was the only power she had, the only strength.

Hunter refused to watch the Conways' buggy pull out of the farmyard. He would not give either Benton or Linette the satisfaction of knowing how they'd torn him apart. He faced the corral, staring sightlessly at the horses, until he could no longer hear the buggy. Then he turned. The farmyard looked desolate. He had to fight an urge to run into the house and up the stairs to the window so that he could look down the road and see the Conways' vehicle until it rounded the curve in the road.

He shook his head as he planted his hands on his hips, cursing himself silently for being such a fool. He kept thinking about the way the sun shone on Linette's hair where it was not covered by her silly little tip-tilted hat. The sun's rays had turned her deep auburn hair to fire. Hunter remembered the first time he had seen her hair down. They had been riding, and her hat had come flying off, pulling loose several strands of hair. They had stopped and he had ridden back to retrieve the hat. When he returned, she had taken the pins out of her hair in order to put it back up, and it had lain like a fall of russet-colored water across her back and shoulders.

The sight had taken his breath away. He had slid off his horse and walked over to where she sat on a boulder, waiting for him. He hadn't said a word, just pulled her off the rock and into his arms and kissed her as if there would be no tomorrow.

Linette had been like a flame within him all the time they had been courting. He had been young and bursting with love and desire for her. Every second around her had been a sweet, painful torment; he had felt he would die away from her, and yet all the time he was with her he was so on fire with desire for her that it was torture. It was almost impossible to be alone with her; there was always a chaperone around. Their kisses were stolen and few, whenever they could escape for a few moments from a dance or a party and find a spot by themselves in the garden. But they stoked his passion.

On that particular day, they had been riding with a group of other young people, but he and Linette, better riders than the others, had left the group behind, and for these few minutes they were utterly alone. His mouth had sought its fill of her, even though he knew that that was something he could never achieve. Her mouth was warm and honeyed, open to his advances, and he had grown hot and pulsing, eager to taste her.

Hunter had kissed her face and neck, fumbling at the buttons of her high-necked riding habit until he had exposed her white throat and chest to his exploring lips. His mouth had moved down eagerly across her milk-white chest to the swell of her breasts, and Linette, groaning, had laced her fingers through his hair and pressed his head closer to her. The evidence of her desire had increased his even more, and it had been all he could do to seize control of himself and not pull her down to the ground right there.

Just remembering it sent heat sizzling through his veins. Hunter closed his eyes and growled with frustration. "Damnation!"

Wasn't he ever going to get that woman out of his blood? It seemed as if she haunted him like a curse.

He turned and strode over to the corral. He unsaddled the horse he had been riding earlier and put the saddle and bridle on the buckskin cow horse that he always rode. Jupe was not as fast or well bred as the stallion that had been shot out from under him at Manassas, but he had seen Hunter through many a tough time in his days of cowboying in Texas, and Hunter was convinced that there was no horse more hard-working, clever, or loyal than his Jupe. Jupe seemed in tune with Hunter, quick to obey the slight-est tug of the reins or pressure of Hunter's legs. Most important, he had heart. Countless other cowhands had offered to buy him from Hunter, but Jupe was one horse Hunter would never sell.

He saddled and bridled him quickly. Jupe's ears quirked forward, and he regarded Hunter with a bright, intelligent eye. "Hey, boy," Hunter told him softly, running his hand down the horse's neck. "You ready to run a little?"

Jupe stamped and blew out, and Hunter chuckled. He patted the horse, then led him out of the corral. Swinging up into the saddle, he trotted out of the farmyard and into the meadow. Then he nudged him with his heels and gave Jupe his head, and the horse thundered across the meadow. Hunter leaned for-ward, thrilling, as always, to the feel of the air rushing by, the sound of the hooves pounding the ground. Riding was the one thing that would take him out of himself, set him free from all thoughts and troubles and pain. When he rode, he felt at one with the horse, a creature of instinct and power—not a man who had seen too much of the world.

At last he reined in the horse and looked around him, getting his bearings. They had ridden almost to town, though circling it to the south. The creek wasn't far, and he turned Jupe toward it. Jupe picked his way down to the creek, and Hunter dismounted. Absently, he stroked Jupe's mane as the horse drank from the rocky water. It was spring, and the creek was running pretty high. In summer it would get much lower, gurgling around the smooth flat rocks.

Where he and the horse stood, it was fairly open around Pine Creek. Farther down, cottonwoods and other, smaller, trees grew close to the water's edge. Holding Jupe's reins, Hunter strolled long the creek into the trees. Bushes, too, grew along the banks. It was grassy and lush, a still, private place. Hunter remembered it well.

He continued to walk, as if he were looking for a particular place. Then he found it and he stopped, looking around him. It had been ten years since he was here.

There had been changes, of course—more bushes had grown up. One of the trees had fallen and now made a natural bridge across the shallow water. But essentially it was the same—hidden in a curve of the stream, a ledge of rock jutting out into the creek, shaded by an oak, wider and taller now, and sheltered by a thicket of wild plum bushes.

He and Linette had come here the night before he left for the war. She had been crying, and her eyes were huge and luminous, their beauty cutting into him like a knife. They had met at Shelby and Tess's house, and the two of them had left the young married couple and walked down to the creek and aimlessly along it, holding hands. Finally, here, Linette had pulled him to a halt.

"Please don't go," she had whispered, gazing up at him. It had seemed to him as if all the love in the world had shone out of her eyes at him.

He had swelled with love and pride that this lovely girl cared for him enough to cry and beg him not to go away. He had smiled down at her, wiping the tears from her cheeks. "Don't cry, sweetheart. It'll be all right. I'll be back before you know it. You'll see."

"It's war, Hunter!" Her voice broke on a sob. "What if you don't come home at all!"

He had chuckled with all the thoughtless confidence of youth. "Come on, Lin. I won't get killed. You know I ride better than anyone in this county, even Shelby, and he's probably the only one better with a gun than I am."

"I'm scared." Linette had looked at him, eyes wide and brilliant blue.

Hunter had surged with emotion, love and excitement bubbling within him. He was twenty-two years old, and he had never tasted fear. There had never been anything he couldn't conquer, any woman he couldn't charm, any race he couldn't win. He was a beloved son of a close-knit family, and he loved and was loved by the most beautiful woman in the world. No Tyrrell ever backed down from a fight, least of all Hunter; there was something in him that thrilled to danger, that raced to meet a challenge. But it touched him that Linette was scared for him; his heart swelled with love for her.

He leaned down and kissed her lightly on the lips. "You don't need to be scared for me. Nothing's going to happen to me. We'll chase those Yankees back to Baltimore, and it'll all be over by the end of the summer."

"Then why even go? Couldn't you wait and see what happens? Lots of men aren't going yet."

"What?" Hunter looked horrified. "And miss everything? I can't do that. 'Sides, Shelby and I've already joined up. We've signed our names. We're honor bound to leave tomorrow."

"Oh, Hunter . . ." Tears welled in Linette's eyes. "I don't want you to leave." She stretched up on tip-toe and kissed his cheek, his chin, his lips, in feather-light brushes, covering his face with sweet kisses. "Please don't go. Don't leave me."

"Linette, don't . . ." Hunter groaned. Desire was never very far from the surface when he was around Linette, and now it flamed anew, sparked by the touch of her soft lips on his face and mingling with the excitement already coursing through him.

He put his hands on her waist, and as she pressed her lips quickly against his, his mouth seized hers and kissed her lingeringly. They had kissed this way before, lips open, tongues leisurely exploring, until both of them were searing with sexual heat, panting and eager. It was rare that they were alone for as long as they liked. But this evening no one would be stepping outside to look for them; there were no other people in their party to catch up with them. Linette had come out today to stay with Tess and be with her after Shelby left the next morning. But Shelby and Tess were wrapped up in their own parting, and Hunter knew that neither one of them would come looking for them. They would be utterly alone tonight. Undiscovered.

The thought sent sparks of excitement shooting throughout Hunter. He was aflame. His hands moved up until they reached the soft mounds of her breasts. He drew in an eager, shaky breath and broke off their kiss. He rained kisses all over her face and neck and throat.

Finally, trembling with eagerness and hunger, he pulled away from Linette. It would be wrong to go any further. Disastrous. He would be leaving the next morning, and he wasn't sure exactly when he would return. He could not do anything that might hurt Linette, endanger her reputation. They would be married, of course, when he did come back, but they weren't yet. Linette was a sweet and delicate virgin.

Yet, conversely, just the thought of that made him harder, even more pulsing with passion. He could imagine her opening herself to his invasion, could almost feel her virginal tightness surrounding him, welcoming him. Linette wasn't like other women; there was none of that maidenly shyness and hesitance that there was in so many gently reared girls. She never stiffened and pulled back from him as if she were frightened when he kissed her deeply. She kissed him back, opening her mouth to his, even whimpering with desire. He could imagine how eagerly she would approach their first lovemaking. There would be no tears or denials, only her arms reaching out to embrace him, her deep blue eyes bright with desire.

Now she opened her eyes and looked at him in dazed distress. "Hunter?"

"No." He drew a deep breath, willing himself to be strong. Linette was too innocent to know what lay ahead if they continued this way, but he did. The blood was already coursing through him with a terrible, driving need, a heat that inflamed his very soul. "We can't."

"Why not?" Her big blue eyes seemed to draw him

in. He knew that in her he could find utter peace, utter bliss. He thought of those long, hungry weeks, even months, ahead of him. He thought of the nights and how unbearable they already were without Linette, how he dreamed and thought about her, tossing and turning in his bed, thumping his pillow into shape, until Gideon, across the room, irritably snapped at him to settle down. How much worse it would be without even the prospect of seeing her the next day or the next week, knowing he could not kiss her or hold her!

Hunter groaned. He wet his dry lips, trying to collect his scattered thoughts. But before he could make a coherent sentence, Linette reached up and put her lips to his again, brushing her mouth teasingly across his.

"Please, Hunter?" she whispered huskily. "Please."

"No, we can't. You don't understand."

"No, I don't." Her skin was searing. It shook Hunter to his soul even to touch her.

"I can't," he said raggedly. "If we go on, I'll—I won't be able to stop."

"I don't want you to stop," she assured him softly. "Kiss me, Hunter. Please . . ."

She made a little moue with her mouth, impossible to resist. He kissed her. And all reason was lost.

He had kissed her again and again, and they had tumbled to the ground, tearing off their clothes, and made love there in the shelter of the trees, darkness gathering around them.

Hunter groaned, and he leaned his head against his horse's neck, remembering the moment. He remembered the sweet taste of Linette's mouth, the faint saltiness of her skin as his mouth traveled over her body. She had writhed and moaned in his arms like a madwoman, an exciting combination of innocence and lust. Once he started kissing her, he had known that there was no way he could stop until he was sheathed inside her, and that was the way it had been.

They had rolled across the ground, caressing and kissing, panting with excitement and wonder. Hunter could still remember exactly how soft Linette's skin had been beneath his fingertips, how hot and tight she had been when he sank into her. He had had to thrust hard to get past the seal of her virginity, and Linette had drawn in her breath with a startled hiss. For a moment, he had paused, his ardor shaken by the fear that he had hurt her, but then Linette had moved against him, and he had been hurled back into the blinding heat of desire.

Even now, sweat sprang out on his forehead as he thought about their lovemaking. He'd never experienced anything like it. Linette had clung to him, her legs wrapped tightly around him, and she had moaned with pleasure when he began to rock inside her again. The sound, the feel, had driven him mad with desire. She had encased him so tightly, gloved him with her soft, searing femininity. He had been lost to the world, to everything; he wouldn't have known if an earthquake had exploded beneath them. All he had known was *her:* her love and her molten heat, the little whimpers of delicious torment she made beneath him. And when at last his release rocked him, that had been an earthquake, one that shook his body and soul.

"I love you," he had whispered as he shuddered and collapsed against her, but he had known even then how inadequate the words were, how little they had expressed the cataclysm that raged inside him. For just that one moment, it had been as if he *were* her and she, him, as if they had blended together, nerve, muscle, and bone. They had been one, the way the preacher always said in the wedding ceremony, joined more surely than any words spoken over them in church could ever have made them.

Or, at least, Hunter reflected, that had been the way their lovemaking had felt to him. Obviously, it hadn't affected *her* that way at all. Because when he'd come home from the war, half-broken by years in a Yankee prison, yearning for the healing warmth of her love, her touch, he had found that Linette had married another man. She had married Benton Conway—only weeks after Hunter was captured in battle. And Hunter had learned the bitter depths of betrayal.

4

Linette sat, stiff and silent, in the buggy until they reached their house again. Then she got down from the carriage, not waiting for Benton to come around to help her, and walked, back straight, into the house and up the stairs to her room. She closed her door and locked it, and at last she gave way to tears.

Curling up on her bed, she cried and cried until it felt as if she had run dry. Exhausted, she rolled over onto her back and stared up at the canopy above her head.

She hadn't cried over Hunter Tyrrell in years. She had thought she was no longer capable of such tears, such emotions. For so long she had lived in a state without emotion. She had gone through the days wrapped in cotton batting, protected from the world by the very deadness of her soul. Quite truthfully, she had not cared about anything.

But things had been changing for the past few months—ever since Hunter returned. She had tried to tell herself that it wasn't anything to do with him, that it was simply coincidence. But Linette wasn't able to lie to herself any longer. It was Hunter.

That night almost a year ago when she had been coming down the stairs and had seen him standing in the entry below, a pain she had thought long gone uncurled in her chest. She hadn't even known he had returned to Pine Creek, and the sight of him had struck her like a blow. Since then each reminder of him had stabbed her anew. Her emotions no longer seemed to be dead, at least where Hunter was concerned. Could it be that after all this time, after all that had happened, she still loved him?

Once she had believed that love could endure through all time. During the years since, Linette had grown more cynical. But, now, remembering how she had felt ten years ago when she walked down the stairs with Tess to Tess's engagement party, and she had seen Hunter Tyrrell standing at the bottom beside his brother Shelby, Linette had to wonder if perhaps, in her naïveté, she hadn't been right after all. Maybe there were some loves that one never got over. . . .

Linette had been sixteen and a trifle dazzled with the knowledge that she was the prettiest girl in Pine Creek, probably even the whole county. But her best friend, Tess, managed to keep her from getting too spoiled by all the attention she received. For

Tess, blond, blue-eyed, and petite, was almost as pretty and at seventeen, a year older than Linette, had been firmly established as the county belle before Linette even came out. If it was a heady experience to be surrounded by swains asking for every dance or an opportunity to bring her a cup of punch, Tess was always there, surrounded by an equal number of young men, and would make a wry little face at her, as if to say, "Isn't this the silliest thing?" And Tess, of course, had scored the real coup of the season because, as everyone knew, she had Shelby Tyrrell, the catch of the county, eating out of her hand.

"Tess," Flora Lee Patterson said with a simper as the girls clustered around Tess's mirror, primping before going downstairs to join the men, "what are the rest of us to do? You've already got the only good man in Pine Creek; you know he won't look at anyone else."

Tess laughed and glanced over at Linette in shared amusement. Only Linette knew that the reason for tonight's party was to announce Tess's engagement to Shelby; he was out of any of the other's reach more than Flora Lee even knew. Linette and Tess also knew that Flora Lee was only half-joking when she pouted about Shelby's unavailability.

"Now Flora Lee, you know there are plenty of other men in this town . . ."

"None of them as tall or blond or such a divine dancer," Flora Lee retorted.

"Or so handsome," Pris Clanton contributed, coaxing a curl back into shape around her forefinger.

"Now, that's not true!" Sarah Compton protested. "My Daniel is as handsome as any man around."

"And what about Gideon Tyrrell?"

"Or Hunter!" Another girl exclaimed, rolling her eyes in ecstasy. "Give me a black-haired good-looking devil any day!"

"I declare, Susie, you are downright wicked!"

"Hunter is too good-looking," Pris stuck in.

"Now, how can that be, I'd like to know?"

"What does he look like?" Linette asked innocently.

"You mean you don't know?" Flora Lee gaped at her in astonishment.

"Well, no . . . I've never seen him at a party or anything."

"Give the girl a chance, Florry," her sister Ruthie admonished. "It's only been three or four months since Linette put her hair up and her skirts down."

"And you know Hunter doesn't go to *our* kind of parties much," Sarah added with a virtuous look.

"He runs with a bad crowd," Linette said, to show that she wasn't as naive and unknowledgeable as they thought. "I know that."

"He spends a lot of time in the Flats, I've heard," Flora Lee said significantly.

"Still," Susie stuck in, dimpling, "he's just about the best-looking man I've ever seen. Besides, there's something awfully exciting about a dangerous man, don't you think?"

"Dangerous!" Tess exclaimed. "Oh, for heaven's sakes, Hunter Tyrrell's not *dangerous*. He's Shelby's brother. He's just sowing a few wild oats, and what man doesn't, I'd like to know."

"Well, not my Daniel."

Tess and Susie exchanged amused looks. Everyone in town knew that Sarah worshiped the ground her husband walked on; in her eyes, he could do no wrong, as she was happy to explain to anyone she could get to listen. It had become a standing joke in the community. The truth was, plain, carrot-haired, freckled Daniel Compton was not likely to be a danger to any woman's heart besides Sarah's, nor had his meek soul probably ever strayed toward any stand of wild oats. But everyone was kind enough to refrain from pointing out as much to Sarah.

"Come on," Tess said gaily, picking up her gloves and heading toward the door. "The party can't begin without us, you know."

Smiling, Linette sailed out the door right behind Tess, her wide skirts filling the doorway. They chattered as they walked down the hall and the elegantly curved front staircase of Tess's mansion. Halfway down, looking over the side, they saw Shelby waiting for Tess, chatting with a tall, broad-shouldered man. Shelby turned, hearing Tess's laugh, and the other man turned, too.

The man beside Shelby had thick black hair, a little longer than was proper, and his eyes were green with just a touch of silver, the color of rain-touched leaves. He was well built, as anyone could see even in a formal suit, with a slim waist and hips and the muscular back and shoulders of a farmer and horseman. When he looked up at Linette, her heart had stood still for an instant, and she had almost stumbled on the stairs.

In that moment she fell head-over-heels in love with the man.

By the end of the evening she was certain that she hated him. Shelby greeted Tess, then Linette, and introduced them to his brother, Hunter. Hunter smiled and bowed over Linette's hand, and Linette flashed him her most dazzling smile. She decided she would summarily erase someone from her dance card when Hunter asked her for a dance; she might even be so daring as to give him a waltz even though they had barely met. But, to her amazement—and wounded pride—Hunter didn't ask her for a dance. In fact, he barely seemed to notice her. He chatted with Tess and Shelby for a few moments, then melted into the crowd. During the course of the evening, she ran into him a time or two, but he was merely pleasant to her, evincing none of the moonstruck admiration for her that most young men did. Linette couldn't remember when a man hadn't tried to flirt with her—even some older married men!—yet Hunter Tyrrell virtually ignored her.

Linette was hurt. She was shocked. And she was determined to make him notice her.

After that evening, she saw Hunter several times at parties and other gatherings. In the hopes that she would see him, she took extra care with her dress and hair. When he wasn't at a party she attended, she was disappointed. When he was, she made it a point to flirt vivaciously with other men, hoping that he would notice how many other men were attracted to her, how much others admired her looks and sparkling personality.

Finally, one evening Hunter was one of the guests at a small dinner party at Tess's house. He didn't sit near Linette at the table, but from time to time, Linette glanced up, conscious of someone staring at her, and found Hunter watching her. There was a smoky, slumberous quality to his eyes that sent shivers through her. Linette felt a sudden flash of longing that he would feel some of the same tumultuous excitement that she felt every time she looked at him. It was truly distressing, she realized, how much she thought about him and planned for his presence and worried about what to do to attract him. She had never spent such time on any other man. She wondered if she was an utter fool to feel this way about Hunter. She ought to give up, she thought. Whatever attracted Hunter to a woman, he obviously did not find that quality in her. But the thought of closing the door on Hunter's ever falling in love with her was extremely painful, and Linette knew that she simply could not do that, no matter how foolish it was of her to continue. Rather sadly, she looked away.

Later that evening, as Linette was standing beside one of the long open windows that led out into the garden, Hunter came up beside her and asked softly, "Would you care to take a stroll with me around the garden, Miss Sanders?"

She half turned, eyes widening. "Yes."

Her heart was fluttering wildly as they slipped out the back door and into the dusky light of the flower garden. Linette cast a glance back toward the house, wondering if anyone had seen them. If so, there was sure to be a chaperone out here in a moment. She looked up at Hunter through her lashes. He cast a glance at her, and a mischievous smile lit up his face.

"I've been watching you for weeks," he told her.

"You have?" She stared at him in astonishment. "Why?"

"Surely you must know the answer to that. You're the most beautiful girl in this town."

"I know that you haven't given me a second glance," Linette blurted out bitterly, then could have bitten her tongue for revealing so much of her feelings toward him.

Hunter smiled to himself. "Oh, I've given you more than a second one. Maybe a fiftieth; no, more like a hundredth."

"Are you joking with me?"

"Never more serious in my life." He gazed into her eyes then, and Linette knew that he must be telling the truth. She had to believe those eyes, or she might as well not believe anything at all.

"Then why—why haven't you said anything to me? You've hardly even spoken to me since that night that Shelby introduced us."

"I had no desire to play your little games."

"Games!" Linette exclaimed indignantly. "What do you mean?"

"You know—the games you play with your many suitors, playing one off against the other, giving a smile to one to make another jealous."

"I don't!" Linette cried. "You make me out to be a hardened flirt!"

"No. Not hardened. Just enjoying this first taste of

your power over men. I decided I'd wait until you grew bored with the others."

"Then you've been toying with me." Linette set her mouth. Her eyes flashed. "Ignoring me in order to pique my interest. Isn't that what you're saying? I think it's you who have been the one playing games."

"I wasn't toying with you. Only . . . trying to decide what I was going to do. How could I possibly steal you away from that flock of men always around you?" He smiled sensually, and he stroked a finger down her cheek. "You see, I knew I had to have you to myself."

"Indeed?" Linette tried to look haughty, still smarting a little. "And don't I have something to say about the matter? Perhaps I don't want to be alone with you. Perhaps I prefer the other men's company."

Hunter grinned, a light sparking in his eyes. "Then what are you doing out here with me now?"

His smugness irritated Linette, and she whirled to walk away from him, but Hunter moved quickly, grabbing her wrist and pulling her to a stop. "No. Don't go."

Linette turned. "And why not?"

"Because I don't want you to," he replied, and his face was suddenly wiped clean of all amusement. "Because I don't think I can bear to stay away from you any longer. To see you flirt with other men or favor them with your smile." His voice was low and mesmerizing, and he moved closer to her with his words, until he was only a breath away. "I'm very afraid I'm falling in love with you."

Linette's breath caught. Her pulse was pounding in her throat. "Afraid? You?"

"Yes." He bent toward her, and Linette watched him, fascinated, unable to move, as his face loomed closer and closer. "The thought of losing you would make a coward out of any man."

He kissed her.

Linette trembled under the force of the emotions that rushed through her. She curled her fingers into the lapels of Hunter's jacket and hung on for dear life. The world could have exploded around her, and she wouldn't have noticed. All she could feel, all she could think about, was the warm pressure of his mouth on hers and the sensations that raced through her.

When, at last, Hunter lifted his head, Linette simply stood, stunned, looking up at him. He was breathing rapidly, and his eyes were as bright as those of a man in the grip of a fever. For a moment they remained like that. Then Linette curved her arms around his neck and went up on tiptoe, her lips reaching for Hunter's. Their kiss was deep and filled with promise, and this time when they pulled apart, both of them were more than a little shaken by it. And Linette knew that in the space of those seconds, her entire life had changed. She was utterly, crazily, in love with Hunter Tyrrell; she had found the man with whom she wanted to spend her life.

And Hunter was just as in love with her. Over the course of the next few months, he courted Linette assiduously. Linette had no interest in anyone but him, and her other swains gradually fell away, sadly aware of her disinterest—except, of course, for Benton Conway. He was an older man who had been

courting her since she came out and who had asked
her more than once to marry him. Linette thought
him a nice enough man, but she had never considered
marrying him. He was almost twenty years older than
she, close to middle age, and far too staid for
Linette's tastes. Why, he had a daughter who was
only five or six years younger than Linette! But her
parents favored his suit, often pointing out to her
what a good, stable life she would have with him,
how well cared for she would be, unlike with the
younger, flightier men who courted her. Even after
Hunter came along, her mother continued to push
Benton as a suitor.

"Look at his house; a girl couldn't ask for a more
beautiful place to live," Mrs. Sanders pointed out.
"Why, it's nicer than ours. He could give you anything you wanted."

"But I don't love him." Linette smiled at her
mother, too happy and in love with Hunter even to
get angry. "I love Hunter."

"Him!" Her mother dismissed Hunter with a wave
of her hand. "That wild Tyrrell boy! The Tyrrells are
good people; there's no denying that. But that
Hunter has given them plenty of gray hairs. And he's
the youngest son of the family. What can he offer
you? A life as a farmer's wife? Living out there with
his parents and Gideon? It's different with Tess and
Shelby; the Caldwells have plenty of money and no
son, and Mr. Caldwell is happy to get a son-in-law
who can manage the plantation for him. But do you
think Hunter would want to take over your father's
business?"

Linette smothered a laugh at the idea of Hunter behind the counter at her father's store, counting out nails. Hunter would never be content to stay indoors all day. "No, of course not. But you have Anthony; you don't need a son-in-law to take over the business."

"Maybe not, but what about you? Are you going to be happy sitting way out there on a farm, spending your life putting up peach preserves and shelling peas?"

"Hunter doesn't plan to stay on the farm. He's not made for that life, either."

"And what, pray tell, does he plan to do?"

"Go west to Texas, maybe. We've talked about that. There are acres and acres of land for the taking. Hunter's got some money that he inherited from his grandparents, and we could use that to get started."

"Started doing what?"

Linette paused. "We're not sure yet." She and Hunter had spent many an hour discussing the delightful prospect of their future, but their plans had centered more on the two of them than on what sort of occupation Hunter would have.

Mrs. Sanders sighed. "That's exactly what I'm talking about. You're just a feather-headed girl of sixteen, and Hunter Tyrrell's not much better. You need someone older and settled, someone mature."

But none of her mother's arguments could sway Linette. Because of her parents' disapproval, she saw Hunter primarily at parties or at Tess's. After Tess and Shelby got married, Linette was able to see Hunter at their house frequently. Madly in love, they talked about running away and getting married, but

Linette still wanted her parents' approval. So they put it off, reveling in their secret love, until, in the spring of 1861, Mr. and Mrs. Sanders finally gave in and consented to their marriage—provided that they wait a decent interval before the wedding.

Linette and Hunter had little desire to wait any sort of interval, decent or not. They were full of youthful passion and love, and every day apart seemed like an eternity. But they agreed to her parents' plan.

Then the war had come, exploding Linette's world. Hunter and Shelby immediately volunteered, of course; they couldn't bear not to be in on whatever action was going on. Linette pleaded with him not to go, but her pleas fell on deaf ears.

They met one last time before Hunter and Shelby left for Virginia. Linette used the pretext that she was staying with Tess so that the two of them could support each other the next morning when the Tyrrell brothers left. They would, of course, but the real reason she went to Tess's was to see Hunter. The two of them left Tess and Shelby alone and went riding, winding up at their special spot down by the creek, where they often sat and talked and kissed until they were almost mad with frustrated desire. There, at last, they made love, swept away by passion, spurred by the coming months apart.

The next day when Hunter left, Linette felt as if her world were falling apart. For days thereafter, she found herself bursting into tears at the slightest provocation. She missed Hunter with a raw, unceasing pain.

As the days turned into weeks, Linette began to feel a new dread: her monthly was late. Although everyone did their best to keep young girls completely innocent, Linette had heard enough of the whispered talk of older women to know what that meant. Every night when she went to bed, she added to her prayers that Hunter come home safely and soon, a fervent wish that she was not really pregnant. Yet, with every day that passed, she grew more and more convinced that her prayers were in vain. When she began to feel listless and queasy, she worried frantically about what to do. She started a hundred times to write Hunter, but each time she tore up the letter. It looked so awful, so blunt, in black and white. Besides, she wasn't absolutely positive. She was only a few weeks late. Besides, what could Hunter do? He was in Virginia. With the haphazard state of the mails, it could be weeks before he got her letter, and even then all he could do was write her back. The army wouldn't let him return to marry his fiancée. The only thing Linette could think of was to travel to Virginia and find him, then tell him in person. The thought of going that far alone frightened her. She had never been anywhere out of town without a chaperone, and the farthest she had ever traveled was to New Orleans once with her parents. And how would she pay for the trip? She had no money of her own; whatever she had was a gift from her father.

But she could think of nothing else to do. She would have to work up the courage to tell her parents about her problem; she could see no other way.

In July there was news of a huge battle in Virginia.

Linette's heart leapt in hope; perhaps this would be the battle Hunter had promised, the one big fight it would take to defeat the Yankees. The South won the battle; that news came first. Linette rejoiced with the rest of the townspeople. Then came the casualty lists, the long rolls of names of those killed. And like the others, Linette went to the newspaper office where they were posted. Her eyes ran down the list of the men who had died. *No one from home. No one from home.* Then she saw it, and her heart seemed to stop. There was his name among all those strangers: Hunter Tyrrell.

Her breath left her. She felt suddenly hot and weak, and the hubbub of the people around her faded away as she crumpled to the ground.

5

Her mother took Linette home and put her straight to bed, and Linette remained there for the next few days, numb with shock and grief. At first all she could do was cry for Hunter, but after a while, she began to think about the burden she carried within her.

She was carrying Hunter's baby; that knowledge gave her the only bit of hope and life she had. Otherwise, she thought that she would have been just as happy to die and join Hunter. But she had to stay alive for the baby's sake. She still had a little bit of Hunter left to her, and she had to take care of it. But how? She was only sixteen and unmarried.

Finally, she went to her mother and told her the news. Predictably, her mother stared at her, popeyed, then burst into a wail. "Linette, no! How could you have done this to us?"

"I'm sorry, Mama. I didn't mean to disgrace you. I never thought—I never dreamed that Hunter would die."

"I knew something like this would happen!" Mrs. Sanders went on furiously, jumping up and beginning to pace the room. "I never should have let you see that wild boy."

"Mama! Don't talk badly about Hunter."

"Don't talk badly about him! After what he's done to you?" Mrs. Sanders's face turned red with fury.

"It wasn't just him!" Linette snapped. "I had a little something to do with it, too, you know."

"You were an inexperienced girl. Hunter Tyrrell was a cad to take advantage of you and then leave you this way."

Tears sprang into Linette's eyes. "He didn't die on purpose, I assure you. He was planning to come back, and we were going to be married. He loved me, and I loved him."

"This is awful! Awful!" Her mother put her hand to her forehead. "I—well, we'll send you to your father's sister in Little Rock. No, that's much too close; word would surely get back. My cousin in Mobile—that's it. We'll say you're overwrought with grief."

"And will I have to live there the rest of my life? I don't want that!"

"No, of course not. As soon as the baby's born, you'll give it to an orphanage, and then you can come home, and no one will be any the wiser. Of course, Cousin Maybelle will have to put out some kind of story about your husband being off at the war, or maybe dead, and—"

"No!" Linette stared at her mother in horror. "How can you even think that? I wouldn't give up this baby! This is Hunter's and my child! I'd never give it up. Never!"

"Linette! Be reasonable. You can't raise a child by yourself—unmarried! Why, you'd be the talk of the town! We'd never live down the disgrace."

"I'm sorry, Mama. I wouldn't want to dishonor you and Papa. I can go somewhere else; I'll live by myself, just me and the baby."

"And how will you support yourself, I'd like to know?" her mother retorted heatedly, putting her hands on her hips. "Scrubbing floors?"

Linette thrust out her chin. "If I have to."

"Don't be absurd! A lady doesn't work!" Linette's mother looked as shocked as if her daughter had proposed robbing banks or selling her body to make money.

"I will if that's the only way I can keep my baby." Tears welled in her eyes again, and Linette dashed them away. "Mama, don't you understand? I have to keep this baby! I'll do anything! Anything!"

"And what kind of life do you think that baby would have with you living in some hovel and washing clothes or cleaning house for a living? Have some sense, Linette. Even if you stayed here with us, everyone would know, and you know what they'd say about the child. You would both be ostracized."

"I don't care!"

"You don't care that everyone calls your child a—" she lowered her voice and hissed, "—a bastard! If you don't care for yourself, at least care for your child's sake! Why, it'd grow up like—like that Jesse Crawford. You know, that woman Lucy Crawford's son. No decent person would have anything to do with him."

"No. I don't want that."

"Then give up the child. It's the best thing to do. I'll write to my cousin immediately."

"No. I mean, well, yes, I'll go there. But when the baby's born, I intend to keep it. I'll continue living there, and I'll find some way to support my baby and me."

"Linette, don't be foolish! What kind of life will that be for either of you? You can't do that."

"What else can I do?" Linette burst out in anguish. "I will not give this baby up! I don't care about my life, anyway. With Hunter dead, nothing matters, anyway!" She began to sob. "Nothing except his baby."

Her mother stopped and looked at her daughter, her face twisting with pity. She sighed and went to her, putting her arm around her and trying to soothe her. "There, there, sweetheart. Just hold on. We'll think of something."

Linette wrapped her arms around her mother and cried her heart out. When she was through, her mother handed her a handkerchief and said briskly, "Clean up your tears. I've just had an idea. "

"What?" Linette asked huskily, wiping away the wetness from her cheeks. She felt as if she'd cried a thousand buckets of tears the last few weeks. Her eyes and head ached all the time, keeping company with her heart, she supposed.

"Benton Conway."

"What about him?" Linette looked at her, puzzled, not understanding the sudden switch in subject.

"That man is crazy in love with you and he'd be a good provider, a good father for your child."

"What! Are you suggesting that I marry him?"

"Of course. What else? It's the best solution I could think of. Benton would be willing to marry you, I think, no matter whose child you're carrying."

"No, Mama, I couldn't. I love Hunter. I couldn't marry another man." She shuddered at the thought of another man's sharing her home, her bed. She couldn't bear to kiss him or let him touch her. "That's mad."

"It's not mad. It's practical. Hunter's dead. Right now, you're grieving for him, but eventually you will get over that. Trust me. That's the way of the world. Grief passes; you forget how much you loved someone, even though at the time you thought the world would end if you didn't see them again."

Linette shook her head vehemently. "No. I couldn't possibly. Don't ask it of me."

"Think about it, child! Think what he could give your baby. What he could give you. A home, a husband. Clothes and jewels and—"

"I don't care! I can't do it!"

"Not even for your child's sake? You won't make that sacrifice for your baby? It will need a father and a name more than anything in the world. And how do you think you'll get one when you're an outcast to society?"

"No! Mother, please, don't torment me."

But as the days passed, Linette's mother kept up

her litany of the advantages of marrying Benton Conway. She told her time and again how good it would be for her child, that if Linette did not marry Benton, she would be making her child suffer because of her own stubbornness. Linette worried that her mother was right. She would be denying her child a great deal if she tried to raise it on her own. She had said that she would scrub floors if she had to, but the truth was that no one would hire her even to scrub floors. It was obvious that she had been raised as a lady; her hands were white and delicate, unmarred by calluses or scars. Anyone would know as soon as they saw her that she was inexperienced at hard domestic labor.

And there was no other way she could make money. She had never been studious; she had only learned the things a girl must to function as a lady and catch a husband—she could dance well and sew adequately; she could play the piano and draw a little. The truth was she and her child would starve to death if she moved away from her parents' support and protection.

The smartest thing would be to marry, as her mother had said. Yet Linette shuddered at the thought. She could never be with another man after what she and Hunter had shared!

One afternoon, to her surprise, her mother came to her room, her face alight with excitement, and asked her to come down to the parlor. Linette, sitting curled up on her window seat, looked up at her listlessly.

"Mama, no, I don't want to see anyone."

"You must. Really, Linette. It's Benton Conway, and he wants to talk to you."

"What!" Linette stared, aghast. "He's here? Why? Mother, you didn't tell him, did you?"

Her mother nodded and reached to take Linette's hands. "Darling, don't be angry. I had to. You'll understand; a mother can't stand by and watch her daughter suffer like this. It was the only thing I could think of, the only way out of your dilemma."

"But, Mama!" Linette's cheeks turned pink with embarrassment at the realization that Mr. Conway knew of her condition.

"He was most understanding. He's such a good man, and he loves you deeply. He told me that he would do anything to make you happy. Oh, Linette, please, just come down and talk to him. You can't throw away your baby's future for your stubborn pride! You have to at least listen to what he has to say."

Linette sighed wearily. "All right. I'll listen to him, but that's all I'm promising."

"Wonderful!"

Benton was waiting for her in the parlor. Her mother discreetly remained behind in Linette's bedroom. When Linette entered the parlor, Benton jumped up, beaming at her. Linette forced a small smile.

"Mr. Conway, I'm afraid you've come here for nothing. I don't—"

"No, wait." Benton held up a hand. "Just hear me out, Miss Sanders. That's all I ask."

Linette hesitated, and he came across the room to take her hand in his. "Please," he went on, looking sincerely down into her eyes. "I understand how you feel. Truly. I won't importune you. But you'd be doing yourself and . . . the child a great disservice if you didn't listen to what I have to say."

Linette glanced away, a little embarrassed by the earnest glow in his pale eyes. She didn't have the heart to send him away without letting him say his piece. "All right." She walked away from him and sat down in a chair by the window. Looking down at her hands, she said, "Please, go on."

Benton came closer to her, but he did not sit down. He remained standing, his hands clasped behind his back. His face was solemn. "I believe you know, Miss Sanders, the depth of my feeling for you."

"Yes." Linette looked troubled. "But . . ."

"No. I don't ask that you return it. I don't expect that. Everyone in town knows that you loved Hunter Tyrrell. But he's dead now; I'm sure that your heart is heavy with grief for him." Linette nodded, relieved that he realized the situation. "However, the unfortunate thing is that you need help. Hunter's not here to help you. So I am offering my help in his stead. I'm asking you to marry me."

Linette began to slowly shake her head, but Conway went on hastily, "Let me tell you what I propose: Your mother has explained the situation to me. This is painful for you to discuss, I know, but I think it's important that we be totally honest here. You are carrying a child. Hunter Tyrrell's child. You can't marry the father, and you don't want to give up the baby. You are unable to support the child, and even if you could, it would be a great burden to you. A shame to your family . . . and to the child."

Linette couldn't keep the tears from welling up in her eyes at his words.

"I'm offering to be that child's father. I will accept him as my own, give it my name, raise it. I have money, Miss Sanders. I'm not trying to boast, but I am a well-to-do man; I've always been able to make money, and I know I will continue to do so, no matter what happens with this war. I will provide well for you and your child. You both will have all the material comforts, safety, security."

"That's most kind of you, Mr. Conway." Linette rose agitatedly. "But I cannot marry anyone. I—I love Hunter. I always will."

"I know that." His voice was kind. "I don't expect you to love me. And I would never presume to expect to . . . exercise my marital rights."

Linette's head snapped up, and she stared at him, amazed.

He smiled faintly. "I see that surprises you. Understandably so. You are such a beautiful woman, you would tempt any man. There are many who would insist on you as part of their bargain. But I love you; I would never do anything to hurt you. I realize how repugnant the idea of . . . a relationship with another man must be to you right now. I'm not asking that of you. We would have separate bedrooms. I promise that I would not visit your bedroom. In time, I hope, as your grief lessens, as you come to know me better, you will perhaps grant me such a right, but even if you never did, I promise that I would not ask it of you. I love you far too much to ask you to do something you do not wish to do."

"I—don't quite know what to say. Your generosity is overwhelming."

Benton came over to her, kneeling down on one knee and taking her hand in his. Earnestly he said, "Let me take care of you, Linette. That's all I want. Give your burdens over to me; this is too much for you to bear right now. Let me cosset and coddle you; let me take care of your child now and for the rest of our lives. That's all I'm asking."

Linette looked into his pale eyes, aglow with love and sincerity, then back down at her hands. She did not want to marry Benton Conway. She didn't want to do anything. She no longer felt like a person; there was nothing inside her but a great dark emptiness, a yawning hole where Hunter had once filled her life. She could not imagine moving into Benton's house, becoming his wife, assuming the role of mistress of his household. It seemed absurd, unreal. Why, it was a chore simply for her to get up every morning. The only reason she could make herself do it was because of the baby she carried.

But that was precisely the point, she reminded herself. It was the baby for whom she should do this. She wouldn't have to share Conway's bed; he had just made that clear. All he was asking for was her presence in his house. He would expect her to be his hostess, she supposed, perhaps to be a mother to his daughter, to run his household. But he did not ask for her love or even her affection; he wasn't asking her to pretend; he would not expect her to give herself to him physically. Had he done so, she couldn't have married him, not even for the sake of her baby; the thought of another man touching her was too revolting. But he had not asked that of her. And how could she refuse the offer he had made her? How could she deny all that to her child?

Finally Linette raised her eyes to his. "All right," she said in a faint voice. "I'll marry you."

The wedding was a few days later. Linette was sure that her hasty marriage would start a firestorm of gossip. But she was too numb, too wrapped up in her own sorrow, to care what other people thought. Tess came by to see her, looking puzzled and concerned, but Linette could not confide even in her best friend. She felt too empty and aching inside; she could not bring herself to talk about Hunter and the baby and the reason for her marriage. Later, she thought, she would explain to Tess, and maybe Tess would understand. But right now it was too painful even to see Tess. Looking at her friend's face reminded her of Tess's husband, Hunter's brother, and all the times the four of them had been together. And it slashed her heart anew. The next time Tess came, Linette pretended that she was out.

Linette kept to the house, raising the waistlines of her dress bit by bit to keep from showing her pregnancy. When it became almost impossible to conceal her growing stomach anymore, Benton took her to Louisiana on a belated "honeymoon" trip. They stayed there until the baby was born.

It was a long, difficult labor, and Linette remembered little about it except the pain. She had passed out when the baby was finally born and had been ill and delirious for days afterward. When she finally was herself again, she learned that the baby, a girl, had been stillborn. She did not cry as she had after she heard of Hunter's death; she simply lay in her bed and stared at the wall or fireplace, lost in her mind-numbing grief. Something inside her died with the loss of her child. She no longer really cared about anything.

Three months after the baby died, Benton came to her room, breaking the promise he had made to her before their marriage. Linette struggled, repulsed, and he slapped her hard. Stunned, she lay looking up at him in shock, her eyes filled with tears.

"Stop fighting me!" Benton hissed, a crazed look in his eyes. "I'm your husband. You belong to me!"

"But you promised . . ." Linette said brokenly.

"It's your fault," Benton sneered. "You're much too tempting; no man could be expected to uphold a promise like that. It's only natural for a husband to want his wife, to expect her gratitude and submission in return for all he's done for her."

"You lied to me!"

Benton slapped her again, and she tasted blood as she felt her teeth cut the inside of her cheek. She turned her head, blinking back her tears. She hated Benton. *And she'd be damned if she'd let him see that he had made her cry!*

She stayed dry-eyed through the whole painful process, even Benton's frustrated rage when he was incapable of entering her and completing the act. It did not hurt her, she reminded herself, because nothing could hurt her anymore. She was dead inside.

The final bitter irony came when they returned to Pine Creek and she learned that Hunter had been mistakenly put on the casualty list. He had not died; his horse had been shot out from under him, and he had been wounded and captured by the Union army. He spent the rest of the war in a Yankee prison. The man she loved was alive, but their baby was dead, and she was married to someone else. Had she been capable of feeling, Linette thought, she would have cried for the life that had been lost to her. But she did not; tears were something that she no longer shed.

And so it had been over the years. The pain of losing her daughter, of knowing that the man she loved would never be hers, had lessened over time. The numbness had faded. She had become accustomed to her life and was even fond of Benton's daughter. She had even figured out various ways to avoid having Benton in her bed, and those tricks, coupled with his anger at his impotence, meant that she was forced to endure his attentions less and less over the years. Linette wouldn't have said that she enjoyed her life, but it was livable. But, even so, there was a cold, quiet emptiness deep at the core of her being. Her emotions were beyond anyone's touch.

Or so she had thought.

A timid knock at the door interrupted Linette's reverie. She sat up, wiping the tears from her cheeks, and glanced out the window. The sun had dropped low in the sky, which meant that she had spent most of the afternoon in these fruitless, self-pitying memories. Linette hated thinking about the past; usually she carefully avoided it.

She got up and went over to open the door a few inches. Rosemary stood outside, looking anxious. "Are you all right?"

"Of course. I'm fine." Linette knew that her appearance belied her words. She could feel stray bits of hair straggling down her neck, and doubtless her face was splotched and her eyes swollen from crying. But she knew that Rosemary would abide by her pretense. "I was . . . merely taking a nap."

Rosemary nodded, but her gaze remained worried. "I—I'm sorry about this morning."

"It's not your fault."

"But Father shouldn't have . . . done what he did," Rosemary finished lamely.

Linette smiled. Rosemary was a sweet girl, and she always bent over backward not to say anything that could hurt anyone. Linette reached out and gave her arm an affectionate squeeze. "Never mind. That's over now. I hope I'm not foolish enough to carry on over something that can't be changed."

Linette stepped back, motioning for her stepdaughter to come into her room. Maybe talking with Rosemary could take her mind off herself and her memories, Linette thought. "Why don't we have Cecy send us up a pot of hot coffee, and we'll have a nice little chat?"

"All right," Rosemary agreed with alacrity, following her into the room.

Linette sat down in the rocker by the window, reaching over to the bell pull to summon the maid, and Rosemary seated herself across from her in the blue easy chair, curling her legs up under her in an unpretentious, almost childlike way.

"Now," Linette began brightly, knowing that this would be a topic on which Rosemary could discourse for hours, "tell me what's going on at the library. . . ."

Pride kept Linette going through that day and the next. She didn't want to worry Rosemary, and she refused to give Benton the satisfaction of seeing that he had hurt her. So she went about her everyday life, looking as cool and collected as she could make herself.

The next afternoon she was in the sitting room, embroidering a handkerchief when a maid came to the doorway. "Mrs. Conway?"

"Yes?" Linette looked up inquiringly.

"There's a man downstairs to see you. He's at the back door."

"Who is it?"

"I don't know, ma'am. He didn't say."

"All right. I'll be there in a moment." Linette stuck her needle into the material and set it aside. The fact that the maid had said "man" instead of "gentleman" indicated that the visitor was a tradesman trying to sell something or maybe someone looking for work around the house. She wasn't really interested in either, but frankly she was glad of the distraction. She'd been unable to concentrate on her sewing.

Linette followed the maid down the back stairs into the kitchen. Cecy, the cook, a tall, spare black woman, turned and gave Linette a long look. "He be waiting outside, Miz Linette," she said, pointing with her spoon to the back door.

"Thank you, Cecy." Linette was puzzled. She couldn't read the look the cook had given her. *Was it suspicion? Warning?* It made her wonder exactly who this visitor was.

She opened the back door and stepped outside. Then she understood the black woman's look. The man waiting for her a few steps from the back porch was Hunter Tyrrell.

6

Hunter was turned away from her, gazing out across the yard. He held the ropes of the two horses Benton had bought from him.

"Hunter!" The name slipped out of her in her surprise.

He turned around. "*Mrs.* Conway," he replied with ironic emphasis, his tone and eyes mocking her. "I've brought your horses."

Her heart was hammering. He was the last person she wanted to see. Yet she couldn't suppress the excitement that rushed up in her. It irritated her, and she struggled to remain aloof as she remarked coolly, "Yes, I see. I'm sure that Mr. Conway will be pleased. Why don't you put them in the stables?"

Hunter came closer until he was standing below her at the base of the porch steps. "Don't you want to inspect your merchandise?"

"I believe they were my husband's purchases, not mine."

Something flickered across his face, then was gone before Linette could figure out what the expression meant. He said nothing, just continued to look at her, his expression hard and faintly challenging. Linette found herself walking down the three steps.

"All right. Let's see them." She tried to look straight into his eyes, just to show him that it didn't bother her to see him, but pain sliced through her chest, and she glanced away. *It shouldn't hurt so much after all this time,* she told herself. But it didn't help.

Linette went past him to the horses and walked around them, running a knowledgeable hand down their legs. But she knew that she wasn't really looking them over, just putting on a show; she was far too distracted by Hunter's presence behind her.

"Why don't you show me where to put them in the carriage house, ma'am?" Hunter's obsequiousness was mockery in itself.

"I'm sure you can find stalls," she retorted sarcastically.

"Oh, but I might put them in the wrong ones. I'm not used to such a grand place."

"Stop playing the fool." Linette shot him a flashing glance.

"Don't know how," he responded, his gaze level. "That's what I've always been around you, isn't it?"

Linette whirled around and strode off toward the barn. The new fashion of drawing the front of the skirt back tightly hampered her stride, however, and she wondered, flushing with a combination of anger and embarrassment, whether she merely looked foolish rather than righteously indignant.

However, Hunter, following behind her, found the view of her quick, bouncing stride more enticing than foolish, for it set her small bustle swaying seductively. *I was an idiot,* he thought, *to ask to see her today.* He had known it when he set out, and he had planned simply to leave the horses with the groom or tether them in the Conways' yard. But then, against all his better judgment, he had found himself knocking at the back door and telling the cook that he was there to see Mrs. Conway. He cursed himself for being ten kinds of a fool. But he couldn't tear his eyes away from the delicious sway of Linette's ruffled, bustled skirt.

The desire to punish her burned inside him, as it always did, the need to scorch her with the fierce heat of his rage. Yet, he knew, looking at her, that it was he himself who was in torment whenever he was near her. And that fact only made him wish even more that he could somehow inflict on her the same pain that stabbed him.

Linette jerked open one wide door of the carriage house and stepped into its dimness. Hunter came in after her. She whirled around to face him, gesturing toward the empty boxes at the front. "Those are the only empty stalls," she said tersely.

"Why, thank you kindly, ma'am," Hunter said, tipping his hat with overblown politeness as he led the horses to the stalls and put them inside, then removed their halters. He talked to her as he worked, thickening his accent until he sounded like a rube talking to a princess. "I reckon I wouldn't have had a notion where fine folks like you would put your horses. Heck, I might have just stuck 'em anywheres."

"Would you stop it!" Linette snapped.

"Stop what?" Hunter's eyes were wide with innocence.

"Talking like that, as if you'd never been out of Hampton County. As if you'd lived in a shack all your life."

"Why, ma'am, I'm just a poor old farmboy. We both know that, don't we? And we both know how much money matters to you. How much you'd do to live at the top." His tone was thick with significance and an equal amount of scorn.

"You don't know anything about me," Linette spat, infuriated and hurt. "And you never have."

"I reckon that's one thing that's true," Hunter replied with a thin smile. "I used to think you were an angel."

"Oh, hogwash! You never thought I was an angel any more than I thought you were a saint! The first thing we ever did was argue. As I remember, you told me I was playing games."

"I had the right of it then." Hunter's eyes were dark. "I just didn't realize how serious your games were—or how far you'd take them."

"I never played a game with you!" Linette blazed. No one had ever been able to make her angry faster than Hunter, even when they'd been courting and passionately in love. Now all that was left was the anger.

She stepped closer to him, her face high with color, her blue eyes flashing vividly. She was so beautiful it made him tremble inside. His fingers itched to reach out and grab her arms and shake her—or pull her into him.

"No?" His voice was low and lethal as he leaned forward, looming over her intimidatingly. Linette planted her fists on her hips and refused to back up an inch. "What about all those sweet words you told me? What about those lying kisses?"

"They were never lies!" Linette felt suddenly as if she couldn't breathe. Hunter's eyes were like green fire, and his face, so dearly familiar to her, was also alien with hatred.

"I'm not that naive anymore, my dear girl. I've had a long time to think about it. When I first came back and found out you'd married Benton, I couldn't understand why you had done it. A woman doesn't love a man, then marry somebody else a month after she finds out he's dead!"

"I tried to explain it to you! I wanted to! But you never gave me a chance. That day on the street, I even called out to you, but you walked away. You wouldn't listen to me!"

"Explain! Oh, I'm sure you could come up with some honey-sweet words about how your 'poor heart just broke in two,' couldn't you? But I'm not stupid enough to fall for them anymore. Finally, I realized, you never loved me to begin with; you'd just let me court you because you were trying to make Conway jealous. Probably he wouldn't go so far as to offer you marriage. Isn't that right? So your seeing another, younger man would bring him around. And that's what you did."

"You may have gotten older, but you sure haven't gotten any smarter," Linette blazed back at Hunter. "I never had to make Benton Conway jealous; he wanted to marry me long before you ever showed up. I chose you over him! That should have been obvious even to someone as blind and stubborn as you! I gave myself to you. What woman would do that just to make another man jealous? You know that you were the first man to ever make love to me!"

"But I sure as hell wasn't the last, was I?"

Linette slapped Hunter with all her strength, so furious that she hardly knew what she was doing. Then she stepped back, staring at him in dismay. Hunter's cheek was red where her hand had landed; his eyes above it were like ice. Making a noise of frustration, rage, and misery, Linette whirled away. But Hunter grabbed her wrist and jerked her back around.

"I want to know something," he grated, and the cold light in his eyes made Linette want to shiver. "Did you ever feel anything when I kissed you? Or was that all a show, just to keep me in your web?"

He pulled her closer. Linette tried to hold herself back, but he was too strong for her. Slowly he drew her nearer, until she stood only an inch from him. His face hovered over hers, looming so large that she could look at nothing but his eyes. She felt lost in their depths, shivering and hungry and desperate for the fulfillment that lay only in him. Her lips parted a little as she struggled for breath. His eyes dropped to her mouth. She could feel the rapid rise and fall of his chest, so close together were they.

"You still have the same effect on me," he said huskily, his hands going to her hips and pressing her crudely against him. Linette could feel the hard length of his desire. She couldn't help but remember how he had filled her, huge and male and supremely satisfying. She trembled, her eyes fluttering closed, unaware of how erotically submissive her expression was, showing a passion that was overwhelming and at the same time against her will. She couldn't have said more clearly that she desired him—desired him with a strength that overcame her will and mind.

Hunter drew in his breath, the sharp pangs of desire biting into him with just as much force, just as little volition. "You drive me out of my mind," he whispered, his voice shaking. "You have ever since I stood beside Shelby and looked up and saw you coming down the stairs. I wanted you so much then, I couldn't even come close to you for fear everyone would see how much I wanted you."

"Hunter, no, please . . ." Linette's voice broke on a little sob.

"Oh, yes, please," he replied raggedly. His lips brushed against hers. His mouth hovering over hers, he whispered, "Tell me you still want me. Tell me how you think of this when *his* hands are on you." His mouth teased her lips again.

Linette made a little noise, a whimper born of passion and despair. Hunter kissed her, his lips sinking into Linette's, rocking seductively until her lips parted for him. He wrapped his arms around her tightly, pulling her up into him, and his tongue invaded her mouth. His chest was rock hard against her breasts, his arms like iron around her. She could not move, could hardly breathe. Yet she wrapped her arms around his neck, clinging as if she might slide from his grasp. Years of yearning rose up in Linette. She kissed him back fervently, her tongue twining around his.

Hunter's breath was hot against her cheek, his skin searing hers wherever it touched. Linette felt suddenly, wildly alive, every nerve in her body tingling, myriad emotions exploding within her. She wanted to cry; she wanted to laugh; she wanted to wrap her arms and legs around Hunter and melt into him. Aching heat flowered between her legs. She dug her fingers into his shoulders.

Hunter held her head with his hand at the nape of her neck, as though fearful she might try to move away from his kiss. His mouth consumed her.

"Linette . . . Linette . . ." Hunter murmured her name. His fingers dug into her bright hair, popping pins loose and sending strands tumbling down, brushing like silk across his fingers.

Linette let out a little sob of loss as Hunter tore his mouth from hers. He trailed kisses across her cheek and down her throat until he was stopped by the high collar of her dress. With a growl of frustration, he reached up and began to undo the buttons at her throat, his fingers clumsy with haste. Linette's head fell back, exposing every inch of her white throat to his greedy mouth, and Hunter seized the opportunity to taste it. His hand came up and cupped her breast.

The mound was soft and pillowy beneath his fingers, slightly larger than he remembered, and as he touched her, the nipple hardened and elongated, a hard button beneath the cloth of her dress. Hunter moaned softly, and his thumb circled her nipple. Slowly he moved around the hard bud, over and over, and all the while his lips explored her throat.

Linette moved restlessly, squeezing her legs tightly together. She ached to feel his hand on her naked flesh again, to have his mouth on her breast. Remembered pleasures tumbled wildly in her mind, blocking out all thought of the present, all reason and propriety.

"Hunter . . ." she whispered, lost in his kisses. "Oh, Hunter, love."

Hunter went suddenly still. He straightened, his hands falling away from her. Linette looked up at him, startled. They stared at each other for a moment. Hunter breathed in short pants. His eyes glittered, and his face was flushed. Then he drew a long breath and said harshly, "Don't say it."

Linette blinked, confused. "Don't say what?"

"Love!" He fairly spat the word out. His face was etched with contempt. "You don't know the meaning of the word. You never loved anyone in your life but yourself."

Linette stumbled back, blanching. She felt as if Hunter had struck her. She wanted to hit him back, to hurt him as he had hurt her. "You're right," she spat at him. "I don't love you. I never did—I was just too young and foolish to realize that all we ever had was lust, not love!"

"Yeah?" Hunter's smile was bitterly mocking. "But you sure felt that, didn't you? You still do; I just proved that. Whatever that old man can give you, it ain't enough to make up for this, is it?"

Linette's lip curled. "Get out of here. I don't want to see you again. Ever."

"With pleasure, ma'am." Hunter reached down and picked up his hat from where it had fallen on the floor during their kisses and set it back on his head, giving it a sharp tug. "With pleasure."

He walked out the door, shoving it back so hard that it slammed against the wall. Linette sat down on a bale of hay. She was trembling all over, her knees too weak to support her any longer.

If Hunter had upset Linette before, he did so doubly now. For days after his visit, merely the thought of him filled her with fury. How dare he treat her with such contempt, as if she were a villainess and he merely the poor, unknowing victim! God knows, she had been wrong to marry Benton, and she had bitterly regretted it many times. But she was not the only person at fault.

Hunter had made love to her and then gone off to play war with his brother, never giving a thought to whether or not he might have planted a seed in her womb. Even the few letters that she had received from him before Manassas never mentioned any concern about leaving her pregnant and facing an awful future. No, he had gone off to do what he wanted to do, without a thought in the world about what might happen to her. About what she might have to face.

She had been the one to face her pregnancy alone, who had had to do the best she could for her baby without a father. Perhaps it had been wrong, but she had been young and numbed by grief, and what she had done seemed like the only course possible for her and the baby. Then, when Hunter returned, he hadn't even been willing to listen to her explanation. He hadn't come to see her, as she thought he would, demanding to know why she had married Benton. When finally one day she saw him on the street, he had looked straight at her, then turned on his heel and walked away. She had called out to him, but he didn't even look back. He hadn't tried to find out what really happened. He simply assumed that she had been unfaithful to him. He had believed the worst about her.

Obviously time hadn't altered his opinion in the slightest. Rather, it seemed to have set it in stone. *He had been so contemptuous in the carriage house, so hurtful and cutting!* Hunter had always had a temper; even when they were in the first throes of love, he and Linette had quarreled frequently. He was also stubborn, a trait generally acknowledged to be common among the Tyrrells. But the years had made him hard and cold, too. He was no longer as quick to cool off as he was to fire up, and his stubbornness wasn't tempered with the saving grace of his ready laughter or flashing smile. He was bitter and sharp, and he hated her with a vitriolic anger. Certainly, Linette had known he no longer loved her; she had expected his resentment. But she had not expected this burning hatred; she had not thought Hunter would despise her, that he would treat her as if she were something noxious and evil.

But at least the fire of Linette's anger carried her through the days in better spirits than the pain that had dogged her after she saw Hunter at the horse farm. She had planned not to ride the horse he had sold Benton. But when she thought about it, she realized that to stay away from the beautiful animal would be to admit to Hunter how deeply he had wounded her, how much she had cared for him. She was furious enough now that she wanted to prove to him—and to Benton—how little Hunter mattered to her. The best way to do that would be to ride the horse, just as she would if they had gotten it from a complete stranger. *Let Hunter see that I can ride the horse and not think once of him! Let him see that I'm in control of myself!*

She took the horse out every day, determinedly steeling herself not to think about Hunter. She could not block out the memories that came flooding back, but each time she shoved the thoughts out of her mind. She found that once she overcame her memories, she enjoyed riding again. There was a freedom in it that she hadn't felt in years. With the powerful horse beneath her and the breeze upon her face, she could believe, at least for a moment, that she was young and free again, that she was not bound in a loveless marriage, tied by the bargain she had made so long ago to a man she disliked. She could pretend that she could just keep on riding and never stop, ride away from this place and this life.

Linette returned from her rides refreshed and renewed. She thought she detected some chagrin on Benton's face when he saw this result of his scheme, and the thought gave her a little secret pleasure. Even if she hadn't enjoyed the rides, it would have been worth going out just to turn the tables on Benton. Perhaps next time he would think twice before he started one of his nasty little plots.

One day she returned from her ride late, and she had to hurry to get dressed and down to the dinner table on time. "Well, my dear," Benton said bitingly, taking out his pocket watch and looking at it pointedly. "I'm so glad that you could join us."

"Why, thank you, Benton," Linette replied smoothly, sliding into her place at the foot of the table.

Rosemary smiled sympathetically at her from her place at the table. "Hello, Linette," she said, hoping to draw the conversation away from Linette's tardiness.

"Hello, dear. How—"

Benton interrupted her gruffly, "You certainly seem to be spending a lot of time on that horse for someone who didn't want it."

"Yes, I am." Linette responded, turning toward him. "I was wrong; I find I love riding still. You were right to buy him."

She smiled sweetly, knowing that she was complimenting him when he had really done it only to upset her. She felt a spurt of amusement when Benton's brows pulled down into a glower.

"Dammit, Linette, if you think that you can play

fast and loose with your marriage vows, you have a lot to learn about me even yet."

"Papa!" Rosemary gasped. "No! Oh, please, you mustn't say such a thing!"

Linette arched her eyebrows, infusing her look with contempt. "Don't worry, Rosemary," she said calmly, her eyes remaining steadily on Benton's face, "I'm sure that your father knows how foolish an idea that is. Don't you, Benton?"

"Goddammit, don't toy with me!" Benton growled, slamming down his napkin and rising to his feet. He pointed a warning finger at Linette. "If I found out you've been sneaking off to meet Hunter Tyrrell, you'll rue the day you were born. I promise you."

"The only time I've seen Hunter Tyrrell was when *you* arranged for it!" Linette retorted, her eyes blazing.

Benton sneered and strode to the door, where he turned and glared back at Linette. "Just remember what I said."

He turned and walked away. A moment later the front door slammed behind him.

Rosemary and Linette sat in an embarrassed silence, staring down at the table. Finally Rosemary began softly, "I—I'm sorry. I'm sure Papa didn't mean what he said. I think it's just that he—he loves you so much that he gets jealous without reason."

"Of course." Linette's mouth twisted bitterly. But then she raised her head and looked at her stepdaughter, who was watching her with such a woebegone expression that Linette forced herself to smile. "Don't worry, dear. Really. I'm sure that everything will be all right. Now, tell me, what did you do today."

Rosemary's face lit up. "Oh, Linette! Mrs. Vance and I went to visit Tess today. We saw her baby, and, oh, he is so darling!"

"I'm sure he is." The same bittersweet ache that she had felt when Maggie Prescott first told her the news filled her chest again. She thought of Tess's baby, of holding him in her arms, and the longing that filled her was so strong that it shook her.

"You have to go see him," Rosemary continued enthusiastically. "You would adore him."

Linette shook her head. "No, I don't think that would be a good idea."

"Why not? I'm sure Tess would love for you to come."

"The Tyrrells and I are not exactly friends."

"But that's so far in the past! And I know Tess doesn't think that way. She asked me about you. She said that she would love to see you."

"No. Really, Rosemary, I don't want to."

Linette avoided babies whenever possible. She preferred not to be around children of any age, but babies were the worst, and a Tyrrell would be bound to upset her even more than another child.

However, over the course of the next few days, Linette found that she could not get the idea of Tess's new baby out of her mind. She thought it was probably fair-haired and blue-eyed like both Gideon and Tess. But Hunter and Maggie were dark-haired, like Mrs. Tyrrell's side of the family. Linette had always wondered whether her own child would have outgrown its baby hair and become a redhead like herself or black-haired like Hunter.

Scalding tears filled her eyes at the thought, and sternly Linette blinked them back. She told herself that she was being foolish, thinking about Tess's baby. She had nothing to do with Tess or her baby. Gideon would probably be furious if she dared to step inside his house.

But one day, almost a week later, when Linette went out for her daily ride, she found herself turning down the road that led to the Tyrrell farm. She kept her face straight ahead and her eyes firmly on the road as she passed Hunter's farm, not even glancing toward it.

When she came to the turnoff to the Tyrrell farm, she pulled her horse to a stop. The palomino blew out, shaking his head with impatience while Linette gazed up the path to the farmhouse. She knew that there was no reason for her to go to Tess's house, no reason to see Tess or her baby. She reminded herself that if she went, she would regret it as soon as she stepped inside the door. It would be asking for punishment to look at a new baby, to see an old friend. To face Hunter's brother.

Linette was about to turn the horse around and ride back to town, but she hesitated, then tapped the palomino with her heels and started up the drive that led to the Tyrrell place.

7

Linette came to a stop in front of the large white farmhouse. It was a roomy, welcoming place with a wide porch that ran around three sides of it. She had been there only a few times, but she had always felt at home and welcome here. She remembered the way Jo Tyrrell, Hunter's mother, had come down the steps to greet her the first time Hunter brought her out for Sunday dinner. Jo's warm face had been wreathed in smiles and she had stretched out both hands to take Linette's and give them a friendly squeeze. Her gray eyes had sparkled with both curiosity and warmth, and Linette had liked her immediately.

That was so unlike the last time she'd seen Jo Tyrrell, when Jo gave her a short nod and said, "Mrs. Conway."

Linette let out a breath and swung down from her

horse, tying him to the hitching post in front of the house. She went up the steps and knocked at the front door, then waited, her stomach jumping, for someone to answer the door. She had been prepared for Gideon or Mrs. Tyrrell to open the door. She hadn't been expecting Maggie, however, and when Maggie opened the door, she stared at her, her carefully prepared little speech flying right out of her head.

"Oh, Maggie, it's you," she said foolishly, then blushed to her hairline. "I mean—I'm sorry, I wasn't expecting you."

Maggie gazed back at her, her eyebrows raised, obviously equally surprised to see Linette Conway on her doorstep. "Linette." Maggie glanced back over her shoulder into the hallway. "Won't you come in?" she asked finally and stepped back to let Linette enter.

"Rosemary told me yesterday that she'd been out to see the baby," Linette began, her voice light and fast with anxiety. "She told me how sweet he was, and I thought—well, Rosemary said Tess asked if I was coming to see him, so I thought it would probably be all right."

"I'm sure it is," Maggie said quickly. She glanced over her shoulder again. It seemed to Linette that she was nervous about something. "Why don't I take you up to Tess's room?"

She started across the entryway to the staircase, and Linette began to follow her. Just at that moment, two men and another woman came out of a room at the back of the hallway and started down it. Linette saw only one of the group—Hunter Tyrrell. Her heart began to skip crazily in her chest. Linette silently cursed herself for coming out here.

The last person she wanted to see was Hunter. Her face burned at the thought of the last time she had seen him and what had happened between them. What if Hunter thought she had come here expressly in the hopes of seeing him again? She remembered how he had bragged about her response to his kiss in the stables. He had been so damnably sure of himself, so openly contemptuous of her!

Linette wished that she could disappear magically. She thought of turning and running back to her horse, but she refused to do something so cowardly. Instead, she braced herself, raising her chin a notch.

"Good morning, Mrs. Conway." The woman beside Hunter spoke as she continued down the hallway toward Linette, and for the first time Linette actually looked at the woman and man who were with Hunter.

The woman's face was carefully devoid of expression as she looked at Linette.

"Good morning, Mrs. Tyrrell," Linette answered, grateful that her voice came out steadier than she felt.

"Linette's here to see Tess and the baby," Maggie explained.

"I see."

Linette did not smile, just looked back at Hunter's mother calmly. She wasn't about to try to ingratiate herself with this woman or anyone else. If Jo Tyrrell hated her that much, then she'd just have to tell her to leave.

"Mrs. Conway," the other man said, holding out his hand toward her. "I'm Dr. Prescott. We met, I believe, but you may not remember me."

"Oh, yes, at Mrs. Dowden's house." Linette smiled faintly at him and put her hand in his, relieved that there was one person here who was fairly neutral toward her. He was married to Maggie, of course, so he had probably heard an earful about her. But at least he was new in town and not a Tyrrell.

"I can attest that William Alan Tyrrell is worth seeing," Dr. Prescott said, giving her a crisp smile. "I delivered the boy myself."

Linette smiled back at him, but her eyes slid over to Hunter. She wondered if he was going to say anything or just stand there, looking darkly at her. She drew a breath and said calmly, "Hello, Hunter."

He looked at her for a long moment, then said only, "I'll put your horse away."

He walked around her and out the front door. Prescott glanced after him, faint surprise on his face. Linette felt a blush rising in her cheeks. "Well," she said brightly to Prescott and Mrs. Tyrrell, "if you will excuse me, I was just on my way up to see Tess."

"Of course."

Jo Tyrrell nodded.

Linette turned and hurried up the stairs after Maggie.

Maggie softly opened a door down the hall and stuck her head in. "Tess? You up to seeing a visitor? Linette Conway's here."

"Linette!"

Linette heard Tess exclaim within the room, and

Maggie opened the door all the way, stepping back so that Linette could enter. Tess was sitting up in a big oak four-poster bed, pillows propped behind her back. She held out her hands toward Linette, motioning her toward the bed. "Come in, come in. It's so nice to see you!"

Linette smiled back. "I would ask you how you're feeling, except that it's easy to see that you're the picture of health."

Her words weren't merely polite. Tess looked radiantly healthy and happy. Her pale complexion was tinged with pink, and her blue eyes sparkled. She smiled and nodded.

"I know. I feel wonderful. Aunt Charlotte told me it was positively unladylike to look as robust as I do less than two weeks after giving birth."

Linette chuckled. She was familiar with Tess's aunt Charlotte's pronouncements on propriety; she and Tess had giggled over them frequently when they were girls.

Linette walked around the foot of the bed to Tess's side. She saw the cradle lying on the floor, a few feet away from the bed, and she hesitated, her chest squeezing within her. She wondered if she had been very foolish to come here.

Tess saw the direction of Linette's gaze, and she smiled, misinterpreting Linette's hesitation. "Oh, it's all right. You won't wake him up. He's been awake for several minutes now; I've been listening to him gurgling. It won't be long before he wants his lunch and really tunes up."

Tess slipped out of bed and went over to the

cradle, bending down to pick up the baby. Linette's hand went out to the poster of the bed to steady herself. Her stomach twisted within her, and she knew that she should not have come. Why had she been so foolish as to think that she could face seeing Tess's baby?

"Here he is," Tess said, turning back toward Linette. She cradled the baby in her arms, a tiny bundle of white, and she was smiling down at it, her entire concentration on the little scrap of flesh. "Master William Alan Tyrrell," she pronounced, her voice filled with both humor and pride.

She glanced up at Linette and came closer, holding out the bundle. "Here, would you like to hold him?"

Panic rose in Linette. She looked down at the baby, which Tess was now holding out to her. Linette glanced up at Tess, then back down at the baby. His eyes were open in his small, perfectly formed face, and he gazed up at Linette with a solemn expression. Pale blond fuzz covered the top of his head. His eyes were blue and unfocused. His tiny fists had broken free of the swaddling blanket and he was waving them around wildly. He looked so beautiful to Linette that she felt almost physically ill.

"I don't think I'd better," she said, putting her hands behind her back. She continued to stare at the baby, filled with a strange combination of fear, awe, and excitement.

"Don't be silly," Tess laughed. "He won't break. Here, take him."

She pushed the baby toward Linette, and Linette's arms automatically curled around him. He felt tiny and light and soft in her arms. An almost unbearably painful sweetness filled Linette. She gazed down at the baby, hot tears welling in her eyes.

"He's so beautiful," she whispered.

Tess smiled proudly. "I know. Isn't it wonderful? Sometimes I look at him and I can hardly believe he's mine. It's a miracle."

Linette blinked the tears from her eyes. She thought that she could stand here with this baby pressed to her breast forever. Yet at the same time, feeling his small soft warmth cuddled against her started a cold lonely ache deep within her that swelled rapidly, threatening to overwhelm her.

At that moment the baby screwed up his face and began to whimper. "Oh, no!" Linette gasped, horrified. "What did I do?"

"Nothing, silly." Tess chuckled and reached out to take the baby. "I imagine he's just getting hungry. You should hear him yowl sometimes."

Tess bent her head down over him, cooing to the baby, and his whimpers stopped, at least for a few moments. Linette watched them, envy and longing creating a bitter taste in her mouth.

"I better go so that you can feed him," Linette said.

"But you just got here," Tess protested. "I don't mind. Why, what modesty can I have around you, considering all the times we got dressed together and helped lace each other up and everything?"

Linette smiled but shook her head. "No, really, I didn't mean to stay long. I rode out here on impulse." She gestured down at her riding habit. "I mean, this is hardly the proper attire for calling on someone."

"Will you come back, then?" Tess asked, frowning in concern. "I mean it, Linette. I'd like to see you longer, talk to you."

"Of course, in a few weeks, when you're feeling stronger." And when there weren't so many family members around, she added silently. The only one she hadn't run into yet was Gideon!

"All right, then, if you promise." Tess reached out toward her, and Linette stepped forward quickly and kissed her on the cheek. She glanced down at the baby again, wondering if she really would come back. She had avoided such pain for so long; it seemed insane to start courting it now. Yet her arms felt strangely empty without the baby, and she knew that she wanted to hold it again.

Quickly she turned and walked out of the bedroom. She closed the door after her and stood for a moment in the blessedly empty, silent hall, her eyes closed, drawing in a deep breath.

Finally she opened her eyes and squared her shoulders. She could not let any of the Tyrrells see how much this visit had shaken her. Quietly she moved down the hallway to the stairs and stood for a moment, listening and peering over the stair rail. She did not want to have to face any of the Tyrrells again if she could possibly help it. There was no one below in the portion of the hall that she could see. She imagined that they had all returned to the back sitting room or, more likely, the kitchen. Perhaps if she sneaked down the stairs as softly as she could, she could get out the front door without any of them knowing. Linette doubted that they wanted to see her any more than she wanted to see them, but if they heard her, politeness would demand that they come out to bid her farewell.

Linette went down the steps cautiously, pulling on her gloves as she went, and paused again at the bottom. She heard the rumble of a male voice from the back of the house, followed by light feminine laughter. She tiptoed across the wooden floor and opened the front door, wincing when it creaked. She stopped and listened, but there was no abatement of the talking from the other end of the house. They hadn't heard the door; no doubt the noise had sounded ten times louder to her than it really was. Quickly she slid through the open doorway and pulled the door shut behind her with a soft click. Now that she was out of the house, she no longer needed to be quiet. All she wanted was to get away from the farm and from Hunter and that sweet baby as fast as she could. She turned toward her horse and stopped in surprise when she saw that it was not there. Then she remembered that Hunter had said he would put it up in the barn. She grimaced in exasperation. Lifting her skirts up to her ankles, she hurried across the farmyard to the barn.

Linette walked quickly through the dimly lit barn, glancing in the stalls for her horse. She saw his head come over the door of the farthest stall as he nickered and she walked to him.

Linette could not believe her bad luck when she saw that Hunter was standing in the stall beside her horse, brushing him.

Hunter looked up and straightened when he saw

her. "Linette! I didn't expect you to return so soon." He glanced down at the brush in his hand, looking rather embarrassed, as if she'd caught him doing something he shouldn't. "I was rubbing him down a little. I thought you'd be here for a while, so after I took off his saddle, I . . ." He ran down and blew out a gust of air. "Sorry. I'll saddle him up for you."

He started out of the stall, and Linette stepped back hastily. "That's all right. I can do it."

Hunter snorted. "Sure. I'm going to stand around and let a lady saddle her horse."

"I know you don't want to do anything for me," Linette replied stiffly.

"I was raised to be polite. It doesn't matter what I think of you; you're a guest here." He didn't look at her as he spoke, just walked past her to the bridle that hung on the wall.

Linette watched as he returned to the stall and fitted the bridle over Rubio's head, carefully ignoring Linette. He moved with economy and a certain grace. His hands on the bridle were quick and sure. Linette remembered those hands on her body, lovingly stroking her breasts and legs. The thought made her blush, and she turned her face away. *Thank God at least Hunter didn't know what she was thinking!*

But he knew how easily she responded to him; Linette couldn't deny that. That day in the carriage house when he had kissed her, she had kissed him back passionately. It was humiliating to be still so easily aroused by him, when he obviously no longer cared anything for her—indeed, even hated her.

Hunter swung the saddle onto the palomino and

bent down to fasten the girth beneath his belly. He straightened and took the reins and handed them to her. Linette's gloved hands brushed his fingertips, and it seemed to her as if she could feel them even through her gloves.

"Thank you." She kept her face turned away from him. Hunter stepped back, and she started to mount the horse. Hunter's hand on her arm stopped her. She turned to look at him, startled.

"Why did you come here today?" he asked. His face was taut, his eyes burning. Linette sensed that his question wasn't really what he had wanted to ask.

"To see Tess's baby," she replied, struggling to keep her voice even. Hunter always made her feel so unsettled, stirring up the old feelings that had once lain in her for him, yet also scaring her and making her angry, all at the same time.

"Why?" he asked harshly, and his fingers remained on her arm, digging in a little. "What do you care about Tess? Or a Tyrrell baby?"

Pain clutched Linette's heart again, as it had when she had looked down at Tess's little boy, seeing his perfect, tiny hands and nails, his fine blond hair, his little shell-like ears. She swallowed hard.

"Tess is my friend."

"*Was* your friend," he pointed out harshly. "Just like I *was* your lover. Seems like you were able to drop us both pretty easy when it suited you."

"You know nothing about it!" Linette snapped and jerked her arm away from him. A saving anger swept her, driving out the sorrow for the moment. "All you do is accuse and blame! You never wanted to listen to the truth!"

"The truth!" Hunter's black eyebrows vaulted up sardonically. "What would you know about the truth? You've never told me anything but lies."

"You wouldn't know the truth if it hit you in the face!" Linette barked back, her hands clenching into fists. She took a step closer to him and planted her hands on her hips, glaring at Hunter. "You hear only what you want to hear, see only what you want to see. Nothing penetrates that hard Tyrrell head of yours, does it? I tried to explain to you! I tried to tell you, but you wouldn't listen! You had already judged me and found me guilty!"

"How could I help but judge you? You married Benton Conway as soon as I left town!"

"I thought you were dead!"

"So that made it all right for you to turn right around and marry someone else?"

"I didn't say that."

"Then what are you saying? That I should have forgiven you because you thought I was dead? That I should say, 'Hey, that's all right, darling, hell, three weeks is plenty of time to wait after your fiancé dies before you marry someone else!' Did you think I'd just turn the other cheek? That I was such a worm of a man that I'd come crawling back to you even though you'd married another man? Were you hoping you could have it both ways—a rich old husband plus a healthy young man for a lover?"

"How dare you!" Tears choked Linette's voice. "Damn you! You make me sorry I ever loved you! I gave up my life—my life! so—" She drew a shudder-ing breath. Tears streamed down her face. "And you never even asked me why! You didn't care whether I had a reason. You didn't care what might have hap-pened to me that caused me to do that. You wouldn't even let me explain."

"All right, dammit!" Hunter roared. "Tell me now. Why? Why did you cut my heart out of me? Why did you marry him!"

"Because I was pregnant!" Linette shrieked back at him. "Because I was carrying your child! That's why!"

Linette burst into sobs. Stunned, Hunter stood frozen, gaping at her. She turned and stalked out of the barn, leading her horse.

Hunter came to life. "Linette!" he roared. He ran to the barn door. "Linette! Stop! Come back here!"

But she didn't look back, just sprang up into the saddle and thundered down the drive.

8

Linette rode at full speed, the wind whipping the tears from her face. She hated the world and Hunter Tyrrell especially, and she wished that she could ride and ride forever and never come back. Ride until all her pain and turmoil were gone.

But she knew that could never happen. Gradually she slowed down to a trot, then a walk. She brushed one gloved hand across her cheeks and gave a long, tremulous sigh. She told herself that she shouldn't let Hunter bother her so. He had judged her and dismissed her long ago; she had known since then what kind of man he was, harsh and unforgiving, thinking only of himself. He wasn't worth the turmoil she felt.

She was so engrossed in her thoughts that it took a moment for the sound of pounding hooves on the dirt road to register. When it finally did, Linette's heart speeded up. *Hunter! Had he given chase to her?* She wanted to turn back but didn't, and kept her horse at its steady pace.

Finally, when the sound of hoofbeats was almost upon her, she could contain her curiosity no longer and she glanced back again. It *was* Hunter. He was riding without a saddle, bent low over the horse, almost at one with it. She realized that he had been in such a hurry to catch up with her that he hadn't even stopped to saddle his horse, and, though she knew it was foolish, somehow that fact pleased her.

Linette thought about kicking her horse into a run again and trying to outrace him, but she knew that he would only catch her in the end. Her horse was swift, and she was lighter, but Hunter was without the weight of a saddle and he was the better rider. She could not beat him ultimately. Besides, a fierce desire to face him and have it out surged through her. She *wanted* to have this confrontation. She *wanted* to have the opportunity to tell him the truth at last—no longer because she wanted his forgiveness and understanding, but just finally to have some vindication.

She wheeled her horse around to face him and stood waiting. Seeing her, Hunter pulled back on the reins and came to a dancing halt beside her. His face was thunderous.

"You better explain yourself," he growled.

Linette raised her eyebrows haughtily. For once she was in control of the situation; after all, *he* had been the one who chased *her*. "I don't owe you any explanation," she replied crisply. "You've avoided one for almost five years—why should I bother to give it to you now?"

"Dammit, don't play your games with me!" Hunter's horse skittered nervously at the rage in his voice. "What did you mean just then? I want to know the truth!"

"Then it's the first time you've been interested in the truth!" Linette snapped back.

Fire flashed in his eyes, and Hunter reached out and grabbed the bridle of Linette's horse, moving so close to her that their legs touched. "What did you mean, you married him because you were pregnant? You have no child!"

"I did have! I was carrying your baby when we heard that you'd been killed at Manassas." Linette met his angry eyes unflinchingly.

"Mine or Benton Conway's?"

Linette let out a low cry of rage. "Damn you!" She struck out at him with all her force, crashing her hand into his arm. Startled, he released her bridle. Linette dug her heels in with all her fury, and her horse took off like a shot.

Hunter cursed and urged his horse after her. He drew up beside her and reached out, curving his arm around her and jerking her from her saddle, pulling back on his reins. Linette screamed and struggled, frantically kicking and beating at him with her fists. The palomino, riderless, slowed down and looked at them, then trotted back. Hunter's horse, frightened by the screaming, squirming weight suddenly dangling from one side, began to dance nervously. Cursing, Hunter pulled him to a stop and slid off, still holding Linette.

One of her fists connected with Hunter's face. He winced and let out a low exclamation, but he did not release Linette until he had carried her off the road and into the shelter of a stand of pine trees. Then he dropped his arm from her, and Linette staggered back. She grabbed at a branch to recover her balance and faced Hunter. Her face was dead white, her mouth pinched and colorless, but her eyes blazed forth with a vibrant blue light.

"How dare you!" she spat at him. "You took my maidenhood that night; you know I had never known another man before you! How dare you suggest that I had slept with any other man but you?"

Hunter glared at her. "I was the first. But that doesn't mean that I was the only."

"Of course," Linette replied scornfully. "Until that night I was untouched, but naturally as soon as I slept with you, I would run out and give myself to anyone! Isn't that right? How like a man to think that—you excuse yourself for taking a woman by calling her a slut."

"I didn't take you by force!" Hunter defended himself. "You gave yourself to me willingly."

"Yes, because fool that I was, I loved you! Because I thought that you were a better man than to label a woman a whore because she gave her heart and soul and body to you. But, of course, if I slept with you, then it follows that I would sleep with Benton, too, and no doubt every other man I could find!" Linette retorted hotly. "You said you wanted the truth." Her mouth twisted bitterly. "I should have known better. You only wanted another chance to revile me."

She turned and walked away from Hunter, whistling to her horse, who was now contentedly grazing along the side of the road.

"No, wait!" Hunter hurried after her and took her arm, turning her around. "I'm sorry. You're right; I spoke out of anger. I said that because I wanted to hurt you." He sighed. "I know I was the only man who had slept with you. That's why—" pain rippled across his face, but he brought it quickly under control, "that's why I couldn't believe you had married Benton. I thought you loved me."

"I did! I loved you more than anything in the world!" Linette cried out, all her old anguish tumbling out. "But what was I to do? I was pregnant with your child, and I was beside myself with wondering what I was going to do. You were away fighting. Should I write you? Chase after you to Virginia? I didn't know. And then . . ." Tears started in Linette's eyes, and she dashed them away impatiently. "Then they said you had died! I was crazy with grief."

"Oh, yes, I can tell," Hunter said sarcastically. "That's why you went right out and found another man to marry you."

"What would you have had me do!" Linette lashed back. "Throw myself in the river?"

"No!" he cried involuntarily.

"Well, I thought about it, believe me. It seemed very appealing at the time. But whenever I thought about it, I reminded myself that I couldn't. I was carrying your baby; it was the last bit of you alive. I had to live so that our child could live."

"As another man's child?"

"You think I should have tried to raise her alone? Without a father or a name?"

"You could have gone to my family. They would have helped you. Why didn't you tell my mother? Or Maggie?"

"Don't you know what they would have thought of me? Why should they believe me that the baby I carried was yours? You yourself just doubted me, and no one knows better than you that I had had no other man."

"I wouldn't have doubted you then," he protested. "Before you married Benton. And neither would my mother or Maggie. They would have helped you."

"You don't know that. Certainly I didn't know it. I was afraid that your mother would scorn me. And even if they had been willing to take me in, the baby would still have been born a bastard. Perhaps I would have been brave enough to face what people said about me. I hope so. But I couldn't let my baby grow up as a nameless bastard, the talk of everyone in town. I couldn't let that happen to my baby! Our baby! Besides, what did it matter to me who I married, when I knew that I would never see you again? I felt too dead inside to care."

Hunter looked at her bleakly. "So what did you do? Go to Benton and sleep with him so that he'd think it was his child?"

"No!" Linette's face was stamped with revulsion. "How could you think I would let another man touch me after you? He knew the truth. Benton had asked me many times to marry him. My—my mother told him the truth and he offered to marry me, to take the baby and raise it as his own. He said that he didn't care that the baby wasn't his. He said he loved me and wanted to take care of us both."

Hunter turned away, placing the palm of one hand against a tree trunk and leaning against it. He looked down at the ground for a moment, then said in a low voice, "If all this is true, where is my child? What happened to the baby?"

"She died." Hunter glanced up quickly at Linette. Her face was even paler than before, if that was possible, and her skin was stretched across her cheekbones like a death mask. For once, she did not look beautiful at all, her bright eyes and hair merely a mockery.

"How?" It was all Hunter could manage to get out through his tightened throat.

"At birth." Linette spoke in a lifeless voice, looking past Hunter into a place that only she could see. "Benton took me to his cousin's in Louisiana, so that no one would know how early the baby was born. We planned to come back several months later, with a large, healthy baby who was born the correct nine and a half months after our marriage. But my labor was long and . . . and difficult. And our daughter was stillborn. I was very sick afterwards; I—" she gulped back a sob; tears glittered in her eyes, "I never even held her. I never got to see her. They buried her before I recovered from the fever."

Hunter stepped back. "Sweet Jesus." He glanced around him unseeingly. A child! He had had a child and never knew it! All this time, he had not known it.

"Why didn't you tell me?" he asked, his voice barely more than a whisper. "All this time, you kept it a secret."

"Why didn't I tell you?" Linette repeated with bitter scorn. "You never gave me a chance. I tried to explain to you when you came back from the war, but you turned and walked away from me."

"My God, Linette, what did you expect? I left my fiancée to go to war, and when I get back, she's married to another man. How could I not be angry? I didn't know what had happened."

"No, and you weren't interested in finding out, either!"

"You knew what I thought! You must have known what I felt, seeing you married to another man! You could have made an effort to tell me. But you didn't. You knew the heart was torn out of me, but you didn't care enough to even try one more time to tell me. You could have come to the house and—"

Linette let out a dry, scornful laugh. "Ha! Come to the Tyrrell stronghold? I think not. You wouldn't have seen me. You'd have only told your mother to send me away, and she would have."

"If you had told her the reason, she wouldn't have."

"I'm supposed to tell my secrets to the world, is that it? I should bare my sorrow to everyone? Just because you are too bone-headed stubborn to listen? Because all you cared about was yourself? I don't think so. You didn't bother to wonder *why* I had married Benton. You didn't wonder whether I was happy or how I felt when I thought you were dead.

I didn't see any reason to think that you'd even care whether or not you had had a daughter who died."

"That's not fair!"

"No? Well, how fair was it when you made love to me, then ran off to play war? Did you ever think about the consequences? Did you ever worry that maybe I was pregnant? Did you ever think about the fact that I might be left here alone to face the town's censure for bearing an illegitimate child? No, all you thought about was what you wanted to do! All you cared about was running off with your brother."

"There was a war." Hunter's voice hardened. "I did what I had to."

"Oh?" Linette looked at him contemptuously. "Well, I had my own war to fight, and I did what I had to, as well."

She turned and walked away to her horse. And this time Hunter didn't go after her. He remained in the copse of trees, staring at the ground, until long after the sound of the palomino's hoofbeats receded into the distance.

Finally Hunter got up and mounted Jupe, and slowly rode back to the Tyrrell farm. When he reached the barn, he slid off his horse and saddled him, planning to ride back to his own place. He couldn't go into the house and face his mother and Maggie right now—listen to their questions and struggle to answer them. But, when he swung up on Jupe's back, he hesitated for a moment, gazing out toward the fields that lay behind the farm. On the horizon he could see his brother's form trailing behind the mule and plow. He turned Jupe in that direction.

Gideon glanced up in surprise when he heard Hunter's horse approaching. He pulled the mule to a stop and took off the tied reins that he wore draped around his shoulders so that his hands were free to grip the plow handles. He turned and waited for his brother to reach him.

Gideon was a big man, a good two inches taller than Hunter, who was considered tall himself, and heavily muscled across his back, shoulders, and arms from years of working the fields. His hair, unlike Hunter's thick black mane, was dark blond, streaked lighter by the sun, and neatly clipped, and his eyes were a pale blue, like the winter sky. He was a quiet man whose emotions and loyalties lay deep and true. The only things he loved more than this land were his wife and his new son.

"Hey, Hunter," he said as Hunter drew close. "What brings you out here?"

Hunter slid lithely out of his saddle. "I'm not sure." He paused, studying the reins in his hand as if they might contain the reason for his being here. "I reckon I wanted to talk."

"To me?" Gideon's eyes widened in genuine surprise. He and Hunter loved each other and each, like all the Tyrrells, would do anything to help the other one, but they had never been close in the way that Gideon had been close to Shelby. Hunter had always rebelled against his big brother's authority, and Gideon had always decried Hunter's reckless, impulsive ways. Gideon would have said that he would be the last person that Hunter would want to talk to.

Gideon's expression forced a wry smile out of Hunter. "Yeah. It's strange, I'll admit. But I wanted to talk to you."

"Sure. Just let me unharness the mule and take her to the stream. Then you and I can sit down to that lunch Ma packed for me this morning. I can guarantee it's enough for at least two men."

"I'm sure it is, if Ma packed it." Hunter tied his own horse to a tree in the shade, then helped Gideon with the mule team.

The two men sat down in the shade beside the stream, and Gideon reached into the basket his mother had given him this morning and began pulling out food. He tore off a hunk of bread and held it out to his brother. Hunter glanced at it and shook his head.

"No, I'm not hungry. Go ahead."

Gideon's eyebrows rose. "It's Ma's bread." He couldn't remember when, if ever, Hunter had turned down a slice of their mother's bread. It was known all over the county as the best there was.

"I know."

Gideon shrugged and took a bite out of the bread. He chewed thoughtfully, studying Hunter. "Something powerful must be bothering you, to turn that down."

"Yeah." Hunter glanced at Gideon, then looked

back out over the stream. Now that he was here with Gideon, he found it hard to begin.

Gideon suppressed a smile. Hunter had always been a talker, but now he sounded more like Gideon himself, answering in monosyllables. After a moment, Gideon prodded Hunter, "I'm surprised you came out here. How come you didn't talk to Maggie? Have she and Reid gone back to town already?"

"No. But it's not something I can talk to Maggie about. It's—" Hunter stood up and began to pace restlessly. "Linette came out to see Tess and the baby this morning."

"Oh." Now Gideon understood. "She still cuts you up inside."

"Yes. Of course. Everybody knows that," Hunter replied bitterly. "Seems like I'm no good at hiding it." He bent and picked up a small stone, then hurled it as far as he could across the water. "Dammit all to hell, Gid, I can't get that woman out of my blood!"

Gideon's face creased with sympathetic pain for his brother. "I reckon there are some women like that. I'm sorry, Hunter. I wish there was something I could do for you."

"Oh, it's not that. I just have to live with that. It's what she told me this morning. We got into a fight, of course, and she told me that the reason she'd married Conway was . . . was because she was carrying my baby."

There was a stunned silence behind him. Hunter couldn't look back at his brother. He jammed his hands into his pockets and continued to gaze across at the opposite bank.

"She thought I was dead," he went on in a tight, carefully controlled voice. "She said she was scared and didn't want the baby to grow up a bastard, and Conway offered to marry her. So that's what she did. But then the baby was born dead."

There was another silence, and finally Gideon said, "Do you believe her?"

Hunter swiveled around, frustration and hurt twisting his features. "Christ, I don't know, Gideon! I don't even know *that*. When she was telling me, yes, I believed her; it sounded so real, so true. Looking at her, you couldn't doubt her. But now, when I think about it, I wonder . . . I've thought for years that she was a consummate liar, that all the things she told me back before the war were lies, that she used me and set me up. And if that's true, then she could just as easily be lying now; she could be spinning another little story to get me back in her web. But why? Why would she do that? Why would she care? There's nothing she can gain by telling me this."

Gideon shrugged. "I don't know. Unless she wants you back. Maybe she's tired of her husband."

"She hates me." Hunter's lip curled. "She hates me because I wouldn't listen to her after I got back. Because I went off to fight without even caring whether she was—oh, God, Gideon, she's right." His voice was low and rasping. He squatted down, not looking at Gideon, his elbow braced on his knee and one hand shoved back into his hair. "I knew I shouldn't take her that night. I even thought for an instant, 'What if she got in the family way and I'm leaving tomorrow?' But she felt so sweet in my arms, and I wanted her so much. I couldn't stop kissing her and touching her, and she—she didn't want me to stop. And we kept on, and pretty soon, I couldn't stop. Afterwards, every time I thought about it, all I could think of was how good it was, how much I loved her. I didn't even think about the fact that she might have gotten pregnant. I guess I wouldn't let myself think about it." He sighed and looked up at Gideon with bitter wryness. "I guess you'll tell me that I did it again, got myself in trouble because I was too impulsive. I acted without thinking."

"No." Gideon half smiled. "I'm a man, too, not a saint, you know. I know how it feels to want a woman so bad you don't think about anything else." He thought about the night that Tess had revealed that she loved him. God knows he hadn't stopped or thought then.

"But I'll swear you wouldn't have gone off and left the woman you loved alone and vulnerable. You wouldn't have left her to face that while you charged off to fight some fool war that didn't mean a tinker's damn anyway. I was such an idiot!" Hunter surged to his feet on a wave of cold, biting guilt, slamming one fist into the other, open palm. "If only I'd married her before I left! Why didn't I wait a few more days to leave for Virginia? I could have married her. I was so certain that the war would be over with the first battle and that I might miss it!" His face twisted bitterly. "I thought I'd be back before the end of summer, and then Linette could have the beautiful wedding she wanted, not some hasty, ramshackle thing. I was so full of foolish confidence and so lacking in sense!"

"Hunter, you can't blame yourself for that. None of us realized how long the war would go on or what it would entail. You don't know the future; nobody does. And you can't blame yourself for not preparing for something you didn't know was going to happen. That's like saying you should have known to build your house in a different place because ten years later a tornado came along and wiped it out. You did what you thought was right. You would have married her if you'd known. Why didn't she write and tell you? You could have gotten married. I could have escorted her to Virginia to marry you."

"I'm not sure. She was worried and scared and didn't know what to do. I guess by the time she was sure she was pregnant, my name was on the list of the dead." Hunter sighed. "I'm so confused. Dammit, she should have gone to Ma or Maggie. You all would have taken care of her. She didn't have to marry somebody else. She could have let my child grow up a Tyrrell, at least! Oh, I can see how she might be a little scared of Ma, but she could have told Maggie. You know Maggie would have taken care of her. Or Tess—Tess was her best friend!"

"Maybe she acted hastily, too." Gideon stood up and walked over to his brother. "I'm not excusing her. Hell, I'm not even sure that she's not making this all up. But you have to remember that she was awfully young at the time. She was what—seventeen?"

"Sixteen." Misery colored Hunter's voice. "And it was what her mother wanted her to do. Her mother set it up."

"I can see how a young girl like that would be scared and confused. How she might be afraid your family wouldn't believe her, would kick her out. Even if we'd taken her in, the baby would still have been illegitimate. That's a hard thing for a woman to have to do: bear a baby out of wedlock. Hard on the child, too."

"I know. Oh, God, Gideon, when I think about it, it tears me up inside!" Hunter swung around to face his brother. His eyes were dark and full of torment. "I had a child, and I lost a child, and I never even knew about it. All these years. I had no idea. What did it look like? If I'd been there with her, mightn't the baby have been all right? Linette wouldn't have been unhappy. Probably she didn't eat right or take care of herself like she should. Or maybe it was her traveling to Louisiana while she was carrying it. If I'd been here, she'd have had the baby here, where she belonged, with Ma and Maggie and Tess to help her. She wouldn't have been worried and upset." He drew a long, shuddering breath.

"Hunter, you can't know that." Gideon frowned. "You'll drive yourself crazy if you keep on thinking this way. Rightly or wrongly, whatever happened, happened, and there's nothing you can do to change it now."

"I know that. But when I think about a baby . . ." He looked straight into Gideon's eyes. "Think about how you feel when you hold your son."

Unconsciously Gideon's face softened, thinking of the baby and the sweetness of holding him in his arms.

"And think about how you felt, knowing the woman you loved was carrying your child inside her, curled up under her heart."

Gideon's lips widened sensuously, and a faint color tinged his cheeks. "Hunter, I don't think that this—"

"How would you feel knowing that you missed that? That it could have been yours but it was torn away before you even knew it existed? What if you found out you had a child and that you lost it—lost it years before you even knew of its existence! Dammit, I feel as if I've been robbed!" Hunter swung away angrily. "Why in the hell didn't she tell me! Would it have been that hard? Couldn't she have made the extra effort?"

"I don't know. I imagine there are some men would have been happier not to know something like that."

Hunter shot his brother a scornful glance. "Linette knew me better than that." He gave a little half shrug. "Hell, I guess she was so mad at me by that time that she didn't want me to know. Maybe it was her little piece of revenge on me for leaving her here to face it alone."

He walked over to the stream, scuffing half-heartedly at a stone in his way, and squatted down beside the water. "What should I do, Gideon?"

"What can you do?" Gideon countered, his eyes dark with pity as he looked down at his brother. "There's nothing that can be done now. You can't bring back the dead, can't erase the past. You can't make it up to her; hell, she's still married to another man, whatever the reason."

"I know. It just feels as if—I don't know, as if I ought to go talk to her again or something."

"Yes, if you want to prolong your anguish," Gideon replied gruffly. "Think, Hunter. What would that accomplish? Seeing her won't get rid of what you're feeling. You think she's going to forgive you? You think you can say something that'll change the past?"

"Maybe I could at least tell whether she's telling me the truth."

"And maybe you could lose your heart to her all over again! Is that what you want?"

"You know it's not. Dammit, Gideon, you always twist everything around."

A faint smile quirked Gideon's lips. "Well, I feel better; at least you've returned to normal—disputing everything I say again."

Hunter cast him a dark look, but then he, too, had to smile a little. "All right, all right. I know you're saying what you think is in my best interest."

"I don't want to see you twisted up into knots again, that's all. Whatever happened in the past, Linette is a married woman now. Anything you have to do with her will only bring you pain."

Hunter sighed. "Yes. I'm sure you're right." He drew a deep breath. "So what am I to do? Just ride on home? Pretend it never happened?"

"No. You can't do that. It happened. You're bound to think about it, to wonder. To wish that things had been different. But your life has to go on. You have to pick up and go on with it."

"Yeah. I'm sure you're right." Suddenly a grin lit

Hunter's face, a flash of the devil-may-care smile that had once charmed everyone Hunter met. "Bet you never thought you'd hear me say those words."

"No." Gideon smiled back. "Obviously you've gotten smarter as you've gotten older."

Hunter grimaced. He walked across the space that separated them and clapped his brother on the shoulder. "Thanks. I'll go and let you finish your dinner in peace now."

"Sure you don't want to stay and help me?" Gideon gestured toward the lunch basket.

Hunter shook his head. "No. I better be by myself for a while."

But when he mounted his horse, he rode, not straight back to the road, but down to the farmhouse again. He went inside and up the stairs. He could hear Tess and his mother talking in his mother's room down the hall. Hunter went to the open door of Gideon's and Tess's bedroom and looked inside. The curtains were drawn, and the room was quiet. He tiptoed across the room to the cradle and squatted down beside it.

Gideon's son lay on his stomach. He had squirmed his way upward in the cradle until his head was almost touching the wood and his blanket had slid off him. Hunter looked down at him, taking in the creamy skin and the button nose, the rosebud mouth slightly open and now and then moving as if sucking an imaginary teat. Hunter smiled faintly at his jack-knife position; Gideon had fondly nicknamed him Frog, and not without reason. Hunter pulled the blanket up over Will's diapered bottom. He couldn't keep from reaching out and drawing a finger down his tiny arm. The baby's skin was the softest thing he'd ever touched.

He looked at the child for another long moment, then stood and left the room. He went down the stairs and out of the house as quietly as he had come. Mounting Jupe, he turned and rode away.

9

Rosemary glanced carefully around her aunt's parlor and into the sitting room beyond, connected by opened pocket doors. She couldn't see any sign of Seth Manning, and she felt suddenly quite low. He had told her only three days ago, when she met him in the yard of the library, that he looked forward to seeing her at her aunt's party, but perhaps he hadn't really meant it.

She looked over at Linette beside her. Linette was gazing vaguely at the mantel, lost in thought. She had been abstracted all the way over here. In fact, she had been that way ever since returning from her ride this afternoon. Linette had told the maid she was tired and wanted to rest, and she had spent the afternoon in her bedroom, not even coming downstairs for supper. Her absence had irritated Benton, but it had worried Rosemary, who could not go to her aunt's party without her stepmother's chaperonage. Benton wouldn't go; he and Rosemary's aunts held each other in mutual dislike, and besides, there was rarely anyone at their parties who could benefit him.

Rosemary had gone up to Linette's room after the meal and asked timidly if Linette felt too poorly to attend the party. Linette had looked weary, even ill, but to Rosemary's relief, she smiled and asked archly, "Tell me, is a certain young schoolmaster expected to be there?"

Rosemary had blushed up to her hairline and confessed that he was.

"Then, by all means, we must go," Linette had said, smiling, and got up from her chair. She had even done Rosemary's hair in a pretty cluster of curls over one shoulder and insisted on her wearing a rich green silk evening dress.

However, it was obvious that Linette was not her usual self, and Rosemary wondered what was the matter. She hoped that she hadn't come even though she felt sick just because Rosemary had wanted her to.

"Why don't we sit over there?" Rosemary asked solicitously, pointing toward a pair of straight-back chairs by the fireplace.

Linette nodded, and they crossed the room to sit down. Linette glanced up and out into the hall and smiled faintly. "I believe I see Mr. Manning."

Rosemary's heart began to pound, and her breath caught in her throat. "Where?"

"Just coming in the door." Linette gave her an intent look. "You're really interested in this man, aren't you?"

"Is it that obvious?" Rosemary's forehead knotted anxiously.

"No, not to someone who doesn't know you as well as I," Linette lied calmly.

"He's such a nice man. And he's so interesting to talk to. I wish—oh, I wish for just this once I could be pretty, like you!" Rosemary whispered fiercely.

"But, darling, you *are* pretty."

Rosemary cast her a glance of disbelief, and Linette continued stoutly, "Well, you are! And I wouldn't be surprised if Mr. Manning recognizes that fact, too. See, he's looking around—for you, I'm sure."

Rosemary lowered her gaze quickly, suddenly terrified that he would catch her eye. "Linette, please tell me what to do. What to say."

"I don't know." Linette frowned. "I would think that he likes the kind of thing you usually say; you've talked many times before."

That was true. Seth often stopped by the library on his way to his lodgings in the small house behind the library. He knew books as well or better than Rosemary herself, and they had had many an enjoyable discussion about them. But Rosemary had to admit that she yearned for something more than a discussion of books with Seth Manning.

Rosemary shook her head, feeling foolish. *Why would any man want to do anything else with me?* Once she had heard her father tell someone that she was born to be a spinster, and Rosemary knew that that was the truth. Still, she couldn't keep from hoping for something different from life.

"He's seen you," Linette whispered. "He's coming over."

Rosemary snatched off her spectacles and stuck them in her reticule. At least she looked a little prettier that way—or she thought she did; she wasn't sure since with her glasses off she had to get up right in the mirror to even see her face.

Manning came to a stop in front of them. "Good evening, Mrs. Conway. Miss Conway."

"Good evening, Mr. Manning," Linette answered smoothly. "How are you today?"

Rosemary looked up and murmured a greeting. Without her spectacles, his face was blurred, and she could not read his expression. It was difficult even to tell whether he was looking at her or not. She wished now that she hadn't taken her eyeglasses off, but it would be too foolish to bring them out and put them back on.

Seth remained standing before them, chatting with Linette. Rosemary, though she racked her brain, could think of nothing to say.

After a moment Linette rose, saying, "There's my cousin Martha over there. I should go speak to her, if you will excuse me. I haven't seen her in weeks."

Rosemary was rather surprised to hear this information, since Linette had never gotten along with her cousin and it had been in reality months since they had seen each other. Then she realized belatedly that Linette was giving her a chance to talk alone with Seth, and she blushed. Would Seth see through Linette's ploy? And what would he think?

"Your stepmother seems to be a very nice woman," Seth commented as he took the seat Linette had vacated.

"Yes, she is," Rosemary replied, conscious for the first time in her life of a spurt of jealousy of Linette. She wondered if Seth had come over to see them because Linette was there; most men were attracted to her beauty. Rosemary disliked herself for feeling this way; Linette had always been so kind to her. Just tonight she had done her best to make Rosemary look pretty.

"I must admit, however," Seth went on, "that I'm very glad she left."

"You are?" Rosemary looked up at him, her eyes widening in surprise. She was completely unaware of how pretty she looked at that moment, her big eyes dreamy and a little vague, a sweet smile curving her lips.

"Yes. It gives me a chance to be alone with you."

Rosemary smiled and glanced back down at her hands, feeling a little flustered.

"I'm sorry. Have I offended you?"

"No. Oh, no . . . it's just that—I'm so terrible at this!"

"Terrible at what?" He sounded puzzled.

"Oh." Rosemary waved her hand around vaguely. "All of this. Parties. Making social conversation."

"I don't much like them, either," Seth confessed, a smile stealing onto his face. "The truth is, I probably wouldn't have come tonight except that I knew I would see you here." He stopped abruptly, then went on, "I'm sorry. I shouldn't have said that."

"It's all right." Rosemary didn't dare look at him. *Could he really mean what he said?*

There was a short silence, then Seth began again, "Would you like some refreshments? Could I bring you something? Or perhaps you'd like to come and choose what you want?"

Rosemary was utterly uninterested in refreshments, but she liked the idea of taking a stroll anywhere with Seth Manning, so she nodded and stood up. He held out his arm to her, and they started across the room.

She misjudged how close a small table was, and her skirts hit it, knocking over a figurine. Seth deftly caught it and returned it to the table, then offered his arm to her again. Rosemary blushed scarlet. Someone said hello to her, and she smiled vaguely, wondering who it was. She felt horribly insecure without her spectacles, and she was afraid of what error she might make next.

When they stepped into the hall, she almost walked into the hat stand. She stepped back quickly and bumped into someone behind her.

"Oh, pardon me. I'm sorry." Rosemary's face burned with embarrassment.

"Would you like to step outside?" Seth asked her in a low voice, bending down to her.

"Yes, please." Rosemary could hardly look at him. She felt like such an idiot. What must Seth think of her?

He led her out the front door and onto the porch. They strolled across the wraparound porch and along the side. Rosemary was grateful for the darkness, which hid her flaming cheeks.

"I'm sorry," she murmured, releasing his arm. She didn't dare look up at him. "You must think me a terrible fool."

"Not at all," he assured her. He reached down and took her chin in his hand, turning her face up so that she had to look at him. He was smiling in a way that soothed her ruffled feelings. "However, I was wondering why you weren't wearing your spectacles. Don't you think you could, uh, make your way better?"

"Of course." Rosemary grimaced and dug into her reticule for her eyeglasses. "I was being stupid—I thought I would, well, I wanted to look better, so I took them off." She bit her lower lip in exasperation. Now Seth would think her vain, and somehow vanity seemed a far worse sin in a plain woman than in a beauty. He would probably be thoroughly disgusted with her.

She unfolded her spectacles and settled them on her face. The world came into focus once again. She looked up into Seth's face. He was so close! And there was a warmth in his eyes that made her heart start to pound.

"Perfectly understandable," Seth commented, smiling. "What woman doesn't want to look her best? Or man, either, for that matter? But you know, I think you look fine with your spectacles, too."

"Really?" Rosemary looked at him in astonishment. She couldn't recall how many times her aunts or her father, even her beloved mother, had bemoaned the fact that Rosemary had to wear spectacles, hiding her eyes.

"Really." He looked solemn, even intent, all traces of amusement fled from his face. "You're a beautiful woman."

Rosemary could only stare at him, sure now that he had taken leave of his senses. He filled her vision, so close she could feel the heat of his body and smell the scent of shaving soap that clung to his skin. Her eyes went to his lips, firm and sharply defined. She wondered what his lips would taste like. Unconsciously she swayed a little toward him.

He bent and his lips brushed hers. Rosemary trembled at the touch, and she went up on tiptoe, her arms stealing up to clasp his neck. His breath rushed out, hot against her cheek, and his arm went around her like iron, pulling her tightly to him. He kissed her deeply, dazzling her senses, and Rosemary clung to him, lost in a maelstrom of pleasure she had never before experienced, indeed, had never even guessed at.

His mouth was incredibly soft and warm on hers, and strange, delightful sensations were darting all through her body, making her warm and weak. When at last he pulled his mouth from hers, Rosemary gasped at the loss. But then he began to trail kisses down over her jaw and onto her throat, and she shivered with pleasure at the velvet touch. Her head lolled back, exposing all of her throat to him. His hand moved over her back, then around and up her front until his fingers reached the soft swell of her bosom. Softly his hand curved under her breast. A throbbing started deep in Rosemary's abdomen, and she made a soft noise of surprise and pleasure.

Suddenly Seth broke away and stepped back, gasping for air. His chest rose and fell rapidly, and his cheeks were flushed, his eyes glittering in the darkness. "Oh, God!"

Rosemary gazed at him, too stunned by the loss of his lips and hand and all the delightful things he was arousing inside her to be able to speak or even form a coherent thought.

"I'm sorry," he panted. "Please, forgive me. It's just that you looked so lovely here in the moonlight, and I couldn't resist. It's impossible, of course; you could never—your father wouldn't allow it."

Allow what, Rosemary wondered, but she couldn't get out the words. Her head was still spinning.

"I'm sorry," he repeated. "I was a cad to take advantage of you like that. Please tell me you'll forgive me."

"Of course." His obvious distress touched her even through the roiling mass of emotions his words aroused in her.

"Thank you. I'm afraid I don't deserve it." He took a step back from her, wiping his hand across his face, and seemed to regain some of his composure. "I think it's better if I leave you now. Please make my apologies to your aunts."

With that he was gone.

Rosemary slumped back against the railing of the porch. She closed her eyes, feeling slightly sick. She couldn't go back inside yet, not until she had regained some semblance of calm. Why had he kissed her like that—and then left? And what had he meant about her father not allowing it?

She wondered if he meant that her father would not allow him to court her, to marry her. Benton would certainly be against it; he would consider a schoolteacher far beneath her. *But surely Seth could not mean that he wanted to court me!* He was so handsome, so wonderful; any woman would want him. Rosemary could not imagine that he would consider someone like her. He must have broken off their embrace because he had been appalled at her boldness in kissing him back. A lady would not act that wantonly.

Rosemary blushed, embarrassed by her actions. She didn't know how she could ever face Seth again. She blinked tears away, realizing that she had managed to destroy everything between her and Seth tonight. They could never be comfortable together again. Anytime they were together, they would both remember how brazenly she had acted.

Rosemary swallowed hard. She couldn't dissolve into tears here on her aunts' porch, no matter how awful she felt. She had to pull herself together and go inside and find Linette. She would tell Linette that she wasn't feeling well, and Linette would be happy to leave. Rosemary had to get away from here; there was no way she could return inside and calmly chat all evening.

She still could not quell that treacherous, quivery feeling in her abdomen. She could not forget how her body had responded to Seth's kiss, to his touch. It had been the most wonderful thing she had ever experienced. Surely that couldn't be bad.

Rosemary could not help but wonder: what if Seth

had felt all those wonderful sensations, too? What if Seth, just like she, was falling in love?

Linette was grateful that Rosemary had wanted to leave the party early. It had been all she could do to go to it. The confrontation with Hunter this morning had left her utterly drained. She wouldn't have made the effort if she hadn't known that Rosemary wanted so much to go.

Rosemary was silent all the way home. Linette wondered why, but she hadn't the energy to talk to Rosemary about it. That would have to wait until tomorrow. Tonight all she wanted to do was drag up to her bed and go to sleep.

But when they walked in the front door, Benton came out of his study. He narrowed his eyes and lurched forward, his gait unsteady. Linette realized with an inward groan that he must have been drinking steadily while they were gone.

"Linette! I want to talk to you. Rosemary, go upstairs."

"It's late, Benton," Linette protested as Rosemary obediently started up the stairs. "Can't we talk in the morning?"

"No. I want to talk to you right now. Come into my study." He turned and weaved his way back down the hall to his study.

Linette considered not following him, just running up the stairs to her room and locking it. But, as drunk as Benton seemed to be, he was likely to make a scene, to come after her and pound on her door until she opened it. It would probably be easier to get it over with now. So, with a sigh, Linette followed him into his study.

Benton closed the door behind her and made his way over to his desk, where he picked up a brandy snifter. He took a long sip, then held it out toward Linette in a mocking toast. "Shall we drink to my lovely wife? My *faithful* wife?"

"You're drunk," Linette snapped. "It's no point talking to you at all."

She started toward the door, but Benton blocked her way, moving with surprising swiftness considering his inebriated state. "You're not going anywhere until we've had our little discussion. I know where you were today."

Linette's heart began to pound, but she raised her eyebrows in a calm, contemptuous look. "You mean, my ride?"

"I mean your tryst with your lover!"

"What! How dare you!"

"You can't deny it." Benton started forward, stumbling slightly. The liquor sloshed over the glass and onto the rug. "I know, Linette. I know all about it. Someone saw you meeting him today."

Linette stared. "Who could have seen that?" Her eyes narrowed. "You followed me!"

"I don't have the time to waste on your affairs, I assure you. I hired someone to follow you."

"What!" Linette was furious. "You hired someone to spy on me?"

Benton shrugged. "Of course. When I noticed how frequently you went riding, I realized that something more must be going on. I suspected you were meeting your lover."

"Hunter is not my lover!"

"You don't deny meeting him."

"I don't deny that I saw him today. I have nothing to hide. We didn't *arrange* to meet. I rode out to see Tess's baby. Hunter just happened to be at the Tyrrell farm, too."

"How convenient." Conway's voice dripped sarcasm.

"It wasn't convenient or otherwise. It was simply chance."

"And I suppose it was 'simply chance' that the two of you disappeared into a stand of trees on the way back into town!"

"We did nothing wrong!" Linette snapped.

"You don't consider a rendezvous with your lover wrong?"

"For the last time, Hunter is not my lover!" Linette's temper was frayed. "We were having an argument, and we chose not to do it on the road in full view of the world. Believe me, it had nothing to do with love!"

"You're a lying bitch," Conway said almost dispassionately. "I've always known that you were."

"I will not stand here and listen to you revile me!" Linette whirled away, but Benton reached out and grabbed her by the wrist, jerking her back around to face him.

"Dammit, you'll listen to whatever I have to say! I'm not some weak-kneed boy to let you get by with your little tricks."

Linette tried to pull away from him, but his grip

tightened until her hand began to go numb. She stopped struggling and stood facing him defiantly. "This is absurd," she said in a calm voice. "Hunter despises me."

"*Hunter* despises you. I notice you didn't protest that you did not want him. I'm sure you'd be glad to toss up your skirts for him, wouldn't you?"

Linette couldn't help but remember that day in the carriage house when Hunter had kissed her and she had responded to him. Color rose in her cheeks.

"I knew it!" Benton snarled, enraged, and he jerked Linette forward. She staggered and lost her balance, and Benton pulled her down hard onto her knees before him. The fall jarred her head and spine, stunning Linette for a moment. "You're panting for him. And he'd be happy to take you up on it. What does it matter that he despises you? You don't need to like a woman to get between her legs."

Linette's eyes blazed at the insult. She started to her feet, but her skirts impeded her, and Benton pushed her back down.

"Stop it! Let go of me!" Linette protested. "This is insane! I have not dishonored you in any way."

"You think I'm blind? You think I don't know where you go on all those rides of yours? 'Don't buy me that horse, Benton, I won't ride it,'" he mimicked her tauntingly. "Then every day you can't wait to get on that horse and ride out to your lover!"

"You're mad! I didn't ask for that horse. I would never even have seen Hunter again if you hadn't forced me to go out there. I didn't want to go to his farm!"

"Oh, so now it's my fault that you're cuckolding me?"

"I am not!"

His hand lashed out, hitting her across the cheek and knocking her to the floor. Linette let out a cry of surprise, quickly repressed, and struggled to rise. Benton slapped her again. She fell backward and rolled across the floor, coming up hard against Benton's desk. Pain stabbed through her back where she struck a leg of the desk, and she lay for a moment, stunned.

"Damn him to hell!" Conway ranted, his face red. "I thought I'd gotten rid of him when he died at Manassas, but no! He rises up again like some specter from the grave." Benton glared at Linette lying on the floor. "I had you!" he said, reaching out and closing his fist in the air as if grasping something. "Right here. I married you and bedded you; I even got rid of his brat. You were mine! And then he comes waltzing in and you're right back in his bed."

Benton turned away, slamming his fist into the wall, then plopped down in a chair, his mood switching suddenly from rage to self-pity. Linette froze, staring at him blankly. It took a moment for her to grasp what Benton had actually said.

"What?" she breathed at last through bloodless lips. She struggled to her feet. The ache in her back and her cheek, the blood in her mouth were completely forgotten. "What did you say? You 'got rid of his brat'?"

Benton blinked stupidly, then cast a sly, sideways look at her. "I fooled you there, didn't I? You never did guess."

All air seemed to have left Linette's lungs. She was afraid she might faint. "My baby?" she asked, her voice strangely high-pitched and breathy.

Benton nodded, beginning to look uneasy, and he hunched his shoulders.

"You killed my baby?" The words rasped out of Linette, as cold and hard and rusty as iron. Her face was rigid, all trace of beauty fled; with her bloodless skin and wide, fixed stare, she might have been a death mask or the image of some vengeful goddess.

"No." Benton hunched his shoulders, and his voice took on a whine. "Of course not. I wouldn't hurt a baby. I gave it to Cousin Louisa and told her to take it away somewhere. Give it to someone."

Linette stood rooted to the spot. Disbelief, joy, and rage tumbled and fought within her, rendering her incapable of coherent speech or any sort of movement. *Her baby was alive?*

"You took my child from me?" Linette's voice trembled, and rage began to sweep through her like a red wave, washing everything else away. "You told me my baby had died! You took her from me!" With a screech, she launched herself at him, kicking and clawing. "I'll kill you! I'll kill you!"

Benton backed hastily away, raising his arms to defend himself from her attack. Linette beat at him with her fists, screaming incoherent invectives, tears streaming down her cheeks. Benton shoved her away with all his strength, and she staggered back across the room, slamming into the wall. The blow momentarily stunned her, knocking the air from her.

"You never cared for me!" Benton grated out, his breath coming in heavy pants. "I thought that without the baby you'd forget about him; I could make you love me. I loved you . . . so much . . . for so long. But all you ever cared about was Hunter and that damned baby. I gave you everything a woman could want! A beautiful house, all the money you could spend, the most expensive clothes! But you were always cold as ice."

Slowly Linette straightened. Her cheeks were tear-stained, and her bright mass of hair had come loose from its pins and tumbled down around her shoulders. Hate streamed from her eyes. She looked wild, even mad, yet somehow vividly, breathtakingly beautiful. Even her cut lip and the harsh red mark on her cheek could not take away that beauty; they only added to its savagery. Life and emotion had come back to her in an instant.

"You think that clothes and money can buy a person's love?" she asked in a voice that shook with outrage. "You think that a mother can that easily forget about the child of her heart? You don't love me; you never did. You couldn't; you have no understanding of love. You're incapable of feeling it. All you wanted to do was possess me, to own me. You wanted to be able to say that your wife was the prettiest woman in town, just as you wanted Tess's house so you could have the grandest house in town. That's all you care about—what you can possess! You're an inhuman, unfeeling monster!" She whirled and ran out of the room.

"Linette!" Benton staggered a few steps after her,

scowling, then stopped and turned and weaved back to his decanter of liquor.

Linette darted up the stairs and into her room. Quickly she hauled a large carpetbag from the top shelf of her wardrobe and began to stuff clothes into it. She took both her riding habits, as well as a couple of blouses and skirts and a pair of sturdy shoes, the plainest, simplest clothes she had. She added a brush from her vanity and underthings from her dresser drawers. She stood for a moment, looking at the jewelry box that sat on her dresser. She would have liked to leave the jewels behind, as well as everything else Benton had ever given her. But even in her rage, she realized that she would need money to do what she had to now. It was only fair that she use Benton's jewels to finance her journey.

Linette threw the box into the carpetbag, too. She closed the bag and swung it off the bed, starting toward the door. She hesitated and swung back around to open the bottom drawer of her dresser. She dug through the clothes to the back of the drawer and pulled something out which she stuck into the pocket of her riding habit. Picking up her bag again, she marched out of the room and down the stairs.

The door to Benton's study stood open, and Linette went straight to it. She paused in the doorway. Benton was seated behind his desk, steadily drinking his way through another snifter. Linette's lip curled contemptuously.

"Where did your cousin take my baby?" she asked crisply.

Benton looked up, startled, and stared at her. "What?"

"To whom did you give my child?"

Benton shook his head in a befuddled way. "I don't know."

"Benton! Tell me!"

"I don't know. My cousin didn't tell me where she took the brat, and I didn't ask. I didn't want to know."

"I might have known." Linette swung away and started toward the front door.

"Wait!" Benton lurched to his feet and followed her. "Goddammit! Where are you going?"

Linette made no answer. She simply continued to walk out the door and across the yard to the stables.

Benton pursued her at a much slower pace, weaving and stumbling. "Are you going to your parents? They'll just tell you to stop being foolish and go back home to your husband."

Linette spared a single icy glance for him. "I have no husband." She turned and thrust open the stable door and went inside. She began to saddle and bridle her horse, ignoring Benton as he followed her inside the barn, still arguing.

"How do you think you will be able to survive? You think your lover will take you in? He won't want used goods, I can guarantee you. And even if he did take you in, you'd be ostracized by the entire town. You won't like not having enough cash to buy any little frippery that strikes your fancy. You won't enjoy having women draw back their skirts when you pass so they won't be contaminated by the touch of a slut."

Linette led Rubio out of the barn, still paying no attention to Benton.

Infuriated, Benton snapped, "Are you listening to me? Don't you understand? Without me you have no position in this community! Are you insane?"

Linette stopped and gazed at him, her blue eyes calm and cold. "I must have been to have stayed with you so long, to have listened to all your lies. I was mad to believe that I owed you a duty to stay with you, no matter how awful it was, no matter how painful or humiliating, because you and I had made a bargain—while you had broken your part of the contract from the very first. But, thank God, at last I've regained my senses. Good-bye, Benton."

She swung up onto her horse. Benton reached out and grabbed Rubio's bridle. "You're not going anywhere. My wife doesn't leave without my say-so."

Linette pulled her hand out of her pocket and aimed a small gun at Benton. "Not when I have this. Now move out of the way."

Benton stared in amazement at the derringer. Then, slowly, he released the bridle and stepped back. "Don't think you can get away with this," he hissed. "I'll find you wherever you go. I'll come after you. My wife does not leave."

"One way or another, all your wives leave. But I don't plan to have to die in order to do so like your first one did. Now you listen to me: if you come after me or try to make me return, I will tell everyone in this town exactly what you did. I don't care if I'm branded a fallen woman; I don't care if I have no money or position. There won't be a person in this town who will talk to you after they hear what you did with my baby. Even your fine Yankee friends won't know you."

"Why, you little bitch!" Hatred flared in Conway's eyes. "You're a lying, deceitful whore!"

"Good-bye." Linette clicked to her horse, and he trotted out of the yard.

"You'll be back here in two days," Conway shouted, stumbling after her to the fence and leaning over it, staring at her as she rode down the street past the house. "Where the hell else are you going to go?"

Linette cast him a single, chilling look and, as she rode off into the darkness, said, "I am going to find my baby."

10

Linette didn't stop to think about where she was going, she just turned Rubio toward the road leading west out of town—the road that ran by Hunter's house.

She was in a hurry, but she could not ride fast; it was too dark, and her horse might easily stumble or hurt himself. It seemed to take forever to reach Hunter's house. When she finally did reach it, her heart sank. It was dark, no sign of a light burning anywhere. Linette remembered how late it was, especially for someone who kept farmer's hours. Hunter had probably been in bed for hours.

Linette hesitated, but only for a moment. She slid off her horse, tied it to the hitching post, and walked up the steps. She rapped sharply at the front door. Hunter would be mad, of course, at being awakened, but that anger was slight compared to the rage he already felt for her; her news was more important than either.

Minutes passed, and Linette knocked again. From inside she heard Hunter's voice, impatient and irritated. "Hold your horses. I'm coming."

She heard the sound of a bolt and the door opened, revealing a slice of Hunter's face and body. He held a revolver.

"Linette!" He stared, letting the door open; the hand holding the pistol dropped to his side. "What the hell—"

"I'm sorry to disturb you so late." Linette found that her voice trembled. She hadn't expected to feel this jolt all through her at the sight of Hunter. He had paused only long enough to pull on his trousers. The muscled expanse of his chest was bare, and the smooth skin of his naked shoulders and arms gleamed in the lamplight. His shaggy hair was rumpled, his face slack with sleep, giving him a vulnerable look that was in sharp contrast to the gun in his hand. He looked dangerous and sensual, a potent combination that both stirred and frightened her.

Hunter laid the revolver on the small table beside the door and picked up the oil lamp that he had set there when he opened the door. He stepped back to allow Linette to enter, sending a suspicious glance at the darkened yard beyond her. He closed the door behind her and turned to face her, holding his lamp up.

"Now, why don't—" Hunter stopped abruptly, seeing now in the full light the brutal red mark across her cheek and the thin line of blood on her swollen lower lip. "Good God, what happened?"

He moved quickly to her, reaching out to take her chin and turn her face up to his keen gaze. His touch was so gentle, his eyes so worried, that tears came into Linette's eyes. What Benton's brutality had not done to her, Hunter's concern did, and she began to cry.

Hunter curved an arm around her, pulling her gently against him. "What is it? What happened to you? Did you fall off Rubio?"

Linette shook her head, sobs wrenching her body. She hated to cry, and knowing how Hunter felt about her, she hated especially to cry in front of him. But she could not seem to stop. Her emotions had received too many blows today, and it felt so warm, so comforting, so *right* to be here in Hunter's arms. She could not stop crying, nor could she bring herself to pull away.

"It's all right," Hunter murmured, resting his cheek against her hair; his hands moved soothingly over her back. "Shhh. I'll take care of it. Just tell me what happened."

Finally her tears stopped. Linette rested her head against Hunter's chest for just a moment longer, gathering strength. She lifted her head and looked up at him. His face was close to hers, his piercing green eyes dark and soft with concern. He reached up and wiped the tears from her face; the skin of his hand was rough, but his touch was light. The feel of his fingers on her sent a shiver through her. Linette stepped back; her feelings were too raw and unprotected right now for her to deal with the sensations Hunter always evoked in her. She swallowed and wiped the remaining tears away from her face.

Hunter, too, stepped back, his face changing subtly, as he realized how differently he was acting toward her. "Now tell me what's going on. What are you doing out here at this hour? And what happened to you?"

Linette made a little gesture of dismissal with her hand. "It doesn't matter. I came here to tell you something."

"Doesn't matter!" Hunter echoed, his eyebrows rising. "You come in here looking like you've been in a fistfight and you tell me it doesn't—" He stopped abruptly, understanding dawning on his face. "Jesus Christ! That's it, isn't it? Conway hit you, didn't he?"

"Yes." Linette turned her face away, feeling strangely ashamed. "But that isn't why I came."

Hunter's eyes lit up with an unholy fire, and his face was suddenly as taut and cold as a mask. "I'll kill that son of a bitch!"

He started toward the stairs, his face grim. Fear sliced through Linette, and she ran after him, grabbing his arm and tugging him around to face her.

"No! Hunter, wait!"

Hunter turned and looked down at her. His eyes were fierce and wild, his jaw set. It was obvious that his brain was clouded with a rage so strong it overcame reason. Linette hadn't a doubt, looking at him, that he would carry through with his threat.

"Listen to me," Linette pleaded, praying that she

could make reason reappear in his eyes. "You can't do this."

"Let go of me."

"Hunter, no!"

"I warned him what would happen! I told him last year what would happen if he ever hurt me or mine again," Hunter growled. "Goddammit, nobody can hurt you like that and get away with it." He stopped abruptly and looked away. His body was still taut with anger, but at least his eyes no longer had that strange, vaguely unfocused look.

"Hunter . . . please. You mustn't go after Benton. Sit down and think. What good would it do?"

"It'd do *me* a hell of a lot of good," he retorted. "And I would think it would do you good, too! What's the matter with you? Why are you trying to protect him, after what he did to you? Do you love him that much?"

"No!" Linette's tone was indignant. "I don't love him at all. I never did."

"Then why the hell are you trying to save his sorry ass?"

"I'm not! I wouldn't care if he dropped dead this minute! It's you I'm worried about."

"Me?" Hunter shrugged out of her grasp and walked a step or two away from her. "You think I can't handle Benton Conway? Have a little faith."

Linette heaved an inner sigh of relief. Hunter was no longer in the grip of a blind rage. He was talking, and surely that meant that he could be made to see reason.

"Don't be ridiculous," Linette went on sharply.

"We both know that you can hurt Benton Conway. But then what would happen? Benton has lots of important friends in the government and the army. They wouldn't let you get away with it. The law would come after you and throw you in jail."

"No," Hunter replied coldly. "I'll never be in prison again."

"So what would you do? Run away to Texas? A lot of good that would do me. I need you! And you won't do me a bit of good in jail or hundreds of miles away. Forget about Benton; he doesn't matter any more. I came out here about something a lot more important."

Hunter scowled. "Dammit, Linette!" He slammed his fist against the wall. "I can't let him get away with hitting you! He'll do it again."

"No. I won't be there anymore."

Hunter went still. "You left him? For good?"

Linette nodded. "Yes. I could never live with him again. I found out something tonight that—that makes it impossible. That was why I came to see you, not because Benton hit me. I'd completely forgotten about the way my face looked. Anyway," she added, almost mischievously, "Benton will still be here when we get back. If you want to bash his face in, you can always do it then."

A faint smile touched Hunter's lips. "I reckon you're right about that." Hunter sighed. "All right. Come in to the kitchen, and let me see what I can do for that cut. Then you can tell me about what's so important."

Hunter took her arm with one hand and picked up

the lamp in the other and led Linette into the kitchen. He pulled out a chair for her before getting the washbasin and a rag. He set the basin down on the table and dipped the rag into it, then wrung it out and gently wiped the trace of blood away from Linette's lip. His touch stung, but Linette tried her best not to wince.

"I'm sorry," he murmured. Hunter rinsed the rag out and held it to her face, covering her swollen lip and cheek. The washrag was pleasantly cool against Linette's skin, and she closed her eyes at the sensation. It was odd to sit this close to Hunter, to have him touch her once more with gentleness and concern. It had been so long since they had said even a pleasant word to each other, let alone acted with any kindness toward the other. Yet, at the same time, it seemed natural, as if all the years in between had never been.

Linette opened her eyes and looked into Hunter's face, weathered by years in the sun and wind, hardened and aged by experience, and the illusion of time standing still vanished. The years had been there, all right, and they had moved Hunter and her so far apart she doubted that they could ever be close again.

Hunter cleared his throat and moved back. He dipped the rag in the cool water again and wrung it out, then handed it to Linette. "Here, hold it on your cheek. Maybe the coolness will ease the pain a little."

He went around the table and sat down across from her, putting distance between them. His face had settled back into the familiar cool, expressionless lines. He crossed his arms and waited, watching Linette.

Linette drew a breath. It seemed suddenly such a monumental task to explain this whole tangle. "I'm not sure where to begin."

Hunter shrugged. "Just start. I'll catch up eventually."

"All right. Tonight Benton and I argued, as you probably guessed. He was very angry and jealous— he's been having me followed. I didn't know it. I ride Rubio every day, and he's gotten it into his head that I've been riding out to see you."

"Me?" Hunter quirked an eyebrow. "I would think I'd be the last man you'd be carrying on a passionate affair with."

"I know. But Benton doesn't realize how you feel about me. He thinks that you're still in love with me, that I'm still in love with you. I tried to tell him how wrong he was, but he wouldn't listen."

"That's when he hit you?"

Linette nodded and looked down at her lap, picking nervously at her skirt. Would Hunter believe her, or would he dismiss it all as a lie? She needed his help; she wasn't sure she could do it without him. "But that's not the important thing. He had been drinking, you see, and he was in a rage and not very rational at all. And he said something about . . . about getting rid of my 'brat.'"

Hunter stiffened, but he said nothing.

Linette raised her face and looked earnestly into Hunter's eyes. "Hunter, our baby didn't die."

Even Hunter's impassive facade cracked at that statement. "What!" He leaned forward onto the table, his eyes boring into her. "What are you saying?"

"Benton said tonight that my baby wasn't born dead. They only *told* me that. They didn't bury her; they gave her away!"

Hunter stared. "I have a child," he said tightly, "living somewhere?"

Linette nodded. "Yes." She, too, leaned forward, her big blue eyes pleading. "I have to find her."

Hunter stood up, running his hand back through his hair. "I'll leave at first light."

Linette was flooded with warmth at Hunter's words. Without hesitating, without questioning, Hunter was going after their child. She had been right to think that she could rely on him even after all that had happened between them.

"Oh, Hunter, thank you." Linette stood up and went to him, her face glowing.

He glanced at her, surprised. "For what?"

"For believing me. For helping me."

"What else would I do? You're talking about my child, too. You think I would just sit here and do nothing if there was even a possibility that I had a child somewhere?"

"No, of course not." Linette halted.

"Besides," Hunter continued, "why in the world would you make up such a story?" He glanced away from her, his face troubled. "What you told me today must be true."

"Thank you," Linette said softly.

Hunter shrugged, as if pushing away the burden of

the heavy emotions. "I guess we better get started. I'll
have to take my string of horses over to Gideon's.
He'll take care of them for me while I'm gone. You
can go there as well. I could take you to your parents,
but you'd be better protected at Gideon's if Benton
came after you."

"Wait a minute." Linette's eyes widened with surprise as she realized that Hunter intended to set out
alone. "I'm not staying anywhere. I'm going with
you."

Hunter, deep in his plans, looked at her in equal
surprise. "Going with me? Don't be silly; you're staying here."

"I'm not. I'd like your help; that's why I came here.
But I'm going with or without you."

"That's absurd. You can't go chasing all over the
countryside. Who knows how long we'll be gone?
That's too hard a life for you."

"I'm not made out of glass, Hunter," Linette
retorted crisply. "I'm a good rider. I have an excellent
horse; you should know that. It's true I'm not used to
camping out on the ground, but I daresay that it's
something I can manage."

Hunter scowled at her. "No. I refuse to allow you
to do it."

"And how do you plan to stop me, may I ask?"

"Blast it!" Hunter took a step toward her, his eyes
flashing. "You didn't use to be so obstinate."

"Perhaps I've changed. One does over the years.
As I remember, you didn't use to be so dictatorial!"

"I'm not taking you with me!"

"Fine!" Linette shot back, thoroughly irritated, and

leapt to her feet. "Then I'll find someone else to help me. There must be someone for hire who can do such things. Since I am the one who knows where to begin searching, you can sit here by yourself and enjoy being alone."

She started toward the hall, but Hunter grabbed her arm, whirling her back around to face him. "I'll be damned if I let you do that!"

Linette cast a glance down at his hand, firmly gripped around her slender arm, then looked coolly up into his face. "As I said, how do you plan to stop me? I think it's fairly obvious that I can't be beaten into submission."

Hunter's face blanched. He released her arm as if it had singed his fingers. "I am not Benton Conway. I have never laid a finger on you or any other woman, and you know it. Don't you ever, *ever* dare to lump me in with that garbage again."

Linette was immediately contrite. Hunter had angered her so that she'd spat out the first insult that came into her head. "I know," she said quickly. "I'm sorry."

She went back to the table and stood for a moment, tracing a whorl in its rough wood. Hunter turned away, too, clearing his throat, and walked over to the dry sink. He stood for a moment, hands braced on either side of the sink, staring out the window at the night-blackened yard. "You're right. I have no control over you. You're free to hire someone to help you track her down. But we're talking about my daughter, too. You know I'm going to go looking for her. It makes more sense to let me do it."

"That's why I came to you," Linette replied. "What I want is your *help*. I don't plan to sit at your brother's house waiting for you to return with my child. I'm going after her, Hunter, one way or another. And since I am the one who has the information and the means with which to finance our search, I think you have little choice except to go with me."

"The means?" Hunter turned, his eyebrows going up.

Linette reached up and touched the pearl stud in one ear. "Benton is going to pay for finding the child he stole from me," she said in a cold, hard voice. "I took my jewelry case when I left. I didn't realize when he gave me those baubles over the years that he was probably trying to salve a guilty conscience."

"Benton Conway has no conscience," Hunter retorted gruffly. It made an icy knife turn in his gut to think of Conway giving Linette gifts—no doubt draping a jeweled necklace around her neck, then bending down to kiss that elegant white throat. His fingers curled up into fists at his side.

"Perhaps not," Linette agreed tonelessly and sat back down in her chair. "Well . . . do you agree to my terms or shall I go on my own?"

Hunter grimaced. "You know I have to agree. You're the one who knows what he did with her. Of course, I could get the information out of Benton, I suppose, but it would slow me down. Besides, I can hardly let you go off by yourself. But have you thought about your reputation?"

"To hell with my reputation!" Linette snapped, her eyes blazing. "That's what I was concerned about before—and look what happened! I lost my baby! My only concern now is getting my daughter back. I don't give a damn any more what the old biddies of Pine Creek have to say about me." She shrugged. "Besides, I don't see that my reputation's any of your concern. You don't have any responsibility for me."

"That's true." Hunter's mouth hardened. "And thank God for that."

He strode back to the table and plopped down into a chair. "All right. We're agreed. Come on, then. We'd better start making plans."

Releasing a little sigh of relief, Linette sat down across from him.

"I only know where to start. We were staying with Benton's cousin in Fairfield, not far from Baton Rouge, when I had her. All Benton would say tonight was that his cousin gave the baby away. I would presume that she didn't go any farther than Baton Rouge, but Benton swore that he didn't know where she took her."

Hunter's lips thinned. He leaned back in his seat, crossing his arms. "Maybe I ought to pay Benton a visit tonight. Perhaps I could persuade him to tell me more."

Linette looked alarmed. "Hunter! You said you wouldn't do anything to Benton. You won't be any use to me at all in jail!"

Hunter grimaced. "I won't be in jail. Would you quit worrying about that scum?"

"I'm not worrying about *him*. I told you that." Linette shrugged. "Anyway, I think maybe he was telling the truth. Benton likes to keep his hands clean;

he usually gets others to do the dirty work for him. I suspect that he gave the baby to his cousin to take to an orphanage and washed his hands of the whole thing. Surely even he would have told me tonight if he knew."

"Are you sure it was an orphanage?"

"No. Just guessing. She could have given her to anybody."

"The thing to do is to locate his cousin and find out where she took her. So tomorrow morning, we'll leave for Baton Rouge." He paused. "That'll be a long trip."

Linette arched an eyebrow. "Don't start that again, Hunter. I won't stay behind. I can ride a lot farther than Baton Rouge."

"All right. But it will take several days. I'll have to take a pack horse for supplies." He stood up. "I'd better get those supplies together. We'll leave as soon as it's light." He paused, looking strangely uncertain.

"What's the matter?"

"Well, I just realized—where are you going to stay tonight?"

Linette hadn't given the matter any thought. But now, considering it, she blushed. She and Hunter would be alone tonight under the same roof. It was anything but proper. Worse than that, the very idea sent all sorts of strange, long-dead sensations running through her. But what else was there to do? She could hardly go back to Benton's house to spend the night.

"I—I suppose I could take you to your parents' house tonight," Hunter began. "Or maybe we could pack up now and ride on out to Gideon's to spend the night." There wouldn't be any question of impropriety with both Tess and Jo Tyrrell there.

"Going back to my parents would simply waste more time tomorrow morning," Linette pointed out. "Besides, if Benton should decide to look for me, that's the first place he'd go. And by the time we'd get packed and ride out to Gideon's farm, it'd be the middle of the night. We can't wake all of them up at that hour."

"Then what do you suggest we do?" Hunter asked with some irritation.

"I'll simply stay here, of course. I'll sleep downstairs on the sofa."

"Don't be absurd." Hunter scowled.

"What's absurd about it?" Linette countered. "We're going to be camping out together every night. What's different about this?"

"Both ideas are foolish. If you were smart, you wouldn't do either one."

"I would never have believed that you, of all people, would turn into such a prig."

Hunter gave her a dark look. "Obviously the same can't be said for you."

"And what is that supposed to mean?" Linette's voice was dangerously silken.

"Only that you're charging headfirst into this without even a thought as to what will happen to you afterwards."

Linette's eyebrows floated upward derisively, and Hunter had the good grace to look embarrassed. "All right. I know. I'm hardly the one to talk about being too impulsive. But, dammit, Linette, I'm only think-ing about your good."

"Thank you, but I think that I will be in charge of what is good or not good for me."

Hunter grimaced, obviously irritated by her crisp words. "Do whatever you like. It makes no difference to me. There's no sense your sleeping on the sofa, though. Take Ty's old room upstairs."

Hunter thought about sleeping in the room next door to Linette, only a thin wall separating them, and his palms began to sweat. Sleeping outside by a camp-fire was one thing, but lying only a few feet away from her, enclosed in the same house, was another matter altogether. It made his pulse skitter even to think about it, and Hunter knew it was a more foolish idea for him than for Linette.

"On second thought," he went on, "you can have my room. The bed's more comfortable. I'll take the room in the barn."

"Oh, Hunter, no, I couldn't ask you to do that. That's too much."

"You're not asking me to; I volunteered. So be quiet and take advantage of it. I'll be in and out, any-way, getting our things ready for tomorrow; it makes more sense for me to stay out there."

Linette hesitated. It would be more comfortable with Hunter out of the house. "If you're sure . . ."

Hunter nodded and handed her the kerosene lamp. "Here, take this and go on up. I'll get to work."

Linette was bone weary, and the thought of lying down and falling asleep was appealing, but she felt vaguely guilty about leaving Hunter to do all the work. "Perhaps I should stay to help you."

Hunter shook his head. "I'll be fine. I know where everything is; I can do it faster by myself, really."

"All right." Linette took the lamp and went up the stairs, leaving Hunter behind her.

It felt odd to be climbing these strange stairs to bed, Linette thought, and odder still to think that Hunter Tyrrell was on the floor below. She reached the top of the staircase, where one door stood open and the other closed. She walked through the open door and paused. It was obviously Hunter's. A masculine shirt in dark plaid colors was thrown across the back of a chair. No pictures decorated the walls, and the dresser was completely bare; it was a plain, functional place, and Linette suspected that the room's occupant spent little time here.

The bed was turned down, the covers rumpled, as if someone had jumped out of bed in haste. Linette walked over to the bed. There was still a shallow dent in the pillow where Hunter's head had lain. It gave her a strange shivery feeling to think that she would be lying down in the bed Hunter had just vacated, almost as if she would be sharing it with him. She reached out her hand and laid it on the bed, half-expecting to feel his warmth still there. It was cool to her touch, and Linette reminded herself that there was a vast difference between lying in Hunter's bed and lying with Hunter.

Linette set the oil lamp down firmly on the bedside table and took the pins from her hair. She sat down on the bed to take off her shoes. She was unbuttoning her dress when she realized that she did not have her nightgown with her. She had left her bag out on the horse when she came in to talk to Hunter. With a sigh, she picked up her shoes to put them back on and go retrieve her baggage. Just then there was a knock on her door.

11

"*Linette?*" *Hunter's voice* sounded outside in the hall.

Her heart began to pound, and Linette moved quickly to open the door. Hunter stood in the hall, her carpetbag clutched in one hand.

He glanced down at her swiftly, his eyes coming to rest on her bare toes peeking out from under her skirt. He jerked his head back up and said stiffly, "I put away your horse. And I found this."

He held out her bag, and Linette reached out to take it. "Thank you."

Their hands grazed each other. His skin was hot and rough, and merely touching it sent a shiver through Linette. She stepped back quickly, hoping that she had concealed her reaction. Hunter continued to look at her a moment, then he turned sharply and trotted back down the stairs.

Linette closed the door and went back to the bed. She sat down on it, hugging her carpetbag close to her chest. Hunter's presence was all around her. Linette tried to ignore how affected she was by being in his room. She stretched out on her side. The pillow smelled like him. She sat up quickly, her nerve endings pulsatingly alive. She had to stop thinking like this!

She had to remember what she was doing and why. It was the baby who mattered, not Hunter or her. She had to find her child, and that was the only thing she could think about. Anything else was a distraction.

Linette touched her cheek where Benton had struck her. It was sore, but she was glad, for the pain took her mind off Hunter and reminded her of how much Benton had taken from her. *That* was what she needed to be thinking about.

She squared her shoulders and stood up. Opening her carpetbag, she pulled out her nightgown and began to change clothes. Then she climbed into bed and shut her eyes determinedly.

Downstairs in the kitchen, Hunter efficiently folded the blanket over the tin pan and the few cooking and eating utensils, then rolled them up tightly and tied them. He glanced around, mentally checking off the list of what they would need to take. He had already made another bedroll with a few eating essentials such as coffee, beans, and jerky stuck inside it. He was also going to take an extra rifle and revolver on the pack horse, as well as Linette's bag and his own clothes. Packing his things would have to wait until tomorrow morning, though. He hadn't thought to get them out before Linette went to bed, and there was no way he was going up to that room again. Linette still had such an effect on him.

He thought about the way she looked when she'd opened the door to him earlier. Her face, swollen and red from Benton's brutal attack, made him angry and vengeful all over again, but those feelings had been quickly overcome by the desire that coursed through him. Linette's rich auburn hair had hung loose around her shoulders, thick and soft and glinting with fiery highlights. He had wanted to sink his hands into it, the old familiar longing for her tightening his gut. Her form was still the kind to make a man's senses reel, so soft and sweetly contoured, and somehow the sight of her bare feet peeking out from under her dress, reminding him that she was getting ready for bed, had jolted him with desire.

It wasn't something he wanted to feel. He tried his best not to feel it. But after everything that had happened today, his guard was down. His emotions had been too battered and stripped raw; they seemed to be lying right on the surface.

Hunter grimaced and stood up, gathering up the bundles around him. It was a good thing he was going to be out in the barn sleeping tonight, he thought. Anywhere in the house would be too damn close; it would be too easy to get up and walk into his room. That was why he had rejected the idea of her sleeping in Ty's room. He had known that he would be unable to sleep, that he would lie awake, thinking about

Linette in the room next door and thinking how easy it would be to walk those few steps to her bed.

But a few minutes later, when he was in the small room at the rear of the barn, lying on the narrow bed, he found that it wasn't much better sleeping out here. Now he was thinking, not about Linette being next door, but about her going to bed in *his* room. He could see her moving about among his things, brushing her hair in front of his mirror, putting her delicate feminine things out on his dresser. He could just imagine her in a lacy nightgown turning down his bed and crawling in between his sheets.

Hunter stifled a groan and rolled over. It was crazy, he knew, to think about things like this. But somehow he couldn't stop. He wondered whether his sheets would now smell like Linette's perfume; he pictured her hair spread out across his pillow like silken flame.

He sat up abruptly, letting out a curse. He had to stop thinking this way! No matter what had happened, no matter how badly Linette might have been hurt, he could not afford to be caught in her web again. Perhaps she hadn't been the evil person he had thought she was, but he had been just as badly hurt by her. His heart had been as broken, his pride as tattered. Hunter had learned the hard way that the only way to avoid such heartache was simply not to give his heart to any woman again. No woman, especially Linette, would ever have the opportunity to destroy him as he had been destroyed when he found out she'd married another man.

He wished for the hundredth time that Linette was

not going with him to look for their child. But that was impossible. He was stuck with her for the rest of the trip, however long it took, and he could only hope that Linette would not seem so tempting when they were camping under the stars as she did now lying in his bed.

Sighing, Hunter lay back down and threw one arm across his eyes. Resolutely he shoved all thoughts of Linette out of his mind. Instead he thought about his daughter, his little girl, out there somewhere. The idea was extraordinary, incredible. He wondered what his mother would say when she found out, and that thought made him smile. He knew what she'd say: not to rest until he had brought that little Tyrrell home to her family. He suspected that the idea might not set too well with Linette. Well, they'd cross that bridge when they came to it. For right now, they had to find the girl. Nothing else could be allowed to interfere with that.

Benton Conway awoke late the next morning, his head pounding. He sat up gingerly, bracing his head on his hands, and let out a small moan of pain and self-pity. His head felt swollen twice its size, and his stomach lurched as if he were on a boat. Then suddenly he jumped out of bed and staggered to the chamber pot, where he emptied out the contents of his stomach. After that he sat down with a cool cloth over his face and tried to remember exactly what had happened the night before.

What he remembered did not lessen his pain. Had

he really blurted out the truth to Linette in his drunkenness? He cursed himself for being a fool; he had always known that he could never tell Linette what had really happened to that brat of hers.

He lurched out the door and down the hall to Linette's bedroom. He stopped just inside the door and looked around, the bitter truth sunk in on him. The doors to Linette's wardrobe stood open, and several drawers were pulled out. A few articles of clothing lay on the bed and the floor, as if discarded or accidentally dropped. Linette really had left. It had been no alcohol-induced nightmare.

Benton leaned back against the wall and tried to think. Finally, he turned and went back to his room, where he shaved and changed into clean clothes. He still felt shaky, but at least he looked a trifle more presentable. And he had come up with an idea.

He didn't wait for breakfast, just drank a cup of hot black coffee and walked down to the shabby rooming house in the Flats where Packer stayed. He had used Packer a few times before for some jobs too dirty for his own hands, and Packer had handled them competently. In fact, it had been Packer whom Benton had sent to follow Linette on her daily rides and find out whether she was meeting Hunter.

Packer was furious, of course, at being dragged from his sleep so early in the morning, but money always talked with Packer, and after a while he gave his surly assent and rode off to Hunter's farm to see if Linette had gone where Benton suspected. While he was gone, Benton waited impatiently in his study, checking his window every few minutes for a sign of

Packer or pacing the room or just fidgeting in the big chair behind his desk. It seemed to him as if hours had passed, and he couldn't understand how it could take that long for the man to ride out to Hunter's farm and back.

There was a soft knock on the door, and Benton jumped, startled, and whirled around. "Yes? Who's there?"

He was across the room and already reaching for the door handle when the soft reply came from the other side of the door. "Father? It's me, Rosemary."

Benton grimaced. The last thing he needed, he thought, was to have to talk to his silly, soft-hearted daughter. On the other hand, if she was determined enough to talk to him that she had actually disturbed him in his office, a thing she was usually too timid to do, she would probably come back later, perhaps at an even less convenient time. So he jerked the door open and stared out at her forbiddingly. "What?"

Rosemary took an involuntary half-step back. "I— I'm sorry to disturb you, Father." Behind her round spectacles, her brown eyes were worried and faintly scared. She clasped her hands together tightly. "I wouldn't except—" She glanced around. "Might I come in to talk? It's not something for the servants to hear."

Benton sighed and stepped back, letting Rosemary in, but he remained standing close to the door, not asking her to sit or go farther into the room, hoping that would encourage her to leave.

Rosemary drew a breath, facing her father, and started again. "The thing is I'm . . . worried about

Linette. She's not in her room. She hasn't been all morning, and it looks messy and . . . and odd. Do you know where she is?"

"How the devil should I know where she is?" Benton barked. He should have known that Rosemary would ask awkward questions. The whole town would once they realized Linette had left him.

"Last night I thought I heard you two quarreling down here in your study," Rosemary went on. "But then everything got quiet and I thought it was all right. But, now—" her voice dropped. "Did Linette leave?"

"Well, obviously she did," Benton snapped.

"But why?" Rosemary looked anguished. "Where has she gone?"

"I don't know, I just told you!"

"Back to her parents?"

"Perhaps. Or maybe she's run clean out of town. She was out of her head."

"Why? What happened? Linette wouldn't leave like that for no reason! Without even saying good-bye!" Tears glittered in Rosemary's soft eyes.

"She said ample good-bye to me," Benton replied grimly. "It's none of your concern why she left."

The whole town would be wondering the same thing, he knew, and the prospect ate at Benton. He had never had any difficulty shutting up his daughter, but the people of Pine Creek were another matter entirely. He would be at the center of a storm of gossip; all the old biddies would be delighted to cast him in the role of the villain in the little drama. Benton was well aware of how thoroughly he was disliked by the loyal Rebels around here; they all considered him a traitor just because he wasn't as big a fool as the rest of them. His power and wealth made him feared, but he wasn't liked or accepted; only his daughter's position among Pine Creek society kept him from being completely ostracized.

But not even Rosemary's status in the community would help him if everyone found out what he had done years ago with Linette's baby. His only hope was that Linette would not want to hurt her own reputation by admitting that she had gotten pregnant out of wedlock. But she had been angry enough last night to spread the news, even if it meant her own social downfall.

It made Benton's blood run cold even to think about what would happen if she told everyone. Shady business practices were one thing, but taking his wife's baby from her and abandoning it was something that no one would forgive. Benton shuddered at the thought. His position in the community was important to him. He'd always hungered after respect and acceptance and had sought to attain them in whatever way he could (including marrying Rosemary's dull mother). He could hardly bear the thought of being ostracized by everyone, including his rich Yankee friends like Farquhar Jones. Worse yet, if he lost their friendships, even his business could suffer.

He could not, simply *could not*, let Linette tell her story. He had to stop her. And if she'd gone to that damn Tyrrell, it'd be even harder to do. Benton was flooded with a harsh mixture of jealousy, rage, and fear, and he hated Linette with as much strength as he'd always desired her.

"Father!" Rosemary cried, and Benton glanced at her. She was watching him, her eyes scared, and he realized that what he was thinking must show on his face.

Benton frowned at her. "What? For mercy's sake, Rosemary, don't have hysterics on me."

"I wasn't! I just—I want to know what happened to Linette!"

"You'll find out soon enough. Just go back to your room and read one of those stupid books you're always mooning over. If she's in this town, she'll soon be back in this house."

"If she's in this town!" Rosemary repeated in astonishment. "You mean she may have left Pine Creek? But why? Where would she go?"

"Would you stop asking all these questions!" Benton roared. "Dammit! I don't know where she is!"

Rosemary opened her mouth as though she would say something else, then shut it firmly. Whirling around, she hurried back down the hall and out the front door.

Benton watched her leave with disfavor, then resumed his position at the window. There was still no sign of Packer. Rosemary's visit had made him more agitated than ever, bringing forcefully home to him what he would be facing from everyone else in town. He needed to get Linette back. He had to have her here under his control again, otherwise . . . the only solution would be to make sure she never talked again at all. And if she had told Hunter, Hunter would have to be taken care of as well. Benton smiled to himself at that thought.

There was the sound of a horse outside, and eagerly Benton looked out. A square, muscular man was climbing down from his horse and tying it to the hitching post out front. Benton let out a hiss. He had told Packer many times to leave his horse in the stables out back. Benton didn't want anyone knowing that he ever conducted business with trash like Packer. But Packer was either dense or defiant, Benton wasn't sure which, and he persisted in being far too open about contacting Benton.

Benton opened the floor-length window and gestured for Packer to come in, avoiding the front door. Packer slouched across the long verandah to him and bent to climb inside. He stood for a moment, looking around him at the study.

"Quite a passel of books you got here," he commented, chewing away at a twig with his tobacco-stained teeth. His hair was sandy-colored, as was his bushy mustache. The mustache, too, bore signs of his tobacco-chewing. He was of medium height, but he had the heavy chest and shoulders of a man much taller. His face was large and his neck thick. One eyelid drooped from scar tissue, and his nose had obviously been broken, probably more than once.

"Yes, yes, so you've said before," Benton remarked impatiently, going around the desk to his chair. "I thought I told you not to tie your horse out front. The less people know about our connection, the better."

Packer shrugged indifferently, and Benton sighed. "All right, never mind," Benton went on. "Tell me what you found out. Was Tyrrell there?" He couldn't bring himself to add the question that was uppermost in his mind: Was *she* there, too?

"Nope." Packer plopped down in one of Benton's leather chairs and stretched his feet out in front of him, lacing his hands across his stomach. "Nobody was there."

"No one?" Benton's eyebrows went up.

Packer shook his head. "No one and nothing. Not even any animals in the pens."

"The horses? There weren't any horses there?"

"Not that I could find. I checked all around; that's why it took so long. I looked in the barn and all." He shrugged. "Nothing. Nobody answered when I knocked at the door, neither, so I checked the doors and windows. All locked. You didn't say nothin' about breakin' in, so I didn't go inside. I looked in a window or two, though, and it looked dark inside. I'd say nobody's home."

Damn the woman! Benton kicked his desk and jumped up, his face flushing red with fury. Obviously Linette had run straight to Tyrrell, just as he'd feared. He had known it, even though he'd clung to a small remnant of hope that she had gone home to her parents. They must have packed up and left as soon as she told him, this morning at the latest. It was clear that they had left expecting to be gone for some time, or else Tyrrell's horses would still be there. Linette must have convinced Hunter to go searching for that brat with her.

Benton paced the room, cursing at some length. His life was ruined. Ruined! Everyone would know

now that Linette had left him, that she had run off
with Hunter. Everyone would laugh at him and call
him a cuckold. Worse, they had probably told that
damn family of Hunter's all about the baby Benton
had given away. The Tyrrells were notoriously clan-
nish. They would spread it all around town.

Benton wouldn't dare show his face anywhere.
Everyone would drop him, even the Yankees—even
Farquhar Jones, perhaps. God knows, Jones and some
of the others weren't exactly saints; Farquhar
wouldn't care about the morals of what he had done,
but he might very well not want to be associated with
Benton, fearing that the taint would rub off on him.

He would be destroyed! With a groan Benton
plunged his fingers into his hair and pulled at it. He
hated Linette and Hunter with every fiber of his
being. He wanted them punished for what they had
done to him. He wanted them dead!

Packer watched Benton's movements with interest.
"Never seen you so mad before," he commented.
"What happened? Your woman run off with this
Tyrrell feller?"

Benton whirled and fixed him with a fierce glare.
"Who told you that?"

"Nobody. I just reckoned it must be something like
that to get you so riled up. Hardly nothin' gets a man
so beside hisself like a woman." He paused. "So . . .
you want me to follow them?"

"Yes! Immediately. You can catch up with them. I
know where they're going."

Packer looked faintly surprised. "Where are they
headed, then?"

"It's a small town close to Baton Rouge. Fairfield. My cousin's house. Here, I'll show you." Benton grabbed a piece of paper and scrawled a crude map on it, then thrust it at the other man.

"All right." Packer shoved his thick body out of the chair and took the map. "It all right if I take another hand along? He's good with a gun, and since there's the two of them . . ."

"Yes, yes, I don't care. Take whomever you like. Just make sure they don't come back." Benton's eyes blazed wildly. He looked half-mad. "Do you understand me? I want Hunter Tyrrell dead! Out of my life!"

Packer nodded. "I understand. Your wife, too?"

Benton hesitated, thinking about Linette. Thinking about her in Tyrrell's bed. If she wasn't there already, no doubt she would be soon. He could see her moaning and writhing as she never had for him. "No," he said finally, his voice a hiss. "Not unless it's absolutely necessary. I want him dead, and I want her back in this house. I want to take care of her myself. By the time I'm through with her, she'll beg me to let her be a good little wife again."

12

Hunter idly poked the fire with a stick, his eyes straying across to where Linette sat, patiently grinding up beans for their coffee, using the butt of his revolver. She was intent upon her task, her smooth brow furrowed with effort as she crushed the beans. Hunter tore his eyes away from her and looked back down at the rabbit meat sizzling on a stick over the fire. He had spotted the animal just before they camped and quickly brought it down, glad to have a respite from the everlasting beans and jerky they had brought along.

It had been three days now since they had left his house. They had ridden to his brother's farm and left his horses there, explaining to Gideon and the others what had happened and where they were going. Linette had flushed and looked away as Hunter told them, embarrassed to have his brother, mother, and

Tess know about her pregnancy and the child. But to her (and Hunter's) surprise, Jo had not said a thing about the immorality of what Linette and Hunter had done. She had looked at Linette with understanding and said in a considering voice, "I see."

Predictably, Gideon had thought that he should accompany Hunter, though all of them convinced him that he was needed too much right there to leave. Tess had worried about Linette undertaking such an arduous task, saying softly that she should stay there with them while Hunter went alone.

Linette had started to make a vehement reply, but to her surprise it was Jo Tyrrell who jumped in first, saying firmly, "No. She couldn't bear to sit here. It's her child." She turned her shrewd gray eyes on Linette, then back at Tess, nodding toward the baby lying in Tess's arms, quietly sleeping. "What if it were your own little boy? Would you be content to stay here while Gideon went looking for him?"

"No. Of course, you're right."

They left soon afterward, not wanting to waste any time, and had traveled hard ever since, not stopping to camp at night until it was dark and rising the next morning at first light to be on their way. Amazingly enough, Linette had neither complained nor slowed him down. If anything, she was usually the one who wanted to push on a bit farther or get a faster start in the morning. She seemed driven by an inner fire, all of her actions as determined and intent as the way she was pulverizing the coffee beans now. It was as if she felt that every little thing she did would bring her one step closer to her all-important goal.

Hunter reached out and gave the wooden spit a quarter turn to brown the meat evenly. His eyes strayed back to Linette. He had done his best to remain aloof from her, keeping in mind his determination not to fall under her spell again. It would be all too easy to do, given the enforced intimacy of this trip. They rode together, ate together, slept only a few feet apart every night. A man would have to be inhuman to be around a woman as beautiful as Linette every minute of the day and night and not feel stirrings of desire, Hunter told himself. But that didn't mean he had to give in to those feelings. He did his best to ignore them—and to ignore Linette. He spoke little as they traveled, and even in the evening as they made camp and ate, he didn't engage in idle conversation with her. He knew where talking with Linette was likely to lead. It would mean that he had to look into her face, would see the lively animation of her features, the sparkle of her eyes, the lovely curve of her lips, the flash of her teeth. He would begin to know her again, to learn her mind and soul once more. He didn't want that; he wanted to remain a stranger to her.

A little to his surprise, Linette seemed content to leave their relationship on this plateau of polite exchanges. She didn't initiate any conversations, either, unless they had to do with some practicality at hand. She made no effort to smile at him or flirt or talk to him about the events and time that lay between them. As best he could tell, Linette had no desire to know him, either. Her mind seemed to be entirely on her daughter.

That was as it should be, Hunter acknowledged. After all, that was the purpose of this trip, and it was what Hunter himself was thinking about as well. But, strangely enough, he discovered that he resented her silence a little. He found himself wanting to talk to her about the baby they shared. He had to stop himself from asking her questions about her life for the past few years. He wanted to tell her about Texas and his life on the ranches where he'd worked, the people he'd met and the places he'd seen. Sometimes, he had to clench his teeth against the words that threatened to tumble out. It annoyed him, but that wasn't the worst of it. The worst was the desire that continued to lurk inside him for her.

He could not keep from looking at her. He would glance over at her as they rode, saying to himself that he was just checking on her, making sure that her form was right and that she wasn't drooping with tiredness. But deep inside he knew that he looked at her not for those reasons but simply for her beauty. He remembered how when he had been courting her, he had never tired of looking at her. It seemed as if he was always discovering some new facet of her beauty, as if with each glance his love grew stronger. He no longer loved her, of course, but he could not deny the pull she still had over him. The sun touched her creamy skin with gold, so that she seemed almost to glow, and it lightened her vivid blue eyes. When she took off her hat for a moment to let the breeze cool her, the sun struck off her hair, turning it to flame, and it sent a wave of desire washing through Hunter just to see it. Her breasts were sweetly rounded beneath the military cut of her riding habit, her waist so small it invited a man to span it with his hands, her hips flowing out richly from him.

At night it was just as bad, maybe worse. The soft, warm darkness was seductive, hinting at the pleasures of her body in a way that stirred him even more. He could not keep from remembering the night by the creek when they had made love. It had been so brief and so long ago. Sometimes he wondered if it could really have been as magical as he remembered it, as exciting and soul shaking.

It wouldn't be the same now, he told himself. Then they had been starry-eyed romantics, swept up in a great romantic love. Now he knew better; he had grown old and cynical. If it happened now, it would not be any more special than it had been other times, with other women. It would be pleasurable, no doubt, but not shattering. *Surely that was how it would be.*

Yet, when Hunter watched her sit at the edge of the fire's light and brush out her hair, the burnished tresses catching the glow of the fire with every movement, desire twisted so sharply in his gut that it almost made him gasp. And he knew that making love to Linette could never be ordinary. Just to touch her would make him tremble. He thought of those old sensations rushing over him again, the intense love and heat sweeping him away, and he felt both excited and disturbed, almost frightened at the prospect of feeling that way again.

Linette was everything a man could want in a

woman—and she could cut his heart right out of him. No one knew that better than Hunter.

She turned toward him now, holding out the small tin pot with the coffee grounds. "All done."

Hunter nodded. "Go ahead and put it on. The meat's almost done."

Linette carefully set the pot on the small flattish rock at the fire's edge, then stood up, stretching her cramped muscles. Hunter stood up, too.

Something hit a tree behind him, sending bark flying, and a loud crack sounded some distance beyond them. Linette glanced around, puzzled.

"What in the world—"

Hunter, however, recognized the sound, and instinctively he grabbed Linette and dove to the ground just as another shot whined past his head. They hit the ground with a thud, knocking the air from Linette, and Hunter covered her with his body, reaching down for his gun as he did so. *Damn!* It wasn't strapped to his leg. Linette had been using it to grind the coffee beans and it was lying back on the rock. Hunter wriggled closer to the large rock, pulling Linette along with him.

Linette struggled futilely, gasping, "Hunter! What are you doing!"

"Shut up, dammit, and move!" Hunter wrapped his arms around her and rolled over against the rock, taking Linette with him. There was another whine, accompanied by a puff of dirt flying up where their bodies had been only an instant before.

Linette let out a shriek, then quickly swallowed. "Hunter! Is someone shooting at us?"

"Of course!" he snapped. "You think I'm rolling around in the dirt for fun?"

He twisted back, feeling along the edge of the top of the large stone. Finally his searching fingers encountered the butt of his revolver, and he wrapped his hand around it, pulling it down to his side. Ideally, he would have preferred to have his rifle, but it, he knew, was propped against the stack of their possessions on the other side of the campfire. It was close, but to reach it he would have to cross an open space, clearly backlit by the firelight, which would make him a perfect target for the gunman.

Propping himself on his elbows above Linette, Hunter peered around the edge of the rock and fired. He had no hope of hitting anything; he hadn't the least idea where their attacker was, but he wanted to draw the gunman out. Sure enough, right after he fired, he saw a flash among the trees, and a bullet slammed into the rock that protected them. Hunter took careful aim at where he'd seen the brief light and fired his pistol again.

He fired once more toward the spot. After that there was only silence. Had their attacker left? Or was he simply trying to outwait them, hoping that they would decide they were safe and stand up again? Worse yet, perhaps the gunman had left his position and was even now circling around through the dark in order to come up on them from behind.

Hunter closed his eyes, putting all of his concentration into his hearing, waiting for a snap of a twig or the sound of a boot striking stone or the soft slide of a foot in the dirt. The night was perfectly still. Then, in the distance, he heard the sound of a horse running.

Whoever it was had ridden off, no doubt deciding it was futile to stay and exchange gunfire in the dark. Hunter relaxed, relief washing through him. His heart was pounding, his nerves supremely sensitive in the aftermath of danger. It always affected him this way, leaving him almost sick, yet wildly alive, his heightened senses alert to every sound or smell or sight.

He was acutely aware of Linette's soft body beneath his. He could hear the soft, shallow intake of air coming from her, feel the rise and fall of her chest beneath his skin, her breath moving in rhythm with his. He could smell the faint lavender scent that lingered in her hair. Their position was extremely intimate, a mimicry of lovemaking, and it sent heat coursing through him. He shifted a little unconsciously, changing the close contact of their bodies ever so slightly, and the faint friction stirred him. He was suddenly hot and aching, the readiness for danger turning abruptly into desire.

Linette's face was only inches from his. Her eyes were huge and dark, alluring pools that beckoned a man to drown in them. Hunter's eyes went to her mouth, soft and imminently kissable, lips slightly parted. He longed to taste that mouth. He wanted to cup her breast in his hand, to feel its inviting softness. He began to lower his head, drawn inexorably to that inviting mouth. Linette's eyes widened, and she sucked in a breath.

Her movement broke the spell, and Hunter realized what he was doing—exactly what he had promised himself he would not. He'd let the excitement and his treacherous body carry him away from the sensible course he had begun.

Letting out a curse, Hunter pulled back abruptly and jumped to his feet, heedless of exposing himself to the sniper if by any chance he was still in the woods.

"Hunter!" Linette exclaimed agitatedly. "What are you doing? What if they start shooting again?"

"I heard them ride away." He moved to the fire, turning his back on Linette. He knew his desire would not subside as long as he was looking at her. He squatted down beside the fire. "Damn!"

"What?" Linette sat up, straightening her clothes, and glanced over at him.

"One of their bullets managed to hit our meal. Half of it's in the fire now."

"Oh. Well, I confess I'm no longer very hungry, anyway. You can have it."

"Don't be absurd. We'll share. You'll recover your appetite in a little while; it's just a reaction to danger." He turned the spit, inspecting the meat. "It's a trifle burned, but I think it'll still taste all right."

Linette moved over and squatted down beside him. "Hunter, who shot at us? Why would anyone want to kill us?"

Hunter cast a sideways glance at her. "Well, I can think of one person who would probably like to see me dead, if not both of us."

"Benton?"

Hunter nodded. Gazing into the fire, he went on, "He hates me for what you and I were to each other before you married him. He hated the idea so much he gave away your baby because I was the father, not him. I doubt he'd balk at killing me."

"Benton's no sharpshooter. He couldn't possibly shoot that well from that far away."

"No. I can't see him riding after us himself, anyway. It's more his style to send someone. A hired hand."

"You mean you think he's paid someone to kill us? But why? I mean, why wouldn't he have gotten rid of you before?"

Hunter shrugged. "You've never run away from him with me before."

"I didn't run away with you!" Linette retorted hotly.

"Benton doesn't know that." Hunter looked at her gravely. "All he could know is that you and I left together. He's bound to realize that we're going after our child. It wouldn't be unreasonable to assume that—" he turned his face aside, "that the three of us would go west somewhere and live as a family."

"He *is* jealous of you," Linette admitted. "He doesn't realize how much you dislike me." Hunter gave her a quick glance, but said nothing. "Or maybe he's simply afraid of my finding Julia—that's what I named our baby—and bringing her back to Pine Creek. He would be terrified if his friends found out what he'd done. Benton couldn't bear it if he lost all position in the community."

Hunter snorted. "I don't know what difference it makes. Everybody in town knows he's a son of a bitch now."

"Well, it does make a difference to him. He doesn't care so much if the townspeople talk behind his back, just so long as they're polite to him and have to admit him in some way into their society—and so long as he has all those Yankees and carpetbaggers to give him power and prestige. But if he fell into disgrace, and they all turned their backs on him, he'd be humiliated. Worse than humiliated. It's very important to him, being a powerful person."

Hunter lifted up the spit and threw dirt over the fire. If the gunmen came back, he would just as soon not make a perfect target for them in front of the firelight. He cut off a hot strip of meat and handed it to Linette. "Here. Careful, it's hot."

She took it gingerly between her thumb and forefinger, but she didn't attempt to eat it, just sat holding it, her forehead knitted in thought. Hunter glanced over at her as he tore off another strip and ate.

"On the other hand," he went on, "it could have been a gang of thieves that saw us and our horses and equipment and figured we were easy pickin's."

"Do you really think so?"

He shrugged. "Could be. It could even be someone who took exception to our camping on their land and decided to scare us off."

Linette looked a little relieved. "Maybe so. They did quit pretty easily; they wouldn't have done that if they'd been someone Benton hired, would they?"

"I don't know, Lin. 'Course, it's safest to be careful. We'll have to keep our eyes open."

Hunter cut off another strip of meat and ate it. He doubted that the thief theory had any validity, and the landowner one had even less. It was too great a coincidence, and Benton Conway seemed to him exactly the type of man who would hire someone to kill his wife and the man he suspected of being her lover. Hunter had suggested the other theories mainly to ease Linette's mind. He wasn't sure why he didn't want Linette to worry. It was stupid; she had asked to come on this trip, after all, and had assured him that she wanted no special favors. Frankly, it would be better if she were frightened into returning to Pine Creek while he went on with the journey. Still, something made him want to reassure her.

He frowned, wondering if he was being a fool, and he glanced over at Linette. She was nibbling at her food, and he had to smile to see the dainty way she ate it, tearing off little strips and eating them, using only the tips of her fingers. Her back was as straight as if she were sitting in an elegant dining room. She could ride hard and fast and never complain, but, Southern lady to the core, she wasn't about to drop any of her manners.

Linette, feeling his gaze, cut her eyes toward him. She frowned. "What are you grinning at?"

"Just you, trying to eat a piece of charred rabbit straight off the fire and still look elegant doing it. I reckon if they'd had a bunch of Southern ladies in that prison I was in, they'd've all been giving the guards lessons in manners—while they embroidered monograms on the prison linens."

Linette had to smile. "They might at that. My mother always said, no matter how unpleasant something was, it was still no excuse for not acting like a lady."

Hunter gave a nod of his head. "That's exactly what I mean."

They were silent for a while, concentrating on their eating. Then Linette said, quietly and a little tentatively, "Hunter, I was always—I felt so bad about your being in that prison. I—I worried about you."

Hunter looked at her, his expression cool and blank, discouraging any further talk. "No need for you to feel sorry about it; you had nothing to do with it."

Linette raised her eyebrows, feeling rebuffed. "Of course not, but that doesn't keep one from feeling bad about something awful happening to a person one . . . knows," she finished a little lamely.

Hunter stood up abruptly, tossing the bone from his meal away from their camp. "I survived. That's all that matters. I don't think about the rest of it."

His tone effectively cut off all further discussion of the topic.

Linette looked down at the bit of meat in her hand; she was suddenly, decidedly, not hungry. "I see."

Hunter turned and looked at her. "No. I doubt that you do. But it doesn't matter. Just believe me: there's nothing to talk about concerning my stay in a Yankee prison. It's over."

Linette nodded, not meeting his eyes. Hunter's

mouth tightened. He swung away, saying, "Let's set up camp. We need to get an early start tomorrow."

Hunter strode over to the stack of their possessions and pulled out their bedrolls. He felt like a brute for snapping so coldly at Linette when she had been trying to offer him sympathy for his suffering. But he wasn't about to lay bare his soul for Linette.

He walked away from the campfire, where he had originally intended for them to sleep, and began to spread out the blankets in front of two large stone outcroppings that formed a natural barrier on two sides. Linette followed and crouched down to help him smooth out the blankets.

"Why are we sleeping over here?" she asked, eyeing the second set of blankets which he was spreading out close to the first one.

"Protection," he replied succinctly. "Just in case our 'friend' takes it into his head to come back for another visit. He'd expect us to be close to the campfire. I'd like to have a little surprise on my side."

"Oh. I see."

"And I don't want us too far separated," Hunter went on, answering the question she hadn't asked. "It'd be hard to protect you if you're clear on the other side of camp."

"You think they'll be back?"

"I don't know. But I'd rather be prepared."

Linette nodded. "Me, too. Do you think we should keep a watch? Sleep in shifts?"

He looked up at her, a little surprised. He wouldn't have expected her to be this calm and practical. He kept forgetting that this Linette was an older and changed person from the light-hearted, flirtatious girl he had known before.

"I don't think that'll be necessary," he told her. "I'll keep my gun by me, and I'm a light sleeper."

He didn't add that he intended to sit up, leaning back against one of the rocks, and merely doze through the night. He had slept that way before, and he knew that the slightest noise would awaken him. Hunter didn't plan to be caught unawares a second time.

He indicated to Linette to take the blanket closest to the rock. In this way, she was sheltered on three sides, by the two rocks and by his own presence on the open side. It was as much as he could think of to protect her.

Linette did as he directed, sitting down on the spread-out bedroll and taking down her hair, preparatory to going to bed. Hunter settled onto his own bedroll, trying to keep his eyes from straying toward her. Linette's bedroll had been laid out several feet away from his on previous nights; he was not used to witnessing her nightly routine this close up, and he found it very disconcerting. He could have reached out and touched the shining fall of hair that tumbled down as she took out the hairpins. He could see quite clearly how thick and rich it was; even his memories had never been able to do it justice. He remembered its softness in his fingers, sliding across his skin like silk. He remembered how many times he had wanted to bury his face in it.

Linette took a brush from her carpetbag and began to pull it through her hair. She would brush it for several minutes, Hunter knew, pulling the brush through it until it crackled and curled around her fingers. Hunter closed his eyes and leaned back against the hard rock. It would be better if he didn't look. He wished that he did not have to go through this torture every night. Yet, perversely, every evening he found himself waiting impatiently for the moment to come when she would take down her hair and brush it. His nerves would tighten, waiting, and desire would begin to coil in his abdomen, treacherous and yearning. He would have been disappointed, even angry, if by chance she had decided to skip the routine.

Even though he was no longer watching her, the sound of the brush against her hair played upon his raw nerve endings almost as much as the sight of it did. He wondered if Linette had any idea how she affected him and if she did it on purpose. Was she teasing him, trying to prove that she could still arouse in him the fierce passions she had once inspired?

Hunter opened his eyes and studied her for a moment. Linette looked utterly calm, even indifferent. It was deflating to admit that she probably hadn't any idea what she was arousing in him— doubtless because she herself felt none of the same sort of sensations coursing through her. She had long ago lost all feeling for him; no doubt she hated him for turning against her without even giving her a chance to explain why she had married Benton. Worse yet, she must have hated him for leaving her pregnant and alone, running off to war like an irresponsible boy, without a thought as to what might happen to her.

Guilt bit into Hunter, as it had many times since Linette revealed to him why she married Benton. It was even worse when she revealed what Benton had done to her child; Hunter knew that ultimately he was responsible for her losing the baby. If only he'd stayed, if only he'd thought about Linette's future, she would never have had to marry Benton and therefore lose her child.

For the hundredth time, Hunter checked the revolver beside him under the blanket and the rifle propped against the rock behind them, using the activity to push unwelcome thoughts from his mind. It didn't help much. Guilt and desire roiled in him, making it supremely difficult to remember his vow to stay aloof from Linette, to protect his heart from another bruising.

Hunter sighed and closed his eyes, squirming in an attempt to find a more comfortable position against the rock. He heard Linette set her brush aside and begin to pull off her boots. Hunter gave in to the temptation to watch her again, opening his eyelids a slit.

Linette pulled off one boot and set it aside, then the other, each time revealing a flash of stockinged leg. It was little enough, but still it affected his equanimity.

Linette glanced over at Hunter, starting to speak, then hesitated when she saw his eyes closed. She could not read the expression on his face. Hunter was so remote, so utterly removed from her. There was a coldness to him that chilled her. She had not expected them ever to recapture their old relationship; something like that couldn't come a second time. But when Hunter had agreed to accompany her on this trip, she had hoped that it meant an easing in his attitude toward her. She had thought that they might talk, might even establish some sort of friendly rapport. There was their daughter to talk about, their hopes of finding her, their speculations on what she might be like. Such thoughts filled Linette's mind almost constantly.

But Hunter obviously had no interest in even a friendly, casual relationship with her. He hardly spoke unless it was absolutely necessary, and though she could not ask for a better companion as far as strength and safety went, much of the time she felt almost as if she were alone.

It wouldn't have been so difficult, she thought, if being around Hunter didn't remind her so forcibly of the days when they were in love. He was still the most handsome man she had ever known, perhaps even better looking now that his body had filled out and his face had become etched with lines of experience. She found herself watching his hands, large and agile and masculine, and remembering how they had felt on her. She could not keep from watching him as he rode and thinking how powerful his thighs were around his horse, how easily he handled the strong animal, and the heat that had died in her so many years ago rose up in her again, flooding her loins with liquid desire.

She hated the direction her thoughts took. Yet she

could not seem to keep her mind from returning again and again to Hunter. *He,* she thought with some bitterness, *obviously has no such problem.* Hunter managed to ignore her with ease.

Finally, Linette turned away and crawled between the blankets. She curled up on her side, and before long she was asleep.

Hunter watched her for a time. Her pale face was highlighted by the moonlight, her long lashes dark against her cheeks. Her lips were barely parted, and he could glimpse the edge of her white teeth. He thought about those delicate teeth grazing his lip or nibbling at his earlobe, and a deep, heavy throbbing started in his abdomen. Being with her was torture; he wanted to reach over and run his hand down her form, to coax her awake with kisses. Why couldn't he be indifferent to her? Why couldn't his body remain as cautious as his heart?

Hunter forced himself to turn his head from her and close his eyes, but it was some time before he slept.

Nothing untoward occurred during the night, though Hunter was startled awake several times by a noise and sat, gun at the ready, waiting for something to happen, until finally he decided that the noise had been caused merely by some animal or the wind in the trees. In the morning they arose early, as had been their custom on this trip, and started out after a quick, cold breakfast.

Hunter was alert in a way he had not been before, his eyes carefully searching the road and the land around them, the memory of the attack the night

before never far from his mind. They passed one or
two other travelers as they rode, both of them unex-
ceptional. Hunter was beginning to think that perhaps the attack the night before had been nothing
more than the work of stray thieves, after all. Then
they rounded a curve and amid the shrubbery and
trees on a small rise before them, Hunter saw a brief
flash as the sun struck upon something metal—something like a gun.

13

There was a stand of trees beside the road ahead of them, and beyond that lay a stretch of open road, where they would be clearly visible to anyone on the hill above. As soon as they entered the cover of the trees, Hunter grabbed the bridle of Linette's horse and pulled her to a stop. Linette glanced over at him, startled.

"Hunter! What are you—"

Hunter, who was already sliding off his horse, made a shushing gesture with his hand.

Now alarmed, Linette dismounted, too. Hunter handed her his horse's reins and the lead attached to their pack horse. "Stay with the horses underneath this tree. Don't go out onto the road."

"I won't." Linette spoke in as soft a tone as he. "But what is the matter?"

Hunter pulled his rifle from the scabbard on his

saddle and handed it to her, "I don't have time to explain. But I saw something up on the hill. Just trust me. I better check it out. You be ready to use this if anybody comes."

"I will." Linette had no qualms about entrusting her life to Hunter. "Is it loaded?"

"Yes." Hunter flashed a grin at her, pleased with her quick acceptance of what he had said. Linette might have been a grand lady the past few years, but she still had the heart of a fearless girl.

He pulled his revolver from his holster and disappeared silently into the trees. Linette settled the rifle into the crook of her arm and glanced around her. She had no idea what Hunter had seen, but she was sure that he hadn't acted without reason, and she was determined not to let him down.

While Linette waited warily, Hunter cut through the trees and circled around to the rear of the hill. Moving almost noiselessly, he climbed the hill, his progress slow but careful. For a long time, his search went unrewarded, but then, at last, off to his right and a little behind him, he heard a soft jingle and the blowing sound a horse makes. Hunter whirled, peering through the trees, but the foliage was dense enough that he could not make out any sign of a person or horse. He worked his way through the brush, careful not to make a sound, and at last he came to a small clearing.

There was a horse, hobbled, munching away at the leaves of a small bush, and not far from him, kneeling behind a rock, his rifle resting on it, was a man. Hunter immediately crouched down behind a bush, studying the situation. The man was tall and lanky, and though he was dressed in scruffy clothes, the gun he held was of the best quality. His back was to Hunter, his face fixed on the road below them, and every line of his body spoke of patient waiting. A saddle lay on the ground on one side of him, and he leaned against it a little as he waited.

Hunter stepped out into the clearing, clicking back the hammer of his gun. "Drop your rifle." His voice was cold and calm, deadlier than any shout, and the waiting man knew it. Immediately, he set the rifle down on the rock and drew back from it. His movements were slow and careful, and his hands went up. It was obvious that he had had a gun held on him before.

"Turn around." The man did so. His face was long and narrow, weasel-like, and his eyes were as flat and cold as death. Hunter looked at him coolly and asked, "Am I the one you're looking for?"

The man didn't answer.

"Move over there." Hunter motioned slightly with his gun, and the man edged to the right. When he was far enough away from the gun, Hunter moved quickly over to the rifle, keeping his eyes and gun on the man. He picked up the rifle and walked toward the man he had captured.

"Move over to your horse and unhobble it." The man followed his order. At Hunter's instructions he saddled and bridled it as well.

Hunter took the reins from his captive and motioned to him to start walking. Slowly they went back down the hill, Hunter keeping the gun trained on his prisoner.

Linette heard the men's approach well before they got there, and she brought her rifle up to her shoulder, sighting down it. A strange man came into view, and when he saw Linette training a gun on him, he came to a quick halt, letting out a curse.

"Good girl," Hunter said approvingly, coming up beside the stranger. "But I've got him tied, so you can relax."

"I am a woman, not a girl," Linette replied primly, but a smile danced in her eyes. "I'm very glad to see you; I was beginning to get worried."

"Sorry. It took a while." He turned toward the other man. "Get over there against that tree, hands up on the trunk where I can see them." Without looking at her, he went on, "Lin, bring some rope."

The man looked back over his shoulder at Hunter, his eyes wide with fear. At first Hunter didn't understand what had caused this sudden look of terror in the man's eyes, but then it occurred to him that the man was afraid he was about to hang him. A wicked grin spread across his face. He took the rope from Linette and handed her the rifle.

"Here. Keep this trained on him."

Hunter strolled over to one side of the man, motioning to Linette to go to the other. Linette leveled the rifle at the base of the man's skull, the cold metal circle flush against his skin.

"Put your hands behind your back," Hunter ordered, and the man relaxed and did as he said. Hunter quickly and expertly tied his hands, sawing off the section of rope with the Bowie knife attached to his belt. Then Hunter came around in front of his prisoner and looked into his face.

"What's your name?" he asked. The stranger said nothing, just stared sullenly back at Hunter. "Who sent you to kill us?"

The man shrugged. "I don't know nothin'."

"Generally, I'm sure that's true," Hunter responded. "But about this one particular subject, I think you know a great deal."

"I don't know nothin'."

Hunter shrugged. "That's too bad." He began to work with the rope casually, forming a noose. The other man's face went white. "I reckon we don't have any use for you, then. I've been in Texas the past few years, and out West, see, you're a long way from the law lots of times. People there administer their justice on the spot. Steal a horse and you get strung up. I'd say bushwhacking is as bad as stealing a horse, wouldn't you, Linette?"

The stranger rolled his eyes toward Linette, obviously hopeful that a woman would show more pity toward his plight. But Linette, who had been staring aghast at Hunter an instant earlier, quickly wiped all expression from her face and replied coolly, "I suppose so. It's a rather infamous thing to do."

"There you have it." Hunter gave a shrug and adjusted the knot on the noose. "Lin, why don't you bring the fellow's horse over here?"

With the man no longer looking at her, Linette cast an uncertain glance at Hunter, but she went over to the man's horse and led it toward Hunter.

"Mister!" the man said, panicked, "I didn't do nothin' to you! You cain't kill me for nothin'!"

"Well, it's not so much the nothing that you did," Hunter said conversationally as he fastened the saddle firmly on the horse, "but the something that you were going to do—and will doubtless try to do once again if we were to release you. You must see that if we let you go, we would have to worry about our backs the rest of the way."

"No! Honest, I swear! I wouldn't come after you again. This is enough for me."

"Come, now, you can't expect me to take your word for that. A man who won't answer any questions or even reveal his name? Now, if you were some use to us, it might be worth our while to let you live. You know, if your memory were not so poor . . ."

The man glared at him. "I ain't no informer."

Hunter turned and flung one end of the rope over a sturdy limb of the tree.

"All right, get on the horse."

"No. You cain't make me."

Hunter pulled out his revolver and cocked it. "Is that right? Let's see now, shall I start with your legs first or your arms? A shattered elbow's a powerfully painful thing, but not, I think, as bad as a torn-up knee. But I'm not sure if I should start with the least painful and work up or just go for a quick conclusion and start with the worst."

The man looked as if he might faint. For a moment he could not speak. Hunter stood and leveled his revolver at the man's elbow, not six inches away. Huge beads of sweat popped out on the man's brow, and with a convulsive movement he went to his horse's side.

"I cain't git up 'thout my arms," he pointed out, waggling his tied hands behind his back.

"You know, you're right." Hunter pulled a mockingly thoughtful face. Then his face lit up with an idea. "I reckon we'll just have to hang you standing up."

He reached behind him and pulled the noose down and dropped it over the fellow's neck. He tightened it securely, then walked the horse to the other side of the limb and began to wind the rope around the saddle horn.

Linette, watching him, thought that *she* might faint. She was almost certain that Hunter was only bluffing. He wouldn't kill a man in cold blood like that, even if the man had been waiting to shoot them. But, then, this was no longer the Hunter she had once known. Had prison and his life in Texas changed him this much? Linette didn't want to find out.

Hunter cast a last dispassionate look at the man and turned back to the horse, raising his hand to bring it down on the horse's rump. A scream rose up in Linette's throat, and she had to choke it down, covering her eyes against the sight. The man, who had been watching Linette, suddenly went limp at the knees.

"Wait!" he cried hoarsely. "Wait! I'll tell you."

Hunter turned back around. "What?"

"Whatever you want to know. Everything."

"I'm glad to hear you say that." Hunter walked back toward him. "Let's start with your name."

"Pauling. Jackson Pauling."

Hunter stopped in front of Pauling, staring straight into his eyes. "All right. Now: why were you lying in wait for us?"

"Seemed like the easiest way to do it." Pauling shrugged. "Catch you unawares." He shifted uneasily, glancing from Hunter over to Linette and back. Finally, he said, "I was supposed to kill you. Take the woman back."

"Take her where? To whom?" Hunter waited for the answer he already knew.

"A rich old coot back in Pine Creek. I don't know his name."

"I do." Hunter paused, then said, "You working alone?"

"Yes. I always work alone."

Hunter nodded and turned toward Linette. She cast him an anguished look.

"I'm sorry, Hunter. I never thought he would do this. Maybe it'd be better if I went on by myself. He's not trying to kill me. Just you. I won't be in danger. You're the only one who is."

"Don't fool yourself. He could change his mind any minute. Besides, you have no idea what he plans to do with you once he gets you back home. He may simply want the pleasure of killing you himself instead of letting his henchman do it."

"No, I'm sure not. He simply wants me under his thumb again."

"And is that where you want to be?" Hunter asked caustically. "Locked up in Conway's house, still not knowing where your daughter might be?"

"Of course not."

"Then I'd say your best bet is to stick with me." He motioned over his shoulder toward Pauling. "Unless you think you can handle the next one he sends after you on your own."

Linette nodded reluctantly. "No doubt you're right. It makes sense. It's just—oh, I can't bear it if you were to be killed helping me!"

Hunter smiled and reached up to take her chin gently between his thumb and forefinger. "If it makes you feel any better, I don't plan to let anyone kill me." He shrugged. "Come on. We need to get going. We've wasted enough time." He turned and walked back to Pauling, where he busied himself untying the man's hands and retying them in front. He held Pauling's horse tightly as the man swung up into his saddle, then tied his bound hands to the saddle horn. He motioned to Linette to take the lead rein of their pack horse, and he himself took the reins of Pauling's horse to lead it.

"What are we going to do with him?" Linette asked curiously as they rode out onto the road again.

"Turn him in at the next town we come to. I suspect that a sheriff might be pretty interested in talking to our friend here. I wouldn't suspect that this is the first time he's broken the law."

None of them glanced down the road behind them, and so they did not see the man who had pulled off the road into the trees. The man, squarely built and with one scarred eyelid, stood watching after them until they were almost out of sight; then he mounted his horse again and followed them.

*   *   *

Hunter and Linette rode into the next town and left their prisoner at the sheriff's office. It took some time to explain to the lawman's satisfaction what had happened to them, and by the time they were able to leave, it was well into the afternoon. Hunter, impatient to make up for the time they had lost, rode harder than ever. He was even less communicative than he had been on the trip up till now, and the expression on his face was grim. Linette had the uneasy suspicion that he was dwelling on the idea that she was in danger and should not be on the journey with him.

Determined that he should have no cause whatsoever to argue that he would do better without her, Linette kept right at his side and did not even protest when he continued riding even after the sun had gone down. When Hunter did at last pull to a stop, she slid off Rubio and efficiently took care of him, then helped Hunter make camp. She could feel Hunter's eyes on her now and then as she moved around, gathering kindling for the fire or filling their pot with water from the nearby stream. She did not turn to look back at him, unwilling to betray even the slightest notice of his mood. To do so, she was afraid, would initiate conversation about the wisdom of her presence here, and she didn't want that.

Of course, she could and would go on even if Hunter refused to let her accompany him; there was no way she would remain behind when her child was at stake, but she hated the thought of traveling by herself. Hunter might not be the most agreeable companion, but she felt safe with him. He was strong and she had never seen him be anything less than fearless in any situation. He could ride and shoot, and he had been in other dangerous situations. More than that, she trusted him in a way that she could trust no one else in the world; Hunter had the same interest in this child that she did, and he, just as she, would search for Julia until the bitter end.

Linette was squatting down beside the fire, stirring a pot of beans, when Hunter finally spoke, and his words surprised her. "You thought I was going to hang that lowlife, didn't you?"

Startled, Linette raised her head and looked at him. He was standing just beyond the fire, his features shadowed. She automatically started to protest that of course she had not, but then she shrugged and replied truthfully, "I wasn't sure. At first I thought you were bluffing, but then when it went so far . . . and I don't really know how the years might have changed you. You're a harder man than you used to be."

Hunter picked up a small branch that had fallen from a tree and began to strip it methodically, keeping his eyes on his task. Linette was surprised that he seemed concerned about what she thought of him. She wasn't sure what to say; it made her feel funny to think that she had hurt him with her doubt.

Finally she said, "I'm sorry that I doubted you. That I wasn't sure whether you would have gone through with it. I should have known you wouldn't."

"How do you know I wouldn't?" Hunter asked harshly. "He gave in before the moment of truth.

How do you know that if he hadn't talked, I wouldn't have strung him up?"

"Would you have?"

Hunter grinned crookedly. "You're supposed to say, 'Because I know you, Hunter, and you wouldn't have done such a thing.'"

"But I don't know you, not anymore," Linette responded reasonably. "Any more than you know me. People don't stay the same for ten years."

"I don't think the essential things about you have changed." Hunter looked as if he would have said more, but then he pressed his lips together and turned his head. Tossing aside the bare branch, he said only, "I wouldn't have hanged him. I saw it done to a man in Texas once. No question but what he was guilty, but it's not something I want to see again."

Linette smiled softly. "I'm glad."

Hunter came closer and squatted down across the fire from her. The flames lit his face almost eerily. "All the wrongs I did weren't done from malice, Linette. I would never have hurt you intentionally. What I did, I did because I was young and reckless and stupid. I didn't think. And I'm sorry."

"Sorry? For what?"

"For what I did to you." Hunter looked uncomfortable, and he glanced away, unable to meet Linette's eyes. "I didn't think. I wanted you so much, and I was so sure of myself, so sure that everything would come out the way I wanted it to. I didn't think about all the things that could happen—I didn't think about your getting pregnant or my getting killed or captured. Ah, hell, face it, I didn't think at all. I just wanted. And I took what I wanted, without any regard to the future or to your well-being."

Linette stared at him, amazed; his words were so far from anything she would have guessed he would say that she didn't know how to reply to them. Hunter had never been the kind to regret or reflect; he was a man who acted instinctively, boldly, and let the devil take the hindmost. It made for problems, God knows, but Linette couldn't deny that it was also part of his forceful appeal. One always knew where one stood with Hunter and what he wanted, what he would do. When he moved, it would be swiftly and competently, with no hesitation.

"Anyway," Hunter went on when she said nothing, "I can see now how wrong I was. I've blamed you all these years because you married Benton, and I can see now that I was the one who was to blame. You were innocent, and I took that away from you."

"Hunter . . . no. . . . You're too hard on yourself." Linette was moved by the raw self-loathing in his voice. "I *wanted* you to make love to me." Her voice dropped down almost to a whisper. "You know that."

"Yes, but I didn't think!" Hunter retorted fiercely. "I didn't protect you or make any kind of provision for you. I said I loved you, yet all I thought about was myself and my own selfish need. I'd have shot any man who treated my sister that way!"

Linette reached out and laid her hand on Hunter's arm, not thinking, wanting only to allay his pain. "No, please, don't blame yourself. What good will it do either of us? What happened, happened. We were both young and foolish, and we acted without thinking. I—"

she hesitated, then went on, "well, I encouraged you to make love to me. I wanted it to happen. I wanted to grasp at what might be my only chance to—to be with you. But I've thought sometimes that I did it, at least in part, hoping that that way I would be able to keep you with me. I hoped that if I gave myself to you, you wouldn't leave, that I could keep you with me that way. Scarcely a very noble motive, was it?"

Hunter studied Linette for a moment. Where her hand touched his arm, his skin seemed to burn. "No, perhaps not, but very understandable. It was the act of a woman very much in love. A brave woman."

Linette looked at him. His eyes were dark in the moonlight, but something in them sent a thrill straight through her. "Impulsive, I think," she said softly, "not brave. But I was very much in love."

"So was I," Hunter responded, and his hand went up to cover hers where it lay on his arm. "Linette . . ."

He brought her hand up to his mouth and pressed his lips softly into her palm. Linette trembled at the touch of his mouth on her flesh, feeling suddenly hot and giddy and scared.

"Yes?" she breathed.

"It's so hard to think around you," he mumbled, his mouth moving slowly across her palm, breathing in the scent of her, glorying in the sweet taste of her skin upon his lips.

Linette closed her eyes, barely suppressing a moan. Hunter was right—it was hard to think. It was hard to do anything but feel when he touched her like this. She wanted to give herself up to the feeling, to luxuriate in the pure sensual joy of it. Yet her brain nagged at her, urging her to stop, to think, to consider what would happen.

"Hunter . . ."

"Mm-hmm?" He slid her sleeve up on her arm and kissed the thin skin on the inside of her wrist. Linette shivered, and he continued up her arm.

"Uh . . . perhaps . . . perhaps we shouldn't."

"Perhaps." It was obvious he hadn't heard her words, at least not with his mind, for his arm went around her shoulders, pulling her to him, so that he cradled her against his chest, her back supported by his jackknifed leg. She leaned against him without a murmur of protest. She was turned sideways to him, her legs extending over his other leg, her body caught between Hunter's legs, her bottom firmly snuggled against his crotch.

Hunter nuzzled her hair, rediscovering its silken feel, its sweet smell. He was lost in the moment, all his former good intentions having fled as soon as he felt and smelled and tasted her. He brushed his lips against her temple . . . beside her eye . . . upon her cheek. Linette turned her head toward him. His mouth found hers.

Suddenly his arms were around her, hard and tight, pressing her into him, and his mouth was devouring hers. Years of pent-up hunger poured out then, bursting into flames with all the swiftness of a match to dry tinder. Linette threw her arms around Hunter's neck and clung to him, trying to wriggle even closer to him. Her movements brought a groan from his throat, and his hand went down to her hips, pressing her to the hot center of his desire. His fingers dug into her flesh. His breath was hot against her cheek, his tongue eager and searching inside her mouth. There was no thought in him, only passion.

Hunter's hand slid up until it cupped Linette's breast through her blouse. She jerked and groaned at the touch, an exquisite pleasure blossoming in the center of her breasts. Hunter felt her nipple turn into a hard bud beneath his hand, and it aroused him even more. He wanted to touch her with no cloth to impede him; he wanted to see her naked; he wanted, with a tremendous, driving need, to be *inside* her.

Panting, he pulled his mouth from hers, looking down at his hand upon her chest, brown against the pale cloth of her blouse, hard around the softness of her breast. The contrast was exciting, and he gazed with hot eyes at his thumb as it circled Linette's nipple, turning it harder and thrusting beneath the cloth. He wanted to watch, wanted to move slowly all over her, undressing and caressing her, all the while seeing the effect of desire on her body, watching her arch toward his fingers, hungrily seeking his touch, or shiver with delight. Yet at the same time, he could not bear to wait; he wanted to rip her clothes from her and thrust deeply into her; he wanted to see her eyes widen as he filled her, hear the low moan of satisfaction; he wanted to feel her hips begin to move beneath him, urging him on.

He groaned and hurriedly began to undo the buttons of her blouse, his fingers clumsy with haste. The first few buttons exposed the white expanse of her throat and chest, and Hunter had to stop to kiss the inviting flesh, his lips moving lower and lower until they touched the soft mounds. He shoved down the top of her shift, pushing aside the blouse as well, and exposing her breast to his greedy gaze.

Her breast was fuller than it had been when he had made love to her before, and its center was a deep rose, the nipple hard and elongated. Hunter touched her nipple with his forefinger, and Linette gasped, her head lolling back against his shoulder. He glanced up at her. Her eyes were closed, her skin glowing and translucent, her lips slightly parted and still moist from his kisses. She was so obviously a woman given up to pleasure, eager and hungry for his touch, that it made him throb with an even hotter, stronger passion.

He bent and ran his tongue across her nipple, and she bucked at the touch, catching her lower lip between her teeth. Hunter smiled and did it again, but then he could stand the teasing no longer himself, and he took her nipple into his mouth, caressing it with his tongue as he sucked on it. Linette's fingers dug into his shoulders, and she whimpered incoherently.

It had been so many years since she had felt any pleasure of the flesh. She had for a long time thought that she had simply dried up, turned into a passionless, desiccated woman. Until Hunter had come back . . . until he had kissed her that day in the stables and turned her body to fire. Ever since, her body had been alert and waiting for him, quivering to feel again those delicious sensations. Now they rushed through her like a powerful river, spreading throughout her body and turning her to fire. Desire bloomed in her abdomen, hot and molten, spreading, beginning a throbbing between her legs. She ached for Hunter to fill her, and her hips moved and lifted involuntarily, begging silently for what she wanted.

His mouth on her breast was pure delight, satisfying yet stirring up an even larger hunger within her, until she hardly knew what she wanted.

But Hunter seemed to know. Tearing at her blouse and chemise, he exposed her entire torso to the night air. Her nipple, wet from his mouth, tightened even more at the touch of the air upon it. He groaned at the sight, wanting to explore her reactions even further, but wanting even more to taste her other breast, still untouched by his mouth. He kissed the other nipple and drew it into his mouth, and as he did so, his hand went down and pulled up Linette's skirt, sliding under it and up her leg until he found the hot, damp juncture of her legs.

Linette groaned and moved her hips, still nestled against Hunter's groin, and the motion sent a white-hot spear of pleasure through Hunter. He thought he might explode right there, and he knew that he could wait no longer. Quickly he moved, lowering Linette to the ground and stretching out on top of her.

14

Linette let out a soft cry, running her hands eagerly over his back and chest. She wanted to feel his bare chest, but his shirt impeded her, and she was too jittery and fuzzy-headed with desire to make much headway with the buttons. As soon as her fingers found one and undid it, she would have to caress him again, leaving the buttons to roam his chest. Then Hunter's fingers started to work between her legs, and she lost all hold on rationality. Her fingers dug into him, and little shivers shook her as he stroked and caressed her. Had she been capable of thinking, she would have been embarrassed at the flood of moisture between her legs, dampening her undergarments, but at that moment she was aware of nothing but the wish that the cotton cloth was not between her skin and his.

As if in answer to her wish, Hunter's hand moved

up and fumbled with the drawstring of her under-pants, pulling it loose and tugging down the garment. His movements were hasty and clumsy, and there was a ripping sound as he jerked the pantalettes down. But Linette didn't even notice. She felt as if she were on fire, and there was nothing that could soothe her except Hunter's touch. Then his fingers were back, touching her, sliding along the slick folds of her flesh, caressing and separating, matching her heat with a fire equally intense.

He was saying her name over and over, murmuring thick, incoherent words of yearning, as he rained eager kisses over her torso. His mouth moved down to her soft, flat stomach as he slipped an exploring finger inside Linette, startling and arousing her. She arched upward at his touch, her heels digging into the ground.

"Please . . . oh, please, Hunter."

"Oh, God!" Hunter could stand it no longer. He tore at the buttons of his trousers and pulled them down and off, freeing the thick, hard shaft of his man-hood.

Wordlessly, Linette opened her legs to him. He moved between her legs, lifting her buttocks, and probed at the mouth of her womanhood. But Linette moved her hips, taking him further inside her, and her gesture shot Hunter past all thought of care and gentleness. He thrust deep inside her, groaning. Linette met him eagerly, taking in the full length of him and delighting at the stretching, filling sensation. It was precisely what she hungered for, and the aching emptiness inside her was filled.

He began to pull back out, and she gasped, her fingers digging into his back, trying to pull him back to her, but then he thrust deeply into her again, and the sensation was even more exquisite. He began to move in a slow rhythm, but the feel of her slick, tight flesh cupping him was too exciting, and he could not keep from moving faster and faster, pounding into her until finally he exploded, crying out, and poured his seed into her.

Hunter relaxed against her, his shaft still inside her. Linette turned her head, pressing her lips into his arm. She felt wonderful and fulfilled and yet . . . there was still an unassuaged heat deep within her, a restless yearning. She stirred a little unconsciously, not knowing how she could feel this strange frustration at the same time that she felt so deliciously loved.

But again Hunter seemed to know her better than herself, for he propped himself up on one elbow, and his other hand went down between them, finding the tender nub of flesh between her legs. Linette sucked in her breath, looking up at him with questioning eyes.

"I'm sorry, sweetheart," he said in a low voice, his expression tender and sated. "I couldn't go slow enough; I wanted you too much."

"That's all ri—oh!" Her eyes widened as Hunter's caressing thumb touched a spot so pleasurable that it deprived her of all speech. She could only moan and twist as he continued to play with the sensitive little nub, sending fierce, hot arrows of sensation through her. She closed her eyes, her fingers digging into Hunter's shoulders and back, unaware that Hunter was watching her face with great interest and delight as sensation after sensation chased across it. It was obvious that what she felt was as new to her as if she were a virgin, and there could have been no better proof that her husband had never touched either her heart or her passion.

Watching her, Hunter began to harden inside her again, and Linette gasped as this new sensation touched her. She moved restlessly, her head turning. Something huge and powerful was building up inside her, and she was racing to meet it, afraid that it would end before she could reach it.

"Shhh . . . shhh . . ." Hunter murmured. "Just relax. I won't stop. You'll get there; I promise."

"Oh!" A broken sob escaped her. "Oh, Hunter!"

"Yes. It's all right; I'll take you."

"Stop—no, don't stop. I mean . . ."

"I know." He smiled down at her taut, intense face. Her eyes were closed, and she was lost in sensation, trembling on the brink. It made him feel immensely powerful and male that he could bring her to the final explosion of pleasure. He paused for an instant, and she tightened all over, arching up toward him in mute appeal. Then he pressed his thumb firmly against her, circling.

It hit Linette like a wave, the pleasure so intense it was almost a blow, and she cried out, jerking and trembling, as it washed upward through her. Heat flooded up her chest and throat into her face and spread throughout her. She had never felt anything like it, and she was lost at that moment in mindless pleasure.

Finally, she went limp, damp with sweat and incapable of forming a thought. They lay for a moment that way, as the violent sensations began to subside within her. Incredibly, Hunter began to move inside her again. Watching her climax, feeling her convulsions around him, had made him hard again. This time, the edge taken off their appetites, he moved slowly, stoking their desire until it was again white hot and molten, surging for release. And when, at last, that release came, it exploded in both of them together, blissfully, an earthquake of pleasure.

Afterward, they curled up together, pulling the blanket up over them, and slept, exhausted and sated.

Linette awakened later than usual the next morning, and lay for a moment blinking in surprise, before she remembered what had happened. She began to blush, and since that memory was followed almost immediately by the realization that she was completely naked beneath the rough blanket atop her, her blush deepened into a bright scarlet. She sat up hesitantly, holding the blanket tightly to her, and glanced around. Hunter was squatting beside the campfire, stirring the coals and adding bits of kindling to it, coaxing it into flames.

She must have made a sound, for he turned to look over his shoulder at her. His face was unreadable, though Linette searched anxiously for some sign of his feelings there. She didn't know what to say—or even what to think. What did he think of her? What did he want? What, indeed did *she* want?

Their lovemaking last night had been wonderful; she had no doubts about that. Her body still felt deliciously, sensually languid. Obviously nothing had changed concerning their physical response to each other. But everything else *had* changed, and in the light of day, no longer borne on the tide of desire—and looking at the blank, even grim, look on Hunter's face—Linette was suddenly scared. What if the night before had been a dreadful mistake?

"Hunter . . ."

"Linette . . ." They spoke at the same time, then stopped. Hunter glanced away from her. "I'm sorry. Go ahead."

"No. You first." Linette had no desire to talk. Her stomach was tightening with each passing moment.

"I—I wanted to say that—I'm sorry."

Linette's stomach plummeted, her uneasy feeling now justified. Hunter regretted making love to her last night. She looked down, her eyes stinging. She would not let him see her cry. At least she had some pride, even if she had jumped with such humiliating eagerness into his arms last night. She shook her head, unable to speak.

"I started out meaning to apologize to you, that's all, and I wound up making the same mistake I did ten years ago." Hunter's voice was filled with disgust, wounding Linette almost as much as his words. Even though she, too, had almost the same thought, it was painful to hear Hunter refer to that sweet scorching passion they had shared as a "mistake."

"Damn!" Hunter rose to his feet, snapping a final piece of kindling between his hands and flinging it away. "I'm sorry," he repeated, his voice quiet and strained. "I acted again without thinking. Being around you seems to turn my brain to mush. But it was foolish and unforgivable. We aren't young anymore; you'd think we could act more like adults."

"I would think that what we did would usually be classified as 'adult,'" Linette put in coolly, stiffening her spine and making herself look at him. She was determined to present as calm a front as Hunter.

"We're all wrong for each other. We can't get along. There can be no future for us."

The awful thing was that he was absolutely right on all counts. Even when they had been young and madly in love, they had often disagreed—although then the arguments had always ended in a kiss. Such a relationship hadn't bothered them then, but now that they were mature, now that they were no longer in love, Linette could see that it would be impossible to live that way. Not that there was any possibility of their living together anyway. She was, after all, married to another man, however much she might despise him; making love to Hunter had been committing adultery. She and Hunter could never be together in any permanent way.

All that could possibly lie before her with Hunter was heartache—and she had had quite enough of that to last a lifetime! The thought of being in love with Hunter and brokenhearted all over again made her blood run cold. The pain she was experiencing right now listening to Hunter coolly destroy the beauty of the night before was nothing compared to what she'd gone through when she lost him the first time. She would not go through that again; she could not!

"You're right." Linette kept her voice as calm and dispassionate as Hunter's own. "It should never have happened. The best thing to do is to agree that it won't happen again. We will have to forget about it, put it out of our minds, and go on. We should concentrate only on finding Julia."

There was a frozen moment of silence, then Hunter agreed colorlessly, "Yes, that's what's important. That's why we're here, after all." He turned and walked away, saying, "I'll take the horses down to the water."

Linette scrambled out from under the blanket and gathered up the pile of clothes that she had so hastily discarded the night before. She dressed as quickly as she could, then brushed her hair and wound it into the tightest knot she could at the nape of her neck, as though by skinning her lush hair into a sexless, unattractive bun, she could somehow deny the fire that had leapt out of her last night at Hunter's kisses.

By the time Hunter returned, she was dressed and her expression sternly schooled. She had even rolled up the blankets, obliterating all evidence of their earlier passion. Hunter glanced around the camp, and without looking at Linette, he began to prepare their breakfast.

*　　　*　　　*

Rosemary hurried down the street and turned up the walk that led to Dr. Prescott's house. She hesitated for a moment on the porch, then rapped decisively at the door. She had to know. She had to find out why Linette had left. Linette had been gone for days now, and the gossip was all over town that Hunter Tyrrell had disappeared, as well. The implication was clear that they had run off together, but Rosemary was certain that something must have happened to make Linette do it. Rosemary could not forget the sounds of an unmistakable argument that had drifted up the stairs from Benton's study.

Whenever she asked her father about it, he refused to say anything. But he just kept acting stranger and stranger. He closed himself in his study after supper every night and drank continuously. Several mornings Rosemary had discovered him still there, passed out at his desk, when she came downstairs for breakfast. He rarely went to his office, and he questioned Rosemary in detail every night about every caller and about every bit of gossip she heard at the library or around town. Rosemary tried to pretend that no one was gossiping about Linette's abrupt departure, but she knew that he didn't believe her. Rosemary loved Linette and she was sure that Linette must have had a good reason to leave her father, but still Rosemary couldn't help feeling sorry for him. He looked wretched and haggard, and he never saw anyone except for the times he rode over to Sharps to visit Mr. Jones.

This morning Rosemary had made up her mind bright and early to visit Maggie Prescott. She had to find out why Linette had left and why her father was acting so strange. If anyone knew the truth about what had happened to Linette and Hunter, Rosemary was certain it was Maggie. The Tyrrells were a close-knit family.

"Why, Rosemary!" Maggie cried when she answered the door, looking first delighted, then uneasy. She wore a loose dress of the style commonly known as a wrapper. It was unsashed and hung loosely around her, and it seemed to Rosemary that Maggie looked rather thick around the waist. She wondered if Maggie were pregnant, but it would be impolite to ask her. One didn't talk of such things except in the vaguest of ways, especially if one was an unmarried woman like Rosemary.

"Come in, come in," Maggie said, leading Rosemary into the parlor. She turned to face her, chewing at her lower lip in a troubled way.

"Please tell me," Rosemary began without preamble. "I can't bear not knowing. Do you know anything about what's happened to Linette? Why did she leave? Did Hunter go with her?"

"Oh, Rosemary, I don't know what to say. . . . You know how much I like you. I can't—well, I'm not sure you really want to hear it."

"I do. I have to. I love Linette; she's been so good to me, not like a mother, but like an older sister or a dear, dear friend. I can't believe she's done anything wrong."

"Well, we all make mistakes. But she's been more sinned against than sinning." Maggie hesitated.

"Then it must be my father," Rosemary said. "I'm

right, aren't I? If Linette is not to blame, then it must be Papa. That's why you don't want to tell me, isn't it?"

Maggie shrugged, making it clear that Rosemary had guessed correctly. Rosemary released a long sigh. It was what she had suspected, no matter how much she longed to believe it wasn't true. But she knew that Linette wouldn't have left without reason, especially without even saying a word to Rosemary. Her father had to have done something that sent her away.

"Did she go to Hunter?"

"Yes."

Rosemary nodded. "She still loves him."

"I don't know. But, well, he was the natural person to turn to."

"Please tell me what happened. I have to know. No matter what my father's done. It's worse not knowing."

Maggie looked at her for a moment, then sighed and took Rosemary's hand, pulling her over to the couch and sitting down. "All right. I will."

As tactfully as possible, Maggie repeated the story her mother had told her, how Hunter and Linette had gone to Gideon's farm and told them about the child Linette had borne. Rosemary listened, her eyes growing wide with astonishment.

It made sense now—why Linette had left her father after all these years, why she and Hunter had left town, why Benton was lurking in the house, drinking and not showing his face outside. He was afraid that everyone would turn against him when they found out the truth of what he had done; he was scared of the gossip flying about—and with good reason. Everyone was talking about him and Linette and Hunter, and even though word had not yet leaked out about what Benton had done to Linette's child—the Tyrrells were a tight-mouthed bunch—it was inevitable that before long the whole story would be known. Benton would be treated like a pariah, even among his friends.

It made Rosemary sick to think what her father had done. And to think she had even felt sorry for him! She had tried all her life to excuse Benton, to find reasons for what he did, to pretend that there was good inside him, somewhere beneath the bluster and the harsh sarcasms, hidden behind his cruelties.

Rosemary knew that she could no longer lie to herself. Her father was a wicked man. She didn't know how she could continue to live with him.

"Thank you," she told Maggie shakily, rising to her feet.

Maggie's eyes were shadowed with worry. "Are you all right, dear? Maybe I shouldn't have told you."

"No. I'm glad you did. I appreciate it." Tears roughened Rosemary's voice, and she had to blink to keep them out of her eyes. She looked down, hoping that Maggie hadn't noticed.

At that moment there was the sound of the back door slamming and Maggie's son calling, "Ma! I'm home. The schoolmaster walked home with me."

Maggie smiled and went out into the hall. Rosemary trailed after her to the doorway, murmuring, "I really must go now." She had seen little of Seth Manning since the night of the party, when they had kissed; she suspected that he had been avoiding her. She certainly didn't want to have to meet him now, when she was on the verge of tears.

But she was not able to escape. Ty and Seth were already inside. "How do you do, Mrs. Prescott? I hope you don't mind my intruding like this, but I had a question I wanted to ask the doctor."

"Of course. He'll be happy to see you—as are we all."

Seth saw Rosemary, and a smile broke across his face, his somber brown eyes lighting up. "Miss Conway! I didn't expect to see you here."

Rosemary was warmed by his patent pleasure at seeing her. Perhaps he hadn't been avoiding her—or, if he was, perhaps it wasn't from disgust at her forwardness.

She smiled back at him. "Mr. Manning."

But then she thought of her father, and her sudden spurt of happiness fled. She wondered what Seth Manning would think of her if he knew what her father had done. The thought sent pain and fear stabbing through her.

"Thank you, Maggie," she said faintly. "Goodbye." She nodded blindly in Manning's direction. "Good-bye, Ty, Mr. Manning."

Hurriedly Rosemary escaped through the front door and almost ran down the steps.

Hunter and Linette continued toward Baton Rouge in silence, scarcely looking at each other. Much of the time, they rode single file, and it was only partially because the trail was sometimes narrow or muddy or they met someone along it.

Linette missed the more comfortable, easy manner that had sprung up between them as the trip had progressed. Now they were stiffer and more uncomfortable than they had been even when they first set out. Worse than that, she found that she could not dismiss their lovemaking from her mind. She kept thinking about it, and even though she would resolutely push the thoughts from her mind, in a few minutes, they would be right back: treacherous, heated memories of his hands and mouth on her flesh, of her own shivery sensations, of the thunderous explosion of pleasure that had shaken them at the very end.

It was bad enough during the day, for the long stretches of riding gave her ample time to think. She found that the rocking motion of the horse made her remember all too forcibly Hunter moving rhythmically between her legs, and as she rode, she began to grow aroused. She glanced at Hunter, his muscled thighs clamped tightly against his horse's sides, and she thought that he must be even more aware of the motion than she, sitting astride. Linette thought about riding her own horse without the woman's sidesaddle, her legs on either side of the horse, and the thought made her flush. Her state was made even worse by watching Hunter throughout the day. She couldn't keep her eyes off his hands, so strong and brown upon his reins. She remembered how his work gloves had looked on his hands, somehow accenting the masculinity of his muscled arms. His thighs were rock hard; Linette well knew the force of them. She wanted him to make love to her again; she had to admit that to herself. She wanted to feel Hunter inside her again. She wanted to close her eyes and give herself up to that wild maelstrom of pleasure.

It might be dangerous, but it was also breathlessly exciting, and sometimes Linette had trouble remembering anything but the excitement.

The situation was even worse at night, when the velvety dark night surrounded them, with only the light of the fire or the dim glow of the coals. Then Linette's imagination ran wild. Only a few feet separated them—how easy it would be for Hunter to cross it, or for her. She remembered looking up into his face as he moved above her, only the limitless sky and stars above him, and the heat and the darkness and the sensuality stirred and mingled in her until she could hardly breathe.

Linette wondered if Hunter had any trouble keeping his distance from her, or if it was only she who was eaten up by desire. His face was always so remote and studiedly blank that she could read nothing in it.

Linette could not wait to reach their destination.

Fortunately it did not take them much longer. Fairfield, where Louisa Barbour lived, was a small town about ten miles north of Baton Rouge, and they came upon it late in the afternoon. It wasn't difficult to find Mrs. Barbour's house. It lay a mile and a half out of town, on a narrow road that turned into little more than a track once one passed the Barbour house. Many years earlier, before Benton's cousin married into the Barbour family, a large sugarcane plantation had surrounded the house, but her husband's father had lost almost all of their money by the time Louisa married Tom Barbour. Within a few years, the remainder of their money, as well as most of the land, was gone, and the only thing left to them was the large house. It was square and white, fronted by verandas on three sides, both upstairs and down, with the long, shuttered windows typical of houses in southern Louisiana.

There was a closed look to it, Linette thought as they road up the drive toward the house, no sign of people or life. Though it was dusk, no lamplight shone through the front windows. Linette's heart sank. Had Benton gotten a message to Louisa warning her of their arrival? She doubted that one could send a telegram to such an out-of-the-way place as Fairfield, but perhaps he had had a telegram delivered here from Baton Rouge.

They dismounted and tied their horses to the peeling black wrought-iron hitching posts. Linette's stomach boiled with nerves as they climbed the shallow steps to the porch. Hunter knocked loudly at the door. They waited for a long moment, but there was no answer. Hunter pounded again, and finally the door opened a crack to reveal a suspicious face. It was Louisa herself, Linette realized in some surprise, several years older but undeniably the same person. Dark blond hair streaked with gray hung in stiff curls on either side of her face in the same way as when Linette first met her. She was a short, squat personage, her figure made even more so by the great circular hooped skirts she wore, almost as out-of-fashion nowadays as her hair.

Louisa Barbour would have been a comical figure had it not been for the steely determination of her jaw and the sharp, shrewd eyes set deep in her doughy face. Just looking at her, a great shiver of hatred ran through Linette, surprising her a little with its intensity. Her fingers itched to reach out to grab the woman, and it took considerable restraint for her to curl her fingers into her palm and remain silent behind Hunter.

Louisa looked at Hunter, snapping, "Who are you? What are you doing here?"

"I'm Hunter Tyrrell."

Louisa said nothing, continuing to frown at him.

"I need to ask you a few questions," Hunter went on, placing his hand on the door and pressing against it, opening it a fraction more.

"Well, I got no need to answer them," Louisa retorted abruptly as she shoved the door.

But Hunter stiffened his arm, pushing the door open, startling the woman, who stumbled back a step or two. Anger mingled with fear flashed across Louisa's face. "Stop that! Get out! You can't come in here!"

Hunter stepped into the entry, and Linette entered after him. "Cousin Louisa, it's me." She managed to keep her voice steady despite her anger.

Louisa goggled at Linette, her jaw dropping. "Linette! What—what are you doing here?"

"I've come to talk to you."

Louisa glanced from Linette to Hunter, recognition beginning to dawn on her face. "You! You're the one—"

"Yes," Linette bit out. "He's the one who was the father of my baby. My Julia—the child who was *not* born dead here in your house. The child you stole from me and condemned to an orphanage."

Louisa swallowed visibly, and she clamped her lips tightly together, as if to forcibly keep any words from tumbling out of her mouth.

"We know what you did. There's no point in trying to hide it." Hunter's voice was stern and implacable. Linette was glad it was not she whom he was glaring at with his cold green eyes.

However, Louisa seemed to have little trouble returning his gaze. She crossed her arms over her chest and stared back at him mulishly. "I don't know what you're talking about. I want you two out of my house."

"We're not leaving until you tell us what you did with my baby," Linette snapped.

"I thought you knew all the answers," Louisa sneered.

"Tell us where you took the child," Hunter growled.

Louisa cast him a contemptuous look. "Or what? Are you planning to beat the information out of me?"

"If I have to."

"Ha! You might be able to do that to a man, but not to an old lady. Even one you hate. I can see it in your eyes. You're too much a gentleman for that."

Frustration swept Linette. Louisa was right, and they all three knew it. No matter how hard or tough

Hunter had become, he would never be the kind of man who could strike a woman, especially one old enough to be his mother. How were they ever going to be able to make Louisa tell them?

"What would it take to get you to tell us?" Hunter kept his voice even with an effort, trying to sound reasonable.

"Well, gold is never out of place."

"How much?"

Louisa pursed her lips, thinking.

"It's no use," Linette said, her hands knotting at her sides. "She might take our money, but you'd never get an answer out of her."

"Information first," Hunter told Louisa firmly. "Then we'll give you the money. I'm sure you'll be able to rely on my word since you consider me such a *gentleman*."

Louisa shook her head. "No. I don't hand out information unless I have the money right in the palm of my hand."

"What did I tell you? She won't tell. She knows Benton'll pay her to keep her mouth shut." Frustration and anger swelled in Linette until she felt as if she might burst. She had to find her baby! She could not leave here until she knew where this evil woman had taken Julia. But even from this distance Benton was still managing to thwart them.

"Why?" Hunter asked calmly. "Why would Benton pay any more to keep it a secret? We already know what he did. What you did." He gazed levelly at Louisa. "I imagine you've bled him for a pretty penny all these years. Why would he be willing to pay you any more for a secret that's useless to him? All we need to know is the name of the orphanage where you took the baby." Hunter's voice softened almost into a wheedle.

It was a tone that Hunter had used many times over the years, a tone that was usually guaranteed to get what he wanted out of a female—of any age. Even though Linette knew why Hunter was using it, it irritated her. Hunter had always used his charm entirely too much—and to hear him wheedling this wicked old lady was the worst.

"Come on," Hunter went on. "There's no reason not to tell us any longer. You don't have to lie for him now. What's the point?"

"The point is I promised Benton," Louisa said firmly, staring back at Hunter, unmoved by his coaxing. "Until he tells me different, I'm not telling anybody anything." A malicious grin touched her lips. "And I'll be bound that Benton won't be doing that, will he? Otherwise, you'd know already where I took the baby."

"Benton didn't know," Linette retorted. Then she hesitated, doubt flooding her at the gleeful look in Louisa's eyes. "He said that you took care of it."

"Uh-huh. That's sounds like what he'd say. But he knows where I took her. He just didn't want to tell you. And I won't, either."

Murderous rage boiled up in Linette. She whirled and rushed out of the house. Hunter looked after her in surprise. For an instant her eyes had lit with such an unholy fire he thought she was going to go for Louisa's throat with her bare hands, but then she left.

He wasn't sure whether to go after her or stay here and try to force this woman to tell him what they wanted to know.

Then the door was flung back again and Linette stormed into the room. Hunter's eyes widened. She looked like an avenging angel, her auburn hair glowing like dark fire in the dim light of the kerosene lamp, her eyes glittering with hatred and an untamed rage. She carried one of the rifles, and she raised it now, sighting down it at Louisa.

"All right, goddammit, now tell me!" Her voice was thin and high, filled with fury.

Louisa shifted nervously and glanced at Hunter. He shrugged. He had no idea what Linette was going to do. Frankly, the way she looked, it wouldn't surprise him if she did blow the woman's head off.

"Hunter may not be able to hurt a woman, but I sure as hell can!" Linette went on, moving closer and closer to Louisa. "I won't have a qualm about it. You stole my baby and left me years of sorrow and grief. Time after time I wished I was dead. But now the only person I want dead is you." Her voice was calm and icy, and her eyes shone with a demonic light. "You and Benton. If I can't find my baby, the only thing left to me is revenge. You understand? And my revenge will be seeing you and Benton suffering for eternity in hell. Nothing could make me any happier. I wouldn't even mind winding up there, too, so long as I can watch you and Benton."

Louisa backed up from Linette until she hit the wall and could go no further. Her eyes widened with terror as Linette continued to come closer, until finally the end of the barrel touched Louisa's cheek.

"This close," Linette hissed, "nobody could miss. Your brains'll splatter all over the wall when I pull the trigger. And you know what? I'll be happy to see it. You tell me what I want to know, and I'll let you live."

Louisa blinked her eyes, shivering. She began to talk.

15

"*St. Anne's!*" Louisa gabbled. "I took it to St. Anne's orphanage in Baton Rouge."

Linette shoved the rifle deeper into Louisa's skin, and Louisa let out a shriek. "I swear! I'm telling you the truth! I promise that's where I took her!"

"You better be telling me the truth. Otherwise I'll come back here and kill you . . . piece by piece. You understand?"

Sobbing, Louisa nodded, and when Linette stepped back, pulling the rifle away from her face, the woman slid down the wall and collapsed in a weeping bundle of flesh on the floor. Linette turned and strode out the door. Hunter followed her, closing the door quietly behind him. Linette reached the end of the porch and stopped. Hunter came up beside her.

Linette's face was starkly white in the pale light of the moon, and her eyes were huge. She began to tremble violently. Hunter reached out and pried her fingers from the stock of the rifle, and as if that had somehow held her up, Linette sat down abruptly on the top step, shivering. Her hand went to her stomach, and then she leaned over the side of the step and was violently sick.

Hunter squatted down beside her, one hand going to her forehead to support it and the other clasping her shoulder, holding her as the spasms shook her body.

Finally she sat up, groaning. "Oh, God, I'm sorry, Hunter."

"It's all right." Tenderly he took out his handkerchief and wiped her mouth. "I've seen far worse, believe me. You'll be fine in a little while. It'll pass. Here, put your head down and take some deep breaths."

They sat that way for a few moments until the wave of nausea passed and Linette's shivering subsided. Hunter held her quietly in the warmth of his arms, letting his strength and warmth seep into her. Finally he said, "Come on, we better ride, or else that witch may recover from her fright and come after us with a shotgun."

Linette smiled weakly and stood up with him. Her knees were peculiarly wobbly, but once Hunter boosted her into the saddle, she was able to take the reins and ride. She followed Hunter without a word, her brain still numbed by what had just occurred.

Hunter didn't ride far before he stopped to camp for the night. He was relatively certain that Louisa would not come looking for them or ride into town to set the law on them, so they didn't have to put much distance between them and this town. He stopped beside a small brook, following it down to a stand of trees that would provide shelter for them, and there he quickly set up camp.

He didn't feel much like eating, and he was sure that Linette was even less interested in food than he was. He built a small fire, more for the comfort of it than anything else, and spread out their blankets beside it. He glanced around and saw that Linette was still sitting on the log where he had directed her when they dismounted, her knees pulled up to her chest and her arms wrapped around them.

He went over to her and laid a hand on her shoulder. Her trembling was almost stopped, but she seemed still in a state of shock. "Come over and sit by the fire with me."

She obeyed him, sliding off the log and walking with him to the blankets he had spread out. They sat down side by side, facing the fire. Hunter cast a sidelong glance at Linette, then said wryly, "Just tell me something: Would you have done it?"

Linette recognized the words she had used with him the other day when he threatened their assassin, and she had to smile faintly. She shook her head. "I don't know. I've never done anything like that before in my life! But I was so furious . . . I couldn't let her get away with it. And all the while I was doing it, it was almost like I wasn't even myself." She shivered and wiped her hands across her face. "Oh, Hunter, do you think I would have really killed her if she hadn't told me? Did I go insane?" She turned and looked at him earnestly. "Do you think I've become a little mad?"

"Of course not." Hunter reached out and drew her into his arms, not thinking of caution or keeping his heart whole and free or of anything else except the need to comfort Linette. "You did what had to be done. You're a mother searching for her child—I know my mother or Maggie would have done the same thing." He paused, smoothing his hand down her hair, then said, meditatively, "You were beautiful in your rage, my love. I don't think I've ever seen such fire in my life."

"Oh, Hunter!" Linette buried her face in his chest, wrapping her arms around him tightly, and burst into tears. "Hold me, please, just hold me."

Hunter did so, keeping his arms around her even after she had fallen into an exhausted sleep upon his chest. Careful not to awaken her, he lay down on the blankets, carrying Linette with him, and twitched one of the blankets over them for cover. And for the rest of the night, they slept, still entwined.

Linette awoke slowly, conscious of a delicious warmth around her, and she snuggled more deeply into it before she realized that the warmth was Hunter's body, pressed against her own. She was nestled on her side, against his chest, and his arms were around her, one leg thrown casually over her. It was so sweet and comfortable that she almost wished that she could stay there forever, if only it wasn't so awkward. Hunter had been kind to her last night, holding her as she cried. He hadn't tried to make sense of her agitation, as many would have, but had simply allowed it to flow out of her.

But his kindness had been just that, nothing more, and didn't mean that he wanted any kind of deeper relationship with her. It didn't mean that he had changed his mind about their lovemaking. To wake up in this intimate position would be embarrassing for both of them.

Carefully Linette turned her head and looked back over her shoulder at Hunter. He was still sound asleep, his eyes closed, thick black lashes against his cheek giving him a curiously vulnerable look. Linette steeled her thoughts against such foolish softness. There was nothing vulnerable about Hunter. He was as hard as nails. He'd sealed his heart off years ago, and he had made it clear that he meant to keep it safely behind its wall. Linette knew that to give in to any tender feelings about Hunter would only end up with her being hurt. Hunter would never allow himself to fall in love with her again.

In love? The thought shook her. *Is that what I'm doing—falling in love with Hunter again?* Immediately she told herself that it could not be. She did not love Hunter. She was heart-whole and just as determined as Hunter to remain that way. Wasn't she?

Linette felt suddenly a little sick. She did not like the way her thoughts were going. Just because she had been weak enough last night to have given in to tears and to allow Hunter to comfort her didn't mean that she needed or wanted him, any more than Hunter's uncustomary kindness meant that he felt anything for her. And the passion they had shared the other night wasn't love, either. It was physical desire, that was all, brought on by the excitement of their situation and the dangers they had shared, just a left-over hunger from their courting days when they had been so overflowing with desire for each other. None of this was love. It was her years of loneliness and the passion that had been so long stifled in her.

But Linette was too honest not to question that thought. If it had been only loneliness and years without passion, if it had been only the closeness of riding together day after day, then the same thing could have happened with any other man she might have chosen for this trip. But Linette *knew* that that was not true. She was not a loose woman; she was not someone so easily aroused that she would have slept with any male who happened to be with her, no matter how long it had been since she had felt pleasure, no matter how much time they spent alone together every day! It was Hunter who had sparked the desire in her, just as Hunter alone had done it so many years ago.

And perhaps she didn't love him any longer, but if not, what did she feel for him? She thought of her and Hunter's passion so many years ago, and she felt like crying. *Am I doomed to repeat my mistake with Hunter over and over again? Am I falling under his spell once more, clearing the path for another heartbreak?*

Determinedly Linette shook off her thoughts and slid out of Hunter's grasp. He shifted and mumbled something, but his eyes remained closed, his face slack with sleep. Letting out a sigh of relief, Linette moved away, shaking out her legs, numbed by the weight of Hunter's leg sprawled across them, and walked out of sight toward the stream to pull both her clothes and her thoughts into composure.

Hunter woke up with a start, his eyes flying open. He was alone, and his arms felt strangely empty. He reached out involuntarily before he remembered where he was and how he and Linette had fallen asleep the night before. He grimaced and sat up, glancing around for her. It annoyed him that her absence should make him feel as though something were missing.

He got up irritably and began to break camp. A few minutes later when Linette returned, he barely gave her a glance. They ate a quick breakfast and mounted up, setting off toward Baton Rouge.

They rode hard, for both of them were eager to reach the city. With every passing mile, Linette's excitement and nervousness grew. She couldn't keep from breaking into a grin now and then for no visible reason, yet at the same time, her stomach was clenching tighter and tighter. Soon she would be at the place where her daughter had been taken. For the first time in her life she was close to being with the child she had mourned so long. At last she would be able to discover where Julia was. It was even possible, though she dared not let herself hope, that Julia might still be at the same orphanage.

When they reached the outskirts of Baton Rouge, they stopped and inquired about the location of St. Anne's orphanage. Linette wanted to go straight there, but Hunter disagreed.

"No. First we'll need to wash up and change clothes."

Linette cast him an exasperated look. Was he trying to be difficult? "What does it matter?"

"A lot," he retorted bluntly. "We're going to be trying to get them to tell us what happened to a baby they took in nine years ago. They won't be disposed to tell us, you know. If nothing else, they won't want to go to the trouble of digging through their records. We have a lot better chance of getting them to do what we ask if we look like a gentleman and lady instead of two ragtag riders covered with the dust of the road."

Linette grimaced, wanting to retort angrily, but she knew that he was right. She couldn't ruin their chances just because she was impatient. She had been around Benton long enough to know how much easier it was to get what you wanted if you looked wealthy and influential.

So she abandoned her argument and they went to a hotel. It was strange to be in such a place with Hunter, Linette thought, and she hoped that she didn't look as awkward as she felt. She followed Hunter upstairs, hoping that she was not blushing. Alone in her room, she looked around at the furnishings, luxurious in comparison to the way she had spent the nights recently. It would be wonderful to sleep in a real bed again, and even more delightful to take a bath, which the porter had promised would be carried right up to her. But despite these pleasant prospects, her spirits were flat. She chafed at having to wait until the next morning to find out about her daughter, but in addition, she felt a curious loneliness.

She missed Hunter. They had been in each other's constant company for so many days now, and it seemed most peculiar not to have him there with her, to know that he was several doors away from her. She knew it was a foolish feeling, but somehow Linette could not shake it. The bath in the metal tub the maids brought up and filled with warm water helped revive her spirits, but it wasn't until later, when Hunter came to her room and escorted her down to dinner that the nagging emptiness vanished.

Hunter raised his eyebrows and gave a low whistle of appreciation when he saw her. Before her bath, Linette had given her clothes to the maid to be laundered. She had also handed her the one clean blouse and skirt remaining in her carpetbag, and the maid had pressed it for her. Dressed in clean, pressed clothes and with her freshly washed hair swept up into a cascade of curls, she looked every inch the fine lady. More than that, Linette could tell by Hunter's expression that she looked beautiful.

Hunter had obviously visited the baths and gotten a haircut and shave, and he had added a jacket to his attire. He still looked devilishly handsome, and Linette felt a spurt of pride at walking into the dining room on his arm.

Their meal was good, a welcome change from the fare they had been eating on the trail, but Linette found she could not really enjoy it. She was in a fever of impatience, and all she could think about was their visit the next day. She fidgeted through the meal, and after Hunter escorted her back to her room, she paced and thought, sitting down, then standing up, going to the window to look out, then walking back to the bed or the door or the chair, until finally, tired of her own restlessness, she gave up and went to bed.

She got little sleep that night, though, and the next morning, she was up at first light and dressed in only minutes. She could not eat, her stomach was in such turmoil, and she noticed that Hunter, too, left much of his breakfast untouched. Afterward, they walked to the orphanage.

The large red-brick building was drab and foreboding, and Linette's stomach quivered with fear and excitement as she gazed at it. At last, she was going to find out about her daughter. She glanced up at Hunter beside her, wondering how he felt at this moment. His face gave nothing away. Feeling her gaze, he turned his head and looked down at her.

"Ready?"

"I think so," Linette answered a little breathlessly. She wanted to find out what had happened to her baby more than anything in the world, yet at the same time she was scared to death. What would they learn? What if she had died, after all? What if she had been adopted by someone horrible and cruel and had spent her years in misery?

What if she was still here?

"All right. Come on." Hunter took Linette's arm and they walked through the gates to the front door.

Children dressed in plain gray smocks played in the side yard, and they turned to look at Linette and Hunter. Linette glanced at them, and pity stirred in her heart. They seemed unnaturally quiet at their play, and their cheap, dull uniforms added to the general drabness of the orphanage. She hated to think of her daughter growing up in a place like this.

Hunter knocked authoritatively on the front door, and a moment later it was opened by an older girl dressed in the ubiquitous uniform, with a timid, subdued air.

"Hello. We'd like to speak to someone about a child who was brought here several years ago," Hunter told her.

The girl blinked vacantly.

"The mother superior, perhaps," Linette suggested.

"Oh." The girl's face cleared. "But she's not to be disturbed."

"Then her assistant." Hunter smiled winningly at her.

The girl, after another long pause, nodded and said, "Wait here. I'll fetch Sister Mathilde."

The girl hurried off down a dark hallway. Linette cast a wry look at Hunter. "I wonder how effective your smiles will be on the good nuns."

Hunter gave her a lazy grin, the corners of his eyes crinkling up in the way that had always made

Linette's heart beat faster. "No harm in trying," he commented reasonably.

"Just don't offend them," Linette snapped. "Remember, they're *religious* sisters."

Hunter quirked an eyebrow. "That doesn't mean they're dead, does it?"

Linette rolled her eyes. "Honestly. I think you've gotten worse as you've gotten older."

"Actually, I'm quite mild these days. I used to flirt just to see you get jealous."

"I wasn't jealous."

"Then or now?" Humor lit his green eyes.

"Either!" Linette glared. Sometimes Hunter seemed determined to be utterly obnoxious.

There was the sound of heels on the cool stone floor, and a moment later, a tall, spare woman dressed in a black nun's habit appeared. She came to a stop in front of them, her hands folded patiently in front.

"I am Sister Mathilde," she announced in a crisp voice. "How may I help you?"

"We're here to find a child who was brought to your orphanage nine years ago," Hunter began.

"I'm sorry. I don't understand. Do you wish to adopt a child? A specific child?"

"No. This is my daughter—our daughter," Linette spoke up, her voice urgent. "It's very important that we find her."

The nun frowned, her gaze sweeping down over Linette's obviously expensive clothes. "You say you gave her to us nine years ago? What was her name?"

"I—I'm not sure." Linette's voice faltered. "I didn't

bring her here. Someone else did. A Mrs. Barbour, Louisa Barbour. I don't know if she just left her here or gave her a name or what. I—I was going to call her Julia."

The nun looked at her oddly, but said only, "Well, why don't we go to my office, and I shall look among our records."

"Thank you."

Hunter and Linette followed the woman to her office. It was a large room, sparingly decorated, and wooden file cabinets lined one entire wall. Sister Mathilde motioned her visitors toward a pair of straight-back chairs in front of her desk while she walked over to the filing cabinets.

"Nine years ago, you said?" she asked as she walked alongside the cabinets, examining the identifying tags on the front. "That would be 1862?"

"Yes."

"Do you remember what time of year it was?"

"Of course!" Linette stared at the nun indignantly. "My daughter was born on February eighteenth. I—I guess the woman brought her as soon as she was born."

Sister Mathilde pulled open a drawer and began to go through it. Finally she pulled out a piece of paper and perused it.

"Yes, here, one baby girl was left with us on February nineteenth. She had no name, so we baptized her with the name Jane Alice Renard."

Linette's heart seemed to stop, and her chest tightened. "Yes." Her voice came out a whisper. "Yes, that must be she."

"She had black hair and blue eyes, no birthmarks."

Linette listened to the woman talk about her child, soaking up the tiny bits of information. "Please, what happened to her? Where is she?"

"I will look that up now." The nun went to another filing cabinet and began to go through it. She stopped. "Oh."

Fear stabbed Linette. "What? What's the matter?"

"Nothing's the matter. But the child's file is inactive. Apparently she was taken out of the orphanage." She went to a large storage cabinet and opened it. Inside were stacks of boxes. She opened one of the boxes and pawed through it, coming up with a file at last. She opened it and perused it.

"Yes. A couple wanted her. She was only a baby."

Pain clutched at Linette's heart. Somehow she had believed deep down that her child would be there waiting for her. Unconsciously she groped for Hunter's hand and he took it, squeezing it firmly.

"Who took her?" Hunter asked. "Where did she go?"

Sister Mathilde closed the file and put it back into the box. "I'm sorry." She stood up and left the closet, closing the door behind her. "We are not allowed to reveal information like that. All our records are kept strictly confidential."

"But—" Linette stared. "But that's my child!" She rose to her feet.

"I'm sorry," the nun repeated, her face unrelenting. "But it's better that way."

"Better! For whom!"

"For the child. Well, for everyone concerned.

Sometimes when a mother gives away her child, she starts to feel guilty later, and she comes back, wanting the child again. But it's hardly fair to the couple who have adopted the baby to take it away from them."

"Fair!" Hunter exclaimed, jumping up and advancing on the nun. His face was hard and dangerous, and the woman backed up involuntarily. "I'd like to know how fair it is to snatch a baby away from her mother and give her away! How fair is it to tell her mother that she's dead? For her to never get to see her or hold her or—"

"Hunter!" Linette cautioned. It warmed her heart to hear Hunter defending her, but she mustn't let him frighten or anger this woman. The nun held the key to her baby's whereabouts, and somehow they must cajole it out of her. "I'm sure it's not Sister Mathilde's fault that my child was taken away from me. And . . . and I'm sure that there are rules she must follow."

"That's right." The nun gave a triumphant nod.

Hunter swung around to Linette. "Have you gone insane? How the hell do—"

"Hunter!" Linette gave him a fierce look. He grimaced, but shut his mouth and walked away, folding his arms across his chest. Linette turned toward the nun and smiled placatingly. "I'm sorry, Sister Mathilde. But you must see that this isn't like other situations. I didn't give my baby to you. I was wronged. Deeply wronged."

"No doubt you were." The nun's expression clearly showed that she believed exactly the opposite. "But that doesn't change the rules. Once a child is adopted, we cannot open the file to her parents."

"But you had no right to give her away. She was *my* child! I didn't give her up. A mother's rights come first, don't they?" Linette's voice was tinged with desperation. "I have to find her! I have to get her back!"

"That's exactly why we can't tell you. What about the people who took her? She's their child, has been for almost nine years. She's grown up thinking that they are her parents. It would hurt everyone for her mother to come around now."

"What about the way I've been hurt for the past nine years!" Linette exclaimed. "What about the pain I've suffered?"

"Obviously she doesn't care about that," Hunter put in gruffly. "Come on, Linette, we aren't going to get anywhere with her." He walked back to the nun and Linette. "Let's talk to the mother superior."

"Mother Superior will tell you exactly the same thing I have," Sister Mathilde replied primly. "It is her policy, as well."

Hunter looked at her for a moment. "You aren't much of one for showing Christian charity, are you?"

If possible, the nun grew even stiffer. "I hardly think you are in a position to judge, sir. It seems to me as if someone was exceedingly *careless* regarding this baby's birth."

"No, not careless. Just exceedingly wicked." Hunter's eyes were cold and hard. "And, believe me, he'll pay for it."

Linette went closer to the nun, looking at her

pleadingly. "Please, Sister. I'm begging you to help me."

Sister Mathilde looked at her, then away. She shook her head. "I'm sorry. I can't."

Linette's heart sank. She couldn't have come all this way, just to find out that her daughter was as lost to her as ever.

16

Linette swung toward Hunter, her face stamped with frustration and despair. "Hunter!"

"Come on." He took her arm and began to lead her toward the door. "Let's go. We're not getting anywhere here."

"But, Hunter, we can't leave!" Linette protested.

He drew her inexorably to the door, saying in a low voice, "Give it up, Lin. She'll never give you permission."

"But, Hunter!" Linette's voice cracked and tears started in her eyes. "I have to try! I have to do something!"

Hunter turned toward the nun. "Good-bye, ma'am. Thank you for your time."

Sister Mathilde nodded. "Good-bye. I'm sure that if you'll reflect on it, you will see that this is the best way."

"The best way!" Linette burst out, anger surging in her. But Hunter pulled her out the door, and the nun quickly closed it behind them.

Linette dug in her heels, trying to turn back to the office. "Let go of me! I have to talk to her! What is the matter with you? Hunter!"

Hunter pulled Linette against his side, and as they walked away down the hall, he bent his head and whispered, "She's not going to give in. There's no point in arguing anymore. I'll have to come back tonight and break in."

"What!" Linette gaped at him, but she let herself be pulled along.

Hunter smiled grimly. "Surely you didn't think I would give up that easily."

Linette relaxed. For a moment she *had* been afraid that Hunter was giving up, that this search for their daughter meant no more than that to Hunter. But, of course, he had not. She should have known better. She could trust Hunter. Tears gathered in her eyes.

"Thank you," she whispered.

They walked down the hall toward the front door. Hunter was glancing around, seeming casual, but Linette suspected he was making plans for breaking in to get the records.

"Pssst!"

They stopped and glanced around.

"Hey, mister!" the loud whisper came again, and they turned. A tall window was set into the wall, hung with heavy, long drapes. One of the drapes was held away from the wall a little, and a freckled face peered out at them from behind it.

Linette and Hunter stared. The gap opened wider, revealing a thin face and scrawny body in a shapeless gray smock. It was obviously a child; Linette wasn't sure what age—from the size, she could have been as young as seven or eight, but her face had a much older look to it.

"Hello." Linette smiled at the girl, surprised to find that it no longer hurt to see a child, now that she knew that her own was still alive.

The child opened the drape wider and craned her neck to peer first up, then down the hall. When she was certain that there was no one else around, she stepped out. The child's smock was smeared with dirt, and one stocking, once white but now gray with repeated washings and dirt, had fallen down around her ankle, revealing a spindly shin. A mop of dirty blond hair covered her head, stray curls spilling down onto her forehead. Dirt smudged her nose. Red-brown freckles ran across her cheeks beneath wide gray eyes. She was not an attractive child, and her looks were not enhanced by the small scab on her chin.

Then she grinned, and her gray eyes lit up with mischief, and to Linette's surprise, she looked somehow appealing. Linette glanced over at Hunter. He, too, was observing the child, a ghost of a smile playing at his lips.

"Hello," he said to her. "I'm Hunter Tyrrell."

"I'm Mary Margaret Keenan." The faint trace of a lilting accent clung to her speech. "Are the two of you looking to get a child?"

"We're looking for our daughter," Hunter told her.

The girl stared. "Get on with you! Here? What would a daughter of folks like you be doing at this hellhole?"

Linette drew in a sharp breath of surprise at her language. Mary Margaret cut her a sideways glance and grinned.

"And were you thinking I was a 'sweet little thing'?" Her last few words were delivered in a broad Southern accent, syrupy sweet, and she chuckled. "I'm not. Sister Marie Louise says I'm the 'spawn of Satan.'" She paused and added judiciously, "That's not true, though, 'cause I'm really Fightin' Jimmy Keenan's girl."

Neither Hunter nor Linette was able to think of anything to say in response to her speech. They simply continued to look at her.

"I'm thinking you didn't find your daughter here, did you? Why not take me? I'm a hard worker, and I don't eat much. If I try, I can keep from cussin', too, at least most of the time. Da always said I was a sharp one. Even Mother Superior says I'm clever." She grinned and added honestly, "Well, too clever by half is what she says."

Linette couldn't keep from chuckling. "Mary Margaret, I'm sure someone would love to adopt you. But we're looking for our daughter, and I'm afraid that she's the one we have to find."

Mary Margaret shrugged philosophically. "Did Sister tell you where she was?"

"No, I'm afraid not." Sadness tinged Linette's face. "She said that she couldn't tell us what was in her file."

"In Sister's office? In one of them big wooden things?"

"In the big storage cabinet."

"Oh. Them's the ones that are gone, then. Lucky souls—they made their escape one way or another." She crossed herself hastily. She paused, her face taking on a crafty look. "I could help you, now . . . providing you were to make it worth my while."

Amusement lit Hunter's face. "Could you, indeed? And how, I'd like to know, would you be able to do that?"

"I could do something out in the yard that'd get Sister out of her office. Create a stir, I'm thinking. Course, what you'd do in there while she's gone is up to you."

Hunter rubbed his hand across his mouth to hide a smile. Linette said drolly, "Why, Hunter, it seems you've found a kindred spirit."

He flashed her a look that she'd seen many times before, one that challenged and mockingly promised retaliation. It was a teasing, very masculine sort of glance, one heavily laden with sexual implication. Suddenly Linette felt a little weak in the knees, the way she always used to. A flush rose in her face, and she looked away, confused and embarrassed. Hunter's eyes remained on her a moment longer, then he turned back almost reluctantly to their self-appointed assistant.

"How old are you?" he asked.

"Now, what's that got to do with it?" Mary Margaret asked scornfully. "I'm eleven years old, if you have to know."

Hunter cocked one eyebrow.

"Oh, all right. I'm ten . . . in two months. But that don't mean I can't hold up my side of the bargain. I never go back on my word—ask anybody! I'll even show you where you can hide close to Sister's office so you can slip in there."

"I'm sure you're a woman of your word," Hunter responded gravely. "I'm just wondering how someone your age is such an accomplished trader already."

"Get on with you!" But a faint pink of pleasure stained her pale cheeks. Linette thought wryly that Hunter's charm worked on females of any age.

Hunter glanced at Linette, a question in his eyes. Linette shrugged. "We might as well try it. It sounds safer than what you were suggesting earlier."

He nodded. "All right." He turned back to Mary Margaret, reaching into his pocket and taking out a silver coin, which he flipped to her. "Will that be enough to purchase your abilities?"

The girl expertly caught it in midair, her eyes widening as she looked at it. "Mary, Jesus, and Joseph! I'll keep her out for half an hour for that!"

"It shouldn't take us that long." Hunter smiled.

"Come on, then." Mary Margaret started off on tiptoe down the hall toward the nun's office. Hunter and Linette followed her.

Linette's heart pounded with excitement. She wasn't sure whether to believe the child or not. And it was probably reprehensible of them to encourage her misbehavior like this. But Linette knew that she would do things far worse in order to obtain that file on her daughter. Nothing was going to stop her from finding out what had happened to Julia and where she had gone. Knowing that they were this close, that in the next few minutes they would actually get the file, made her almost dizzy with hope and fear.

Mary Margaret turned off the main hall into the small side hall where Sister Mathilde's office lay. Holding a grimy finger to her lips, she sneaked past the office to the door beside it and eased it open. Inside was a broom closet. Against one wall were stacked brooms and mops, and two buckets sat on the other side, while shelves of rags and various supplies covered the back. Linette looked at it doubtfully. It was probably a marvelous hiding place for a child, but there was very little space for two adults.

Mary Margaret grimaced at them and jerked her thumb toward the closet. Hunter stepped inside, pulling Linette in after him, and Mary Margaret closed the door. It was very dark inside. Linette could see Hunter's face, but she couldn't make out his expression, and his eyes were dark. He looked down at her, and she glanced away breathlessly. They were close together, their bodies almost touching. Linette thought that she could feel the heat of Hunter's body; she could smell the faint scent that was distinctly him. Suddenly she thought of the creekbank so many years ago, and she could almost smell again the heady odor of the wild roses that grew there, mingling with the scent of their heated bodies and the sharp tang of a crushed mint plant.

Linette trembled slightly. She didn't want to remember those things.

Hunter put his hands on her arms. Linette jumped,

startled, and glanced up at him. He was gazing down at her. His hands were suddenly hotter; she could feel them through the cloth of her dress. She knew, as she had always known with Hunter, that he wanted her, that her body pressed up against his had reminded him of the past, too—or perhaps of just the other night. The closet suddenly was stiflingly warm to Linette. Unconsciously, she swayed toward Hunter.

A loud knock sounded out in the hall, making them jump. "Sister! Sister Catherine needs you right away in the courtyard."

They heard the door open and Sister Mathilde's voice say, "What's the problem?"

"It's Mary Margaret Keenan, Sister."

Sister Mathilde heaved a sigh. "Of course."

Their footsteps clicked on the stone floor, growing fainter as they turned the corner. Hunter sneaked the door open a fraction and put his eye to the crack to make sure there was no one still standing there. Then he opened the door and quickly slipped next door into the nun's office, with Linette on his heels. He went straight to the sister's desk and opened the top drawer. Pulling out the ring of keys, he went to the tall cabinet and fitted key after key into the lock. Linette watched him anxiously, her palms sweating. Finally one of the keys opened it. Hunter pulled out the box of files and began to dig through it.

"Renard. Here it is." He opened the file and started to scan the first page, murmuring, "Girl, seven pounds three ounces, black hair, blue eyes." His face softened, and he glanced up at Linette.

Tears stood in her eyes. Making a soft noise, he

ripped the pages from the file and folded them up, sticking them in an inside pocket. "Let's look these over in more leisure."

He stuck the empty file back into the box and closed it, shoving it back into the cabinet. He closed the door, re-locked it, and dropped the keys into the top drawer. They started out the door.

They heard the sound of approaching voices in the outer hall. ". . . veritable imp of Satan! Mary Margaret, what am I going to do with you?"

"I don't know, Sister," a familiar child's voice replied loudly, its brogue thicker than when they'd heard it previously. "Faith, and it's sorry I am. But, truly, sometimes I just don't know what comes over me."

Quickly, Linette grabbed Hunter's arm and tugged, turning to the broom closet in which they had hidden earlier. Hunter followed her as she ducked inside the small room, and he pulled the door nearly closed behind them, leaving a tiny crack through which he could peer into the hall.

The nun's voice grew louder, and Hunter, peeking through the slit between the door and the frame, saw the woman round the corner, dragging the urchin Mary Margaret after her. "Don't you know that you offend God when you act like that? Why, Jesus weeps at the sins you commit."

"Yes, Sister, I'm sorry."

"Don't you try that penitent air with me, young lady." Sister Mathilde paused at the entrance to her office, gazing down sternly at Mary Margaret. "I know you too well. You're not the least bit sorry for putting a frog in the chapel. It's not the first time you've done it. And it gave Sister Catherine quite a turn, I'll tell you. I'm surprised she didn't drop down in a faint right there."

Linette clapped a hand over her mouth to keep from letting out a chuckle. Hunter glanced down at her, and his eyes danced with merriment. Linette remembered a story he told when they were courting about a frog he put in his older brother's bed, and how Gideon had chased him clear to the creek behind their house.

Sister Mathilde marched into her office, pulling Mary Margaret with her. "It's my duty to turn you into a God-fearing, respectable young lady, though the Lord only knows why he has put so many obstacles in my path. Now, pull up that skirt, missy." The nun closed the door behind her, drowning out her next words, though their tone was unmistakable. The sharp slap of something against flesh was equally discernible, if somewhat muffled.

Linette frowned and looked uneasily at Hunter. His brows rushed together and he glanced toward the office, then back to Linette.

"Hunter . . . we can't let her be punished like that for doing something to help us," Linette whispered urgently. It made her chest hurt to think of that child's merry, mischievous little face contorted with pain—and for nothing more than a childish prank!

"I know. But what? She has to stay here. We have no authority over her or the 'good sister.'" His tone was laced with irony.

There was a sudden exclamation in French from

the room beyond, followed by a cry of, "Why, you little she-devil! How dare you!"

Next came a clatter of something falling. Hunter could stand it no longer. He left the broom closet and pounded on the nun's door.

"Not now!" Sister Mathilde snapped from inside. "You'll have to come back later."

But Hunter pushed open the office door, disregarding her command, and stepped inside, with Linette right on his heels. Both the occupants of the room whirled at the noise and froze when they saw Hunter and Linette standing there.

Mary Margaret, holding a wooden ruler in one hand, had climbed up on top of the wooden filing boxes. The nun, her face bright red with fury, stood below her, a long thin wooden pointer in her upraised hand, obviously about to strike the child.

Linette gasped. "No!" and ran to the nun and grabbed the pointer. "Don't you dare strike that child!"

The nun stared at her, nonplussed. "What!" She tugged hard on her end of the wooden stick, but Linette refused to let go.

Linette had thought she was as angry as she could be at Sister Mathilde when she had refused to give them the name and whereabouts of the people who had adopted her daughter, but that fury didn't compare to what she felt now, seeing this woman about to hit a little girl with a stick. She jerked back with all her strength, pulling the pointer from the nun's hand and hurling it behind her onto the floor. Hunter, somewhat more calmly, bent and picked up the stick, casually breaking it in two. He dropped the pieces in the wastebasket.

Sister Mathilde's face grew even redder, if that was possible. "How dare you interfere! This child is in my charge!"

"That doesn't give you the right to beat her," Hunter returned easily.

"I was not beating her! I was disciplining her. I have a duty to discipline her, to raise her to be a good Christian girl!"

"And you accomplish that by whacking her with a stick?"

"I was not! I merely slapped her legs with my ruler—until the little demon kicked me and grabbed my ruler!" Sister Mathilde retorted indignantly. "She has no respect for her elders or her betters."

The nun turned and cast a dark glance at Mary Margaret, who was now crouched on top of the cabinets, watching with interest the unusual scene being played out before her. "The little wretch!" The nun said feelingly. "She's just like her father, God have mercy on his soul, who was a drunk and a fighter up until the day he died. In a saloon brawl."

"That's not true!" Mary Margaret burst out. "You're a liar! Da was not a drunk, and it's no sin to be a fighter! It's fighting that gets you anywhere in the world."

Linette's eyes widened. "How can you say something like that about her father right in front of the child? And you call yourself a Christian! Why, you haven't a drop of Christian charity or kindness in your veins!" Linette's hands doubled up into fists at her sides. "When I think of all the years I longed for my baby, ached for her—yet women like you are allowed to have charge of children! Hurting and humiliating them! It's criminal."

Sister Mathilde raised her chin. "I think I know better than you, young woman, what my duty is. It's to see that these poor benighted children have a roof over their heads, clothes on their backs, and food in their stomachs. To make sure that they grow up into dutiful, sober, hard-working men and women who can take their proper place in the world. It is *not* to coddle or baby them or allow them to get away with wild, undisciplined behavior."

"All you can talk about is duty," Linette retorted coldly. "There's no love in you. That's what children need—love! Not just food and shelter and discipline!"

"What *you* think doesn't matter," Sister Mathilde pointed out. "You have no place here. I am the one responsible for this girl. I'm the one who is in charge of her."

"That is shameful." Linette blazed back. Her eyes were sparkling, her body regally straight, and she seemed almost to shimmer with her anger.

Hunter, looking at her, was struck anew by the glory of her full, mature beauty. Linette had never been anything less than lovely, but now, with emotions once more animating her beauty, she was positively breathtaking. Emotion welled up in him.

"Shameful? And who are you to judge, may I ask?" A haughtily righteous look stamped the nun's features. "A woman who bore an illegitimate child and gave it away? I haven't noticed you offering to take one of these orphans off our hands. I haven't seen you asking to feed and clothe and look after this hoyden here! I think you best look to your own sins before you start upbraiding me about mine!"

Linette looked stricken. Hunter quickly stepped forward and took her arm. "You're wrong, Sister. That's exactly what we intend to do. That's why we're here. We want to take one of these children with us." He glanced up at Mary Margaret, watching him with eyes wide and mouth agape. "And this is the one we choose to take."

17

"What!" Sister Mathilde's mouth dropped open, and she stared at Hunter, pop-eyed.

Mary Margaret, on her perch atop the filing cabinets, looked stunned, and Linette swung around to stare at him with astonishment. Hunter gazed at the nun coolly, then glanced over at Linette, his eyebrows raising a fraction in question.

"Y—yes," Linette stammered. "That's right. We want to take Mary Margaret home with us. We met the child on our way out and she enchanted us so that we decided to turn around and come back and get her."

"Mary Margaret?" The nun repeated in disbelief.

"Yes." Linette's voice was firm now, and she gave the other woman a quelling look. "Mary Margaret Keenan. We want to take her with us."

Mary Margaret let out a yell and jumped off the

top of the file cabinet, landing on the floor and bouncing up to hug Linette around the waist, then prudently taking up a position behind Hunter, at some distance from Sister Mathilde.

The nun straightened, her dark eyes narrowing, and snapped, "Take the child, then. I wish you well of her." Her tone clearly indicated that she doubted such a possibility. "No doubt the three of you will suit each other quite well."

"No doubt," Hunter agreed blandly.

Sister Mathilde looked as if she would like to say more, but after a brief internal struggle, she turned away and marched to the file cabinets. "Sit down," she ordered over her shoulder as she searched for a file and found it. She turned and slapped the file down on her desk. "There are a few formalities we have to go through."

Rosemary glanced over at her father uneasily. He had been acting more and more strange with each passing day. Today he had come home late to supper, and all through the meal he had been watching her covertly, shifting his gaze away whenever she looked up at him. She was certain that he was up to something, though she didn't know what.

When he was through eating, Benton put his utensils down and turned to his daughter. "Rosemary, I want to talk to you in my study."

"Couldn't we just talk here?" Rosemary asked, her stomach tightening. She hated even going into her father's study, the way he hid in there and drank himself into oblivion every night. She could understand his need to drink; his conscience must be heavily burdened by the things he had done. But she hated to be around him when he drank—indeed, she was finding that she could hardly bear to be around him any more at all.

"No. Don't be stupid." Benton stood up and strode out of the room, presuming that his daughter would follow.

With a sigh, Rosemary did so, steeling herself for whatever encounter lay ahead. When they reached the study, Conway closed the door behind them, and to Rosemary's relief he did not head immediately for the liquor cabinet, but turned to face her.

"I spoke to Farquhar Jones today," he began.

"Oh?" Rosemary's stomach knotted a little at the man's name. Was her father going to urge Jones's suit upon her?

"Fortunately, he still wants to marry you. He reiterated his offer for your hand today."

Rosemary gaped at him. "What?"

"He's still willing to marry you!" Benton snapped. "Aren't you paying attention?"

"But I don't want to marry him!" Rosemary retorted hotly, color tinging her cheeks.

Benton stared at her in amazement, as though he could not believe that she had refused him. "What did you say?"

"I will not marry Mr. Jones."

"What!" he thundered, though this time the word carried no question, only outrage. "I have already accepted his offer!"

"You can't be serious! The two of you just agreed on my future without even bothering to consult me?"

"Of course. It's perfect. Once you're married to him, none of them will dare turn their shoulder to me, including that cold bitch of a Thompson woman. No one will listen to the rumors with his power behind me."

"Perfect!" Rosemary exclaimed. "Perfect for you perhaps. But what about me? I'm the one who would be marrying him, not you!" Rosemary flared, a little surprised by her own temerity. She had never faced her father down before, but strangely enough, it was rather exhilarating. Frightening, but emboldening as well.

Benton's face darkened dangerously. "You little fool! This is a far better offer than you have any hope of receiving. I don't see any other suitors pounding at the door. You'll never get another chance if you turn Farquhar down."

"I don't care! I do not love him, and I will not marry him."

"What does love have to do with it? Jones is a rich man, wealthier by far than I am, and he's influential, too. I can't imagine why he's taken the notion into his head that he wants you, but I can only thank God that he has. It will mean the saving of us."

"You mean the saving of you! I can't believe that you, even *you*, would sell your daughter to a man she despises, just so you can maintain your position. Well, I can tell you, it won't even help you with anyone but your Yankee friends. The real people of this town will still hate you."

"A bunch of stiff-necked Rebels!" Benton dismissed the people of Pine Creek contemptuously. "I can live without them. I don't know why I ever bothered to worry what any of them thought about me anyway. They have no power."

"They and their families will be here long after the Union army and your carpetbagger friends have all left! They're the people who belong here, who love this place, who have paid for it with their sweat and blood. Your friends just walked in here on the backs of all their dead soldiers!"

"I will not be defied in my own house!" Conway roared, his face purpling with rage. "You *will* marry Farquhar Jones!"

"No! I will not!" Her father's rage frightened her, damping her momentary courage. But Rosemary was determined not to back down. She could not, not about this. Marrying Farquhar Jones would be condemning herself to a life of misery. "I cannot!"

"You can, and you will." Conway's eyes were cold bits of glass. "You get up to your room and you stay there and you think about the duty you owe your father. And don't come back down until you're ready to do as I say."

Rosemary swallowed nervously and jumped up from her chair. Picking up her skirts, she fled out of the room and up the stairs.

She heard her father slam the front door. Rosemary knew he was furious, and his anger frightened her. She began to pace her room, her stomach knotting with nerves. *What am I to do?*

She wished that Linette were here to advise her,

to help her. Rosemary quivered to think of facing her father again. She had never stood up to him before, and he would be sure that she would give in this time, too. Rosemary was scared that she would not be strong enough, that she would surrender eventually, just as he thought. And that would be disaster. She would be letting him ruin her life just the way he had ruined Linette's—and countless other people's.

She thought of the way her father had tried to take possession of Tess's house, of the people he had forced off the land or out of business. Until recently, she had refused to admit how utterly ruthless her father was, but she forced herself to face it now. He would stop at nothing to get what he wanted; he cared for no one but himself. Even the supposed love he had carried for Linette was a warped and twisted thing that only took for himself and gave nothing back.

One thing was certain. She had to get away from him. She could not remain here. She must flee, just as Linette had.

Not really thinking of where she would go, just filled with the urgent need to get away before her father came back and decided to lock her in her room, Rosemary stuffed a few necessities into a carpetbag, adding the small locked box in which she kept her money and the pieces of jewelry her mother had left her. Then she peeked out her door and quietly slipped down the back staircase. Cecy, the old black cook, glanced up as she crossed the kitchen to the back door. Rosemary was sure that she saw the carpetbag in Rosemary's hand, but she said nothing, only smiled faintly and returned to her work.

Rosemary hurried across the darkened backyard, afraid to take the street in front of their house for fear she might run into her father. Instead she slid through the trees that bordered the back of their large property and emerged on the road beyond. Instinctively she turned toward the edge of town, hurrying through the lengthening shadows of evening. It would be dark soon, but the thought didn't scare her. She welcomed the darkness, for then no one would be able to see her.

She would go to her aunts. They would take her in; they despised her father. But they were old, and Benton would do his best to make life miserable for them. That would be the first place he would look for her. Perhaps it would be better to go someplace else. But where? She didn't know anyone well enough to ask protection from them against her father. No matter how much the town might have been buzzing with gossip about him recently, he was still a powerful man.

She stopped, drawing a shaky breath, and took stock of her surroundings. She must not panic. She had to think.

The library was not far. If she cut across this lot and the next, she would come to its back door. At least it was familiar, and there were plenty of empty bedrooms upstairs, since Tess and her mother moved out. No one would bother her, and perhaps her father wouldn't think of looking for her there immediately. It would give her a little time to think.

So Rosemary hurried through the trees and across the street, creeping past the small house where Seth Manning lived. At last she reached the back porch of the library and slipped inside. She lit a lamp that stood beside the back door and made her way upstairs. After a bit of looking, she chose a small room near the back stairs. With a sigh, she dropped her bag and sank down into a chair. She closed her eyes, sinking back into the big comfortable chair. It felt wonderful to relax at last.

"Raise your hands!" a voice snapped from the doorway behind her. "Who the hell are you and what do you think you're doing here?"

Rosemary let out a little shriek and jumped to her feet, whirling around, her eyes huge and round with fright. A man stood in the doorway, holding a gun on her. She stared at him blankly. He stared back.

"Rosemary!" he burst out. "What in the world?"

"Oh, Seth!" Rosemary went limp with relief. "I'm sorry. You scared me! I—I didn't expect to see anyone."

"Neither did I. That's why when I saw someone sneaking across the backyard I decided to investigate. I thought some vagrant had broken in. Or a thief."

"I—I guess I am a vagrant in a way." She began to tremble, and, to her horror, tears started in her eyes. "Oh, Seth, I don't know what to do!" She raised her hands to her face.

"Rosemary! What's wrong?" He crossed the room to her in a few quick strides, and setting the pistol down on the nightstand beside Rosemary, he took her into his arms. "Darling, what is it?"

His tender words seemed to trigger the roiling emotions that had been swirling chaotically within her. Rosemary burst into tears, burying her face in his chest and clutching his shirt. She cried in great, wrenching sobs, and Seth wrapped his arms around her, holding her against the storm.

Finally, she quieted into little hiccuping sobs and pulled away in embarrassment. "I'm sorry."

"Don't be. Here, wipe your eyes and tell me what's wrong." He handed her his handkerchief.

Rosemary did as he said, pouring out the whole story of what her father had ordered her to do, "But I can't marry Farquhar Jones! I just can't! Not even if it would save Papa."

"Of course not!" Seth's voice shook with outrage. "How could he have even suggested such a thing? A lovely, delicate young woman like you marry that scum!"

"But what can I do? I know Papa will come after me, and where can I go that he won't find me? He'll make me marry Jones; I've never been very brave, and I'm so afraid that I might give in to him finally."

"That won't happen."

"You don't know what he's like."

"I won't let it happen," Seth told her firmly.

Rosemary's heart warmed at his words. *He wants to protect me.* But she could not keep from asking pragmatically, "But how?"

"First of all, you can't stay here. He'll come here first thing."

"You're right. As soon as he checks at my aunts' house and finds I'm not there, he'll think of the library. I came here just to buy some time to think."

"You need to stay with someone who will stand up to your father. But a woman, of course, for propriety's sake. Otherwise, I'd take you back to my house."

Rosemary's breath caught. That idea sounded lovely to her, and for a moment her fear disappeared in a stronger feeling of love and desire.

"What about one of the Tyrrells? I may not know much about this town, but I've been here long enough to know that there's no love lost between the Tyrrells and your father."

"That's true. I think Maggie Prescott or Tess would take me in. Or even Mrs. Tyrrell. They'd all be happy to thwart my father in any way they could. But it would be so presumptuous of me. I have no claim by blood or marriage. I couldn't expect them to take me in. At least, not for any length of time."

"No. Certainly that's only a temporary answer. In the long run, I think the only answer would be—" he hesitated and looked away, "—a husband."

Rosemary gaped at him, stricken by his words. "No! I told you—I can't marry Mr. Jones!"

"Not him!" Seth exclaimed. "Me!"

"You?" Rosemary's eyes opened wide. Suddenly it was difficult to breathe. "You mean that *you* would marry me?"

"Yes. Until you marry, your father will continue to have a claim on you. No one could deny a father's rights over his child, no matter how much they might hate the man."

"I'm of age."

"Even so, practically speaking, you know the law

would not step in and protect you from him. But a husband . . . a husband would have every right to protect his wife, even from her father."

"But . . ."

Seth took her hand and gazed down into her eyes. "Would it be so terrible to be married to me? I thought that night at your aunts', that you were not . . . entirely indifferent to me. I would be a good husband to you, I promise. I'd take care of you, protect you, treat you with kindness and respect."

But what about love? Rosemary felt like bursting into tears all over again. She pulled her hand away. "I can't let you do that. It would be too great a sacrifice. You can't ruin your life just to save me from my father."

"Ruin my life! You can't be serious. It would hardly be a sacrifice."

"I know that you don't love me," Rosemary said hurriedly, not daring to look at him. She didn't want to say these things; she wanted to throw all caution and fairness to the winds and grab this opportunity that he had presented to her. But she loved Seth too much to do that. "You left me there. You haven't spoken to me in weeks. I was too bold."

To her amazement, Seth began to laugh. She raised her head, her eyes great pools of hurt, and he hastened to explain, "No, no, I'm not laughing at you. Just at myself and what an idiot I've been. I was afraid I could not control myself. I wanted you more than anything in the world. I have for months. Rosemary, I love you!"

"You love me?" she breathed, gazing at him with stars in her eyes.

"It's I who don't deserve you. That's why I turned away and left that night. I knew your father would never accept my suit. And, frankly, to even try to engage your affections would be criminal of me. I'm not the proper man for you. I'm only a schoolteacher, a man with no wealth and no prospect of wealth. I could never give you the things you deserve, the things you're used to.

"It's presumptuous of me to ask you to marry me; I would never have done it except that I—it would be a help to you now. It would free you from your father."

"That's not a reason to marry," Rosemary said gently.

Seth's face fell. He cleared his throat. "Yes. You're right. You shouldn't marry me. We'll think of another way."

"The reason I want to marry you," Rosemary went on, "is because I love you. And I will, but only if that's the reason you want to marry me."

He gazed at her for a moment, surprised, but then he smiled. "Yes. God, yes, that's why I want to marry you."

Seth reached out and pulled Rosemary close to him, and his lips found hers.

18

Hunter and Linette walked back to their hotel, Mary Margaret Keenan skipping along beside them. Linette glanced over at Hunter, wondering what they had just done. *What in the world are we going to do with this child?*

Hunter felt her gaze and turned to look at her. He shrugged, a sardonic smile touching his face, and murmured, "What else could we have done?"

Linette didn't know. She and Hunter both glanced down at Mary Margaret, and Linette was certain, all over again, that there was nothing else they could have done. She simply could not leave the little girl there in that woman's care.

Mary Margaret grinned up at Linette, her pale eyes bright in her freckled little face. "You won't regret taking me, ma'am. You'll see. I can do a ton of things—wash and carry water and launder clothes—

I've done almost everything there is to do in the orphanage." A dimple popped into her cheek as she added irrepressibly, "I got booted out of every one of the jobs, so I've tried all of them. But it wasn't 'cause I couldn't do the work, ever; I know how to do them, and if I try, I can be real careful."

"I'm sure you can," Linette told her, smiling. "But we didn't take you away from the orphanage to turn you into a drudge."

"Why did you take me, then?"

"Well, I—we couldn't bear to leave you there, with that woman beating you—and all for something you'd done to help us!"

"But you'd paid me for that," Mary Margaret assured her earnestly.

"Not to be beaten with a stick!" Linette returned, horrified.

The girl smiled and reached out to take Linette's hand and squeeze it reassuringly. "It's all right. Don't worry yourself about it. It's not the first time I've had a few licks with a stick, ma'am. My father always said that it'd take more than a few blows to keep a Keenan down."

"I'm sure it would," Linette replied, not sure whether to laugh or weep at the girl's words.

When they reached the hotel, they went straight to Linette's room. Hunter pulled out the pages he had torn from their daughter's file and pressed them flat on the dresser in the full light from the window. He and Linette bent over them eagerly, their eyes scanning the page. Mary Margaret looked at them curiously, but she could see that they were blind to everything and everyone else at the moment, so she wandered away and busied herself investigating the room.

"Name: Jane Alice Renard," Linette read at the top of the page. "Oh, how could they name her something as dull as that? When she must have been such a beautiful baby." As she read the physical description of the baby, her forefinger skimmed lightly over the words, as gently as if she were touching the child herself.

But Hunter's eyes ran quickly down the page until he found what he was looking for. "Ah, here it is: December 12, 1862, she was given to 'Josef and Gerta Scherer, recently of Amite River.' Not very specific as to their location, is it?" Hunter frowned.

"Amite. It's French; it must be around here, wouldn't you think? Nobody would have traveled here from very far away just to get a baby; there are plenty of orphanages everywhere."

"Yes, I'm sure it's nearby." Hunter turned the page. "Wait, look. Here's a note: 'The Scherers expressed a desire for a baby girl and were very pleased with Jane. They are concerned about the war and intend to move shortly to a German settlement in Texas.'" He stopped reading abruptly.

"Texas!" Linette's eyes flew to his in alarm. "They took her to Texas!"

Her hand went up to her chest, and tears filled her eyes. She had been so sure that her daughter was close by, that she would find her soon. "But that's so far away. And how are we ever going to find her in Texas?" Tears began to course down her face. "Oh,

Hunter!" Her shoulders shook, and she turned away, trying to hide her sobs.

But Hunter put his arms around her and pulled back against him. "Shh . . . don't worry." He bent his head to hers. "We'll find her. I promise. It's not that bad. Look, right here, it says the name of the town: Fredericksburg. All we have to do is go there, and we'll find her. It will take a little more time, that's all. But we *will* get her back."

Linette nodded, pulling herself together. "I know." She summoned up a smile. "It was just that I thought we were so close."

Hunter smiled and kissed her gently on the forehead. "We're a hundred times closer than we were a week ago. Just remember that."

Her smile grew a little more genuine. "I will."

"Good. Then I'm going to inquire about the riverboats to New Orleans."

"You'll need some money. We must be running low. You'll have to sell the jewels." Linette rummaged through her carpetbag and found the small box. She went back over to Hunter, opening the box and holding it out. "Here. I suppose you might as well sell all of them at once, if you can get a decent price. Or perhaps we ought to wait until New Orleans. You could probably get a better price there."

Hunter hesitated, frowning. "Dammit, Linette, I hate to sell your jewels."

Linette gave him a faint smile. "How else, pray, do you think we're going to make it to Texas? I know you've been using your money this far."

He shrugged. "Our expenses haven't been exactly great."

"Well, there was this hotel, for one thing, and food. It's hardly fair since I'm the one who asked you to come along."

"Linette . . . she's my daughter, too."

"I know. And we aren't going to find her if we don't sell this jewelry. So stop being so stubborn. Anyway, it's not *my* jewelry. Benton gave me all of that." She looked at the lovely jewels contemptuously. "I would never wear any of it again. I would have left it with him except I knew we'd need it on this trip."

Hunter glanced down at the jewels, and after a moment longer of internal struggle, he acquiesced. "All right. I'll take them." He reached in to scoop the jewels out.

"No, wait! There is one thing I want to keep." She reached into the back corner of the box and pulled out a ring.

Her fingers curled over the ring quickly, enclosing it in her palm, but not before Hunter caught a glimpse of it.

"Wait a minute. What is that?" he asked, reaching out and unfolding her fingers from the object. He looked at it for a long moment. "That's the ring I gave you." His voice was slightly unsteady, and he looked up, his eyes searching her face.

Linette lifted her chin a little and met his gaze defiantly. "Yes, it is."

"And you kept it?"

"What was I supposed to do? Throw away the only

memento I had of you? I know you think me heartless, but I loved you and I —I truly mourned you."

He continued to gaze down into her deep blue
eyes, and his thumb moved caressingly over the back
of her fingers. "Linette . . ."

Out of the corner of his eye, Hunter caught a
movement across the room. It was Mary Margaret,
leaning forward interestedly to catch their lowered
words, and it reminded him suddenly that they were
not alone. He dropped her hand, glancing over at
Mary Margaret.

Linette followed his gaze, and she colored a trifle.
"Oh," she said softly and turned away from him.

"I'll take the rest of the jewelry then and see what
I can do. I'll purchase tickets for New Orleans. But,
Linette . . ." He moved closer to the door, taking her
by the elbow and pulling her with him. In a lower
voice, he said, "What are we going to do about
her?"

He nodded his head toward Mary Margaret, and
automatically Linette glanced over at her. She stood,
watching them closely, a mess of a girl with a halo of
tangled curls and eyes that somehow made one want
to smile whenever one looked at her.

"I don't know," Linette groaned. "We can hardly
take her with us. That's a long trip—sailing on a ship,
and then once we get there, we'll be riding and camping out again."

"No, that's hardly fit for a child. If we could just
send her back to my mother, everything would be
fine. Mama would be happy to take her in and care
for her." A slight smile touched his lips. "Straighten

her out, too. By the time we saw her again, we probably wouldn't recognize her."

A gurgle of laughter rose in Linette's throat. "I don't know. I'm tempted to put my money on Mary Margaret."

"You're right; she might be a match even for my mother." Amusement lit his eyes, but then he sighed. "But I can't figure out any way to get her back to Pine Creek. If only we knew someone traveling to Arkansas, we could entrust her to them."

"Yes, but we don't. And I don't know anyone in Baton Rouge or New Orleans that we could leave her with."

"You're not planning to foist me off on somebody, are you?" Mary Margaret spoke close to them, startling them both. They had been so intent on their conversation that they had not seen her creep closer and closer, and now she stood only a couple of feet away, her hands on her hips, glaring at them balefully.

"No, no, not 'foist' you off on someone," Linette assured her hastily. "It's just that now we have to go to Texas, and that's hardly a fit journey for a child."

"Oh, no, I promise you, ma'am, I won't slow you down. I'm no pantywaist; Da always said I was tough as an old boot, and indeed, I am! I won't be lagging behind."

"Well, it wasn't exactly that," Hunter put in. "But it's a hard journey for a child. Texas is still pretty wild, and you have to ride for days to get anywhere."

Mary Margaret looked supremely offended. "I told you: I'm no pantywaist! I can take it. If a fine lady like *her* can manage it," she pointed out, jerking her thumb toward Linette, "then so can I. I've lived rougher than she ever has, I'll warrant."

Linette and Hunter glanced at each other. That much was true, no doubt; the girl was obviously used to an unkind life.

"And I can help," Mary Margaret stuck in. "You'll see. I'll make it easier, not harder. I can fetch water and cook and clean the dishes up."

"I've never seen a child so eager to work," Hunter teased, his eyes twinkling.

"Well, I'm a good worker," Mary Margaret retorted defensively. "I can be, anyway."

Hunter suppressed a smile at the candor of her last statement. He turned toward Linette. "The devil of it is, I don't know what else to do with her."

Linette shrugged. "I don't either." It didn't seem right to subject a girl to the rigors of the journey— and it chafed at her to think of slowing down their pace so that Mary Margaret could rest. But what other choice did they have?

"All right, you little imp," Hunter told Mary Margaret. "I guess we'll have to take you with us." He raised a warning forefinger. "But you better not be up to any tricks on the way."

"Oh, no, sir!" Mary Margaret looked horrified. "I wouldn't, not with you."

Hunter smiled. "You remember that, because, believe me, I know *all* the tricks that children can get into."

Mary Margaret returned a conspiratorial smile, and Hunter turned to Linette. "I'll be on my way, then. You stay here with Mary Margaret and rest. I'm sure it's something both of you could use."

Linette nodded. For once, she was willing to comply with Hunter's orders. She felt too dispirited to want to go anywhere. Nothing was happening as she had hoped. She had not found her daughter, and it would be weeks before they did—if, indeed, they were able to find her at all. Texas was a huge place, and it would have been so easy for the family that had taken Julia to go to a different town than the one they had intended or to have moved somewhere else in the intervening years. And now she and Hunter had a child encumbering them.

Hunter left, and Linette sat down on a bench at the end of the bed, sighing. Mary Margaret came over to where she sat and squatted down beside her on the floor, gazing up into Linette's face.

"I can put lavender water on a handkerchief and bathe your forehead," she offered. "One of Da's particular lady friends liked that when she was feeling under the weather."

Linette looked at the girl's earnest little face and smiled. "Oh, Mary Margaret, you put me to blush. Here I am feeling sorry for myself because things didn't happen exactly as I wanted them to, and you are offering to do things for me." She studied Mary Margaret's stained smock and smudged face and her thick, half-combed curling hair. "I'm the one who should be doing something for you."

Linette stood up, feeling new energy. "The first thing, I think, is a bath. It looks like it's been far too long since you've had a decent one."

"A bath?" Mary Margaret's face turned wary.

"Yes. A new dress and stockings won't do much good if the body underneath them is as dirty as ever. And why try to bring all these curls into a semblance of control if they'll still be sticky?"

"A new dress?"

"Yes. New shoes, too." She looked down at Mary Margaret's rough shoes, too large for her feet.

Mary Margaret, too, looked down at her shoes, then back up at Linette. She still looked uncertain, but she didn't argue against Linette's plan.

Linette ordered a bath sent up. Mary Margaret stared in awe at the slipper-shaped metal tub and the two maids who filled it with buckets of water. Shyly, turning her back to Linette, she undressed. Linette tactfully turned to look out the window while the girl undressed and slipped into the tub.

It took some time to wash away all the dirt, especially in her hair, which had obviously encountered a sticky substance at some point in the past and had become almost hopelessly snarled and matted. However, Linette, working patiently on her knees beside the tub, managed to work the rose-scented soap through each tangle and comb it free. Finally, Mary Margaret was deemed clean enough, and Linette let her out of the tub, wrapping her around with a bath sheet.

Linette was tempted to give Mary Margaret's old garments to the maid to use as rags, but she realized that the poor child had nothing else to wear until they purchased new things, so she relented and ordered them laundered as soon as possible. In the meantime, she gave Mary Margaret one of her own shifts to wear, which pleased the girl no end, even though it was ludicrously too large.

She sat Mary Margaret down on the bed and rubbed her hair with a towel to dry it, then combed through it. She was surprised to find that it was a much lighter shade of blond than she had earlier imagined, almost golden, in fact. Mary Margaret's hair fluffed as it dried, creating feathery curls around her face, and Linette brushed the ends of her hair into long curls around her finger.

Linette sat back and admired her handiwork. "There, I think that will do very nicely. A ribbon would add just the right touch, I think, don't you?"

Mary Margaret climbed off the bed and advanced toward the vanity mirror, an awed expression on her face. "Is that me, ma'am?"

Linette chuckled. "Of course it is, you goose. Who else would it be?"

"But I've never seen my hair look like that. The sisters used to put it in braids, but it would never stay that way for long."

"Oh, no, your hair's too curly for braids. This will suit you much better. Of course, it's more trouble. You'll have to remember to brush it well every night and morning."

"I will," Mary Margaret breathed, gazing into the mirror as if enchanted.

Afterward, Linette went out, leaving Mary Margaret luxuriating in the room; she returned sometime later with a seamstress, who measured Mary Margaret for a new smock. The girl, stunned, obedi-

ently stood, raising or lowering her arms as
requested, while the woman crept around her, deftly
using a tape measure.

"Here's a swatch of the material I bought for the
new smock," Linette said after the seamstress had finished and left, holding out a piece of pink calico to
Mary Margaret. "Do you like it?"

"Oh, ma'am, it's beautiful! Is that for me?" Linette
nodded. "But—but it's pink!"

Linette's smile faded. "Don't you like pink? I'm
sorry; I thought it would be an excellent color for
your hair and coloring."

"Oh, no, ma'am, I like pink. It's lovely, but . . .
well, it's just that our dresses are always gray or
brown. It's so much more serviceable." She primmed
her mouth, her voice a faithful imitation of Sister
Mathilde's.

"No doubt. But pink is much prettier. I'm sorry
that I could get only one dress; we'll probably leave
tomorrow, and the seamstress couldn't make up more
than one dress by then, even a simple smock. Perhaps
in New Orleans we can purchase some more."

Mary Margaret simply gaped at her.

Linette merrily untied the parcels she had brought
with her. Inside one lay new white cotton underthings
and stockings. In the other was a new pair of shoes.
Linette glanced over at Mary Margaret, grinning.
"Well? What do you think?"

"You're teasing me," the girl gasped, reaching in
reverently and taking out the shift that lay on top. It
was plain except for a single eyelet ruffle down the
front and a little pink ribbon that was threaded

through the neckline and tied in a bow in the front. "Is this for me?"

"Who else? It's much too small for me."

"Oh, ma'am!" Mary Margaret clutched the garment to her chest, raising tear-filled eyes to Linette's face. "I've never had anything like this. It's so pretty and new and—and all mine!"

It nearly broke Linette's heart to see the poor child's gratitude over a few simple pieces of underclothing. She wondered if her own little girl was living the same sort of life, relegated to hand-me-down's and 'serviceable' clothes.

"Why are you doing this for me?" Mary Margaret asked wonderingly. She looked down, her face screwing up worriedly. "You don't know me very well. I'm not, well, I'm not a good sort of girl. I'm forever getting into scrapes. All the sisters say I've plenty of the devil in me, and I'm thinking they're right. I don't want you thinking you've got another kind of girl or something. You'd be terrible disappointed."

Linette smiled a little sadly. "I'm not thinking you're a different kind of girl. I can see exactly what kind you are—brave and resourceful, and honest, too. Hunter and I didn't take you out of there because we thought you were an angel. It's obvious enough that you have a tendency to get into scrapes. But, you know, sometimes people like that are much more interesting than perfect little angels."

"They are?" Mary Margaret grinned, her freckled face lighting up, and she looked again like the mischievous urchin they had met earlier. "That's what Da used to say, too!"

"Well, see? You should always listen to your father."

"That's what he said, too," Mary Margaret admitted with a chuckle. "But—I still don't understand why you're getting me all these things. I'm not anybody to you. I'm not the girl you're looking for. I mean, you're still going looking for her, aren't you?"

"Yes, we're going to continue searching for her. She's our daughter. But that doesn't mean that I can't buy you a few things. You don't have to be someone's mother to give her a present. Besides, you need these." Linette smiled at Mary Margaret's uncertain expression and took both her hands in her own. "Let's just say I'm practicing being a mother, so when I do find my daughter, I'll know what to do. How's that?"

"All right." Mary Margaret smiled at her, then startled Linette by throwing her arms around her and hugging her hard. "You're the best and nicest person I ever met."

"Hardly that, I'm afraid." Linette smiled, smoothing her hand over the child's hair. She bent down, putting her arms around Mary Margaret, and laid her cheek on the girl's head. Mary Margaret felt so soft in Linette's arms and smelled so delicious. Linette closed her eyes, and for the first time in years, did not brace herself against the tender feelings welling up in her.

Hunter returned not long afterward, and when Linette admitted him to the room, he stopped in the doorway and stared at Mary Margaret. Theatrically, he placed one hand over his heart. "Miss Keenan! Here you've turned into a beauty while I was gone."

Mary Margaret giggled, pleased by his effusions. "Go on. I'm no beauty. Miz Linette just cleaned me up and fixed my hair." She cast a look at herself in the vanity mirror and smiled, adding with an innocence that made Hunter chuckle, "But I am pretty, aren't I?"

"Indeed, you are." Hunter came in, closing the door, and bent to plant a kiss on the top of her forehead. "I'll have to keep an eye on you in New Orleans, so no one will steal you from me."

Mary Margaret blushed and laughed, throwing her arms around his neck and squeezing hard. "Am I going to New Orleans, then?"

"Yes, we all are. Tomorrow morning, on a big beautiful paddlewheeler. Have you ever been on one?"

"No." Mary Margaret's eyes sparkled at the prospect. "I've seen them, though, and, faith, but they're grand. I'll feel like a queen."

"Good. You should." He grinned at her. "And tonight, I propose to take the two most beautiful ladies in Baton Rouge out to eat. What do you all say to that?"

Linette and Mary Margaret admitted that it sounded like a splendid idea, and, after Mary Margaret's newly laundered and ironed dress was delivered to their room, they sallied forth. Their mood was happy, almost frivolous, as Hunter joked and teased them and Mary Margaret giggled. The heaviness that had weighed down Linette's spirits earlier was gone. It might take a little longer for her to find her daughter, she realized, but she *would* find her and, after nine years, what did waiting another few weeks matter?

As they crossed the street after leaving the restaurant, on their way back to their hotel, Hunter paused and glanced around. Linette noticed his gesture, and, frowning, she asked, "What is it? What's the matter?"

"Nothing, I think," Hunter said ambiguously, and stopped on the sidewalk to take another long, careful look at the street all around them. "I just had a funny feeling, that's all, as if someone were watching us. It's not the first time, either. I felt it this morning." He shrugged. "But I didn't see anybody that I recognized."

"Do you think it could be that man? Pauling?" Linette asked in a low voice as they continued on their way, casting a glance at Mary Margaret in the hopes that she was not attending to their conversation.

"What man?" Mary Margaret inquired curiously.

Linette grimaced. She might have known; there was little that the child missed.

"Just a man we ran into earlier," Hunter replied blandly. "But he's in jail, so I don't see how it could be him. Besides, I would have recognized him."

"What if—what if Benton's sent another one?"

"How could he have gotten here this quickly? I mean, Conway would have had to learn that the other man was in jail and then send someone, and they would have had to try to find us."

"No. Benton would have known where we were going. He would know that eventually we'd wind up at the orphanage. All anyone would have had to do is come straight here and wait for us."

"I still don't think he would have had enough time. We're probably worrying ourselves for nothing."

"Or he might have hired someone in Baton Rouge. He knows people here. He could have sent a telegram. Or maybe that man we found wasn't really alone; maybe he just happened to be by himself at that moment for some reason or other."

"What are you talking about?" Mary Margaret interrupted with breathless interest, her eyes rapt on their faces. "Is there somebody after you?"

Linette and Hunter stopped talking and looked down at her with dismay. Hastily Hunter shook his head and assured her, "No, goodness, no. I'm sorry. Did we alarm you?"

Mary Margaret cast him a suspicious look. "No. But it sounded awfully exciting, like someone was chasing you or something."

Hunter sighed, and Linette said, "Well, you're right." She cast Hunter a look and said, "It's no use trying to fool her, Hunter." Then she turned back to the girl. "There was someone chasing us for a while. The same man who took my daughter from me and gave her to the orphanage."

Mary Margaret sucked in her breath. "Oooh, he sounds like a terrible wicked man, ma'am."

"He is." Linette's voice hardened. "But he didn't actually chase us himself. He sent someone after us to try to stop us. But Hunter found him out and put him in jail, so that's all over. And Benton, the wicked man, is back in Arkansas, so we needn't worry about him."

"I see. So you're worried about him sending someone else."

"Oh, Hunter, do you think there's any possibility of it? If so, we shouldn't take Mary Margaret with us."

"I can take care of myself," Mary Margaret hastened to assure them, doubling up her small fists and looking pugnacious. "Now I know to be on the lookout."

A smile touched Hunter's lips, and he cast an amused glanced at Linette. "No, I've probably just got the willies. I'm not a city man; all these people make me nervous. There shouldn't be any danger." His smile faded, and he went on, "All the same, let's keep our eyes open. I don't want to be caught napping."

They turned and continued on their way back to their hotel. A block behind them, a stocky man stepped out of the doorway of a store where he had been idling, watching the passersby, and followed them.

19

Benton Conway poured the whiskey into his glass. His hand trembled so badly that the decanter clattered against the edge of the glass. He swallowed the drink in one long gulp and poured another. He was ruined. Ruined!

He picked up the telegram from Packer and read it again. Hunter and Linette had once more outwitted his man. Worse, they had reached the orphanage at Baton Rouge and had discovered the whereabouts of their daughter. According to Packer, Hunter and Linette were booked on a steamboat to New Orleans and when he bought the tickets, Hunter had also inquired about ships to Texas. Texas! Apparently they intended to chase this brat down to the ends of the earth!

Conway knew where they were headed. Even his cousin Louisa didn't know it, but he had sent someone to the orphanage years ago to find out the whereabouts of Linette's child. He had known for a long time that the girl was living in Fredericksburg, Texas, with a German couple. It had given him a certain secret pleasure every time Linette looked at him in that cold, superior way, every time he had tried to make love to her and failed, to know that he knew where her child was and that she would never find her.

But now that was no longer true. Now Linette would have the damned brat. She would go off somewhere to live with it and Hunter—while he was left here to live amid the ruins of their life. *Damn her! Damn them both!*

They had taken everything from him, and he hated them fiercely. Conway was sure they had told the Tyrrells before they left what he had done, and the Tyrrells had doubtless spread it around. Whenever he went out, he could see people whispering about him. He called at the Thompsons' house the other day when he was in Sharps, and the maid who answered the door told him that neither the colonel nor his wife were at home. But Benton knew better. He was sure that he had seen a curtain twitch at an upper window, and he knew that it was the prissy Lilibet Thompson, checking to see if he'd left.

Tears came with drunken ease to his eyes as he thought about his old friends who were now avoiding him, about the proud, censorious locals who looked at him as if he were dirt. *What did any of them have to be so righteous about? Why, I could buy and sell them all! Even that damn Yankee colonel.*

Then his treacherous daughter had destroyed whatever chance he had of remaining in good standing with the Yankees by refusing to marry Farquhar Jones. She'd run off in the middle of the night and gone to stay with that pig-headed, fiery-tempered Maggie Prescott, who would not even let him in the door, let alone allow him to talk to Rosemary. Two weeks later she'd married that schoolteacher—and out of Maggie Prescott's house, too, just as if she didn't have a father and a beautiful home herself. *That,* he was sure, had only added to all the scandalous rumors being whispered about him.

But there was nothing he could do to Rosemary to punish her for what she'd brought on him. Not with her and her husband living right here in this little town, with the entire gossipy population watching both them and Benton.

However, punishing Linette and her lover was an entirely different thing. Conway straightened, an evil light starting to gleam in his eyes. Linette and Hunter weren't here in Pine Creek, under everyone's eye. They would be in Texas soon. Texas—where nobody knew them or him. Where, according to what he'd heard, lawless acts occurred all the time. Why, one killing would probably hardly be noticed—especially if the killer vanished immediately. And no one here in Pine Creek would ever know what he had done.

It was, after all, what he had sent Packer to do. But obviously Packer wasn't up to the job. The only way he could be sure of getting it done would be to do it himself. Besides, it would be pleasurable to pull the trigger and watch Hunter Tyrrell die. Conway smiled,

his alcohol-soaked brain dwelling happily on pictures
of Hunter writhing on the ground, bleeding to death,
of Linette kneeling before him, Benton Conway, begging him for her life.

Conway jerked open a desk drawer and pulled out
a map, spreading it out on his desk and anchoring it
with his whiskey glass and decanter. He pored over
the map, his stubby forefinger tracing a trail across
Arkansas and down into Texas. If he rode, he could
get there before them. The route Hunter and Linette
were taking was longer, even if more comfortable,
and they would probably have to wait in New Orleans
for a ship to take them to Galveston. Then they'd
have to take the stage or ride up from Galveston to
Fredericksburg, and that would take several days,
too, particularly since they now were traveling with
some child that Packer said they'd picked up at the
orphanage.

But the land route, slanting down through Texas,
was shorter, and a man riding alone, especially with
changes of horses periodically, could make it to San
Antonio much more quickly. Then all he would have
to do was wait for Hunter and Linette to arrive and
follow them when they rode out to Fredericksburg.

Conway didn't relish riding all that way. He was
not a horseman. But the thought of overtaking
Hunter and Linette overcame his dislike of riding
hard and fast and living rough. He could do it.

Suddenly his life had meaning and purpose.
Hunter and Linette were the source of all his problems and if he got rid of them, his life would become
normal again. He was filled with hatred, consumed

with desire for revenge. Linette and Hunter had ruined him, and he would make them pay.

Conway lurched to his feet and stumbled out of his study. He would go upstairs and pack, and tomorrow, at first light, he would leave. A chilling smile played about his lips as he climbed the stairs. *Soon, I'll be rid of Hunter Tyrrell forever.*

Hunter and Linette boarded the big white paddleboat late the following morning, Mary Margaret Keenan skipping along beside them. Hunter had decided to stable their horses in Baton Rouge, reasoning that the journey to Texas on board ship would be easier without them, especially since, with Mary Margaret along, it made more sense to travel by stagecoach once they were in Texas.

Mary Margaret was elated at being aboard the elegant white boat, and she bounded all over it, exclaiming and pointing out every sight, from the wooden curlicues decorating the posts to the elegant Brussels carpet in the main cabin to the ten crystal chandeliers hanging there.

"Yes, it's lovely," Linette assured Mary Margaret, smiling as she glanced around the dazzling white-and-gold room.

"Will you dance in it?" Mary Margaret asked breathlessly. "I've heard that they have a band and people dance in the evenings. I would love to see it!"

"There won't be a dance tonight. We'll dock in New Orleans before evening," Hunter told her, and the girl's face fell.

"Besides, I haven't any gown to wear to a ball," Linette added. But a wistful sigh escaped her lips as she said it. It hadn't been long since she attended a ball, but it had been years since she enjoyed one . . . years since she had been to one with Hunter.

She turned toward Hunter and found him looking at her. Linette knew that he was thinking the same thing: the parties they had been to, the way they had waltzed together or bounced through a hectic reel. Linette could almost feel Hunter's arms around her again, his hand enfolding hers as they spun around the room, giddy with love and excitement.

Linette swallowed and looked away, suddenly breathless. It would be best if she didn't have such thoughts. Hunter no longer loved her; he wouldn't even be here with her if it hadn't been for their child. All that life was lost, and she would be better off if she put it out of her mind.

Hunter turned away, saying gruffly, "Come along. I think the ship is about to pull away from the docks."

Mary Margaret was eager to see this sight, and she bounced away. Hunter and Linette followed her more slowly. The ship pulled away as they stood at the rail and watched, and afterward Hunter was able to persuade Mary Margaret to settle down in a chair beside Linette on one of the decks and watch the bank of the Mississippi slide by. Even then, she was forever up and out of her seat to exclaim over some new sight—a barge on the river or children fishing from the levee. By the end of the day, when they reached New Orleans, even Mary Margaret was exhausted and quite willing to go to bed.

They were somewhat dismayed the next morning to find out that it would be almost a week before a passenger ship would be leaving New Orleans for Galveston. They resigned themselves to the wait, however, and Linette seized the opportunity of their enforced sojourn there to have three new frocks made up for Mary Margaret. Mary Margaret was ecstatic at the idea of these garments and threw her arms around Linette in an enthusiastic hug when Linette suggested at lunch the first day that they visit the dressmakers. She was particularly pleased that though two of them would be smocks, easy to play in, one of them was to be a muslin dress suitable for wearing to church.

"Oh, ma'am, could it be yellow? I've always wanted a pretty yellow dress."

"If that's what you want."

Mary Margaret clasped her hands delightedly in front of her. "And will it have ruffles?" she asked, her eyes shining.

"Yes, indeed!" Linette replied with a chuckle. "It shall have enough ruffles and frills to satisfy any young girl's heart—and ribbons, too."

"With a matching ribbon for my hair?" Mary Margaret countered.

Hunter, listening to their conversation, could not help but laugh. "Linette, see what you've done!" he teased her, his green eyes dancing with amusement. "The girl's becoming a fashion plate, just like you."

Linette flashed him a look of mock exasperation, but Mary Margaret hastened to defend her idol. "Oh, no, sir! I could never hope to be like Mrs. Conway. She's *beautiful.*"

"Yes," Hunter agreed, smiling at Mary Margaret's earnest face, "that she is." He glanced over at Linette, and the amused look vanished from his face. His eyes were suddenly dark and hot, and Linette's gaze quickly fell. She flushed.

"We'd better go, Mary Margaret," she murmured, standing up. She did not look at Hunter before they left; she could not.

Normally Hunter treated her with a politeness that bordered on indifference, which Linette had discovered irritated her to no end. But whenever a certain expression came over his face or he cast her a certain look, Linette was reminded of that night on the trail when he had made love to her, and she knew that, whatever he said, Hunter still desired her. Whenever that happened, Linette was hard put to behave at all normally around him. Just the hint of fire in his eyes, just the subtle softening of his mouth that bespoke desire, were enough to make her start trembling inside.

Nothing could come of it, Linette knew. For one thing, Mary Margaret was quite an effective little chaperone. She was always with them and even slept in Linette's room with her. But, more than that, even if Mary Margaret had not been there, Hunter would never let himself get involved with Linette again. He had told her so. But what was awful was that Linette knew that she did not have as much control over herself and her desires as Hunter did.

Linette found it hard to be around Hunter all the time, as she was, and not reach out and touch him or hold him or stretch up to kiss him. Most of the time they were on terms of such easy familiarity—being together so much, often teasing or joking as they had in the past—that it seemed the most natural thing in the world, and it was only at the last moment that she remembered how things really were between them and she would stop herself from doing or saying something that would have embarrassed them both.

It seemed that as time passed, Linette grew more and more conscious of Hunter and the desire she felt for him. She thought it was in part because they were together at the hotel, waiting for the ship, with nothing to occupy their minds. It left her too much time to think, to remember, to feel.

As the week wore on, Linette could tell that Hunter, too, felt the tension. He seemed to grow more irritable and the lines around his mouth were tauter. He went out more often for long walks, and there was a nervous, even jumpy quality about him. There were even times when he snapped at Mary Margaret when she was noisily playing or asking ceaseless questions. He always apologized afterward, explaining once that he was tense from waiting, but Linette suspected that it was from something more than that. Surely his nerves, too, were beginning to fray under the constant scrape of unsatisfied desire. Sometimes Linette wondered how they would manage to make it through the long journey to Texas.

At least here they could escape outside of the hotel, Linette going shopping with Mary Margaret or Hunter taking one of his walks. But what would they do on board the ship to Texas, where there would be nowhere to go except one's cabin or the deck? Linette

didn't look forward to the prospect of spending the
entire voyage hiding inside her cabin. As the sailing
date drew closer, her nerves stretched tighter and
tighter.

The day before they were to sail, Linette and
Hunter seemed particularly on edge. Mary Margaret
had gotten her new frocks and had spent the afternoon excitedly jabbering about her dresses and trying
on each one over and over and modeling it for
Hunter, who had had luncheon with them in their
room. She continued to giggle and jump, making silly
faces and talking loudly until finally Hunter rebuked
her sharply, and she fell silent, her face drooping dis-
consolately.

Hunter let out an exasperated oath and jumped up
from his seat, saying, "I'm sorry, Mary Margaret. I'm
a cross old bear and not fit for human company
today."

Then he left and didn't return until several hours
later, when he knocked on the door and gave a formal
bow as Linette opened it. "I have come to make
amends for my bad temper, ladies."

Mary Margaret, who had been subdued since he
left, grinned and bounded over to him, saying, "I'm
sorry for being such a jack-in-the-box; I know it
wears people's nerves out. Even Da used to say so."

"Not so fast, Mary Margaret," Linette drawled,
shooting a teasing glance at Hunter. "If you want to
be a successful belle, one thing you have to learn is
not to let a man off the hook that easily. It's much
better to keep him dangling. You look at him consid-
eringly, like this, with just a touch of pain still in your

eyes, and say, 'I'm not sure I can forgive you just yet, sir.'"

"Don't you listen to her, Mary Margaret," Hunter chuckled. "Believe me, it will earn you the admiration of all men."

"Oh, fiddle!" Linette responded stoutly. "Nothing makes a man notice you more than making him suffer a little, and nothing makes him more complacent and self-centered than giving in to him."

"You mean to tell me that you ladies are going to hold a grudge against a man who proposes to take the two of you out in your best finery to an elegant restaurant tonight?"

"Do you really?"

"I do."

"Can I wear my new best dress?" Mary Margaret, whose only regret in her new dresses was that she had no place to wear the elegant one, gazed at him with stars in her eyes.

"But of course. That's exactly what I intended for you to do."

Mary Margaret turned her shining face toward Linette. "Oh, ma'am, can we?"

"May we," Linette responded automatically, but a smile belied any strictness. "Yes, we certainly may. It's only foolish to turn down an invitation to dine elegantly. And much more ladylike to forgive."

So they dressed and went out and had a long and leisurely supper. When they finished, it was late in the evening, but, being New Orleans, there were still many people about. They strolled the few blocks home to the hotel, enjoying the pleasant evening.

They turned down a side street to cross to the hotel. It was dark, and there were no other people on it, but Linette and Hunter were deep in discussion and paid little attention. Mary Margaret skipped on ahead. There was a step down as they went past an alley, and just as they reached it, a dark figure came swiftly out of the alley and swung at Hunter, a knife glinting in his hand.

Fortunately Hunter had caught a flash of movement out of the corner of his eye and instinctively stepped to the side, pushing Linette out of the way. As a result, the knife merely sliced through his jacket and shirt, barely cutting his skin.

Quickly he twisted and grabbed his assailant's arm, and the two men struggled in a grim, silent dance. Linette, who had been pushed unceremoniously to the ground by the force of Hunter's movement, cried out and tried to jump to her feet. But her feet got tangled in her long skirts, and she could not get up. Impatiently she jerked at them, and something ripped, and then she was able to lurch to her feet.

She started toward the two men, but just at that moment, a little whirlwind of fury that was Mary Margaret came whizzing past her. The girl launched herself full tilt at Hunter's assailant. She thudded into him with her entire weight, knocking a loud "oof" out of him, and her fingers went straight to his head and face, scratching and clawing. The man let out a roar and reached back with one hand and tore Mary Margaret from his back, sending her flying into the street.

His movement left him unprotected, however, and
Hunter landed a hard punch in his stomach that doubled him over. Then Hunter grabbed his knife arm
with both hands and slammed it into the wall behind
them. The knife went flying.

Linette hurried over to pick up the knife, then
returned to where Mary Margaret lay in the street,
trusting that Hunter would be able to hold his own in
a fistfight. She bent over Mary Margaret solicitously
and helped her up. She was pale and had the wind
knocked from her, but she was conscious and staggered to her feet with Linette's help. They both
turned back to check on Hunter.

He and the other man had tumbled off the sidewalk, fists flying, and they rolled across the street,
stirring up dust. Linette watched anxiously, trying to
figure out which was which in the dark now that both
men were covered with dirt. She would have liked to
grab Hunter's pistol from his holster and put an end
to the fight, but they were moving too swiftly for her
to be able to grab anything.

Then they stopped, one figure on top of the other
one, fists raining down on the other's face. Linette
recognized the slender torso of the victor as Hunter's,
and she let out a sigh of relief.

She glanced down at Mary Margaret, who was taking in the fight, wide-eyed, and she tried to turn her
aside from the bloody sight.

But Mary Margaret stubbornly turned back, craning her neck around Linette to see. "No, wait! Let me
see Hunter finish him off!" She grinned up at Linette,
excited and not in the least horrified. "He's a devil

with his fists, ain't he? Even Da wasn't no better'n him."

Linette, whose heart was still pounding, grimaced. "Hunter! Hunter, stop! You'll kill him."

She ran over and grabbed Hunter's upraised fist as he knelt over the man. "Hunter!"

He glanced up at her, then drew a long breath and relaxed.

His hand dropped, and he let go of the man's shirt, letting his head fall back to the ground. Hunter stood up, brushing back his hair from his face. "Son of a bitch!"

Linette peered down at the man on the ground. "Why, I've seen him!"

"You have?" Hunter looked surprised. "Who is he?"

"Well, I don't mean that I know him, precisely. I don't know his name. But I think he lives in Pine Creek. He's done work for Benton; I saw him coming out of Benton's study once." She raised her face to Hunter's as the full implication of her statement hit her. "He's someone Benton sent to kill us?"

"Or at least me. That would be my guess." Hunter shrugged. "Well, that's one I don't think we need to worry about anymore. He won't be getting on the ship to Texas tomorrow."

"How many people did Benton send after us?" Linette asked, shaken. "Do you suppose there are others out there?"

"I'd guess not. Otherwise I would think they'd have ganged up on us tonight. Conway may decide to sic someone else on us, but we'll be long gone by then. Don't worry about it."

"I can't help but worry." Linette sighed and looked back down at the supine figure. It seemed unnaturally still to her. "Do you suppose he's dead?"

"No." Hunter's face twisted contemptuously. "Worse luck. He could have hurt you or Mary Margaret."

"He could have *killed* you," Linette retorted.

"Nah." Hunter shook his head, then grinned at her. "He wasn't good enough."

Linette cast an exasperated look at him. There was blood trickling from the corner of his mouth, and his cheek was red, his eye beginning to swell. Another cut above his eye dribbled blood down his face.

Linette pulled out a handkerchief from her pocket and wiped away the blood from Hunter's face. He winced and reached up to take her hand.

"Not so rough! You'll finish off the job *he* started," he told her.

"Don't whine," Linette told him, making a face. Then she saw the front expanse of his shirt, which his upraised arm had exposed. "Hunter! Oh, my God, you're bleeding! He stabbed you."

"No, it's just a scrape," he protested, but Linette was already ripping his shirt away to expose the wound, and she gasped at the sight of his bloody side.

"Hunter!"

"It's not as bad as it looks. It just bled a little." Hunter looked down at the top of Linette's head. In truth, he had suffered worse wounds, and it really was not as painful as the marks on his face. But there was something quite satisfying about the look of concern on Linette's face and the gentle way she dabbed away the blood.

Carefully wiping his skin, she could see that it was not bleeding profusely and although it was more than a scratch, as Hunter had maintained, it was not an excessively long or deep cut. She breathed a sigh of relief.

"Still, I need to dress it. Come." She slid an arm around his waist on the uninjured side. "Let's go back and patch you up."

Hunter leaned against her very slightly. That, too, was unnecessary, but he found it comfortable. They walked slowly back toward the hotel, Mary Margaret dancing along beside them. Hunter bent his head and said reassuringly, "The danger's over, Linette. Let's forget about it. Just think about what's ahead of us: Texas . . . and finding our daughter."

20

The sea trip to Texas was long and tedious, taking almost a full week. The first couple of days out, Linette was plagued with seasickness, and she kept to her cabin, trying to ride it out. Mary Margaret, who experienced not even the slightest bit of upset stomach, looked after Linette solicitously, bringing a cool wet rag to wash her face and soothe her brow. The young girl entertained her with stories while Linette grew bored lying in her narrow bunk, and sat quietly when Linette napped. She offered to bring food to Linette from her meals, too, but that kind service Linette adamantly refused.

The nausea gradually subsided, and Linette ventured up on deck and even to the meals. But there was little else to do aboard the ship. It was a small vessel, and there were only two passengers besides themselves, both of them men. One was a newly

ordained minister going to take over a flock in a small
town north of Galveston, and the other was a seedy-
looking character who said little. Linette had no
interest in talking to either of them, and they
appeared to avoid her just as assiduously, which
meant that Hunter and Mary Margaret were her only
companions. And aside from talking to them or walking endlessly around the deck, there was nothing to
do. She hadn't even a book or a bit of sewing to
occupy her.

She was grateful for Mary Margaret, who was a
taking little thing. Her good humor rarely failed her,
and she had a funny way of talking that made Linette
laugh. She could imitate people to perfection and
often amused Linette with portrayals of the sisters at
the orphanage or the captain of the ship or even
Hunter or herself. She had a vast store of humorous
or fantastical stories told her by her father or about
her father, and she was apt to drop in outrageous
comments on almost any conversation. Linette was
never sure what she was going to say, but it was a
given that it would liven things up. Mary Margaret
was thirsty for knowledge and as full of questions as
she was of stories, and she kept Linette on her toes,
trying to come up with answers.

Linette spent most of her time with the child, and
she found herself growing more and more fond of her
every day. She could understand why the sober nuns
at the orphanage found Mary Margaret a trial.
Looking after her was quite a task, for she was never
sure what the child would take into her head to do
next. Whenever Mary Margaret was out of sight,

Linette began to worry about what she was doing and would soon go in search of her. She usually found her plaguing the crew with questions or exploring the ship, and more than once she gave Linette a real scare by climbing the rigging or venturing down into the dark hold. But she was always contrite about worrying Linette, and her quick, sunny smile made Linette abandon her stern lectures halfway through. It was impossible to remain angry or even irritated with the girl long.

Unfortunately, it was not nearly as easy to be with Hunter, which, given the circumstances, Linette was obliged to be much of the time. Just as Linette had feared, it was more difficult being around him here than it had been back in the hotel in New Orleans. They could not escape each other easily, except to retire to their cabins, and since these were both quite cramped, neither of them could bear to spend much time there. They ran into each other on deck often. Sometimes they sat, and sometimes they took a stroll around the deck; at other times, they simply stood by the railing and watched the limitless expanse of the sea around them. Whatever they did, they could not help but be acutely aware of each other—and of everything that had passed between them.

Linette could not keep her mind off the night they had made love, much as she tried, and she was afraid that it often showed in her face. She hoped that Hunter didn't notice it, yet she could not imagine how he could not. All her memories of him seemed to be tangled up in passion, whether they were recent or old, and it did little good to try to keep her mind in the present, for just being beside him stirred up vivid, compelling sensations of desire. Everything about him was lethally attractive, from his slow smile to his piercing green eyes to his supple hands, weathered by work and sun.

One evening, halfway through their voyage, Hunter was standing beside Linette at the railing, watching the night sky over the sea. The air was balmy and tangy with the scent of the ocean. A breeze caressed their faces and lifted tendrils of hair from Linette's cheek. Hunter leaned against the railing, his eyes more on Linette than on the horizon before them.

Almost conversationally, he said, "I think you are the most beautiful woman I've ever known."

Startled, Linette glanced at him. "What?" Then she blushed. "Hunter, really . . ."

He shrugged. "I'm just stating a fact. You must know it. I'm sure more men than I have told you."

"It's a nuisance more than anything. When I was young, I enjoyed it." A small smile played about her lips, and her eyes got a distant look to them. "I loved to walk into a party and see the men turn and look at me. I liked to flirt and hear their pretty compliments."

"I remember."

Her gaze returned sharply to his face. "You weren't one who favored me with them."

"I didn't figure you needed them from me. I'd already laid my heart at your feet."

Her gaze did not waver. "I think that's when I grew tired of compliments."

The air was suddenly charged between them. Linette felt as if something were crushing the air from her chest; she could not look away from Hunter. Some remaining element of common sense kept her from moving closer to him, as she longed to do, but another force, equally strong, would not let her turn away from him, either.

"When I was in that Yankee prison," Hunter said, his voice raw with emotion, "you were what I thought of. You were what kept me from going crazy. I'd remember every inch of your face, the way you smiled, the way your eyes looked in sunlight, clear and blue, or in candlelight, when they were dark and mysterious and beckoning."

"Hunter . . ." Linette protested breathlessly.

"I'd get myself through whatever happened by telling myself that that was the only way I'd see you again. I made plans how I'd kiss you, undress you, take you into my bed."

His low-pitched words made Linette quiver inside. She wanted desperately to kiss him, yet she knew it would be an awful mistake if she did. Hunter would only reject her again, as he had after that other night. But her body stubbornly paid no heed to the thought of hurt ahead; it only yearned for its pleasure.

Hunter reached out and softly stroked his knuckles down Linette's cheek. Her skin was as soft as down, her face so beautiful it made his heart hurt. "I was so crazy-jealous when I came back and found out you'd married someone else. I thought you didn't love me, had never loved me, that I'd been deluding myself all those years."

"I didn't stop loving you," Linette whispered in reply, her eyes glowing, unaware of how much she revealed with that statement.

"Linette . . ." Her name was a sigh on his lips. Hunter closed the distance between them in a step, and his arms went around her tightly. Linette's head fell back, her face lifting for his kiss.

Hunter's mouth came down on hers, the pent-up hunger of the past days flooding into his kiss. His lips dug into hers, his tongue taking her mouth. Linette answered his kiss eagerly. Suddenly they were aflame, their bodies straining against each other. Hunter dug his hand into her hair, and it tumbled loose from its pins, spilling over his hand. The silken feel of it enflamed him even more, and he clenched his fingers around the strands, luxuriating in their softness. He felt as if he were falling, spinning downward in a vortex of passion, forever lost in her spell.

With an oath he pulled away from her. "No! Dammit, we can't do this!"

He stood for a moment, everything within him aching to return to her arms, to seize that sweet mouth again. But all the impossibilities of their situation pounded in his brain, too, holding him back. Furiously he turned away, wishing that he could swing out and break something.

"I'm sorry," he growled. "I should never have done that."

He strode away rapidly, leaving Linette standing limply by the railing, staring after him.

*   *   *

After that evening, the tension was thick between Linette and Hunter. They could not be comfortable together, indeed, could hardly even look at each other. Yet at the same time, they were extremely aware of the other one—where they were, what they were doing, what they said. The days on the ship seemed to go on forever, and Linette's nerves felt as if they were stretched taut as wires. Judging from Hunter's silences and snapped comments, Linette suspected that his nerves were in much the same shape. Even Mary Margaret began to find it difficult to get a smile out of either one of them.

It was a great relief for everyone when their ship docked in Galveston, and they were at last able to leave. Linette and Mary Margaret, who had pictured all of Texas as a sort of wild wasteland, were amazed by the city of Galveston. A busy port, it was a bustling metropolis of almost fourteen thousand people, and its business district, known as the Strand, contained many elegant buildings, most of them decorated with graceful wrought-iron balconies and columns. They spent much of the afternoon walking about the town, getting back their land legs and reveling in their new freedom to roam.

After a night spent there, their party started out the next morning, taking the ferry across from the island on which Galveston was located to the mainland of Texas. The stagecoach trip across Texas was hot, dusty, and seemingly endless, across miles of flat coastal plain, and required numerous changes in the horses at the way stations and sleeping at inns along the way. Linette had never dreamed that the remainder of their journey could take so long. She had thought that once they were in Texas, they would almost be in the town of Fredericksburg. Instead, it took them day after long, dreary day to reach it. The fact that she was cooped up in a stagecoach with Hunter and the active Mary Margaret made the trip seem even longer.

No doubt Hunter had been right when he said that the stage was a more practical way to travel with Mary Margaret accompanying them, but Linette found herself longing for the freedom and speed of riding her horse instead. She would be glad when they finally reached San Antonio, where Hunter planned to hire horses for them for the remainder of the trip north to Fredericksburg.

The last night before they reached San Antonio, the stage stopped at a cozy inn in Seguin, an improvement over most of the other way stations they had stayed at. A smiling woman welcomed them into the inn, handing Hunter the register to sign in.

"Well, Mr. . . . Tyrrell," she greeted him cheerfully, craning her neck around to read his name. "Pleased to meet you. I'm Jewel Brown, the owner's wife. Thank goodness we've got a room left for you and the missus." Everyone they met presumed that the three of them were a family, and they found it easier to go along with the impression than to try to explain.

But at the woman's words now Linette stirred uneasily. "What?"

"I know. It seems plumb unbelievable, don't it, that we could be so full up? Half the time it seems like we're lucky to get three rooms occupied, but tonight, we're just bursting at the seams. Part of it's the dance tonight, I reckon. Some folks come in from ranches so far away, they have to stay the night. Round here, nobody likes to miss a dance. You all are welcome to come to it, too. It's down by the river."

Linette and Hunter looked at each other, hardly hearing the woman's stream of words. Hunter cleared his throat. "Well, actually, we need two rooms."

"Oh. For the little girl? That's all right; she can stay with my own children over at the house. We've got my brother and his wife and their young 'uns staying with us over at the house, so we're sticking all the children on pallets in one room. It's like a regular bunkhouse, and the young 'uns love it." Mrs. Brown paused for breath and looked at Mary Margaret. "Would you like that, missy? Having a little party with the other kids?"

Mary Margaret's face lit up. "Oh, yes, ma'am!" She turned excitedly toward Linette and Hunter. "Can I? I mean, may I? Please? I promise I'll be good."

"Well . . ." Linette wavered. She couldn't bear to say no, looking at Mary Margaret's excited face. But without her there, Linette and Hunter would be stuck in a room together.

"My brother's oldest girl'll be looking after them," the innkeeper's wife assured them. "She'll take them away from the dance early and put them to bed. There's no harm in it."

"Please?" Mary Margaret clasped her hands in entreaty.

"All right." Linette couldn't refuse her. But what were she and Hunter going to do?

Mrs. Brown showed them to their room, continuing to chatter about the dance that night. "You will come, won't you?" she asked, stopping outside their door and bending down to insert the key in it. "Don't feel shy. There aren't any strangers at this dance."

"Well, I really don't have any clothes that are proper to wear for a dance," Linette demurred.

"Oh, that don't make no never mind!" the woman said gaily. "We ain't all fancy here. What you got on'll do just fine, I promise you."

"Perhaps we will." Hunter gave Mrs. Brown a brief smile.

"Good!" She turned the key and pushed back the door with a flourish. "Well, I'll leave you to clean up, then." She turned to Mary Margaret. "You can come along with me, missy, if you want. I'll take you over and introduce you to my young 'uns."

The matron bustled away with Mary Margaret in tow, leaving Linette and Hunter standing awkwardly in the doorway of the open room. Linette hesitated, then walked into the room. Hunter followed her, setting down their bags and closing the door after him. Linette found that she could not look at Hunter. Instead, she glanced around the small room, which seemed, at least to her eyes, to be filled by the four-poster bed, piled high with down mattresses and covered by a colorful quilt.

How were they going to spend the night here together? she wondered. Somehow it seemed so much more intimate than sleeping close together in the open, each wound up inside his or her own blanket and with the open country all around them. Here the very room seemed to press in upon them, binding them together in an atmosphere of intimacy.

"Don't worry," Hunter said quickly. "I won't sleep here."

"But where will you go?" Linette glanced at him in surprise. "She said all the rooms were taken."

Hunter shrugged. "I don't know. The barn, maybe, out under the trees if I have to. I've slept outside before, as you may remember."

"Well, yes, but what if someone sees you? It will seem awfully peculiar."

"I'll make up some excuse—say you and I had a fight and you kicked me out." His eyes twinkled. "Anyway, what does it matter? We'll never see any of these people again. Who cares what they think of us?"

Linette started to protest that she felt guilty about sleeping inside on a comfortable bed while he lay on the ground or in the barn outside, but then she realized that she might sound as if she *wanted* him to sleep here in the room with her. So she kept her mouth shut. She wasn't about to give Hunter cause to think that she was so filled with desire for him that she wanted to lure him into her bed.

"You're right," she said coolly and walked over to the washstand. She still felt a little uncomfortable with Hunter in the room, but there was nothing she could do about it. He could hardly go out and hang around in the barn now. And he had seen her do such personal things as wash her face or brush her hair many times now; it was nothing new except for the location.

Hunter sat down in the only chair in the room, watching Linette as she poured a bit of water in the washbowl and wet a rag in it to wash the dust of the road from her face and hands. It *was* something that he had seen several times before, but he found that it still didn't leave him wholly unaffected. Besides, there was something very different about watching her do it here in the suggestive environment of a bedroom. Hunter stirred in his seat and tried to think of something else to occupy his mind.

Linette unbuttoned the top two buttons of her blouse to wash her neck, as well. Hunter's eyes followed the path of her rag over her jaw and down onto her throat. He remembered the feel of that supremely soft skin beneath his lips, and heat flared in his abdomen.

"Shall we go to the dance?" he blurted, seizing on the first thing he could come up with.

Linette turned and looked at him, a little surprised. "I don't know. I hadn't really considered it." She thought about being at a dance with Hunter again, and she didn't like the excitement that ran through her at the idea. "I—I'm rather tired."

"Yes, I suppose." He paused, then said. "But it might be better than being cooped up in here all evening."

"Oh." Linette was struck by the wisdom of his words. It would be exceedingly awkward to spend the evening with Hunter in this room, with only one chair and the bed to sit on, waiting for it to be late enough that he could go outside to sleep. It would be better to be at a dance, surrounded by other people, with something to do besides think about Hunter and the bed. "That's true. Perhaps we should. But . . ." She looked down at her travel-stained skirt and blouse.

"Mrs. Brown was telling the truth: people are much more informal out here. You won't find women in ball gowns there tonight. They won't think anything amiss about you wearing something plain."

"Well, I do have a clean skirt and blouse in my bag. That is, if you don't mind going with someone who looks like a Quaker."

Hunter let out a little snort of amusement. "You could *never* look like a Quaker."

Linette flashed him a smile that always had a devastating effect on him. "I'll take that as a compliment."

Linette pulled her skirt and blouse, a plain blue one with a single ruffle down the front, out of the carpetbag and looked at them critically. They were far too wrinkled to wear. "I'll need to press them."

"Why don't you take them down and see what you can get done for them?" Hunter suggested. "I'll get cleaned up and dressed, and then I can take a walk and smoke a cigar while you're getting ready."

"All right." That arrangement would solve the problem of their being in the room together until the dance. She dug out Mary Margaret's Sunday dress, as well as a nightgown and underthings for the child, then bundled them up with her clean clothes and went to look for Mrs. Brown.

Linette found herself feeling lighter and happier by the moment; it would be rather fun to go to a dance.

It seemed so long since she had done anything just for fun.

Linette found Mrs. Brown downstairs, once again behind the front desk, and explained her problem with the clothes. Mrs. Brown immediately whisked the skirt and blouse from Linette's hands.

"I'll have them all pressed within the hour, and I'll send one of the girls up to your room with them," she promised.

"Oh, I can wait for them," Linette offered quickly. She had to stay out of the room to give Hunter time to clean up and change. "I need to give Mary Margaret her dress and these things, anyway."

"That's where I'm going right now; I'll just take them to her. What you ought to do is go right back upstairs and take a little nap. That's the thing—rest up for the dance tonight."

Linette smiled. If she hadn't known better, she would have thought that the woman was trying to thwart her plans to give Hunter some privacy. "Perhaps I will. But first I think I'll stretch my legs a little, take a walk around the yard."

The other woman looked doubtful. "We don't rightly have a garden, ma'am. There's just the yard between here and the stables, and that's not really fit for a lady to be walking in."

Linette was beginning to wonder if she would have to while away the next few minutes just sitting on the stairs waiting for Hunter to emerge, but then Mrs. Brown smiled. "But there's a little bit of grass in front of our house. If you want to come with me, you can see that your daughter's all settled in right and tight and then you can take a little stroll around our yard."

So Linette followed the woman to the white limestone house next door to the inn, half listening to Mrs. Brown's cheerful chatter. There she found Mary Margaret playing tag with the other children in the yard, so she sat on the porch for a few minutes and watched them, then took a short walk and returned to her room.

When she opened the door and stepped into the room, Linette found Hunter standing before the washstand mirror, shaving, wearing only a pair of trousers. Linette stopped abruptly, and a blush spread up her face.

"I'm sorry. I guess I didn't allow enough time. I didn't think about your having to shave."

Hunter shrugged. "Come on in. It doesn't matter." He grinned at her in the mirror. "Leastways I'm decent now."

Linette, looking at the bare expanse of his tanned, muscled back, wasn't at all sure of the accuracy of that remark. Hunter looked entirely too good without a shirt on to be called decent. However, she could hardly say as much without embarrassing herself, so she put on an air of nonchalance and strolled over to the chair, trying not to look at Hunter.

She couldn't help it, though. It fascinated her to watch him shave. There was something viscerally exciting about watching him move the razor smoothly down his cheek, something very masculine and almost mysterious, like a secret male rite. She thought about what it would have been like to have been here and watched him wash, too—the rag in his supple hand moving over his bare skin, sliding over the curve of muscle, the flat plane of his stomach, dampening the hair on his chest so that it glistened and curled . . .

Linette's breath caught in her throat, and she realized that she was staring at him. Had he noticed? Had he seen the raw desire on her face? It would be most embarrassing; Hunter always seemed to be able to keep his own passion perfectly under control. She looked down, concentrating on the braided rug beside the bed.

"Uh, I saw Mary Margaret. She was playing with Mrs. Brown's children and having a fine time."

"Good. No doubt it's boring for her being around adults constantly . . . and all this traveling must be hard on her." Hunter tilted back his head and stroked the razor up his neck, unaware of the way his movements drew Linette's eyes.

"Yes. It'll be nice when we get Julia; the two of them can play together."

"Then you're planning on keeping Mary Margaret?"

"What else would I do with her?" Linette looked at him, startled. "I could hardly just abandon her here."

"I know. But I mean, after you take Julia back. Are you going to raise Mary Margaret, too?"

"I hadn't thought about it but, yes, I'm sure I will."

"My mother would probably be willing to take her."

"But I'm not sure I'd be willing to give her up," Linette admitted almost ruefully. "She's such a taking little thing, and I don't think she ever really means to commit any mischief, whatever those nuns thought. Well, I think I'm coming to love the child."

Hunter cast her another grin in the mirror. "I think it would be hard *not* to fall in love with her—even though there are times when she's enough to turn your hair gray, like when I found her climbing up the mast on the ship."

Linette chuckled, although at the time the incident had put her heart in her throat. Hunter paused and his face sobered. He cast a sideways glance at Linette, then went on carefully, "Linette . . ."

"What?" Linette stiffened. There was something odd and hesitant about his voice.

"What if—well, I've wondered: when we find Julia, what if she's happy? What if she doesn't want to come with us?"

"No!" Linette clasped her hands tightly together in her lap and regarded him suspiciously. "I'm her mother! We're her real parents. Of course, she'll want to come."

"But she doesn't know us," he reminded her gently. He had finished shaving, and he wiped the remaining soap from his face, then came over to Linette and knelt beside her chair. He took her hands in his and looked earnestly into her face. "Not every orphan is unhappy, you know; some people take them merely to get a free servant, but not everyone. She was just a baby when they got her. What if they treated her like their own child? What if they've been kind and good to her?"

Panic and fear enveloped Linette's face. "Hunter!

She's mine! She doesn't belong to them. I've mourned her all these years. Don't you understand? However that woman's treated her, she's not her mother; I am! Are you backing out on me now? Are you saying you're willing to just ride away and leave her there?"

"No. No. Calm down, sweetheart." The endearment slipped past his lips without his noticing. Hunter looked into Linette's distraught face; her eyes were huge and filling with tears. He pulled her to him, though she was stiff and resisting in his arms. "Don't fret. I won't let you down; I promise. When we find Julia, you'll have her back—even if I have to steal her from them."

Linette's arms went around him convulsively, and she clung to him. "I knew I could trust you. I knew I could count on you."

"You can. Always."

21

At first all Linette was aware of was the warmth and security of Hunter's arms, the wonderful feeling of trust after the soul-shaking fear his earlier words had brought up in her. She could rely on Hunter. He might argue, might curse or storm, his green eyes blazing; he might even regard her with scorn and hatred, as he had the last few years, his bitter anger making him refuse to listen to her. But she could rely on him; he would always be there for her, and he would not lie, would not manipulate her for his own purposes. Hunter was direct, honest, his feelings real and true. He belonged to her, as she belonged to him, in a basic, fundamental way that not all the years in between had altered. Linette knew that he would do anything for her, just as she would do anything for him, no matter how much they might try to deny or hide from that fact.

Linette knew that she loved him. She had never stopped loving him, hard as she had tried to get over him, and Linette knew that she would never stop loving him. All those years he had been away, she had been dead inside; robbed of those she loved, she had drifted in emptiness. Yet when Hunter had come back into her life, she had started to live again. She knew that there was no life for her without him.

Deep inside, Linette was certain that he loved her, too. She had felt it, known it viscerally that night when they made love. They were too much a part of each other for it to be any other way. Hunter might not want to accept it, but it was the truth. He was simply too scared of laying himself open to hurt again to admit it. The pain had scarred him so that he did not dare feel again.

But he could not contain the passion inside him. He could not overcome the love he still felt for her. It boiled up in him again and again . . . every time she saw that hot look in his eye, every time he could not hold back from kissing her, every time he laughed with her over a shared joke or took her in his arms to comfort her. His love for her was there, she was certain of it, merely imprisoned beneath Hunter's doubts and fears. Eventually it would grow strong enough to overcome everything else. She just had to wait, and some day Hunter would be hers just as surely as she was his.

Even as she rested here in his arms, Linette could feel the heat rising in Hunter's flesh. He wanted her, and that desire would bring him back to her. The thought started a flickering flame deep in her own abdomen, and a sensual smile curved her lips. She wanted him every bit as much as he wanted her, and it would be pure pleasure to evoke that desire in Hunter. The bare skin of his chest was beneath her cheek; her eyelashes brushed against it, and she felt his tremor in response to her movement.

"Oh, Hunter." Her breath touched his skin. She rubbed her cheek against his chest, as sensual and direct as a cat. Hunter jumped, and his skin was suddenly as hot as fire.

He stood up quickly, pulling Linette with him, and stepped back from her, breaking their embrace. Linette looked up at him. His face was flushed beneath its tan, his eyes glittering. He gazed at her for a moment, frustration and desire in every line of his body. Then, with a sound of exasperation, he whirled around and walked away from her. Silently, with quick, angry movements, he jammed his arms into his shirt and buttoned it up.

"Hunter?" Linette asked worriedly. "Are you angry at me?"

"No," he replied tersely, not looking at her. "You're not responsible for the effect you have on me." He fastened his cuffs. "But I think it's better if I get out of here right now."

Linette made no comment, just turned away politely and looked out their window with feigned interest while Hunter finished dressing. But, after a few minutes, an irritated oath from across the room made her jump and look over at him. Glaring, Hunter threw a black string tie down on the bed in disgust.

Linette smothered a giggle. "Would you like some help?"

He cast one fulminating glance at her and said shortly, "Yes." After a moment's pause, he added, "Please."

Linette came around the bed and stopped before him. Only inches away from him, she reached up with nimble fingers and tied the recalcitrant tie. Then she adjusted the loops, making sure that they lay down flat. She looked up into Hunter's face as she did so. He was staring stonily in front of him, not looking at her. Smiling a little to herself, Linette did not hurry about her task. Finally she completed it and stepped back, giving her handiwork a considering look.

"There. I think that's done it." There was very little to a string tie, after all, other than making sure the loops were even and not crooked. Hunter must have been distracted indeed not to have been able to do it properly.

"Thank you." He looked anything but grateful. Grabbing his jacket, he shrugged into it, then picked up his hat and strode to the door. "I'll wait for you downstairs."

Linette nodded, not permitting herself to grin until after he had left the room. She brushed her hair and put it up into a smooth chignon that was most becoming to her even features. She pulled on her clean underthings, but since no one had brought her pressed skirt and blouse, she could not finish dressing. Wrapping a robe around her, she waited, wondering if she would have to put on the clothes she had been wearing to go search for her clean ones.

Just then there was a knock on her door, and when she opened it, to her surprise, she found Mrs. Brown herself at the door.

"Sorry." The woman bustled inside, carrying a blue dress. Linette glanced curiously at the gown, which was most assuredly not her skirt and blouse. "But just as Maisie was finished pressing your blouse, I had the most wonderful thought! I have some dresses you could wear."

Linette gazed at her blankly.

Mrs. Brown chuckled, saying, "I know, I know. You're thinking anything of mine would hang upon you, and so it would—now. But I used to be much smaller, and I kept some of my prettier dresses. It might be a wee bit large on you, but you could pull the sash a little tighter, and it won't make the slightest difference. I would have let you choose, but there wasn't time, so I just pulled out this blue one—I remembered how pretty and blue your eyes are, you see—and had Maisie press it, too."

"But that's too much to ask of you," Linette protested.

Mrs. Brown waved that objection away. "Now, don't you worry about that. I wouldn't have offered if I didn't want to." She spread the blue dress out on the bed, then laid Linette's blouse and skirt, which she had carried beneath the dress, beside it. "Well, what do you think?"

Linette looked down at the bed. The blue dress was simple, but pretty, a frivolous party dress with little cap sleeves and a low neckline. It was a few years out of style, but next to the plain skirt and blouse, it looked beautiful.

"Why, Mrs. Brown!" she exclaimed. "It's lovely. I don't know what to say. You are too generous. Hunter said that the people out here were friendly, but I had no idea—"

Mrs. Brown laughed merrily. "Well, he's right about that. We believe in helping each other out. Out here, you have to, you know. So you just wear that dress tonight and have a wonderful time at the dance."

Linette nodded and smiled. "Yes. I will. And thank you so much."

Gratified, the older woman nodded her head. "Well, I best run back to the house and get dressed myself or my Jim and I'll be late to the dance."

She left, and Linette turned back to the bed, picking up the blue dress. She pulled it over her head and buttoned the little buttons up the front, pulling the sash tightly so that it fit her waist. Then she looked at her reflection in the mirror, twisting this way and that to see herself from every angle. She smiled, satisfied with what she saw.

The dress fit her nicely, the wide sash with its big butterfly bow in back emphasizing her small waist, and its blue color matched her eyes and set off her fair complexion and auburn hair to perfection. The dainty puffed sleeves showed off her slender arms, and the scoop neckline revealed as much as was decent of her chest, skimming over the tops of her creamy breasts. She looked, she thought, better than she had in years, glowing with life and joy.

Linette waltzed around the room in sheer exuberance. In a few days she would be reunited with her daughter. And tonight she was going to a dance with the man she loved! She intended to dance all night and flirt with Hunter shamelessly. She wasn't sure how Hunter would react, but she knew that she was looking forward to finding out.

Linette swept out of the room and down the stairs into the entryway. Hunter lounged beside the front door, looking out the glass side panel, his back to her. At the sound of her footsteps on the stairs, he turned and glanced up at her. Linette remembered that first night when she had met him, and she stopped abruptly, her heart suddenly in her throat. Hunter's eyes widened as he took her in, and he came forward to the foot of the stairs, gazing up at her in a slightly stunned way.

"Linette . . ."

She smiled dazzlingly at him and came down the last few steps, holding out her hands to him. He gripped them tightly. "You look—how—where did you get that dress?"

"Mrs. Brown lent it to me. I'm afraid it's a little old-fashioned, but I thought it was a vast improvement over my skirt and blouse."

"You look lovely." He had regained control of his voice, and the expression on his face was once again carefully neutral. But as Linette took his arm and walked out the door with him, she could feel the tautness in it, the rigid control, and she knew that he was not unaffected by her appearance.

The air was warm and enveloping, but a delightful

breeze fanned their cheeks, making the evening pleasant. Bright stars dotted the dark sky, and a full, white moon hung overhead, casting a pale wash of light over everything. It seemed to Linette a magical night, full of promise and mystery.

She glanced up at Hunter and found him watching her. She smiled. "I'm looking forward to this. Aren't you? It seems like forever since I've enjoyed a dance."

"Yes," Hunter replied, a little reluctantly. "I am looking forward to it. I want . . . to dance with you again."

At his words, the glow of her eyes put the moon to shame. Hunter sucked in his breath, but he said nothing, and neither did she.

The dance was held in a clearing beside the Guadalupe River. Lanterns had been strung between trees, and they cast a golden glow over the scene. Three men played fiddle, banjo, and harmonica in a lively way, and already several people danced on the hard-packed dirt that made up the makeshift dance floor. More people were arriving all the time, walking as Linette and Hunter did or pulling up in buggies or on horseback. All around the edges of the dancing, people stood in knots, conversing, and farther back, deeper beneath the trees, a group of men stood, smoking cigars and pipes, and now and then a jug passed between them.

The song ended, and the musicians swung into a waltz. Hunter moved to the edge of the dancers and turned to face Linette, holding out his hand to her. Linette drew a shaky breath, wanting to cry and laugh and smile all at the same time. She took his hand, letting him pull her into the moving crowd. His other hand went to her waist, drawing her closer, and they began to waltz.

It might have been only yesterday that they had last danced, they moved so naturally together. It seemed to Hunter that Linette fit into his arms the way no other woman ever had. She was not small and delicate, yet not as tall as his sister, either. She was a sweetly rounded armful, not all pillowy soft or full of angles. He could not keep from thinking about that first night when he had watched her descend the stairs in Tess's house, and he had fallen suddenly, helplessly in love with her. He had hidden it from her then, just as he had hidden his awe this evening when she joined him at the foot of the stairs.

She was beautiful, and she stirred him in every way imaginable. He wanted to press her tightly against him and kiss her. He wanted to feel her soft and pliant in his arms, her mouth opening its hot secrets to him. Nothing had ever tasted as sweet as Linette's kisses, and he could not keep his mind off them now. He felt himself hardening and pulsing in response to her nearness. He wondered how he would ever make it through the evening, and yet he knew that he wouldn't leave, even if he could.

They danced all through the evening. Linette was effervescent with happiness and excitement, and she flirted merrily with Hunter, as bright and sparkling as crystal. She could not remember when she had felt so alive as she did this night, so pounding with love and joy and desire. She wanted Hunter, and she could feel his desire every time they touched, every time he looked at her.

When the dance was over, they strolled back to the hotel. Hunter's hand was searing on her back, and the air between them was thick with sexual tension. Linette's breath was fast and irregular, and she could feel her nerves tightening with every step. She cast a glance up at Hunter. His face was taut, his eyes hot. Linette looked back in front of her, her heart pounding even harder than before.

They entered the hotel and walked up the staircase. Linette's senses were heightened; she was very aware of the swish of her skirts on the stairs, the glossy smooth wood of the rail under her hand, the mellow glow of the oil lamp in the entryway below. They reached their door, and Hunter unlocked it, stepping aside to let Linette enter. He came in after her and closed the door. Linette glanced over her shoulder at him.

He stood against the door, watching her. Now, she thought, was when he should offer to leave, giving her the room to herself. Silently she prayed that he would not. They stood for a moment, their eyes locked. Slowly Hunter walked towards her. He stopped only inches from her, and she tilted her head up to look at him.

Hunter reached slowly to the nape of her neck to remove the hairpins from her chignon, his eyes continuing to stare steadily into hers. Linette's breath caught in her throat. The heavy knot of her hair came apart, sliding silkily over his fingers, and Hunter's eyes darkened at its touch.

"I shouldn't do this," he murmured.

Linette gazed at him, her eyes glowing. "Yes," she

whispered back, "you should. There can't be any other way with us."

He let out a funny noise, half sigh, half groan, and his mouth came down on hers. His kiss was hot and demanding, his lips digging into hers fiercely, and his arms went around her tightly, pressing her into his hard body. Linette kissed him back, her mouth as avid as his. She felt as if she had been starved for the taste of him. The scent of his skin was in her nostrils, his heat enveloping her, and she made a whimpering noise in the back of her throat, lost in the delight of being in his arms. She ran her hands down his chest, his hot, smooth skin beneath the cloth of his shirt. She could feel the hard buttons of his masculine nipples, and she circled them with her thumbs, as she had felt him do with her. His muscles jumped beneath her hands, and his kiss turned even more fierce.

Finally, he broke off their kiss and released her. Gazing down into her face, he began to unbutton her dress. Linette shivered at his touch, heat coursing through her veins. The buttons seemed to take forever, and by the time he was finished, both of them were on fire. Hunter pushed her dress back over her shoulders and down, and it pooled about her feet. He gazed at the white expanse of Linette's chest and below that the delicate white cotton camisole cupping her breasts. Her nipples were dark circles through the thin cloth, and as he looked, they hardened and pushed against the material, arousing him even more. He reached down and untied the strings of her petticoats, and they fell in a heap atop her dress. He looked down at her abdomen and legs, encased in the lace-trimmed pantalettes.

"You are so beautiful," he told her hoarsely, his eyes feasting on her.

Heat thrummed in Linette's abdomen, pooling between her legs. She longed to feel his touch.

Hunter's hand came up and cupped her breasts, his thumbs brushing over her nipples. They grew even tauter in response, hard and yearning. Hunter tugged at the bow that tied her camisole, and it opened, the material parting to expose the soft swell of her breasts. He unbuttoned it and pushed it open, gazing at her bare breasts, full and white, pink-crowned with her engorged nipples. Hunter swallowed and took her breasts gently in his hands, caressing them with loving slowness. Linette trembled beneath his touch, moisture flooding between her legs. She ached for him to touch her there, too, and unconsciously she moved closer to him, stretching up toward him.

He crushed her to him, seizing her lips in a bruising kiss. He picked her up and carried her to the bed, laying her tenderly down upon it. Quickly he stripped off his own shirt, revealing his lean brown body, hard and ready for her. Linette's eyes drifted down over his muscled chest and arms to the flat expanse of his stomach and the thrusting evidence of his desire. Her mouth softened with passion as she gazed at him naked, and the hungry expression on her face fed Hunter's desire. He bent over her, kissing her again, then trailing his mouth down the tender skin of her throat and onto her chest, finally reaching her breasts. With a groan, he curved his fingers around her breasts and bent to kiss one luscious mound. His mouth moved slowly over the pillow-softness of her breast until it reached the hardened nipple. He took it in his mouth, his tongue teasing it into a tight, hard point. His tongue stroked over the bud, sending Linette into a frenzy of desire. She moaned, moving her legs restlessly on the bed.

As he suckled her breast, his hand slid down her body onto the cotton of her pantalettes and still farther down to where her legs joined. His fingers caressed her through the cotton, dampened by her passion, and Linette sucked in her breath, clamping her legs around his hand. He continued to stroke her until her hips began to circle impatiently, thrusting up off the bed against his hand.

He released her then, raising his head from her breast, and reached down to take off her slippers and drop them on the floor. Then he reached up under her pantalettes and took off her garters, rolling the stockings down her calves and off her feet. At last, he unfastened the drawstring of her undergarment and pulled the pantalettes downward, so that she was, finally, naked to his gaze. For a long moment, he studied her naked beauty, and then he climbed on the bed, straddling her.

Linette gazed up at his powerful nude body, heat flushing her body. She reached out and laid her hands on his legs and slid them upward, delighting in the feel of his hair-roughened skin. Hunter sucked in a breath, but said nothing. He just watched her, eyes glittering, as her hands traveled up his legs to the satiny flesh of his abdomen, skimming teasingly around, but not touching, the hot, pulsing shaft. He bent over her, allowing her hands to caress the muscled skin of his chest, exploring and teasing, arousing him almost past reason.

He bent and took her other breast in his mouth as she caressed him, and his own hands were hungrily moving over her body. He slipped down to the thatch of hair between her legs, tangling his fingers in it and drawing a gasp of desire from Linette. Tenderly his fingers slid between her legs, stroking the hot, satiny flesh of her womanhood. Linette let out a soft cry, arching up, and he gave a rich chuckle of masculine satisfaction, separating and stroking the slick folds, finding the hidden nub that gave the most exquisite pleasure and caressing it.

His mouth trailed down her body, following the path of his hands. Linette's hands fell away from his body as her own body surged with pleasure, and she dug her fingers into the sheets, rolling her head restlessly against the bed and sobbing under the force of the desire building up relentlessly in her body. She jerked, amazed yet delighted as his mouth found her most intimate place and began to feast on it. Her breath came in jerky gasps as his tongue worked at her, and she moaned and sighed, tossing on a storm of sexual pleasure. The pressure within her built and built, turning her to trembling fire, until finally she exploded with pleasure. Waves of passion pulsed out from her abdomen, sweeping over her body and suffusing her with intense heat. She cried out, her body jerking as she gave herself up entirely to passion.

Linette lay stunned for a long moment, luxuriating in the bone-melting satisfaction that crept through her body. She turned her head and gazed at Hunter, her eyes glowing. "Oh, Hunter . . ."

Then her eyes went down to his still-engorged manhood, and they widened a little. "Oh," she breathed guiltily, "but you . . . what . . ."

"Don't worry, I shall have my pleasure." He stroked his hand over her cheek.

"But I have been so selfish." She reached out tentatively and brushed her fingers around the base of his shaft.

Hunter closed his eyes, a soft groan escaping his lips. "Hardly. Believe me, my love, I enjoyed watching you come to your peak. Quite selfishly, I'd like to see you do it again."

He gently circled her breast with his fingertips. "And if you would just touch me again, I'll guarantee I'll reach my own satisfaction."

Obediently, Linette curled her fingers around his manhood. Seeing the intense reaction this caused in him, she experimented a little, caressing and stroking him, teasing his hot flesh until finally he stopped her.

"No more, no more. I'm about to burst," he panted, his eyes fiery with desire. "And first I want to touch you again."

He trailed his fingertips over her in feather-light caresses, and amazingly, Linette felt passion rising in her again. Finally, he moved between her legs. She parted eagerly, raising her hips to facilitate him as he entered her. He was hard and full, stretching her damp passage, and the feeling of her tight and hot around him almost made him lose control.

"Oh, God, you feel good," he mumbled as he moved deep into her, his thrust exquisitely slow, then back again until he was almost out. He slid back into her, making Linette whimper with pleasure and frustration. She moved her hips, wanting him to pound into her, but he continued to stroke slowly, teasing her and himself into an almost mindless frenzy.

Then, at last, unable to stand it any longer, he began to thrust in quick, hard motions, rhythmically stroking, building their desire up and up and up until it exploded in a white heat, tearing through both of them. Hunter bucked, pouring out his seed, as a hoarse cry ripped from his throat. Linette wrapped her arms around him, holding on tightly as the storm overwhelmed them.

He collapsed against her, his breath rasping in her ear. "I love you," he murmured in a dazed voice. "Oh, God, Linette, I still love you."

Hunter was awakened the next morning by soft, butterfly kisses over his face. He opened his eyes, smiling. "Good morning."

Linette, who was propped up on her elbow, leaning over him, smiled back. "Good morning. Did you sleep well?"

His lazy smile held hidden meaning. "Very. And you?"

"Yes. In fact, I believe that it's the best sleep I've had in ages."

"Good." His voice was rich with sensuality as he put his hand on the nape of her neck, pulling her down for a thorough kiss. "I think I could learn to enjoy waking up like this."

"Could you?" Linette's eyes glinted with amusement.

"Yes." He paused, then said seriously, "I meant what I said last night: I love you."

Color tinged Linette's cheeks. "Then you don't regret it, like last time?"

"No." His voice was decisive. He went on, "I didn't really regret it last time; I was simply so scared of what I felt for you. All I could think about was protecting myself from hurt again. But last night, when I held you in my arms, I knew that there was no other choice for me. If I don't have you, I don't have anything in my life. Whatever might happen, nothing is as bad as the pain of living without you."

Linette's eyes glowed, and she planted a brief, hard kiss on his mouth. "Oh, Hunter! I'm so glad to hear you say that! I love you so much. I don't think I ever stopped." She paused, and a cloud touched her eyes. "But what are we going to do? I'm still married."

"You'll get a divorce," he said firmly. "I don't care about the scandal. Do you?"

"No, but . . . what if I can't get one? Benton's a very powerful man, and I'm not sure I could prove that he's committed adultery. I think he has, but—" she stopped as a thought struck her, "wait. Is—is nonconsummation grounds for a divorce?"

"What!" Hunter's eyes widened and he sat up. "What are you saying? You mean Benton never—"

Linette looked away, blushing. "No. He tried, but he was never able to complete it. It was awful. He would come to my room and touch me, fondle me."

Hunter's jaw tightened, and his eyes blazed with anger. "Did he hurt you?"

Linette shook her head. "Not really. It was more humiliating than anything else."

"What a worm!" Hunter commented scornfully. He reached out and smoothed a hand down her cheek, then tilted her chin up to look at him. "I'm sorry for the humiliation he caused you. But I have to admit I'm glad to know that he never really made love to you. Oh, Linette . . ."

He pulled her into his arms and held her tightly against him. "I love you so much. And we are going to be together, I promise you. As soon as we get Julia, we'll go back to Pine Creek and start court proceedings to dissolve your marriage. You won't even have to get a divorce, I wouldn't think; a marriage that is never consummated can be annulled."

"But how can I prove it? I know that Benton would never admit it!"

"Then we'll try something else."

"Your mother will hate me for pulling you into a scandal like that."

"I don't live by my mother's opinions. Besides, if this is what I want, my family will be behind me. And, if worse comes to worse, and you can't get out of that travesty of a marriage, then we'll leave. We'll come out here to Texas and start a new life."

"With me being married to another man?"

"If that's the only way it can be," Hunter replied

firmly. "I'll do whatever it takes. Dammit, Linette, I don't intend to lose you again."

"Oh, Hunter, I don't want to, either! It's just that I don't want to condemn you to living in sin the rest of your life because of my mistakes!"

"Your 'mistakes' were as much my fault as yours. And living with you couldn't be a sin. I think it'd be more like heaven. We'd be a family—you and me and our daughter and Mary Margaret, too. There'd be more love and joy in that house than in most families." He paused and looked at her. "Are you not willing to do that?"

"Yes!" she cried, flinging her arms around his neck. "Oh, yes, I would. I'd live with you in a minute. I couldn't ask for anything more in life than to share a family with you. I'll take you anyway I can get you— marriage or no marriage. I've had a marriage without love, and I'd far rather have love without marriage. I don't want you to be hurt."

"I won't be. I can't be, if I'm with you. You're all I need." He looked deep into her eyes. "You're all I want."

Linette smiled and brought her lips up close to his, scarcely an inch away. "If that's the case, then why don't you prove it?"

He chuckled and lay back down on his pillow, pulling Linette with him.

22

Later that morning, Hunter and Linette, rejoined by Mary Margaret, boarded the stagecoach for the last leg of its journey. They arrived in San Antonio that evening, and stayed there for two days while Hunter made arrangements for their trip north to Fredericksburg. After the long and uncomfortable stagecoach trip, it was a relief to spend a little time in a pleasant hotel. The only problem was that now that Mary Margaret was back in the room with Linette, Hunter and Linette could not again spend the night together. However, now the sexual tension between them was more exciting than painful, for they knew that eventually they would have the chance to be together again and satisfy their hunger.

Linette was on pins and needles, however, about the possibility of finding her daughter, which now loomed so close in front of her. Even though she was tired from their long journey, she could not bear to rest long. She had to push forward, unable to rest knowing that her daughter could be so near.

Mary Margaret, watching Linette pace their room waiting for Hunter to return with news regarding the horses he was hiring for their trip, said quietly, "You're real excited about finding that girl, aren't you?"

Linette turned and gave her a tense smile. "My daughter? Oh, yes. Of course I am."

"Are you sure it's the right girl?" Mary Margaret watched her face closely.

Fear flickered in Linette's eyes and was quickly suppressed. "It has to be. She was brought to the orphanage at the right time, just a day after my daughter was born. That's the orphanage where Louisa took her. It has to be; she was too scared to lie to me." She nodded her head decisively. "I'm sure when we get there, we'll see it; there'll be a resemblance. I'll know if it's her; I would know my own daughter."

"Oh. Yes, I guess you would. 'Blood calls to blood.' That's what one of Da's lady friends told me once."

"Yes. It must be that way." Linette glanced out the window, looking for Hunter to return, and did not see the way Mary Margaret's face drooped sadly. By the time she turned back, Mary Margaret had pulled her face back into its normal cheery expression.

Hunter returned with the horses and supplies they needed, as well as directions to the German community they were seeking, and so the next morning the three of them set out on horseback.

Across the street from their hotel a man stood in the shadow of a building, his hat pulled low over his face, his eyes intent on the hotel. When he saw Hunter and Linette ride away with the girl, he went to the hitching rail and untied his own horse, then mounted. He followed them slowly through the city streets, keeping well behind them. When they left the city, he dropped farther back, until finally he could no longer see them. But that was not important now; they had taken the Fredericksburg Road, and he was certain where they were going. The important thing was that they not see him.

Late in the afternoon, Hunter and Linette pulled into Fredericksburg, and a few questions brought directions to the Scherers' house at other end of town. It was a tidy little white stone place with black shutters, freshly painted, to match the low black wrought-iron fence encircling the yard. A girl was in the front yard, squatting down and scratching in the dirt with a stick. She glanced up curiously at the sound of the horses, and when Hunter, Linette, and Mary Margaret stopped in front of the fence, she stood up and began to walk toward them.

Linette swung off her horse, not waiting for Hunter to lend her a hand. Her heart was pounding furiously in her chest. The girl walking toward her might be the very girl they were looking for. Her daughter.

Hunter took Linette's reins from her; she hardly noticed. Nor did she pay any attention to his helping

Mary Margaret down and tying the horses to the fence. She saw nothing except the girl, now standing at the gate and watching them with interest.

The girl had black hair, pulled into neat braids down her back. She was slender and her face was oval, her features beautifully modeled. Her eyes were large and a vibrant blue. Linette stood and looked down into her face. It was eerily like looking at herself as a child. If the girl's hair were red instead of Hunter's black, and if she didn't have that stubborn Tyrrell chin, she would be a replica of Linette at the same age. As it was, she was a curious, unmistakable blend of Linette and Hunter. Their search was finally over; this girl was their daughter, her Julia.

Linette could hardly breathe. She was terrified, yet overcome with joy at the same time. Unable to speak, she glanced at Hunter. He, too, was staring at the girl, and when he felt Linette's gaze, he turned to her, their eyes holding for a moment. It was like a physical touch. They were linked, bound inextricably together and with this child. Tears filled Linette's eyes; she had never felt such a wild uprush of love, both for Hunter and for this child whom she didn't know—yet knew as well as her own heartbeat.

"Hello," the girl said after a moment when no one else spoke. "Who are you?"

"I'm Hunter Tyrrell," Hunter answered in a soft and unusually uncertain voice. "I. . . . This is Linette Sanders, I mean, Conway." He flushed a little and cast an apologetic glance toward Linette.

"And I'm Mary Margaret Keenan," Mary Margaret said, pushing around Hunter to face the other girl across the fence. She studied the girl carefully and turned to the adults.

Linette saw her look, a mixture of happiness, pain, and fear, quickly concealed. For the first time Linette was aware of the conflicting emotions in Mary Margaret regarding the return of their daughter. She must worry what would happen to her when Linette and Hunter had their real daughter back. Linette's heart clenched within her at Mary Margaret's hurt, and she wanted to reassure her that they still wanted Mary Margaret, too. But this was neither the time nor the place to discuss it.

"Are your mother and father home?" Hunter asked the girl.

The girl nodded politely and motioned for them to follow her. "Come. I will call her." Her voice carried a faint accent.

All three of them followed her to the front door. As they reached it, a woman stepped out onto the stoop, smiling and wiping her floury hands off on her apron. *"Guten Tag,"* she told them cheerfully. "How do you do?" She spoke the words with a thick German accent. "I am Frau Scherer. Please, come in."

She was a square, stocky woman with a broad face, red-cheeked from the heat of her kitchen and her work. Her features were ordinary, even plain, but her cheery smile lit up her face.

"You wish to see Herr Scherer?" she asked. "The ironworker, *ja?*"

"Well—frankly we came to see both you and your husband," Hunter said, sweeping off his hat as he followed the chunky woman through the low doorway.

Mrs. Scherer hesitated and glanced back at them curiously. "Oh. Well . . . just sit yourself, and I will get him."

She gestured toward a small parlor, neat as a pin, and disappeared into the back of the house. They heard her raised voice calling in German and a man's deeper voice answering from a short distance. Hunter and Linette sat down in the parlor. Julia followed them and stood watching Linette. Mary Margaret loitered in the wide doorway, her gaze flickering from Linette to Hunter to the other child and back.

"You are beautiful," the girl told Linette candidly. Then she added loyally, "Not as beautiful as my mother, of course . . . but very pretty."

It was, of course, a ridiculous statement; no objective observer would even put the chunky, plain-faced Mrs. Scherer in the same category as Linette. But the girl had spoken as a daughter, seeing Mrs. Scherer with the eyes of love, and it was this fact, the love of Linette's daughter for another woman, that sent a pang through Linette.

Mrs. Scherer bustled back into the parlor a few minutes later, carrying a tray. "My husband is coming," she announced cheerfully, setting down the tray on a serving table. "You wish something to eat, *ja?* You are having a long ride today?"

"From San Antonio," Hunter told her. His eyes strayed to the young girl. "You have a very pretty daughter, Frau Scherer."

The woman beamed. "*Ach, mein Herr,* thank you. She is a . . . a joy. Johanna, say hello to the nice gentleman and lady."

"Good day, sir . . . ma'am." Johanna said obediently, giving them a little curtsy.

"You have a daughter, too, *ja?*" Mrs. Scherer said, nodding toward Mary Margaret in the doorway. "Come here and have something to eat, child."

"No, thank you, ma'am." Mary Margaret shook her head, for once not heading immediately for the food. She seemed almost shy.

At that moment Mr. Scherer came clumping into the room. Like his wife, he was a short, sturdy man. His shoulders and arms were massive, out of proportion to the rest of his body, and Linette recalled that his wife had mentioned that he was an ironworker, a man who used the muscles of his upper body far beyond what other men did. He introduced himself and sat down, taking the plate of food his wife dished up for him. He ate and watched them, a man of few words, while his wife chatted on about the weather and the journey to San Antonio.

Finally he moved restlessly. "Gerta said you wished to see me?"

"Yes. Both of you." Hunter drew a breath. He glanced toward Linette, then began, "Linette and I have a daughter. Not Mary Margaret, but another girl . . . one who is nine years old now."

"But that is our Johanna's age!" Mrs. Scherer exclaimed in a delighted voice. Her husband frowned, looking puzzled.

"That's true. In fact, that is why we are here. You see, a . . . a terrible thing happened to us."

Mrs. Scherer's hand went to her chest, and her face was filled with sympathy. "No. She died?"

"No. My . . . Linette thought she did. Linette was very ill after she had her. I was away, in the war, and I wasn't there to help her, protect her. She had the baby in someone else's house, and they were wicked people. They took the baby and told Linette that she had died."

"No!" Mrs. Scherer's eyes rounded with shock. She looked at Linette, and Linette nodded.

"That's true. I was very ill, and for a while I was out of my head. I didn't know what had happened. I believed them when they said that my baby had died at birth."

"Oh, you poor thing. I don't know what I would do without my Johanna."

Drawn by the tone of Mrs. Scherer's voice, Johanna came across the room to stand beside her. The German woman smiled at the girl, love shining in her eyes, and pulled her close to her, one arm looped around her waist. She rested her head for a moment against Johanna's arm.

Linette, watching, felt a lump rising in her throat. This was her daughter, she was sure of it. It should be she who was sitting with her, holding her, not Mrs. Scherer. She thought of all the years she had missed with the girl, all the love, all the shared joys and sorrows that she would never know. It was Mrs. Scherer who had had all those things with her. *It's so unfair! So cruel!*

"This is true," Mr. Scherer said ponderously. "Last winter, Johanna was sick. Very sick, with the fever and all."

"*Ja*, she could hardly breathe at night," Mrs.

Scherer added, shaking her head, her eyes clouding with sadness at the memory. "I was afraid our Johanna was going to join the angels."

"But Gerta sat up with her all night, every night. She heated the water and put it so the steam formed, see, in a tent around her, so she could breathe."

"I was so scared. Worst of all was when Johanna would look up at me with those big eyes and say, 'Mama, I hurt.'" Tears glittered in Gerta's eyes, and she had to stop and swallow hard.

"But she lived, thanks to Gerta."

"And to you," his wife stuck in, nodding at him decisively. "I wasn't the only one who sat up with her. You took my place during the daytime while I slept." She smiled at him affectionately and turned toward Hunter and Linette. "My Josef is a good father. He loves Johanna very much. You should see the bed he made for her—ach, it is so beautiful."

Linette felt tears gathering in her own throat. She had never thought about the family with whom her daughter had been living. Even the other night when Hunter mentioned it, she had refused to think about it. The only thought she would allow was of having her child back with her. She hadn't considered the years of life and love the Scherers had shared with her daughter—why, obviously the child wouldn't even be alive today if it weren't for this couple and the care they had given her when she was sick. Then there were all the years of ordinary days and nights, of measles and mumps and colds, of birthdays and Christmases, of little dresses lovingly stitched and hair plaited into braids.

Linette thought of her time aboard ship with Mary Margaret and how they had talked and laughed. She remembered brushing out the girl's hair and curling it, of listening to her prayers, of looking at her while she slept. She thought of how her heart had tugged within her as she watched the sleeping child, of how much she had come to care for her in just the short time they had been together. How much more so must it be for this woman, who had lived with this child every day for nine years, who had been a mother to her!

She looked helplessly toward Hunter, tears gleaming in her eyes. She felt heartsick. Hunter reached out and took her hand and squeezed it. Then he turned toward Mr. Scherer.

"Sir, do you think Johanna could go outside and play with Mary Margaret for a bit? We—we'd like to discuss something with you."

"Of course." He looked puzzled, but he turned toward Johanna and said, "Go play, child. We have business to discuss now."

"All right, Papa."

All of the adults waited until the two girls were gone and the door closed behind them. Then the Scherers turned curiously toward Hunter and Linette.

"How can we help you?" Mr. Scherer asked.

"The people who took our child," Hunter began, "gave her to St. Anne's orphanage in Baton Rouge."

Mrs. Scherer gasped. "But that—"

"Yes, ma'am, we know. That is where you got—your daughter."

Fear settled on the German woman's face. "What are you saying?"

"We looked up our daughter's file and found that she was given away to a German couple, to you. Johanna is our daughter, Mrs. Scherer."

"No!" The woman leapt to her feet, her face suffused with anger. "No! Get out of my house! *Johanna ist meine!*" She whirled to her husband and began to talk rapidly in German.

Josef Scherer rose more slowly than his wife, but he faced them with the implacability of a rock. "You have upset my wife. You must go now."

"Please," Linette cried, clasping her hands together and looking at Mrs. Scherer earnestly. "You must understand how I feel. As a mother, you must know. I've been without my daughter for nine years. I mourned her, thinking she was dead. When I found out that she was alive, I was so happy. So overjoyed. I've missed so much of her life, and I can't—"

"Johanna is mine!" Mrs. Scherer reiterated, her face pale, her fists clenched at her side. "I will never let her go. Never!"

"Please, just listen to me . . ."

"No! You listen to me! You gave her away. You cannot have her back!"

"She didn't *give* her away!" Hunter exclaimed. "Johanna was taken from her, stolen from her!"

"Then you should know how I feel! You are trying to take my baby from me! Steal her!"

"No, no." Tears streamed down Linette's cheeks. "Truly. I don't want to take anything from you, but she's my baby! All you have to do is look at her, and you can see that she is ours. Her hair, her eyes . . ."

Mr. Scherer stepped in front of his wife protectively. "I understand how you must feel, Frau . . ."

"Conway."

"Frau Conway. But you must understand, my wife . . . Gerta wanted children so badly. But she cannot have them. We are a little old to be parents to Johanna, as you can see, but that is because we tried for so many years to have children, and we could not. My wife was very sad. Sometimes she did not even want to live. Then we adopted Johanna. She has been a sun in our lives. You and your husband, you can have other children. You have your Mary there. But Johanna, she is all my wife and I have. She is everything to us."

"Oh, God." Linette began to cry in earnest. She put her hands up to her face and sank back down into the chair. Her shoulders shook under the force of her sobs.

"Linette . . . sweetheart." Hunter knelt beside her chair and took her in his arms. "Honey, I'll get her back," he whispered into her ear. "I promise. Whatever it takes. You know me—I'll do it. You remember what I said."

Linette remembered. But she thought about Johanna waking at night to find a strange man carrying her away. Hunter might have to fight with Mr. Scherer, to hurt him to take the girl from them. Johanna would be terrified. This was the only home she knew; for all her life, these two people had been her parents. They had loved her, cared for her. Johanna might be of Linette's bone and blood, but she was this woman's daughter.

Linette could not do that to them. She could not do that to her child.

Linette drew a long shuddering breath and raised her head, wiping away her tears. "No," she said, her voice thick with tears. She looked into Hunter's eyes and saw in their green depths love and determination. He would do exactly what he said, try whatever he could. She knew that no one had ever had a firmer love, a truer passion or devotion. Whatever happened, she would always have Hunter, and on that she would build her new life.

"No," she said again. "I don't want you to. I ruined both our lives once before. I'm not going to do it again to our baby, just to get what I want. Mrs. Scherer is right. Johanna belongs here, with her parents."

She looked over at Mrs. Scherer and tried valiantly to smile. Mrs. Scherer looked at her, and her face, which had been stubbornly set and pugnacious, now crumpled with relief, and she, too, began to cry.

"There, there, *liebchen*." Mr. Scherer put his arm around his wife and patted her shoulder. "It's all right now."

Hunter reached down and took Linette's hand, and she rose. He encircled her with his arm, and Linette leaned gratefully into his warmth and strength. "Thank you," she whispered.

Hunter bent and pressed his lips against the top of her head. "You did what was right."

"Did I?" Linette smiled at him tremulously. "Why does it feel so awful?" They paused at the door and turned back toward the Scherers. "Do you—would it be all right, do you think, if sometime I sent Johanna a little something at Christmas or on her birthday? You could just say I was that lady who came to visit one time."

"*Ja, ja,* that would be fine." Mrs. Scherer smiled at her. "You are a good woman. I am sorry about your baby."

"Thank you."

Hunter opened the door, and Linette stepped outside, but came to an abrupt halt when she saw who was in the yard.

"Benton!" Linette gasped.

Benton Conway, squatting down beside Johanna, was talking to her, while Mary Margaret stood beside her, her arms folded across her chest and her face stamped with suspicion. At Linette's startled exclamation, Benton looked up. He smiled thinly and rose to his feet, one hand going down to clasp Johanna's shoulder.

"Hello, Linette."

"But what—how did you find us?"

He smiled thinly. "Did you honestly think I wouldn't find out where you were going? You may have gotten my man in New Orleans, but he'd already told me where you were going. You all slowed down once you hit New Orleans, so it wasn't hard to catch up with you."

"Why would you want to?" Linette retorted sharply. "I'm certainly not coming back to you." She glanced at her daughter beside Benton and said in as normal a voice as she could muster, "Johanna, I think your mother needs you inside."

Johanna started to leave, but Benton stopped her, his fingers digging into her shoulder so hard that she let out a surprised yelp and looked up at him in astonishment. Hunter started across the yard toward them at a lope, Linette right on his heels.

Benton jerked Johanna up against him and at the same time reached into a pocket of his coat and removed a small revolver. He jammed the gun up against Johanna's temple. Hunter came to a quick halt. Linette gasped and stopped, too.

"Benton! Have you taken leave of your senses?"

He grinned. "No. I've just finally realized that if I want something done, I need to do it myself. Hunter, I want you to unbuckle that gunbelt and drop it." When Hunter hesitated, he pushed the gun against Johanna's head harder.

Quickly Hunter reached down to do as he said. He unbuckled the belt and let it drop to the ground. "There. All right? I can't shoot you. Now let the girl go."

Conway chuckled. "Do you think I'm a complete idiot? This girl is my ace in the hole. I want you to come over here."

"Hunter, no!" Linette snapped. "He'll shoot you!"

"How perceptive of you, my dear," Conway sneered.

"What else can I do?" Hunter asked her in a low voice and started forward slowly.

"Benton, don't be a fool!" Linette exclaimed. "Let the girl go and nothing will happen to you. If you shoot her or Hunter or me, you'll have the law on your trail. You'll hang. This is Texas, not Pine Creek. None of your friends are around."

"Oh, no, we'll get away, you and I and the girl. I was a fool to have gotten rid of the brat in the first place. If only I had known how attached you'd be to her, I would have seen that having her around is the very best way to keep you in line. That's why we're going home now, the three of us together. We'll bring up your daughter in the bosom of our family."

"She's not mine. She belongs to that couple inside the house."

Conway laughed. "You really are an amusing liar, Linette. All anyone has to do is look at her to see whose child she is."

"There are other people in the world who have blue eyes."

"But none who look quite like you." Hunter had almost reached Conway and Johanna by now, and Conway nodded at him sharply. "That's far enough. Turn around and face the house. Hands behind your back."

Hunter obeyed the order. Linette's heart leapt into her throat. He was going to shoot Hunter right there! She could think of nothing to save him.

"Kneel down."

Hunter knelt.

"Benton, no!" Linette shrieked. "Don't! I'll go with you! I'll do whatever you say. Just don't shoot him! Let him and Johanna go, and I'll leave with you right now."

Benton's lip curled. "Don't be a fool. I'll never have you as long as he's alive."

"Please! No!"

Linette stood frozen with terror as she watched Benton raise the gun from Johanna's head and aim it straight at Hunter.

A shot roared out. Linette jumped; a scream tore from her throat. Then, at the same time she realized that the sound of the gun had come from behind her, not from Benton, and that Hunter was still kneeling, unharmed. Benton crumpled, red spreading across his shirt, and the revolver fell nervelessly from his hand.

"Papa! Papa!" Johanna shrieked, running for the house.

Linette whirled around and saw Mr. Scherer standing in the doorway of his house, his face grim. He held a rifle in his hand. Linette let out a sob of relief and ran to Hunter.

"Oh, Hunter! Hunter! Thank God!"

He rose to his feet as she launched herself into his arms, crying and laughing, shaking from the violence of her feelings. An instant later Mary Margaret slammed into both of them, wrapping her arms as far around them as she could.

"Mary, Jesus, and Joseph!" the little girl exclaimed loudly. "I was thinking you were a dead man."

Hunter squeezed them both tightly. "That's the second time I was given up for dead. But nothing can kill me, child. You'll find that out."

"Hunter, how can you joke? I was so frightened I'm still shaking."

At last Hunter released them and walked over to where Conway lay. Mr. Scherer was standing beside the body, looking down at it.

"He's dead," he said simply.

"Thank you," Hunter said, sparing only a glance for his former enemy. He reached out to shake Josef Scherer's hand. "I owe you my life."

Scherer shrugged. "I owe you my daughter's life. He would have shot her if you hadn't given yourself up in her place." Scherer gave him an apologetic smile. "I'm sorry I waited so long to shoot, but I was afraid to do so while he still had the gun pointed at Johanna's head."

"Of course." Hunter glanced back down at Conway. "I suppose we'd better send for the sheriff."

"*Ja.* I will take care of it." Scherer's eyes narrowed shrewdly. "But I think it's better if you and the lady and the little girl leave now. There would be questions I'd as soon not have answered."

"But—"

"Don't worry about me. I will get into no trouble. They know me here. And we know how to deal with madmen who try to harm children." He paused, looking down at Conway. "So this must be the man who stole the lady's baby."

"That's not the only thing he stole, but I daresay it was the worst."

Hunter, Linette, and Mary Margaret, shaken, climbed on their horses and rode away. Linette glanced back to where Mr. and Mrs. Scherer stood in the yard. Mrs. Scherer's arm was around Johanna. Tears blurred Linette's eyes as she turned back around toward the front.

Mary Margaret nudged her pony up beside Linette. "I'm sorry, ma'am," she said earnestly.

Linette forced a smile. "No, there's no need to be sorry. Hunter and I did the only thing we could."

"But it's sad you'll be without your daughter. And after you came all this way to get her and all."

Linette swallowed her tears and reached out to take Mary Margaret's hand. "Daughter? Why, what do you mean? I've already got a daughter, right here."

A smile like sunshine broke across Mary Margaret's face. "Do you mean it?"

Linette nodded. "Of course."

Mary Margaret let out a shriek and kicked her pony into a run, catching up with Hunter in front of them. "Did you hear that? I'm going to be your daughter!"

"Well, and what else would we do with a rascal like you," Hunter retorted jokingly. He looked back at Linette and pulled his horse up, waiting for her to draw even with him. He held out his hand to Linette, and she put hers in it trustingly. He raised her hand to his lips and kissed it. "I reckon we'll be a family after all."

Linette smiled at him. "Yes."

For a moment they simply looked at each other, their hearts in their eyes. Then Hunter said, "Well, where do you want to go, madame? We have the whole world in front of us."

Linette hesitated, then said, "Back home, I think. Where we belong. How could we raise a passel of Tyrrells anyplace else?"

"All right." Hunter grinned. "But first, we're getting married in San Antonio. This time, I'm not taking any chances. Nothing's going to come between us."

Linette smiled at him and replied, "Absolutely nothing."

Hands clasped, they continued down the road, Mary Margaret Keenan trotting alongside.

Epilogue

Hunter planted his elbows on the table and propped his chin in his hand. It seemed as if it had been years since Maggie and Reid had arrived and gone upstairs. He thought it had been hard waiting that night a little over a year ago with Gideon. But he was finding out that when it was your own child, the waiting was sheer torture.

He glanced over at Gideon, seated at the end of the kitchen table, sipping a cup of coffee. Gideon gave him a sympathetic smile. It didn't help any.

With a sigh, Hunter stood up and strolled over to the window to look out into the backyard. Tess was there in the pleasant autumn afternoon with Will, stretched out on a blanket on the grass, watching him take a few wavering steps on the grass and bend down to pick up a twig. He lost his balance and plopped down on his bottom, but the fall didn't seem to bother him. He picked at the twig with an intense concentration that reminded Hunter forcibly of the boy's father. Beyond them, Ginny and Mary Margaret were laughing as they climbed the cherry tree, sending showers of golden leaves tumbling down to the ground.

It was a peaceful, pleasant scene, and Hunter felt at home, watching it. It had been a year since he and Linette had married, and in that time, his life had turned around. All the old restless feelings were gone. He was once more at home and at peace with his family. And now, now there would be one more in the family. He swallowed hard against the emotion that swelled his throat.

"Hunter! Hunter!" There was the sound of steps clattering down the stairs, and Maggie burst into the room. She was grinning from ear to ear, and Hunter went limp with relief.

Maggie threw herself into his arms and hugged him fiercely. "A little girl! She had a little girl!" Her voice was choked with tears, and when she stepped back, Hunter could see the tears shining in her eyes.

"She is so precious!" Maggie went on. "I couldn't wish anything better for you. And just think, she's almost of an age with my Susie. They'll be able to play together and go to parties together and—" Only a few months ago Maggie had had a baby girl herself, a healthy little hazel-eyed, curly haired doll. She had left the baby at Rosemary Manning's house when she accompanied her doctor husband out here today.

"Whoa . . ." Gideon laughed behind them. "Slow

down, Mags, he's still trying to adjust to the news that he's a father. Don't marry the girl off just yet."

"Oh, you." Maggie made a face at her brother.

"How's Linette?" Hunter asked anxiously.

"Wonderful! Go see for yourself."

He did so, taking the stairs two at a time. Reid was just leaving the room, rolling down his sleeves, as Hunter entered, and Reid gave him a congratulatory handshake. Then Hunter stepped inside the room and stopped, gazing at his wife, shaken by emotion.

Linette sat up on the bed, Hunter's mother fussing around her. Her hair was spread out on the pillows behind her, a blaze of auburn against the white. In her arms lay a baby, wrapped round with a soft pink cotton blanket. Linette looked up and saw Hunter, and she smiled, a soft, feminine smile of happiness and contentment.

Jo Tyrrell turned, too, at Linette's expression and saw her son. She grinned. "Well, come on over here. Don't just stand there like your feet have taken root. Just look at this little angel."

Jo gazed down at the baby lovingly and reached out to smooth a finger across the child's forehead. "Have you ever seen anything so beautiful?" she murmured.

"Never." Hunter moved to the side of the bed, and Jo stepped away.

"I'll leave you two alone now," Jo said, walking to the door. There she turned and looked back at them. Great tears gleamed in her eyes and spilled over. "I am so happy. I have all my family back."

She left, closing the door softly behind her. Hunter

turned and looked down at his wife. Linette smiled up at him. Her face was tired and etched with lines of pain from her ordeal of the last few hours, but her eyes were sparkling.

"Look at her, Hunter. Isn't she beautiful?"

She was. She was a perfectly formed little thing, with a mop of black hair and huge blue eyes. She blinked up at Hunter, her arms and legs moving wildly, shoving aside the blanket.

"Already going like a spinning top," Hunter chuckled.

"Yes—easy to tell that she's your daughter."

"Come on, now, she didn't inherit all that just from me."

"No, I suppose not."

Hunter bent and kissed Linette's forehead. "How are you feeling?"

"Wonderful!" Linette laughed and amended her statement, "Well, a little sore, perhaps, but wonderful nonetheless. Oh, Hunter, I'm so happy!" She reached up and took his hand. "I have everything I want—you, my baby, Mary Margaret. My life is so full that I'm almost scared somehow I'm going to lose it."

"No," Hunter replied firmly. "You won't lose it. What you have isn't even half what you deserve. And, believe me, you'll never lose my love."

He squeezed her hand and brought it to his lips, kissing it softly.

There was a wild shriek of happiness in the yard outside that carried up even through the closed window. Hunter and Linette looked at each other and laughed. "That must be Mary Margaret, learning that she's got a new baby sister."

"She'll spoil that child rotten."

"Probably."

They both turned to look down at the baby squirming in Linette's arms. Linette stroked a finger down the baby's cheek.

"Shall we name her Julia?" Hunter suggested.

Linette smiled mistily at him. "That's terribly sweet of you." She shook her head. "But no. This isn't Julia, but a sweet little girl all her own. I was thinking we might call her Jo, after your mother."

"Well, you'll win Ma's heart." Hunter smiled. "Yes, I think Jo would be a perfect name for her. And you're right—she's a completely different person. Just like ours is a whole new life."

Linette nodded. "I knew you'd understand. I love you, Hunter."

"I love you." He eased down on the bed and held out his hands. "Now, here, let me hold that daughter of mine."

FLAME LILY by Candace Camp

Continuing the saga of the Tyrells begun in *Rain Lily,* another heart-tugging, passionate tale of love from bestselling author Candace Camp. Returning home after years at war, Confederate officer Hunter Tyrell dreamed only of marrying his sweetheart, Linette Sanders, and settling down. But when he discovered that Linette had wed another, he vowed never to love again—until he found out her heartbreaking secret.

ALL THAT GLITTERS by Ruth Ryan Langan

From a humble singing job in a Los Angeles bar, Alexandra Corday is discovered and propelled into stardom. Along the way her path crosses that of rising young photographer Adam Montrose. Just when it seems that Alex will finally have it all—a man she loves, a home for herself and her brother, and the family she has always yearned for—buried secrets threaten to destroy her.

THE WIND CASTS NO SHADOW by Roslynn Griffith

With an incredibly deft hand, Roslynn Griffith has combined Indian mythology and historical flavor in this compelling tale of love, betrayal, and murder deep in the heart of New Mexico territory.

UNQUIET HEARTS by Kathy Lynn Emerson

Tudor England comes back to life in this richly detailed historical romance. With the death of her mother, Thomasine Strangeways had no choice but to return to Catsholme Manor, the home where her mother was once employed as governess. There she was reunited with Nick Carrier, her childhood hero who had become the manor's steward. Meeting now as adults, they found the attraction between them instant and undeniable, but they were both guarding dangerous secrets.

STOLEN TREASURE by Catriona Flynt

A madcap romantic adventure set in 19th-century Arizona gold country. Neel Blade was rich, handsome, lucky, and thoroughly bored, until he met Cate Stewart, a feisty chemist who was trying to hold her world together while her father was in prison. He instantly fell in love with her, but if only he could remember who he was . . .

WILD CARD by Nancy Hutchinson

It is a dream come true for writer Sarah MacDonald when movie idol Ian Wild miraculously appears on her doorstep. This just doesn't happen to a typical widow who lives a quiet, unexciting life in a small college town. But when Ian convinces Sarah to go with him to his remote Montana ranch, she comes face to face with not only a life and a love more exciting than anything in the pages of her novels, but a shocking murder.

COMING NEXT MONTH

STARLIGHT by Patricia Hagan
Another spellbinding historical romance from bestselling author Patricia Hagan. Desperate to escape her miserable life in Paris, Samara Labonte agreed to switch places with a friend and marry an American soldier. During the train journey to her intended, however, Sam was abducted by Cheyenne Indians. Though at first she was terrified, her heart was soon captured by one particular blue-eyed warrior.

THE NIGHT ORCHID by Patricia Simpson
A stunning new time travel story from an author who *Romantic Times* says is "fast becoming one of the premier writers of supernatural romance." When Marissa Quinn goes to Seattle to find her missing sister who was working for a scientist, what she finds instead is a race across centuries with a powerfully handsome Celtic warrior from 285 B.C. He is the key to her missing sister and the man who steals her heart.

ALL THINGS BEAUTIFUL by Cathy Maxwell
Set in the ballrooms and country estates of Regency England, a stirring love story of a dark, mysterious tradesman and his exquisite aristocratic wife looking to find all things beautiful. "*All Things Beautiful* is a wonderful 'Beauty and the Beast' story with a twist. Cathy Maxwell is a bright new talent."—*Romantic Times*

THE COMING HOME PLACE by Mary Spencer
Knowing that her new husband, James, loved another, Elizabeth left him and made a new life for herself. Soon she emerged from her plain cocoon to become an astonishingly lovely woman. Only when James' best friend ardently pursued her did James realize the mistake he had made by letting Elizabeth go.

DEADLY DESIRES by Christina Dair
When photographer Jessica Martinson begins to uncover the hidden history of the exclusive Santa Lucia Inn, she is targeted as the next victim of a murderer who will stop at nothing to prevent the truth from coming out. Now she must find out who is behind the murders, as all the evidence is pointing to the one man she has finally given her heart to.

MIRAGE by Donna Valentino
To escape her domineering father, Eleanor McKittrick ran away to the Kansas frontier where she and her friend Lauretta had purchased land to homestead. Her father, a prison warden, sent Tremayne Hawthorne, an Englishman imprisoned for a murder he didn't commit, after her in exchange for his freedom. Yet Hawthorne soon realized that this was a woman he couldn't bear to give up.

Harper Monogram **The Mark of Distinctive Women's Fiction**

ANALISE

Analise Caldwell was the reigning belle of New Orleans. Disguised as a Confederate soldier, Union major Mark Schaeffer captured the Rebel beauty's heart as part of his mission. Stunned by his deception, Analise swore never to yield to the caresses of this Yankee spy...until he delivered an ultimatum.

ROSEWOOD

Millicent Hayes had lived all her life amid the lush woodland of Emmetsville, Texas. Bound by her duty to her crippled brother, the dark-haired innocent had never known desire...until a handsome stranger moved in next door.

BONDS OF LOVE

Katherine Devereaux was a willful, defiant beauty who had yet to meet her match in any man—until the winds of war swept the Union innocent into the arms of Confederate Captain Matthew Hampton.

LIGHT AND SHADOW

The day nobleman Jason Somerville broke into her rooms and swept her away to his ancestral estate, Carolyn Mabry began living a dangerous charade. Posing as her twin sister, Jason's wife, Carolyn thought she was helping her gentle twin. Instead she found herself drawn to the man she had so seductively deceived.

CRYSTAL HEART

A seductive beauty, Lady Lettice Kenton swore never to give her heart to any man—until she met the rugged American rebel Charles Murdock. Together on a ship bound for America, they shared a perfect passion, but danger awaited them on the shores of Boston Harbor.